THEY ALRE
HOW IT WC

"When we make love," Sy said, tracing the back of Susie's hand with his fingertips, "it will be completely—with no busy schedules, no distractions, no doubts." He lifted her hand and pressed her open palm to his lips. "And it will be worth waiting for," he added huskily.

Sy's breath fanned her cheek. With almost dreamlike motion, Susie sought his lips with her own. The ardent merging, the slow soft circling of warm mouths and rippling breaths became a dance of gentle rhythm as the tender languid pressure of their kiss held them suspended in a world of their own.

But when reality returned, this kiss, like so many others, was just a promise. A promise of passion —if only the rest of the world would leave them to love.

*With great admiration for the
Colombos who do their costuming
magic every Mardi Gras season—
and to the DeNouxs for sharing
their friendship, insights, talents,
family, and their city, New Orleans.*

———————◆———————

CHRISTINA CROCKETT
is also the author
of this title in
SuperRomance

TO TOUCH A DREAM

A MOMENT OF MAGIC

Christina Crockett

A *SuperRomance from*
HARLEQUIN
London · Toronto · New York · Sydney

First published in Great Britain in 1985 by
Harlequin, 15–16 Brook's Mews, London W1A 1DR

© Christina Crockett 1983

ISBN 0 373 70103 9

11–0385

Printed and bound in Great Britain by
Cox & Wyman Ltd, Reading

CHAPTER ONE

SUSIE COSTAIN flipped up the collar of her tweed jacket and turned her back against the wind. The cool October breeze skipped up over the levee between the dull brown Mississippi River and Decatur Street sending the dry leaves in Jackson Square swirling in erratic little spirals. Even the pigeons turned their backs to the river, hoping that the bright sun overhead would bring out the lunchtime crowd with all their extra tidbits.

Susie diligently peeled the crust from her sandwich, broke it into small pieces, then pitched them into the air so they scattered in the wind. Suddenly the sky filled with iridescent feathers as the more ambitious pigeons tried to get their share before the crumbs hit the ground. "Lazybones...." Susie grinned at a round-chested, disgruntled pigeon who had refused to leap skyward with the others. The bird blinked at her with disdain, then turned and strolled away toward the next bench. Perhaps its occupant would be less demanding.

Across the Square, directly below the towering statue of General Jackson mounted on his rearing horse, several young women were lining up. *Tour group....* Susie glanced over at them as she sipped her hot coffee and balanced her sandwich so the thick slices of corned beef wouldn't drop out. Then two more females joined the others and Susie hesitated, inspecting their outfits more carefully. *Models*... she concluded silently. Their makeup was too stark for street wear. Their fur jackets and boots seemed out of place for a bright afternoon in New Orleans' French Quarter. Then the group of young women abruptly converged around a tall, bearded man entering the Square from the St. Ann Street side. Laden with two hefty camera bags and a tripod, the rugged-looking fellow was obviously someone they had been awaiting.

"Simon," one delighted voice called out.

"Let's hurry up, I'm freezing," another wailed.

Susie narrowed her eyes and looked intently at the photographer called Simon. His features were obscured by the mass of tousled hair trailing onto his forehead and the well-trimmed, short beard that framed his chin line. There was little to remind her of the slim young portrait photographer who had once been in such demand by New Orleans society. It was at least eight years since Simon Avery had closed his studio in the French Quarter and had gone off to Europe. Susie had been almost sixteen at the time and had barely known him, but she had seen his photographs of prominent socialites and beauties in newspapers, magazines and debutantes' scrapbooks, or framed and displayed in the homes of affluent families.

That younger, clean-shaven Simon had taken outstanding portraits. For years he had "captured" the New Orleans social set and preserved their memories in splendid color. Susie had caught an occasional glimpse of him when he had come to her parents' fitting sessions to photograph a costumed client. He had taken the official coronation portrait of Susie's older sister, Claire, when she'd been queen of a Mardi Gras ball. While Susie was still in high school, pursuing interests of her own, Avery had made portraits of countless costumed queens and maids and dukes and captains in ball regalia designed by Susie's parents and sewn in their work-rooms. Then he had simply disappeared. Susie furrowed her brow, trying to remember gossip about a marriage. Then she shook her head to dismiss the thought. If Simon Avery was back in town, soon enough his per-sonal life would be the topic of considerable attention. Eventually she'd hear the details—accurate and imaginative—about the return of one of New Orleans' own.

By now the wide-shouldered photographer had moved his covey of young beauties to an abandoned wrought-iron bench and meticulously began placing them around it, some seated, some standing, and one with her boot-clad foot braced casually against the arm-rest. They were very young. Susie smiled ruefully as their nervous fingers flitted from their hair to their scarves or jacket fastenings in a constant pattern of checking and rearranging. They were outfitted in pastel woolens and matching short jackets. Without having to look at the labels inside the garments, Susie could iden-tify the stores where they had been purchased and estimate the cost. Expensive. But then, these were not the mere models she had once thought. Susie knew them by the soft lilt to their voices, the glow that surrounded them and the sophistication they struggled to achieve. They were the debutantes. Their names would be promi-nent in newspapers for the next months. The Mardi Gras balls would have them on courts and in tableaux. They would be brunched, dined and set dancing until their final grand ball in the spring. Susie had seen it many times before.

Simon Avery.

Her gaze lingered on the bearded man as he moved his camera from one position to another while the young ladies giggled among themselves. Susie sipped her coffee and sniffed the air. She could smell the hot powdered-sugar-coated beignets from the Café DuMonde, the open-air French doughnut shop on the corner of the French Market. She still had twenty minutes left on her lunch break. Hastily she packed away her napkin and shook a few crumbs onto the grass and strode across Jackson Square toward the source of the marvelous scent. Five minutes later, with a small white bag containing two steaming beignets, she resumed her post on the park bench and watched the man called Simon work his magic.

With a light touch to a cheek, he could transform the broad, intense grin of an eighteen-year-old into a subtle, elegant smile of restraint and elegance. He could tilt a head and add years and style to a slightly overeager teenager. He could charm a group of giggling girls and capture them on film with an aura of majesty, preserving them as they wished they were.

Susie found herself leaning forward, entranced by his skill, as the powdered sugar from the warm pastry she nibbled trailed in tiny snowbursts onto her hand cupped below her chin. When he paused in his work and glanced around the square, Susie abruptly shifted her attention to a nearby pigeon so he would not realize she had been watching him so studiously. She had brushed the sugar from her hand and reached for another beignet when the shadow fell across her.

"Would you mind if I took a few shots of you?"

Nearly black eyes stared down at her. They were brilliant and intent, and the wide mouth neatly framed by the trimmed beard was smiling.

"I hope you don't think this is a come-on," the man called Simon insisted. "I noticed you while I was working over there." He nodded toward the distant bench where several of the young women still lingered. "You have such a great face." He stared openly. "I mean. . . it's a *real* face." He grinned.

Susie plunged the beignet back into the bag and squeezed the top closed. Already her cheeks were getting hot. She knew she was turning deeper shades of red.

"I don't like having my picture taken." She stood hastily and prepared to leave, clutching her purse in one hand and her paper sack in the other. "I've always had this thing about my nose," she added, sounding as if she was apologizing. "And I've probably got powdered sugar all over myself." She began brushing away at her cheek with the back of her hand.

"You look great," Simon insisted. "You have a face with incredible character."

Susie blushed more deeply.

Character. Who in the world wants character. She shuddered.

"I always wanted blond hair and a sizable chest," she joked tentatively with the photographer. "And until they arrive in the mail or in my Christmas stocking—" she stepped past him "—I'd rather not have my picture taken. Probably not even then." She began to walk off.

"Wait. . ." he called after her. "Just a minute, please. Avery. Simon Avery is my name." The footsteps followed her. Then the broad hand flourishing a business card moved into view. "Just Sy is fine. Look, I didn't mean to embarrass you. Taking pictures is my profession." He kept in step with her. "I just saw something special in your face."

Susie stopped and looked down at the card. He held it closer to her. Finally she reached out and took it from him.

"I've seen your portraits." She spoke without looking up at him. "My parents are in the costuming business. Their name is Costain. We do a lot of Mardi Gras balls. You used to take the final portraits of a number of our customers."

"Costain..." Sy repeated. "Bernard and Rose Costain...in Chalmette. I remember them quite well." He paused and regarded her closely. "You certainly aren't the daughter I photographed then. You're too young." There was a trace of laughter in his voice. "Surely you aren't the skinny kid with the faded jeans and big eyeglasses?" He smiled as Susie began nodding.

"I'm Susie Costain." She lifted her chin and smiled back at Sy Avery. "At sixteen I was shy about everything—especially being skinny and wearing glasses."

"Time certainly has a way of making impressive changes," he noted almost to himself as he let his gaze slip down the whole length of her body. Then his eyes were staring back into hers. "In all the picture-taking I did at the Costains' we somehow managed to miss each other. So it's nice to meet you, Susie Costain."

"Nice to meet you...Sy." The words came with a little difficulty. The clear dark eyes that looked down at her seemed to be admiring more than the character in her face.

"Did you follow the family tradition and become a Mardi Gras queen like your sister?" he asked.

Susie shook her head slightly. "I'm a bit of a black sheep," she answered. "No debut, no balls, no college. Just art school and a job in advertising."

"Then I was right about the *character*," Sy leveled a finger at her and smiled. In one quick glance, he assessed her slender form, apparently pleased with what he saw. At twenty-four, Susie was a slender-legged woman with sleek black hair that swayed just above her shoulders and velvety brown eyes. "You look like you belong in the Quarter, not on a society page," he remarked. "There's something about you—the intent way you watch without revealing anything of yourself, a calm exterior, but behind the doorways, secret courtyards," he said quietly. "I can almost hear the Creole blood pulsing in your veins. Looking at you reminds me how much I've missed this city." His voice trailed off into a pensive smile.

"You've been away in Europe, is that right?" Susie changed the subject abruptly. There was an intimacy in the look Sy gave her that made her want to shift his attention elsewhere.

"I lived in France for a while." His eyes moved back to the remaining four young ladies perched on the park bench. "Then in Switzerland," he added almost absentmindedly. Without his expert direction, they had turned back into mere teenagers, with bored expressions and wandering, anxious fingers once again fumbling with errant locks of hair and fading makeup. "But now I've come back here to stay," Sy ended abruptly. One of the girls pouted and crossed her arms petulantly. "I'd better get back to work." Sy shrugged, then he gazed down at Susie once more. "I wasn't kidding about taking your picture." His voice was even and low. "You have a certain quality that I'd like to try to get on film." Again his black eyes appraised her.

"I just couldn't," Susie replied softly.

"It wouldn't be so bad," he asserted. "I'd just set up a few shots until you feel comfortable."

"I'm simply not the model type." Susie stiffened. "I am who I am, and I know what I look like. I'm *not* picture pretty, and I couldn't pretend to be." She backed away, sending up a small cloud of pigeons that had wandered too close to the once-generous lady. "Look, you have lots of eager clients—" she tilted her head toward the waiting debutantes "—they delight in acting like something out of *Vogue* magazine. I don't. You're making me terribly self-conscious." She felt her anger increasing as he continued to study her. "You make me feel like a piece of meat in a supermarket. It doesn't help one bit that you would label my package Real and With Character. I'm not interested in being put on display." Susie's voice quavered just before the last word.

Sy's eyes narrowed, and a slow half smile spread over his lips. He found her discomfort amusing. Susie's jaw tensed in anger at his reaction. Once again she was that awkward teenager, busying herself in the shadows while the beautiful people dressed up and paraded around. And that teenager couldn't trust her voice to utter another word. Bright tears glimmered in her eyes as she turned away and hurried out of the square. She didn't miss a step when he called out after her. She simply sped across the street between two horse-drawn carriages waiting for tourists. Then she increased her pace until she was almost running. She didn't slow down until she turned onto Canal Street and the revolving doors of Blaine's department store whirled closed behind her.

Inside Blaine's everything seemed perfectly austere and calm. The elegant old store even smelled reassuring with its counters full of luxurious cosmetics and expensive perfumes and racks of leather purses on display. Susie pressed her lips together and forced a detached look as she passed through the store to the elevator at the rear. Once inside the small employees' elevator, she jabbed at the button marked Up and pressed her shoulders against the smooth paneled wall. What was it about Sy Avery that had made her lose control like that? What was so bad about having a *real* face—one with character?

I don't want to be different. Susie sniffed back a persistent tear. *I just want to be like everyone else.* She caught herself on that one. She knew that wasn't true. She had always felt set off from the rest of the world— as if she were the observer and everyone else the participants. It was a feeling of separation she had grown accustomed to, and eventually she had learned to make it work for her, not against her. Susie had quietly become the eccentric—the "artsy" offspring of the Costain clan, who could avoid the usual formalities and obligations since she had a talent to develop and required some freedom to create. So when she turned down the offers to be on Mardi Gras courts, no one suspected that Susie simply wished to avoid being conspicuous and that her remoteness came from shyness, not preoccupation with her artwork.

In a family known for its lovely daughters, Susie had been unique. Claire had always been the beautiful one in the Costain family, with her long, wavy light brown hair and perfect features. One cousin was red-haired and green-eyed with a thirty-six-inch bust and perfect size-eleven figure. Even Susie's younger cousin Michelle was lovely and elegant at nineteen, with an aura of sophistication about her that Susie had never achieved.

Michelle had the honey-blond hair and blue eyes that Susie often wished were her own. But Susie was the one with "personality." Her wide brown eyes were too alert, too inquisitive. Unlike the others, Susie had never learned to sit back and let people simply talk around her. She asked questions. She demanded explanations. She asked for information and listened carefully when it was given, but always she could turn the focus of a conversation away from anything personal, anything that might reveal something of herself. But while she insisted she would never be a mere decoration, an object to be admired, Susie Costain had blossomed into a vibrant, intelligent young woman with a vital beauty of her own.

There had been something dangerous about Sy Avery, Susie concluded as the elevator moved to a stop. He saw too much. His eyes looked more deeply and saw more of her than she liked to reveal.

He could have at least said I was pretty, Susie huffed to herself as the elevator doors opened. Somehow that would have made Sy safe—predictable. She knew she would have still turned down his offer to photograph her. She had never liked what she saw in any photograph taken of her. No phony pose would have made her feel better.

"Enjoy your lunch hour?" Ella Jenkins, the advertising manager called out as Susie passed her office door. The edge to her voice was critical, not welcoming.

"Simply divine," Susie answered cheerfully, refusing

to acknowledge the apparent reprimand. Susie was a little late—eight minutes to be precise—but she had made up that amount many times over in unpaid overtime and work carried home. Susie turned into her own cubicle where the advertising sketches she had begun that morning still sat waiting. Next week Blaine's was having a china sale. In slender black lines, Susie was sketching the intricate patterns of a series of plates and teacups for an advertisement that would announce the special event. Without stopping to remove her jacket, Susie started right in where she had left off, glancing occasionally from the sketch to the actual plates spread out across the desk next to her drawing table. As she filled in the minute details with tiny skillful strokes of her pen, Susie bit her lower lip thoughtfully, remembering Sy's dark eyes and how they had swept over her.

When her pen began to feel unsteady in her hand, Susie laid it down and lifted a teacup for a closer inspection. She held it carefully, rotating it in the light to study it closely, trying to recover her concentration. Instead she found herself wondering what Sy had seen in her face. Was she just another subject to him? She had accused him of thinking of her as a piece of meat—a product to be photographed. She arched her dark brows in sudden insight. The cup she held was not simply an object—not like a "piece of meat" she was manipulating. It was something unique in itself, and it dictated to her how exquisite it was. It showed its special qualities and made her stretch her talents to capture them. She found herself wondering if being a photographer presented the same challenge—to let the subject speak its own language through the lens.

That was the romantic in her thinking. Maybe Sy had

that same romantic streak. Perhaps his idea of posing was like her holding the cup aloft, trying it in varying light until it looked right. With a smile she remembered Sy's expert touch, the slight adjustment in a hand or level of a chin that brought out the sophistication of the young debutantes in Jackson Square. If she had been his subject... if she had posed for him, what would he have elicited from her? What qualities would he have captured on his film?

With a sigh, Susie chased the thought away. *I don't need a picture of me, anyhow.* But if she ever did, Simon Avery's card was tucked away inside her jacket pocket.

WHEN SUSIE WALKED into her folks' house that evening, everything was in chaos. Sixteen bolts of satin in a multitude of shades were draped over every available piece of furniture.

"Ah—Souci." Bernard Costain passed along the hallway and greeted her with his pet name for her. His *souci* meant his little marigold. It sounded like Susie but since her childhood it had been their special code. "More bolts of material are in the front bedroom." He arched his bushy gray eyebrows hopefully. "How about it, Souci?" he asked. "Give us a hand before dinner?"

"Sure, dad." Susie turned in the opposite direction and headed for the front bedroom. When Claire was at home, it had been her room. In many ways, it still was. Claire's tall, gowned form smiled down from color photographs along the walls. Her Mardi Gras headdress, the one she had worn as Queen of Aeolus, had been preserved in a glass-covered display case. Then there were Claire and John's wedding pictures. And the one with the proud parents and John, Jr. Susie shook her head and sighed. Claire had done everything just perfectly.

"Black sheep," Susie muttered to herself as she wrapped her arms around two bolts of vivid green satin. She had told Sy she was a nonconformist. However, that didn't mean she liked drawing attention to herself. *No,* Susie thought, *I prefer to stay out of the limelight.* She cast a displeased look at the gallery of her sister's "accomplishments." Susie had rejected the offers to be a queen or even a maid of any Mardi Gras ball. She had attended an excellent local commercial art school instead of college. Unlike so many of her friends, Susie had not married. Her series of beaux had included only one near trip to the altar, and that romance had taught her to be cautious. On the surface, Richard Martin, the successful C.P.A. to whom Susie had become engaged after a swift and idyllic courtship, had been more than acceptable by any standards. Tall, sandy haired and sure of himself, Richard had seemed like any young woman's ideal: attractive, wealthy and a gentleman.

Susie had met Richard at a post-parade ball when she was twenty. Publicly, they appeared to make a perfect match—old New Orleans money on his side and artistry and fanciful Mardi Gras tradition on hers. Richard was convinced from the beginning that Susie was the one for him. He soon had Susie believing it, as well. They dated, became engaged and set the wedding date before Susie realized that what he saw in her was not the person she really was. She began to comprehend that Richard was not what he had seemed to be, either. Behind his polite veneer was a mind with rigid preconceptions for everything—including her.

Richard expected her to mature into a dark-haired version of her sister Claire—decorative, agreeable and domestic. Susie would be expected to join the right ladies' clubs, serve as a pleasant and attractive hostess for social functions, and within a year or two of their marriage she would produce the first of Richard's children. They would have two. Richard assumed that Susie would channel all her energies into their family and his career. His business was expanding; there would be no reason for her to work. She would have him, and she would have the children. She could direct her artistic abilities into making their home a showplace.

"But I'm not sure I want to jump into all that so soon," Susie protested. "Maybe one day," she conceded. "But right now, I like my art classes, and I like my work."

Richard listened and smiled as Susie spoke of her dreams and her ideas. In spite of the countless discussions, something in Richard's eyes indicated he never quite connected with what she said. Susie had the growing uneasy sensation that in spite of how much she cared for him and valued his opinions, her ambitions were relegated to a corner of his mind labeled "temporary." They would pass.

Richard diverted her attempts at discussion with his passion, using kisses and arousing touches to stimulate a sexual response that shifted her focus of attention. Richard was older, experienced and very skilled in lovemaking. And he knew how deeply Susie cared for him. Susie let her own sensuality blossom under his caresses. Desire and a longing to be physically close clouded Susie's vision of caring and commitment. She thought with Richard that they were all part of the same

feeling, or at least they could be when he finally understood how she felt about her art. Drawing allowed her
to release a passion she could not express in any other
form, a passion far removed from the one that Richard
could elicit. Both passions would mature—in time.
When Richard chose one rainy October night to take her
to his apartment for a quiet evening by the fire, he
betrayed her most unforgivably. He decided that there
was no more time. Then he tried to coerce Susie into
having sex with him. First he tried words. When they
were not enough, he tried force.

"You know you want to," he coaxed. "You know
your body is hungry for mine." Richard was right, up to
a point. Susie wanted to experience the mysteries of
making love with a man who was gentle and passionate.
She had believed Richard was that special man. But as
long as questions remained in her mind, she was not going to do anything irreversible that night—not with
Richard.

"I'm just not ready," she replied. "I'd rather wait. I
wouldn't want to get pregnant." Richard argued that he
was ready. He was frustrated by stopping with the pre-
liminaries.

"We're engaged. If you get pregnant, it will simply
speed things up a bit," he replied matter-of-factly. Then
he grabbed her and started kissing her, stroking her
body with strong, knowing hands. "I'll make it good,"
he promised as his voice thickened with desire.

When Susie resisted, Richard became more aggres-
sive, roughly stroking her thigh and sliding his hand upward over her silky panties. "I want you tonight." His
voice held a demanding quality. "You're letting all this
career stuff pull us apart. I want you all to myself. I

want to show you how good it can be, Susie. I want to
make you mine.'' At that point, Susie realized that
Richard had planned this all along. He was using her
own sensuality against her, trapping her in a stifling
relationship by bonding her to him sexually.

"I'll make you want it all the time.'' He thrust his
hand inside the sheer panties and touched the soft moist
area.

"Get away from me, Richard,'' Susie insisted coldly.
"Get your hands off my body.'' She stood rigid and
silent, expecting the biting edge in her voice to be sufficient to stop him.

But Richard only paused briefly as if he were considering his options. Then he started pulling off her
clothing, ripping off the panties with a sudden tug.
"You'll see.'' He forced her onto the carpet, pinning
her down with the bulk of his body. "You'll see that this
is what you really want. I'll take care of you.'' He
ground his mouth onto hers.

For the first time in her life, Susie actually had to
fight—physically hit and kick another human. But
Richard was not quite human anymore. Grasping and
clutching, panting and groaning, he had turned into
some kind of beast, seeking satisfaction from claiming
her body. Susie's frantic resistance finally stopped him
before he succeeded. Weeping and disheveled, Susie
rolled away from him. Richard had sprawled on the
floor, calming himself, then finally smiled sheepishly.
"I didn't want to lose you...'' he confessed. "I could
feel you slipping away....''

Susie never spoke to Richard again. He took her
home, let her off at the front walkway and drove off
into the night. He had done precisely what he had not

wanted to do. He had lost Susie—forever. Susie had lost something precious of her own—her innocence. The world of romance was no longer filled with beauty. She had tasted the power of her own passions and had managed to subdue them before they led her into a marriage for which she was unsuited. Susie had been honest and vulnerable. Now she recoiled, shaken more deeply than anyone realized. She went back to her art classes, her beginning career at Blaine's, and her seasonal job helping her parents with their costuming business, but she locked her sexual instincts deep inside herself so they would not betray her again. She avoided men who desired her and thought of sex and marriage, fearing that they were just like Richard—willing to tolerate her fantasies and ambitions temporarily but intent on fitting her into a mold that would trap her.

Susie's parents had accepted the breakup with Richard resolutely. Susie's father had eyed her cautiously, then nodded at the gleam of determination in her eye, and called her his *souci*. He trusted her judgment. Her mother, Rosie, had managed a stony look of resolve, knowing she would be the one to face the relatives and tell them the wedding for Susie and Richard was off. Within the year, Richard had married someone else. A few months after that the news reached the Costains that the delighted couple was expecting their first child.

Susie dismissed the events without regret, feeling vaguely relieved that Richard's efficient schedule was proceeding without her. In the four years since the engagement had ended, Susie had finished school, gone on to work full-time at Blaine's as an advertising illustrator and had become indispensable in the Costain Costuming Company. She had also never again trusted any man with her intimate thoughts or her secret desires. She had woven a secure cocoon around herself. An admiring young man shared her company for a time, then was replaced by another temporary romance. She was protected by her busy schedule full of friends, family and work. Most of the time that was enough.

"I need to check these with the sketches you made." Rosie stretched up over the bolts of fabric and brushed a quick kiss on her daughter's cheek as they passed in the hallway. "Wait till you see the apricot." She kept up a continual flow of chatter as she headed for more fabric bolts. "It's so gorgeous. And the lime green is a bit sharper than we thought but it will look spectacular with the rhinestones." She had two large plastic-covered bolts of vivid blue tucked under her arms as she hurried up the hallway after Susie.

The second floor of the Costain household had been transformed over the years into a vast storage and work area with shelves for fabrics, suspended doweling to support rolls of sequined and beaded trims and flat smooth cutting tables where Rosie Costain and her crew of seamstresses worked on the gowns. There was a row of heavy, gleaming sewing machines where the pieces were all assembled and at the far end of the large room were headless mannequins whose adjustable bodies would stand in for the actual clients.

Over the double garage behind the sewing room was another square workroom—the remaining space occupied by Costain Costuming Company. This was Bernie's realm—which he gladly shared with his daughter. Here, amid spirals of metal, heavy clippers, soldering irons and models of heads and torsos, Bernie and Susie designed and constructed the elaborate headpieces, collars, backpieces and trains that transformed mere mortals into creatures of fantasy.

All the bolts of satin were placed in specific order on the shelves of the first workroom. Here the three of them—Bernie, Rosie and Susie—would meet, review the stacks of ink and acrylic sketches Susie had done, correlate colors and trims, then approve or adjust the designs.

Susie smiled as she watched her dad sliding bolt after bolt of fabric into place. Already she could feel the pace accelerating. Within the week, the sewing room would leap to life as cutters and seamstresses worked under Rosie's scrutiny. Susie's designs would emerge from flat sketches into flowing, three-dimensional creations.

"Here we go again." Rosie nudged her daughter aside and passed the blue fabric to Bernie. "Like on a roller coaster." She grinned. All the preconstruction work—the meetings with clients, preliminary sketches and designs, coordinating colors with themes of the various balls had been done throughout the summer and early fall at a leisurely pace in the evenings. But now the activity would intensify as October turned into November, and the Mardi Gras season moved closer. Each of the nearly sixty carnival organizations, with membership from a hundred to almost a thousand, had its unique origins and traditions, from the older ones with secret rituals and select entrance requirements to the more recent ones founded by neighborhood groups and young professionals. There were certain similarities among them, however, chiefly the facts that all of them called themselves "krewes" and chose some historical or mythological namesake for their own. These carnival societies scheduled elaborate balls spanning the months leading up to Mardi Gras, then filled the streets of New Orleans and the surrounding parishes with day and night parades in the weeks before Mardi Gras Day. It was the representatives of the krewes who sought Susie and her family to design the costumes for king, queen and court.

Some of the balls were as early as December, but the Costains had their first shipments of costumes due to be ready for the weekend of the eighth of January—a sparkling Friday-night ball for the Krewe of Aeolus, then a Saturday celebration for the Krewe of Merlin. After that, there were five other krewes to accommodate. It would mean a steady stream of fittings and finishings, photo sessions and final touches until the Triton Ball on the fifth of February, where cousin Michelle would reign, and their final krewe ball on the twelfth. On Mardi Gras Day, when the last two krewes paraded, Susie and her parents would be home watching it all on television, happily finished for this year.

"We eat first." Bernie slid his arm around Susie's shoulders. "Our partner looks like she had a long day." He held Susie against him while they crossed the hollow-sounding workroom. "Come on, Rosie," he summoned his wife from her inspection of the shelves. "Feed your loving husband and your darling daughter," he joked, "then we'll get to those sketches. Rosie—" he urged her away from the fabric "—*food*."

Rosie talked nonstop as she moved around the kitchen. "Your cousin Michelle was by earlier," she went on, as she scooped steaming white rice and rich okra-tomato-and-shrimp gumbo onto each plate. "She didn't seem very impressed with the fabric for her gown." Rosie made the comment without expecting an answer.

She didn't get one. Susie eagerly focused her attention on her plateful of aromatic seafood stew, and her father was preoccupied with his parrots.

Bernie kept two of them in a Plexiglas-covered alcove in the far wall of the kitchen—live, multicolored parrots named Rosalind and Marcel. "Come, eat." Rosie nudged her husband with her hip as she bore his plate of gumbo to the table. "Those two birds have done nothing but sleep all day," Rosie muttered. "I don't want them holding up our meal with all their squawking." Both Marcel and Rosalind let out shrill cries of protest as Bernie edged away from them.

Bernie moved his large-framed body across the kitchen and snatched several pieces of lettuce from the refrigerator. Then he dropped one into each compartment of the alcove. Each parrot could munch contentedly in privacy, and the Costains could enjoy their dinner without jungle sounds interrupting the proceedings.

"You know, you could move back in with us for the next few months," Bernie said to his daughter. "All the late hours and you with a job." He poked at a large piece of pink shrimp on his plate. "You know how hectic it gets."

"We don't ever use your room for anything except storing heads," Rosie chimed in. The heads that lined Susie's former bedroom were tagged and molded copies of customer's heads awaiting fittings for hats and headpieces. Each head was numbered to identify the sketch that went with it, and most of the heads bore whimsical, long-lashed faces Susie had drawn on them after the mold had dried.

"I like my own place," Susie answered quietly. After the season had ended the year before she had moved from a furnished efficiency apartment in Chalmette into her own one-bedroom apartment down in the Quarter. Bit by bit she had furnished it herself from outdoor markets, antique shops and her parents' overflow from their garage. It had become her private haven and her home.

"I don't mind the drive out here," Susie insisted. "The apartment is close to Blaine's, so I can walk to work." She didn't look up. She knew her dad would be frowning. "Maybe..." Susie relented, "maybe if it gets terribly busy—" she noticed her father's fork halt in midair "—I'll stay here over the weekends. Maybe even some weeknights, if it seems wiser."

"Anytime you want to stay," Bernie affirmed. "We kinda miss having you around." Now it was his turn to glance away.

"Whatever you want, dear." Rosie patted her daughter's arm. "Your room will always be waiting for you."

Susie stifled a sigh. Rosie meant well but she did tend to worry about Susie's living in "that part of town." Susie was doing just fine out on her own. There was no way she would give up her independence and come running home to mom and dad.

It was after eleven when Susie pulled her little compact car into the parking place marked 2B. In the sloped-roof apartment above, on the second floor of the old slave quarters that had been transformed into two pleasant apartments, Renny Castelot's light was still on. Susie glanced over the dark shrubbery shrouding the high walls that separated the apartment courtyard from the parking area. There was no moon visible this night, and mist from the river hung like a pall over the rooftops, cloaking the narrow streets of the French Quarter in an eerie silence. Some sections of the Quarter weren't the safest places for a lone female to be at night, but Susie's courtyard usually felt like a pleasant sanctuary. Tonight it didn't seem so secure.

Before she unlocked the car door, Susie flicked her headlights off and on. There was no response, so she did it again. This time Renny's mane of wild hair poked out his doorway.

"That you, Susie?" he called down over the dull stone wall that surrounded the courtyard.

"It's me." Susie opened her car door and stepped out. "Boy, am I glad you're still awake." She closed and locked the car door securely and hurried through the metal grille gate half hidden in the bushes. Her heart was beating more rapidly than usual, but she managed a brave smile as she climbed the stairs toward her bushy-haired neighbor. Renny was probably the most gentle man she had ever met, but his tall, gaunt frame and his ever-changing bush of shoulder-length hair made him a frightening sentinel. Anyone lurking in the dark around the parking area would think twice before tangling with this long-armed specter who stood guard over her.

"Have you been painting?" Susie greeted him.

"I've been out lining up some new projects." Renny stepped back from the edge of the narrow balcony to let her pass. "I'm going to sell out. . ." he said dramatically. "I'm going commercial with my massive talent."

"Well, I happen to have a container of my mother's gumbo and rice," Susie teased him. "If I offer you a little food, will you quit being so mysterious and tell me what you're talking about?"

"Feed me and I'll tell you anything you want to know." Renny strolled into her apartment after her and collapsed onto one of the three unmatched dining-room chairs.

"Start talking," Susie said eagerly. "I'll stick this in the microwave. Go on. . ." she urged the lanky artist.

"I am going to paint scenery." Renny assumed his flamboyant pose and flipped his wrist haughtily. "I will be scenic consultant, part-time builder and background painter for *three* Mardi Gras balls. And I'll get six months' rent for my efforts."

"Six months' rent!" Susie clasped her hands in delight. Renny had barely been able to afford food since the tourist trade had dropped off in the Quarter. He had poured all his financial resources into a collection of enormous acrylic abstracts he was preparing for a gallery preview in February. But that was almost four months off. If painting scenery for some Mardi Gras balls would pay the rent, Renny could now afford to eat and buy paints and canvases for his more serious projects.

"That's absolutely wonderful," Susie exclaimed, as the soft chiming of the microwave oven signaled that the food was now hot.

"I may need a little help from you." Renny kept his eyes on the steaming gumbo as he watched Susie ladle it into a bowl. "I think you and your folks are doing the costuming for the same functions. Do the names Merlin, Hyacinth and Sirens mean anything to you?" He had named three prominent krewes that had balls and parades scheduled each Mardi Gras season.

"We're doing the costumes for two of them." Susie sat down across from him while he ate. "We have Sirens and Merlin. I don't know about the other krewe. They must be getting their headpieces and gowns from some other costumer.''

Renny looked up at her and shrugged, then he turned his rapt attention back to the bowl of seafood stew.

"How am I supposed to help you?" Susie propped her chin on her hand and waited for Renny to finish a mouthful.

"Just make sure that nothing *I* do clashes with whatever it is you're making for them to wear.'' He scraped the last morsel from the white bowl and sighed with genuine pleasure. "I'd like to look at the drawings you made for the costumes," he continued, "if that's not too much of an invasion of professional privacy.'' Renny knew that all sketches and plans for Mardi Gras costumes and decorations were scrupulously guarded secrets.

"You can come over and help glue on sequins while you look,'' Susie agreed. "My folks have been very curious about who I hang around with socially.'' She grinned. "I can't wait for my father and mother to get a look at you.'' She knew Renny delighted in shocking people with his outrageous outfits. Today his hair was its normal brownish hue and his faded jeans were unspectacular, but there were weekends in the quarter when Renny went fuchsia or orange from head to toe— hair included. Generally he sold the most paintings on those days.

"You want me in any particular shade?" Renny's pale blue eyes sparkled mischievously.

"Let's keep it simple for the first visit.'' Susie felt suddenly cautious. "I'm trying to assure them that I'm secure and functioning successfully on my own. One of your color spectaculars may unnerve them. They're very picky about who's allowed in the workrooms, anyhow," she noted. "I'd rather you look like a scenic designer and not a part of the show."

"Then I shall moderate my style," Renny promised.

"Just be your off-duty self," Susie stressed. "They'll see the good inside you—eventually." She smiled slyly. "That's the method I keep hoping works for me. Of course, they still haven't made up their minds in my case. I'm still the uncategorized daughter in the clan," she confided. "There isn't much to brag about—especially at family get-togethers where job titles and grandchildren are the main topics of conversation."

"If your mother feeds you this well and your father worries about you getting mugged," Renny said philosophically, "then I think you're safe in assuming they really like you just as you are." He stretched his long thin arms in a satisfied manner, then dropped them abruptly over the pockets of his faded shirt. "I forgot to give you the note!" he gasped, groping into one pocket. "Some guy came by before dark and knocked on your door. He kinda paced along the balcony—seemed a bit uneasy." Renny wriggled his eyebrows dramatically. "So I climbed into your apartment through the bathroom and answered the door for you." Susie shook her head and laughed out loud. The old transom between the boarded-shut doors that separated his bathroom from hers had come in handy more than once when she'd forgotten keys or hungry goldfish needed attending. Now it had been used to surprise some late-afternoon visitor.

"And what did my mysterious caller want?" Susie asked patiently. "For me to buy something or join something? Or did he want anything after he got over the thrill of seeing you instead of me?''

"He didn't confide in me," Renny said grandly. "He just asked if this was where you lived. I said yes. I told him I'd give you a message if he wanted to leave one. He scribbled this note and asked me to give it to you." Renny held out a folded piece of paper. Susie's smile of amusement collapsed when Renny added, "He was a big guy with a beard—nice beard, short, neat, like a Roman gladiator's."

Renny had just described Simon Avery. Susie quickly opened the note.

"It says he's sorry he bothered you and hopes you'll forgive him for upsetting you." Renny had recited the contents precisely before Susie was half finished reading.

"You read it!" Susie groaned.

"It could have been something real important—or real weird!" he said to defend himself. "And it was just folded up. I didn't break any federal mail regulations." He sniffed. "I guess I wanted to check him out before he got too far away."

"You shouldn't have read it." Susie looked at the now-open note that bore the message Renny had detailed. It was signed Sy.

"Who is this Sy and what did he do to upset you?" Renny leaned forward anxiously. With elbows and knees poking out, he looked like a hairy spider about to pounce on its victim.

"None of your business," Susie said coolly.

"You want me to work him over?" Renny tried to sound tough. His pale blue eyes and lean hands betrayed his gentle nature, but the look of concern on his face was genuinely touching.

"I want you to quit reading my messages." Susie barely suppressed a smile. "You did remember to feed the goldfish while you were breaking into the premises?" she asked.

"No, but I will if you'll forgive me for poking my nose in where it doesn't belong." He leaped to his feet and grabbed the plastic container of fish food.

"Feed the fish." Susie gave in. "Then go home and let me get some sleep. I have to be at work at eight tomorrow," she muttered.

"What's this Sy's last name?" Renny tried to sound casual as he sprinkled the flakes over the surface of the water of the aquarium.

"Go home, Renny," Susie waved him out. "And use the door this time—" she chuckled "—so you'll remember how it works." Obediently her tall, gangly friend loped off along the balcony to his own apartment.

"Forgive me for upsetting you. . . ." Susie stared at the note Sy Avery had written. His strong, slightly back-slanting letters spread across the page. Susie studied the handwriting, trying to decipher some message beyond mere words. She wondered if he had been startled to find a man in her apartment. Live-in arrangements were quite common. Perhaps he would assume she and Renny were lovers. Then she wearily tucked the note into her jacket pocket along with the neatly printed business card that bore his name.

"Forgive and forget," she sighed as she slipped off her brown pumps and padded into the bedroom in her stocking feet. But when she finally slid beneath the cool sheets and stared into the darkness, Sy's solemn deep brown eyes haunted her, and a tight sensation in her chest warned her that even without being here he could threaten her self-control.

"Me and my character," she mumbled before drowsiness finally eased away the tension. Perhaps the dark-eyed photographer would leave her alone after this. Sy had come looking for her and found a six-foot-four hairy ostrich of a man who seemed very much at home in her apartment. That would be enough to discourage most men. Whatever Sy had concluded was no longer Susie's concern. This long day was over. Tomorrow would take care of itself.

CHAPTER TWO

SUSIE KNEW Simon Avery had taken the photograph even before she glanced at the name embossed in gold on the lower right corner. Her cousin Michelle looked radiant, like some fairy princess out of an ancient tale, with her pale gold hair billowing in the breeze and her bright blue eyes the identical color of the sky behind her. The portrait had been propped up on the Costains' kitchen counter when Susie arrived there after work.

"Uncle Leo is so proud of Michelle." Rosie leaned over her daughter's shoulder and stared at the color portrait. "She's finally given up that grubby geology student, whatever his name was," Rosie rattled on, "and she's concentrating on her classes at Tulane. She's taking French, you know."

"I didn't know." Susie slid the portrait back into its envelope and placed it on the kitchen counter.

"She has so much to do with the ball this year, fittings and all." Rosie didn't notice that Susie's gaze lingered on the return address on the large envelope. "You can remember how exciting it was when Claire was a ball queen." The dark-haired woman moved around the kitchen rapidly, checking the oven and sprinkling spices into the pot on the stove. "Apparently Leo is having an entire album of this year done for Michelle by Sy Avery. I don't know if he still is terribly expensive," she went on, as she sniffed the casserole in the oven. "He does marvelous work. There will be a lot of delighted people when word gets around that he's back here. Don't you think the portrait of Michelle is wonderful?"

"The portrait is very good," Susie replied pleasantly, then turned toward the hallway that led back to the workrooms.

"Dinner in thirty minutes," Rosie called after her. "Tell your dad."

Susie nodded and kept walking. She needed to get up there amid all the fabric and trims and find a bit of solace simply working next to her father. The picture of Michelle and the name Simon Avery had brought back a flood of conflicting feelings. Part of them revolved around his chocolate eyes and neatly trimmed beard. She remembered how the dark beard outlined his square jaw and gave an intriguing look to an otherwise gentle face. But thinking of Sy also brought back the feelings of self-consciousness when he'd looked at her. She wasn't a golden goddess like Michelle. Michelle was nineteen, five years younger than Susie, and she was following the pattern set by Claire and other friends and cousins before her. She had served as a maid in a ball last year. This year she would be a queen. Then she'd meet a young man with money, marry him...and have children and social engagements.

Susie just couldn't fit herself into that mold, not even to please her family. And she would never look exquisite in a Simon Avery portrait.

"Grab the soldering iron," Bernie greeted her as soon as he heard her footsteps in the rear workroom. Susie picked up the hot, wedge-tipped instrument. "Now give me just enough to hold this in place here—" he waited while she melted a drop of solder onto the joint he indicated "—and here." Bernie blew on the two soldered spots then held up the curlicued metal frame he had crafted. "This is the head of the giraffe...." He turned it upright so it did, in fact, resemble the head of the creature. "You think your old man did all right?" He beamed with satisfaction. Pinned to the workroom wall in front of his stool was the original drawing that Susie had made for the giraffe headpiece. Only a few dark lines indicated where the understructure was crucial. Just as he had done hundreds of times before, Bernie had created the perfect metal support for Susie's complicated design. The Krewe of Merlin would have another breathtaking creature to present at their ball, "Jungle Splendor."

"You did great." Susie placed an affectionate kiss on her father's slightly damp forehead. Already she could imagine the pale, mottled-satin covering and the beaded mane that would transform the giraffe framework into an exquisite headdress. "How about taking a break?" She placed the soldering iron back on the stand and unplugged it. "You look a little overheated." She frowned.

"It was just the strain of doing a four-handed job with only two hands." Bernie put the wired head aside. "Now that you're here, we can wrestle with a couple of other things before your mother calls us to dinner."

"I'd like you to know that we're having company..." Susie began cautiously. "A good friend of mine, Renny Castelot, will be working on the scenery for a few of our balls. He wanted to see the costume designs and colors, just to keep from making any big errors." She waited while her father mopped his brow.

"Now, I know the designs are top secret," she said, anticipating his next remarks, "but Renny is the fellow who lives in the next apartment to mine, the man who protects me from muggers." She patted Bernie's knee good-naturedly. "If he protects my body and my personal belongings and feeds my goldfish," she noted, "I think he can be trusted with our designs."

"So why is he coming to dinner?" Bernie asked slyly. "You got a romance going with this guy?" He didn't try to conceal the hopeful quality in his voice.

"He's coming to dinner because he likes to eat," she replied. "He's another one of those starving artists."

"Is he some kind of nut case?" Bernie asked warily. "I've seen those guys in the Quarter."

"With any luck, tonight he'll be perfectly normal." Susie shrugged. "Just give him a chance, daddy."

"Of course I will," Bernie replied gruffly. "Should I put on a beret and an ascot," he teased. "Maybe your mother's Chinese bathrobe?"

"There's no need to get carried away." Susie giggled. "Renny will be nervous enough as it is. Besides—" she stood and looked down at her wide-shouldered father with his crop of steely gray hair "—you'd look silly in all that stuff."

"Then I'll settle for my gray sweater." Bernie touched the soldering iron to make sure that it had cooled enough that he could leave the room. "Right after you help me straighten a few feet of wire." He and Susie retreated to the bench and vise at the far end of the room where a spool of coiled aluminum wire hung from a wooden spindle. There they cut and straightened two-foot lengths of wire until Rosie called them to dinner.

"I think your friend is here." Rosie met them at the

bottom of the stairway. "*Something* in a cape just leaped off a motorcycle. The motorcycle roared off—" she rolled her eyes toward the front of the house "—but whatever it is is still standing out in the cold."

"I'll call him in." Susie preceded her parents. *Please be normal...* she begged inwardly as she tugged open the front door and felt the chilly gust of damp November air.

The first meeting went more easily than Susie had anticipated. Under his hooded cape, Renny had been neatly clad. His flyaway hair was still its natural sandy brown and seemed to have been combed at one time, in spite of the ravages of riding behind his friend on the motorcycle. But when he bit into Rosie's crabmeat casserole and sighed with ecstasy, Renny gained a friend for life. Rosie loved an appreciative audience.

"These two are spoiled." She grinned at Renny. "They think everyone cooks like this...."

"Only the gods cook like this," Renny gushed. "And maybe a chef or two at Antoine's or Galatoire's." The last remark elicited a smile from Bernie. He knew for certain that no one dressed like Renny Castelot dined at either of those prestigious New Orleans restaurants. So the tall, gawky fellow had a sense of humor. And he looked out for Susie. The guy was all right.

Somewhere in the midst of the dinner conversation, Rosie leaped up and passed the portrait of Michelle to Bernie. "I forgot to show you this," she said. "Your brother Leo dropped it by."

"Simon Avery is back in business," Bernie remarked. "Sy does good work. I'll have to pass the word to our clients."

"Sy...?" Renny's pale blue eyes shifted from the

envelope and the portrait to Susie. It had been more than a week since he'd greeted Susie's nocturnal caller, but Renny recognized the name that the bearded visitor had signed on Susie's note.

"Sy Avery...." Bernie passed the photo to Renny. "He used to do all the debutantes and engagement pictures and anything else that required making someone look good." Bernie took a sip of his coffee. "He married some model gal a few years back. I think she went to France to do some high-fashion work. I guess he went with her. Nice fella. The women all love him."

"I can see why." Renny slid the portrait of Michelle back into the envelope and passed it to Rosie. "He gets the most out of his material."

"Michelle is quite a beauty, anyway," Rosie boasted. "We have a gorgeous group of gals in our family."

"I'll say." Renny smiled. Without looking up from her plate, Susie kicked his leg under the table. "Good old Sy is back." Renny chuckled. "I'll have to keep an eye out for him."

At ten-thirty, Renny had completed his tour of the Costain workrooms, eaten his second piece of Rosie's carrot cake and folded himself into Susie's car on the passenger side.

"So Sy Avery hurt your feelings...." He got right to the point after they'd backed out of the driveway.

"I don't want to discuss it," Susie warned him. "He apologized, it's over, I'll probably not cross paths with him again—unless it's on business, and he's married." She moved through the list a bit too rapidly.

"I guess that about covers it." Renny glanced sideways at her intent face.

"I guess it does," Susie agreed.

Renny let it drop at that. As they drove the few miles from the Costain house in Chalmette into the heart of New Orleans, they spoke only of the costumes and the colors and not of the man who worked magic on film.

SUSIE NOTICED the young boy dining alone in the chilly back alcove of the Napoleon House restaurant in the Quarter when she made her way through the lunch crowd. The sea-god fountain still spouted a thin stream of water even though there was a film of ice around the outer edges of the water's surface in the semicircular base. The open courtyard had been shunned by most of the locals who preferred to eat closer to the heaters indoors. Susie had been cooped up in Blaine's all morning. She and the boy shared a similar desire to sit by the small fountain where the sunshine was visible and listen to the steady trickle of the water.

From the doorway, Susie studied the lad's solemn little face as he sat by himself inspecting the menu.

"Would you mind if I sat with you?" Susie asked him when she'd reached the alcove. "We could leave that other table free for any other daring souls who decided to eat out here."

The boy looked up at her, then contemplated the empty table with four chairs across the patio from him.

"I guess it would be fair if we let some others have that table." He looked up at her warily. "You're not a weirdo or anything are you?" he demanded.

"I'm not a weirdo," Susie assured him. "My name is Susie Costain." She held out her hand. "I work just a few blocks away at Blaine's."

"I'm Tony." The boy shook the hand she offered. "I go to school."

"Apparently not today." Susie grinned as she sat across from him. At lunchtime on a Wednesday in November, school was where a youngster his age should have been.

"I had a dentist's appointment." Tony lifted his chin a little defensively. "My dad said that since I didn't need any fillings, he'd take me to lunch and I could sort of miss the rest of the afternoon at school."

"Your dad is with you?" Susie picked up her purse and started to slide her chair back. She had not intended to intrude on a father-son luncheon. Then she heard the click and whir of the automatic advance of a camera.

"He is now." Tony grinned up at his father who hastily snapped another shot of the twosome at the table.

"This time, I didn't ask," Simon Avery smiled politely. "If you want me to crop off your part of the picture, I'll do it when I print your copy of the shot." There was a trace of caution beneath his tight smile. "It's nice to see you again, Susie," he said, nodding.

"I didn't mean to butt into your luncheon with your son," Susie apologized. "I thought he was alone."

"We didn't want to waste space," Tony explained. "Besides, she works in the Quarter—like you. I checked her out, dad," he insisted. "She isn't a weirdo."

"Leave it to a seven-year-old to be a character witness," Sy blurted before he realized he'd said the word "character." "Sorry." He raised both hands in resignation.

"We seem to be going from bad to worse." Susie smiled in forgiveness at Sy's distress. "Let's back this up a bit," she suggested. "You two were about to have lunch—and I was just leaving."

"I thought you were going to sit with me," Tony protested. "I can eat with my dad anytime."

"Maybe I'm the one who should leave you two alone." Sy winked at his son. "Or maybe we could compromise. Let's just all sit calmly," he suggested as he urged Susie to remain seated. "I'll treat you both to lunch," he offered as he sat down next to Tony, "and I'll act as an unobtrusive chaperone." His eyes locked onto Susie's.

For a moment, she considered refusing. Then she glanced at the bright, upturned face of Tony Avery. "Okay," she said softly. There was a glimmer of change in the set of Sy's bearded jaw—a slight softening that seemed to indicate approval, or maybe it simply meant they had called a truce. Whatever it was, Susie felt compelled to lower her eyes from his. Until now, she had not realized how apt Renny's description had been. The close-trimmed beard and mustache—dark and luxuriant—did give Sy the formidable appearance of a Roman gladiator. His angular profile, softened slightly by the line of the beard, made him striking—and handsome. Handsome—and married.

The white-jacketed waiter had delivered po-boys, thick slices of French bread packed with juicy, meaty fillings, by the time Tony launched into his commentary on the intricacies of his karate lessons. "My dad says that he doesn't want me to be a bully or anything," Tony explained, "but it takes a long time for a little kid like me to get as tall as my dad, and he doesn't want me to get pushed around while I'm waiting to grow."

Susie had to sip her hot coffee to avoid smiling at his sincere narration. "My dad doesn't like fighting," Tony added in a matter-of-fact tone. Then his big brown eyes shifted momentarily to meet his father's.

"Does your mother encourage you in your karate?" Susie hoped that her color didn't deepen visibly with the question.

"My mother isn't interested in sports. Once she bought me some roller skates," he noted. "Then she wouldn't even let me skate in the house."

"It was winter. . . in Switzerland." Sy stared at Susie evenly. "There was nowhere else to skate except in the house."

"And she didn't like the toboggan my dad bought me because she was afraid I'd fall off and get snowy." Tony shook his head. His smooth brown hair, not quite as dark as his father's, swayed gently, then settled down just above his collar.

"Then I guess she doesn't approve of your karate, either," Susie remarked.

"She doesn't know!" Tony grinned. "Dad and I aren't going to tell her until I qualify for a blue belt. By then I'll be able to take care of myself pretty well."

"Doesn't she wonder where you are when you go to the karate lessons?" Susie frowned slightly. Her mother had always kept close track of her; she assumed that was something all mothers did.

"My ex-wife lives in France." Sy had grown impatient with Susie's questions, and he bit off each word with deliberate precision. "Tony lives with me."

"With my dad and Francine," Tony added dutifully.

"Oh." Susie felt her temporary relief at knowing Sy was divorced fade with the mention of a live-in companion called Francine.

Sy smiled smugly, obviously reading Susie's thoughts.

After several long seconds he said, "Francine is fifty, slightly overweight and one heck of a housekeeper." He had no intention of playing games with her.

"Oh," Susie repeated as her color deepened.

"Who do you live with?" Tony asked abruptly.

"That's none of our business." Sy shushed his son. "Let's get on with the sandwich eating," he advised. "Susie has a right to her privacy."

"I live by myself—in an apartment here in the Quarter," Susie answered quietly. "Next to a very considerate neighbor who keeps an eye on me and my goldfish."

Sy paused and looked at her. Then the remoteness in his deep brown eyes faded as that broad grin spread across his face.

"I'm sure Tony is delighted to hear that." Sy stared at her with his penetrating eyes that seemed to strip through her defenses so easily. He knew the information was intended for him. She was no game player, either. Susie wanted to be sure that whatever Sy thought about Renny Castelot's greeting him at her door was corrected. "So, you live alone—we live with Francine." Sy smiled. "Is there anything else you'd like to know about us?" he teased.

Susie lifted her po-boy and bit into it, eager to conceal her embarrassment. She had been pressing Tony for details about his mother, but only to let Sy know she was well aware he was married. Now he seemed to infer she was fishing for information—personal information that was none of her business. Susie cringed at the thought. She always asked straightforward questions—out of curiosity, not for any devious purpose. In his profession, Sy must have found many women—

beautiful, single women—who asked questions for other reasons.

Oh, brother, Susie silently lamented. *He must think I'm just another one.* "I saw the portrait you took of my cousin, Michelle." Susie tried bravely to change the subject. "It was quite good."

"They're supposed to be good," Sy replied easily. "That's what I get paid to produce." There was no arrogance in his remark. He simply was stating a truth.

"I guess that's right," Susie heard her voice quaver.

"What do you do?" Tony asked between mouthfuls. His wide eyes scrutinized Susie's outfit. Her slim gray slacks and cable-knit sweater didn't look like a shop clerk's attire—particularly not at a stylish department store like Blaine's. Susie had a certain informality that Tony appreciated. "I like to try to guess what people do, but I can't figure you out."

Sy and Susie laughed, then a bit self-consciously Susie said, "I have two jobs." She was relieved to have Tony to divert her attention. "I work days at Blaine's drawing everything from ladies' shoes and cosmetics to housewares for advertisements," she said evenly. "After that, during the months leading up to Mardi Gras, I help my dad and my mom in a costuming business. We design and make headpieces, collars, gowns and trains for the members of the courts of various krewes."

"You mean all those guys that ride on floats?" Tony brightened with interest. "The ones who throw beads and doubloons into the crowds?"

"I design the costumes for some of them," Susie confirmed.

"Wow," Tony breathed.

Encouraged by his interest, Susie went on. "Every

year each krewe picks a certain theme, and I design their costumes to fit that idea. But we actually make only some of the costumes," she acknowledged. "We primarily do the ladies' costumes—the ones they wear to the krewe balls when the queen and maids are presented. Later they wear the same outfits in the parades."

"When they throw the doubloons!" Tony said excitedly.

Susie laughed with delight. Now she understood the object of his fascination. "Yes, when they throw the doubloons."

"Can you get me some doubloons and some beads?" Tony asked with a grin. Like most children who knew about Mardi Gras parades, he wanted the trinkets, or "throws" as they were called—the stamped doubloon coins that bore the name of the krewe sponsoring the parade and the gaudy necklaces of plastic beads that the riders on the floats pitched in handfuls to the throngs of eager bystanders.

"Tony." Sy chuckled in exasperation.

"I'll see what I can do," Susie promised. "I'll use my influence to see if I can gather some goodies for you."

"You can drop them by the house or mail them to me," Tony suggested. "Or my dad will pick them up," he offered promptly and good-naturedly. "Won't you, dad?" He turned wide, dark eyes, much like his father's, toward Sy.

Sy tired to frown, but the delight in the boy's face forced a smile to break through. "You get the doubloons." Sy said to Susie, "and I'll find a way to pick them up."

"It's a deal." Susie grinned, relieved to see the glow in Sy's eyes.

"Yeah, well if it's a deal, you have to shake on it," Tony insisted.

Sy promptly held an open palm out to Susie.

Perhaps it was her slight hesitation that made Sy's smile widen. When Susie placed her hand in his, he closed his long, strong fingers around her palm and stared at her until she finally let her eyes meet his. That wide spectacular grin surrounded by the elegant, manly beard simply engulfed her—and the warmth of his grasp spread a tantalizing heat through her body that gradually turned her cheeks a deep rose. What seemed to be simply a handshake had lingered and become an embrace.

"I still find your face fascinating," he said evenly.

"I'd... better go," she stammered when Sy finally relinquished his hold on her hand. "I'm probably well over my lunch hour as it is. Thank you both for the lunch and the company." She stood to leave.

"How will Susie know where to reach us?" Tony wailed. He wasn't about to lose out on the cache of Mardi Gras trinkets.

"She has my card, son." Sy stood calmly and eased the chair out from behind his guest. "Whenever she wants to reach us," he said deliberately, "I'm sure she can find us."

Susie's cheeks were scarlet when she strode out onto Royal Street and turned toward Canal where the comforting austerity of Blaine's awaited her. "Me—call him," she huffed. Her breath made little clouds of gray in the chill November air. "Of all the arrogance...." She stalked past shops with windows already glistening with Christmas displays.

But there was a certain charm about Sy Avery that she

could not deny. There was that sudden burst of light when he smiled—really smiled. It had made her heart leap. It had made her breath catch. And it had made her blush. Ever since she'd broken off her engagement to Richard Martin, she had built a snug wall around her feelings. She had adopted an attitude of self-assurance and independence that even she had begun to think was impenetrable. "I'm not ready for a commitment," she reminded herself whenever a beau became a bit persistent. Until now, it had always worked.

Then Sy had looked at her and smiled. He had spoken of the Creole blood pulsing through her veins. He seemed to sense the sexuality that she was afraid to release.

"Whenever she wants to reach us...." He had said it carefully, as if it were an invitation.

"I'm not ready..." Susie breathed as she neared the entrance of Blaine's.

This time when the big revolving doors swished behind her, they did not close out the world. She could still visualize the smile and the steady eyes above the neat beard. She could remember the lingering grasp of his hand. She could imagine how that same hand would caress her breast or slide down the curve of her spine.

"Why now?" Susie moaned as the elevator hummed up to the third floor. She was up to her eyebrows in headpieces, trains and collars. Her nights were taken up with fittings and soldering and gluing. Why now? She shook her head dejectedly.

"Another long lunch hour?" Ella Jenkins stepped into the elevator just as Susie started out. Her thin lips were drawn into a tight slash of a mouth.

"I guess so." Susie felt as if she had been caught playing hooky. Then she remembered young Tony Avery. He was playing hooky, and he had been thoroughly enjoying it. "It was another divine luncheon," Susie added defiantly as Ms Jenkins's angular face disappeared behind the closing elevator doors. It was a silly, childish, rude thing to do, Susie realized. *But it sure felt good.* However, just in case, she would stay a little late tonight and put in some obvious free overtime to placate the punctual Ms Jenkins.

SUSIE SPENT MUCH of the next two weeks with the Costains, often sleeping over in her old room and stopping at her own apartment only long enough to pick up or drop off clothing. From late afternoon until almost midnight, a steady stream of clients from various krewes came through for their first dress fittings and their initial headpiece fittings. For each of the ladies who would be in the courts, Susie also had to design a smaller tiara to wear at the Krewe ball after the presentation and the tableau. The heavy, elaborate theme headdresses were simply too cumbersome to continue wearing throughout an evening of dining and dancing. A seven-foot giraffe would be spectacular in a presentation tableau, but would be ill-suited for a waltz.

By the weekend of the nineteenth, Susie had lost five pounds by maintaining her rigorous schedule and could barely drag herself out of bed in the morning.

"I think I'll skip the coronation tonight." She propped her head up on one hand while Rosie poured her a cup of coffee. "I'll just stay home and sleep." She lowered her forehead to the kitchen table.

"Now you know it wouldn't look right," Rosie reprimanded predictably. "Michelle is wearing the presentation dress you designed and I sewed. She'll be paraded around in front of all our friends and relatives, not to mention the other krewe members. Besides, your Uncle Leo had every one of *his* children there when Claire was named queen...."

Susie didn't need to listen to the rest. Rosie was right. If Michelle was being crowned Triton's Queen, the Costains had to be there in full force. The coronation dance marked the official beginning of festivities for each krewe that would participate in Mardi Gras. From mid-November until the big Triton Ball in February, Michelle would be a fantasy queen. It had been five years since a Costain beauty bore a queen's crown; when it happened, Susie knew she should be present.

"I don't have anything to wear." Susie looked down at the loose waistband of her jeans. "I get skinny when our schedule gets hectic."

Rosie slid a plate with two blueberry pancakes under her nose, then stood back to take a good look at her daughter. "Maybe I'll take in your plum-colored dress. It has nice soft lines." She bent down and hugged Susie's shoulders. "You look pale; plum will make you look a bit pinker."

"So will a hot bath." Susie sighed and let the golden syrup trickle over her pancakes.

"You eat, take a bath, shampoo your hair." Rosie patted Susie's shoulder. "Let me poke around and see what else I can come up with. We've got closets full of dresses," she assured her daughter. "What I want to know is who will be your escort? You have to go with somebody."

"I'll go with you and daddy," Susie said, stuffing a forkful of pancakes into her mouth.

"How about that nice young man from the telephone company?" Rosie began reviewing Susie's recent beaux. "Or that fellow from the antique shop?"

Susie simply chewed without comment.

"I'll call Renny . . ." Susie finally said.

Rosie stood absolutely still. Her eyes widened with uncertainty. Renny was perfectly acceptable as a friend, but as a date to a fancy coronation dance, Rosie wasn't so sure. "Does he have something suitable to wear?" Rosie ventured to ask.

"I'm sure Renny will come up with something," Susie replied with a trace of a smile.

"Something suitable?" Rosie stressed. Susie smiled again and concentrated on the disappearing pancakes.

"We wouldn't dream of embarrassing you," Susie finally added.

Rosie let out a dubious stream of air between pursed lips. She wanted everything at Michelle's coronation to proceed with the proper decorum. That meant her branch of the Costain clan must attend the function without provoking any unnecesssary concern. Tonight was Michelle's night, and no one should detract from that.

THE KREWE OF TRITON had reserved a double banquet room in the Chalmette Riverside Hotel for the coronation dinner-dance. Unlike the elaborate ball still months away that would conclude the Mardi Gras festivities for the krewe and its court, this function was a less formal, family-style gathering, where the pleasure of dining with old friends compensated for the lack of opulence. Only the tables where the eight maids and their escorts and the soon-to-be-crowned queen and her escort would be seated had special floral arrangements to distinguish them from the other tables in the large room.

"Uncle Leo says he put you near the front at the table next to Michelle's," Rosie said, catching her daughter by the arm before Susie and Renny turned to one of the outer tables. "He says he wants all the pretty ones in the front of the room—" Rosie beamed "—and that means you."

Susie had found a deep crimson gown amid the collection of dresses her mother had stored in the house. Against its scooped neckline with a soft ruffle from shoulder to shoulder, Susie's smooth skin and sleek black hair created a rich contrast. The Costains would make a fine showing.

Even Renny had made himself surprisingly attractive. The slim navy dress suit and sedate tie seemed to subdue the angles of his lanky body, and his customarily unruly hair was brushed into a rakish collar-length Prince Valiant style turned under at the bottom. There was no chance he would be mistaken for a conservative-businessman type, but New Orleans had plenty of bizarre and bohemian characters, and Renny in his suit seemed staid compared to those extremists.

"I owe you one for this." Susie took Renny's arm and moved between the tables toward the area where Rosie had directed them. Initially Renny had groaned, moaned and protested when Susie asked him to be her escort, but he had finally agreed to come along—and he was making a noble effort to conceal his discomfort.

"I'll take it out in time," Renny half joked. "Keep track of how many hours we put in here," he suggested. "Then you come paint scenery with me one night. Now if the food tonight is really good, I'll count off an hour or so.'' He grinned.

"Fine with me," Susie agreed. "I'd like to wander through the scenery warehouse and see what kind of backdrops you're doing, anyway. I might as well help paint while I'm there."

Just as they reached their table, the room began to fill with guests, and beyond the crowd at the doorway, the glare of flashing strobe lights and flashbulbs and the excited laughter of young female voices indicated that the honorees were arriving. Clad in billowing furs, most of them on loan from one relative or another, the maids of the court made their entrance. Behind them all, the golden blond hair of Michelle was visible as she paused beside her parents for a candid photo to record the event.

The dark-haired photographer who snapped the shot was Simon Avery.

"Ah—it's him again." Renny gazed across the sea of heads and shoulders following Susie's unswerving gaze.

"He's been commissioned to do an album for Michelle," Susie explained, "to keep all the memories preserved. It's part of the tradition." Her voice trailed off as Sy slid the camera strap from his neck and took Michelle by the arm.

"It looks a little more sociable than that," Renny noted dryly. Sy now escorted Michelle to the place of honor at the head table. Once she was seated, he took the place next to her. "Maybe she has a thing for older men." Renny pulled out Susie's chair while she sat down. "Or he might have a thing for younger women." He shrugged. Sy was in his mid-thirties and Michelle was only nineteen. "Maybe it's simply a convenience date—like ours," he joked uncertainly.

"It really isn't any of our business." Susie turned her chair slightly so she wouldn't have to look directly at Sy just beyond Renny's shoulder. But her eyes could not resist the temptation to linger on the dark-haired man, elegant and impressive in a suit of deep chocolate brown.

"Let me sit on the other side of you." Renny moved around to her right side. "Then you won't have to deal with them at all." With Renny seated, Susie could turn her back to the twosome at the table of honor, without seeming to be rude. The only trouble was now that she couldn't see Sy, Susie couldn't think of a single thing to say to Renny. She fiddled with her teaspoon, wondering about the relationship between her cousin and Sy. She wanted to look—to see if he smiled at Michelle or the maids of the court the way he had smiled at her.

"I can see that this isn't going to be a stimulating evening, conversationwise," Renny observed. "Perhaps we could get out a pencil and draw pictures on the tablecloth," he said with a mischievous smile.

"Maybe you can talk and I can listen." Susie patted his slender hand. "Then once I get engrossed in what you're saying, I'll just leap in with some golden comments of my own."

"I'd rather draw." Renny chuckled. "Or maybe play Tic-Tac-Toe. I'll be the X's and you be the O's."

"We can dance." Susie brightened. While the late arrivals were exchanging greetings and enjoying a predinner cocktail, the band had started to play.

"I'd still rather draw," Renny protested, but he was out of his chair immediately and ready to escort her to the dance floor at the far end of the banquet area. "When you see how I dance, you might be sorry." He chuckled.

Throughout the dinner, Susie and Renny and the others seated at their table kept up a steady flow of conversation that touched on everything from the game that night in the Louisiana Superdome to the birth of a baby hippo in the nursery section of New Orleans' Audubon Park Zoo. Susie had managed to appear so engrossed in what was being discussed that she had avoided looking directly at Sy. But she was always aware of his presence as if her mental compass continually followed his movements throughout the banquet room.

Finally the official chairman for the evening's proceedings ambled to the microphone and the presentation of the Court of Triton began. Eight dukes, all in their late forties or early fifties, all successful businessmen, were named first. Then eight maids, some the daughters of krewe members, some local beauties or debutantes, were presented next. Then the banquet chairman who would later serve as captain for the Triton Ball, announced the king—Ernest Dufrene, a soft-spoken local mortician who had recently donated ten thousand dollars to the Chalmette Historical Society. There was immediate and loud applause for the slight, white-haired gentleman who would appear months later at the Triton Ball masked and supposedly anonymous. For this krewe, the tradition of keeping the identity of the king and queen a secret, like so many other traditions, had yielded to a more efficient system of honoring the royal pair in advance.

Then came Michelle's presentation. Uncle Leo rose and crossed to her table, offered her his arm, then escorted her to the dance floor for the Queen's Dance. Michelle was slender and radiant in the sapphire blue gown Susie had designed earlier in the fall. For the Triton Ball, with its theme "Fantasy Beneath the Seas," Michelle would be Queen of the Sea Creatures, clad in a costume of luminous greens—but tonight, she looked like a golden nymph, with her pale hair swaying as she danced with her proud father.

"You say it costs six thousand bucks for this honor?" Renny whispered irreverently. Weeks before when he had strolled through the Costain workrooms, Renny had been astounded at the cost involved in making costumes for the regal attendants at these functions. Susie had told him about the money that would go into the preball parties, the trinkets to throw from the floats, the gifts for the members of the court, and the champagne party a few weeks before the ball. Then there was the final parade and another less formal postparade party.

"Six thousand to pretend to be royalty," Renny groaned. "What a waste of money—throwing it away for a couple of parties and a parade. And I'm painting scenery to pay for canvas and framing."

"It's the tradition." Susie shushed him, somewhat uncomfortable defending a custom she had declined to participate in herself several years before. "If they have the money, they should feel free to spend it the way they want to," she professed. "The krewes pay for the spectacles, and all of New Orleans gets to join the celebration and share the fun."

"Tell me that when you're up to your elbows in paint, paying me back for this evening with the social set," Renny remarked, and chuckled. Susie smiled, too, then she heard the relentless click and whir of the camera. When she looked up, Sy was staring down with an inscrutable expression on his handsome face. With a slight shrug, he glanced from Susie to her escort.

"It's for your cousin's album." Sy nodded to them. Then he turned and shot another angle of the adjoining table. "Just doing my job," he commented apologetically, then proceeded to other tables.

"We could dance again," Renny volunteered. "Maybe if we move real fast, we can get there in time to be preserved on film by your friend Sy."

"He's not my friend," Susie sniffed.

"Whatever..." Renny smirked. "He can sure make you change colors," he observed. "You and that dress are almost the same shade...."

"I just get embarrassed having my picture taken." Susie pressed her hands to her cheeks. "And I really don't want to dance again."

She had barely finished the sentence when Sy materialized beside her. "Maybe you would make an exception in this case," he urged her. "Would you dance with me? I can't dance and take pictures at the same time, so you won't have to worry that I'll sneak up on you." Sy glanced at Renny to see if he had any objections.

"Go ahead," Renny insisted. "If I see a single flash go off, I'll come charging over like Lancelot," he promised.

Sy took Susie's hand and led her through the crowded dining area onto the dance floor. When he turned and took her in his arms, Susie stiffened defensively. "I won't hurt you," Sy said gently. "I won't do anything to attract attention. Relax and trust me. I just want to dance with you."

"I get nervous sometimes..." Susie explained. "I don't like—"

"To be in the limelight." Sy finished her sentence for her. "It's dark over here." He held her closer. "We'll dance and no one will even notice us." Susie let her hand rest along the back of his shoulders, feeling the contours of his broad back beneath his deep brown jacket.

"How's the doubloon collection coming along?" he asked, as his warm breath brushed against her temple. "Tony has been pestering me about them."

"It's a bit early for trinkets and doubloons," Susie replied. "After Christmas, when all the krewes begin to get their parade throws, I'll be able to collect plenty."

"You mean that you weren't going to call until after Christmas?" His voice had a teasing quality.

"I'm not sure I was going to call at all." Susie answered honestly.

"I thought we had a deal. I remember shaking on it." Sy held her back a bit and looked intently into her eyes. "I was certain you would keep your part of the agreement," he said softly. "Otherwise, I don't think I would have let go of your hand." Susie started to move away from him, but Sy's arm tensed and he held her tightly.

"I think I'd better get back to...Renny." Susie didn't want to call her friend her date. Sy kept looking down at her, swaying to the music, but refusing to loosen his hold.

"I let you go once before when you promised to call." He regarded her closely while she tried to move away from him. "I won't let you go this time, unless you agree to keep that promise."

The band was finishing the number. Susie glanced at them anxiously. Obviously Sy had no intention of ceasing dancing—whether or not the music stopped. "Please...." Susie whispered. "I can't think when you keep looking at me like that."

"I can't help looking at you." Sy smiled. "When you're caught off-guard, you're like a kid in so many ways—wide-eyed and curious—all your feelings right there on the surface." His dark, liquid eyes softened. "Then you pull up the walls. You're covering up, Susie Costain." He pressed her closer to him. "All those feelings belong to the grown-up woman you've become on the outside, but you keep hiding so much of her trapped inside with that kid. Whenever you set them both free, I want to be around."

"Well I don't think it will be tonight," Susie snapped angrily. "Certainly not here on the dance floor. And the band has stopped playing—" her words came rapidly "—so please let me go."

"I have tried to call you," Sy continued, as if he hadn't heard her protest. "You're never at your apartment, so I'm serious when I say I want you to call me. If you won't do it voluntarily, I'll have to improvise." Sy grinned, holding her closer still. "I want to see you—all of you. And I want you to give me the chance to get to know you," he said softly. "When I look at you and you look at me, we both sense there's some kind of magic possible between us. But you have to make the magic happen, Susie. You have to take the time. Call me...call us," he corrected, "when you want to stop hiding." He kept dancing. They were a study in deepest brown and crimson, arms around each other as they swayed in perfect rhythm to a silent melody.

A few dancers departing from the area cast amused glances at Susie and her bearded partner.

"Call us—doubloons or no doubloons—call me. Promise," Sy said stubbornly. "I want to have some time with you."

"All right," Susie agreed, desperate to get back to her table and off the empty dance floor.

"I'll be delighted when you do." Sy let her step free of his embrace. "And so will Tony. Not for the same reasons, of course," he added with a wide grin.

Susie had to force herself to walk slowly away from him. She wanted to run. Everywhere his hands had rested, every place their bodies had brushed against each other still tingled from the contact. And there was that smile—handsome, strangely gentle, inviting—asking her to make a move. "Call me...call us." The words kept ringing in her ears.

"Are you all right?" Renny stood to meet her. "You look a little flustered. Did he do it again—hurt your feelings?" Renny towered above her, shielding her from the sight of Sy's returning to Michelle's table.

"I'm fine," Susie replied unconvincingly. "But I'm very tired, and I'm ready to go. I think we've done our bit for family unity," she declared. "Let me see if I can persuade my folks to let us leave now. The band is taking a break." She looked out over the tables toward her parents. "All we'll miss is more dancing." Susie didn't choose to get that close to Sy again. She could still recall the soft fabric of his suit beneath her fingertips and the disturbing warmth that seemed to radiate from him. Touching him had prompted more than a physical response in her. It was as if for the duration of their contact they had shared a highly charged experience, which made all Susie's senses become more acute. When the contact had ended, Susie felt both relieved and strangely empty.

"I wouldn't mind getting out of here myself." Renny followed her across the room. "They lost my attention right after dessert."

Rosie insisted on one more observance of politesse before Susie left the party. "Now you can't leave without saying something nice to Michelle." Rosie clasped her daughter's arm and escorted her across the floor to the honoree's table. "Susie is leaving." She rested her hand on Michelle's shoulder. "And she just had to come over and say good-night."

"Oh, thank you, Susie—good night." Michelle stood and hugged her cousin. "And thanks for all the work you did on the dress. And you, too, Aunt Rosie." Michelle literally glowed. "It's so lovely."

"These ladies designed your dress?" Sy picked up on her comment. "Perhaps the three of you should pose together," he suggested, "to show off the dress." There was a look of delight in his dark eyes.

Before Susie could reply, Rosie had lined them all up, with Michelle in the middle. Sy snapped two photos from various angles, then hesitated, apparently satisfied. Rosie and Michelle turned back toward the table of honor. Susie started to leave, then glanced around. No one was looking. Very hastily she crossed her eyes and puckered up her nose and whirled around to make a face at Sy. He clicked it into history before she could uncross her eyes.

"I'll save this one for Tony." He laughed out loud. "He'll get a kick out of it." Sy tucked the camera well out of her grasp. "And he said you weren't a weirdo..." Sy teased. "Don't forget to call." He winked and moved off into the crowd before Susie could respond.

"*Now* we can go." Susie had calmed down by the time she got back to her dad and Renny.

"Let's all go." Bernie hugged his daughter and moved toward the door. Susie heard one more click and whir as she and her father arrived at the exit. This time she was too tired to protest. If Sy wanted a shot of Susie and her dad, he was welcome to it. All she wanted was a hot bath and a snug bed. Tomorrow would be Sunday, and from noon until nightfall there were more clients and more fittings. The Mardi Gras season had officially commenced.

CHAPTER THREE

THE FRENCH QUARTER—the Vieux Carré—that forms
the heart of old New Orleans snuggles against the curve
of the Mississippi River. From the green oasis of Jackson Square and the tall spires of St. Louis cathedral, the
Quarter spread six blocks on either side from Canal
Street to Esplanade, then six blocks deep, from the river
to North Rampart Street. For Susie Costain and most of
the permanent residents of the Vieux Carré, the Quarter
by day was as intimate and friendly as an Old World
village, with its narrow streets flanked by balconied
buildings, its inviting shops and courtyards and its
abundance of delightful and unique restaurants. Those
New Orleaneans who worked in the adjacent business
areas soon found familiar faces and favorite spots to
shop or eat within the Quarter.

By night, the Quarter took on a different personality.
From bistros and bars, the sounds of music spilled onto
the streets. Along Bourbon Street, the Quarter became
boisterous and often naughty, for the bare-bosomed
women danced on runways behind the swinging doors
and the streets filled with the curious and often the inebriated. In the evening, the locals dined in quiet restaurants or stayed at home, sitting on balconies or inside
private courtyards, while the more commercial elements
of their quaint village teased and tantalized the
passersby.

Since Blaine's marked the border between the Quarter and the modern commercial district downtown, Susie had always been able to slip from one world to the other at will. Only rarely did the two worlds intrude upon each other.

"I must have been out when you called." Sy Avery's cheerful voice interrupted Susie's drawing. "I was in the neighborhood and thought it might be time for you to take your lunch break."

Susie jerked upright, startled to find him leaning against the wall of her cubicle in Blaine's advertising department.

"How did you get back here?" Susie gasped. All the doors leading to the art section of the advertising department were labeled Employees Only.

"I just adopted a very efficient look and pretended that I knew what I was doing." Sy shrugged. "It seemed to work very well."

"I guess it did." Susie smiled at last. "And you know good and well that I didn't call you."

"Maybe it was mental telepathy. You *wanted* to call me. And just now I had the strange feeling you might be hungry. How about lunch?" he pressed her. "I have something to show you," he said, patting a brown portfolio under his arm.

"What is it?" Susie crossed her arms and questioned him. From the shape and size of the package, she guessed it contained photographs from the coronation dance.

"If you join me for lunch, I'll show you," he bargained. "Eat first—look later." He waited for an answer. "Your lunch hour starts in four minutes," he warned her. "I'm betting crepes will be an improvement on whatever you brought in that bag." He tilted his head, indicating the brown paper sack on her desk.

"How did you know when my lunch hour started?" Susie countered. "And how did you know I had brought my lunch?"

"I've got my contacts," Sy replied. "And even if you hadn't brought your lunch, crepes would still sound good, wouldn't they?"

"They sound fine." Susie surrendered. "I'll get my coat." When she hesitated before moving closer to him so she could slip it on, Sy laughed.

"I had hoped either your curiosity or your hunger would keep you from having second thoughts," he teased. "Come on, you'll be safe with me. I promise not to dance with you." He took the coat and held it open for her. "My son checked me out. He knows a weirdo when he sees one, and he says I'm okay."

"How is Tony?" Susie asked, somewhat relieved to have something specific to talk about. "How are his karate lessons coming along?"

"He's doing fine." Sy stepped back and let her lead the way through the narrow hallway leading to the elevator. "He has a green belt with two stripes on it," he noted. "I'm not sure what that means, but he certainly seems to be getting lots of exercise doing all those moves."

"Tell him I haven't forgotten about the doubloons," Susie stressed. "I've been thinking of him."

"Just about him?" Sy was apparently enjoying himself.

"I haven't had time to think of much other than work." Susie glossed over his comment. "It's not even December yet—we haven't made it through Thanksgiving—and I'm already doing after-Christmas sale ads here and trying to keep up with my dad at home. I think the family business took on a little more than we can handle this season. But my mother and father are such pushovers." She stopped at the elevator and turned to face him. "They just can't say no to anyone."

"You obviously do not take after your parents," Sy replied evenly. "You have difficulty saying yes."

"I was referring to doing costumes," Susie said coolly. "I think we have more than we can handle."

"How many workers do you have in your operation now? Surely it's not just you and your parents." Sy frowned. He obviously had no idea how the Costains' business had expanded over the years. He had dropped his joking attitude and seemed genuinely interested.

"My mother has six seamstresses who help with the gowns," Susie answered, "but my dad and I have generally managed to do most of the headpieces and collars ourselves. Of course, we recruit friends and neighbors part-time to help with the gluing when things get hectic. Last year we had to bring in two new employees, but this year we've picked up more business, so we'll have to add more help. Perhaps we'll start a separate shift evenings and weekends," she noted, as the elevator doors slid open and they stepped inside. "Last year I was living out in Chalmette and I hadn't been promoted in the art department. This year I have more work at both jobs and living in the Quarter means a lot more driving time. Two shifts may be the only solution."

"Is that why your car is never parked at your apartment?" he asked.

"More of your contacts spying one me?" Susie frowned.

"I did my own spying," Sy confessed. "I've been working late at the studio developing and printing portraits. I call every so often to be sure your telephone is in working order. When I drive by your place, I never see your car there."

"I'll have to tell my father that someone else is keeping an eye out for me," Susie said. "He'd be intrigued by your surveillance system."

"It's my pleasure, I assure you." Sy held open the elevator door so they could both step out. "Watching you could become habit-forming," he said softly. "Stopping by your empty apartment and getting no answer when I telephone is depressing."

Side by side they walked through the central aisle of Blaine's and stepped out into the brisk November air. Sy linked his arm in hers, blocking the force of the wind with his body as they walked beneath iron-lace balconies, past bank buildings and elegant shops with windows full of antiques and art. It was too chilly to linger and look, and they barely spoke until they stepped inside the foyer of the Olde Crepe Shop.

"You weren't exaggerating when you said that your work schedule really wouldn't allow much time for a social life." Sy warmed his hands on his coffee cup as he spoke. "You do burn the candle at both ends."

Susie had the uncomfortable feeling that he was not making casual conversation. "It's a good thing I like to stay busy." Susie said evasively.

"I've got a rather erratic schedule myself. I have to show up at everything from fittings to tea parties—but I can't get you out of my mind. There's a definite affinity between us," he admitted. "You don't happen to have any suggestions what we can do about us—you and me?"

"I'm not really interested in a serious relationship." Susie spoke the words to Sy with less certainty than she had with other men. "The family joke is that doing costumes for Mardi Gras is like riding a roller coaster— once it's started, there's no getting off until the ride ends. This year the slow climb has already begun."

"And you couldn't get free of your horrendous work schedule for an occasional evening?" His soft brown eyes watched her closely. They were eyes Susie could get lost in—eyes that could see into the dark secret places where all her sorrows and joys were carefully hidden away. Her fiancé, Richard Martin, once had looked at her like that, and she had trusted him enough to share her dreams and passions. Richard had listened but had not understood at all. He had used what he knew to betray her. He had taught Susie to doubt—herself as well as anyone who came too close. Learning to trust someone else—even the velvety-eyed Simon Avery— would take time, something Susie hadn't allowed herself.

"I'll be swamped until mid-February," Susie forced a matter-of-fact tone. Unfortunately, with the current workload, she was telling the truth. Her parents had taken on more customers than ever before—primarily because of the success of her designs. Now Susie would have to assume direction of more of the production. New employees would have to be trained and closely supervised to maintain the excellence of the workmanship. Since she knew from the beginning how each costume would look, Susie would have the ultimate responsibility for every aspect of the work. It was going to be a terribly busy three months.

"That's a shame. February suddenly seems a long

way off. A lot could happen between now and then." Sy locked his eyes on his hands momentarily. The disappointment in his voice echoed her own feelings. Then his jaw tensed slightly. When he looked up, his eyes held an unfamiliar remoteness like the chill wind off the river. He was backing off—putting some emotional distance between them. Susie had done the same thing many times herself.

"At least we can eat lunch together once in a while," he said pleasantly.

"We can do that. Just drop by the office and lure me away." She tried to lighten the somber atmosphere. "Now you can show me what you have in the portfolio." She reminded him of the envelope he had brought.

"These can wait," Sy insisted. "When one eats crepes, one doesn't get sidetracked by other things." He gradually regained his lighthearted tone. "If the only time I get to enjoy your company is across a table at lunch," he stated, "then I prefer to hear about you. I've seen your work at Blaine's, now tell me how you come up with the costume ideas in your other business, year after year—if that isn't poking into professional secrets."

Sy had touched a subject Susie couldn't resist. She began by telling him how she had loved fairy tales as a child. Stories of damsels and dragons or ogres and elves, fairies and fabulous beasts had entranced and enchanted her. She'd even studied Latin in high school for the wonderful mythology. Eleven years earlier, when she was just thirteen, the Costains had begun making headpieces in the living room as a means to supplement Bernie's income as a floor superintendent at the aluminum plant. Susie saw the designs her parents made then and eventually began sketching ideas of her own. The creatures in Susie's world of fantasy became transformed into life-size costumes and began to dwell in closets and cupboards in her own house.

"Then everything mushroomed," Susie explained. "My folks did such good work that they kept getting more clients. Everyone in the family pitched in for a while, but besides my parents, I was the one who really stayed with it. I love so much about the business. It's like being able to create a magical world and share it with everyone."

"You didn't ever want to be queen of one of those balls you make so magical?" Sy quizzed.

"I didn't want to be *in* those fairy tales." Susie smiled. "But I do like to draw the costumes, work out entire scenes with all the people in gorgeous outfits. Each ball gives me the chance to bring to life a moment out of a storybook."

"For a world of grown-ups who need a bit of fantasy." Sy nodded. "I feel that way about some of my photographs," he admitted. "I always try to capture something extraordinary. But back to you—it must be a challenge to come up with different designs each time, with so many balls and so many krewes trying to have a spectacular theme."

"You should see the files we've accumulated." Susie stretched her arms to indicate the size of the file drawers. "We keep albums full of sketches and photographs so we know what's been done. Then we always collect clippings and showbills and posters of costumes others have designed," Susie continued enthusiastically. "When we're contacted to do a set of costumes, we look

through our files for ideas. Then there are the books,"
she added with a smile. "I have volumes of period
costumes and designs for theatrical productions," she
noted. "But the best ideas usually come after I've talked
to the committee from each krewe and know what
theme they've chosen. Then I let everything just drift
around inside my head for a few days while I sit and
doodle with colored markers." Her deep brown eyes
sparkled with delight. "You must have that same feeling
when you shoot some of your pictures. Somehow it all
starts to come together."

Sy was grinning at her. It was that wide radiant grin
that had made her breath catch before. There was the
intelligence—the instinctive understanding. From the
look in his eyes, Sy had experienced the some rush of
creativity Susie was describing. He knew precisely what
she meant. Yet there was more in his eyes than just comprehension. There was a distinct gleam of satisfaction,
as if he had suspected they shared a similar passion and
now Susie had confirmed it. Once again he had managed to get her to reveal something more than she had
intended.

Abruptly Susie dropped her gaze. To create, one had
to let instinct, emotions and ideas rise to the surface—
one had to be unguarded—to reveal the inner soul. Sy
saw and understood.

He reached across the table and clasped her hand
beneath his. "That's part of the magic, Susie," he said
softly. "Don't hide it from me."

"You have an uncanny knack for upsetting my equilibrium." Susie shook her head slightly, realizing that she
was slipping, perhaps unwisely, into the dangerous
realm of being too honest. "Or maybe it's my momentum

that you disrupt. I built up a certain pace, shifting from one project to another. I've got more work to do than the hours in the day accommodate. And you come along and everything slides into slow time. I wasn't looking for anything like this. In fact, I wasn't looking for anything—period.'' The color in her cheeks deepened as she spoke. ''I can't risk a highly emotional involvement.'' She withdrew her hand from Sy's grasp. ''There are too many projects resting on my shoulders. It's as simple as that.''

''I've got shoulders you can rest on, Susie.'' His voice caressed her as warmly as his fingers had. Susie looked into the velvety depths of his eyes as a pensive smile flitted across her lips. How much a part of her yearned to lean against his shoulder and have his strong arms surround her. Even for a moment, just to *feel* again.

''I really don't know what you're asking of me,'' Susie said aloud. She realized that every word she uttered gradually unraveled the threads of her self-imposed veil of composure. She was revealing far too much of herself to a man she barely knew. But Sy had been straightforward with her and he deserved the same courtesy. She wanted him to understand that there was no place for him in the delicate balancing act she was performing. She could juggle two jobs and hundreds of sketches and costume pieces, but she could not do all that well and still have time for a lover.

''I don't feel in control when I'm with you,'' she admitted. ''Every time I'm near you, I feel as if I'm on the brink of something precarious. I have learned to be cautious about intimate relationships. They have a tendency to become consuming. I made a mistake before with someone who assumed I would meet his expectations. He thought that a sexual relationship was the solution to all sorts of problems." Again she felt that she was telling him too much. But it was apparent to both of them that their fascination was a mutual one.

"This other fellow was wrong about me, but that didn't stop him from trying to pressure me into a more intimate relationship than I was ready for." Susie stopped herself from being more explicit. "Sy—I'm not saying that you're pressuring me, but I'm afraid you want too much. You're asking for more than I can give."

"I have to admire your honesty," Sy said with a trace of melancholy in his expression. "I'm not sure what I'm asking of you or what I expect, Susie. I've had that same sensation—that precarious sensation—from the first time I saw you sitting in the square with the pigeons, eating beignets with such gusto. Caring for someone is very delicate business," Sy replied gently. "Like Alice and the Looking Glass—neither one of us knows what discoveries lie just beyond the surface. In my work I've seen so many shiny surfaces with nothing beyond them," he said with a touch of cynicism. "I didn't expect to come face-to-face with anyone like you. But I have. And I want to do something about it."

"But this isn't a good time for me," Susie responded, frowning.

"There never is a good time," Sy responded. "Here I am settling into a new house, getting my son adjusted to life in the States, reestablishing my business, swamped with work—and you show up with powdered sugar on your nose and those eyes of yours that speak secret messages to me. This simply happened, Susie. We have to make the best of it. There's something rare and magical happening between us. Here we are—both in the business of making fantasies for other people and we can't find time to claim some of it for ourselves.''

"I'm afraid I've done a pretty good job of tying myself up with the real world," Susie replied. "I can feel the magnetism between us, Sy. Stepping through the Looking Glass with you is one thing. Finding my way back to this world and functioning in it with my schedule is what worries me. Something in me wants to get lost in you. But I feel more like Humpty Dumpty than Alice in Wonderland. I'm more fragile than I appear.''

"I know that." Sy's solemn expression softened. "I won't push you. There is something here too important to rush. But I do want to leave the options open. If at any time in the next few months you reconsider, just let me know. But understand this—after Mardi Gras season, I'll be coming after you like a steamroller.''

Susie looked at him warily. "I don't respond well to force," she said quietly. "I don't like to be overpowered.''

Sy smiled easily. "Maybe my simile was incorrect. Let's say I'll be after you like a moth to a flame.'' His eyes held hers steadily.

"Better," she said, and returned the smile.

"Much better," Sy repeated. "Like a moth to a flame.''

WHEN RENNY CASTELOT directed her to a huge warehouse in Gretna, a business area just over the bridge from downtown New Orleans, Susie barely recognized the new development. An entire section of run-down houses and shops had been leveled and a vast new industrial complex had been built on the site. One of the major float-building companies operated from an L-shaped warehouse that was closely guarded now that the new season was underway. The floats, like the costumes for the balls, were designed and built in secrecy so one spectacular procession after another could be unveiled when each krewe paraded its members and court.

"I have a friend who works there," Renny commented, noticing Susie's interest in the float-storage area. "If you're interested, I'll get you a tour through the premises," he promised. "We artist folk can trust one another," he joked.

"I would like to see them," Susie conceded. As a young girl, she had waited breathlessly amid roadside crowds to see the latest floats and to catch the trinkets thrown by the riders. By the time she had reached her teens, Susie's interest had been more in the workmanship on the floats than in the throws, but the sight of any float could still send those childhood flutters of excitement through her.

"First, take a look at my scenery." Renny led her off in another direction to an adjacent warehouse. Inside, small groups of paint-spattered workers labored or stood around with cups of coffee examining the progress on the huge backdrops. "This one is for the 'Jungle Splendor' theme for the Krewe of Merlin," Renny said, pointing to a filmy scrim, an almost transparent hanging of fabric that was designed to transform under the proper lighting. When lighted from the rear, the gauzelike fabric seemed to disappear and the people poised behind it could be seen, but when floodlights shone down on the front at a certain angle, all the designs painted on the material would catch the light and assume a solid form, concealing any backstage motion from the audience.

"Wait till you see this." Renny loped over to several people standing by a light-control panel. He spoke briefly to a tall, oval-faced young woman with her hair pulled back into a long braid, then he came back to Susie's side. An instant later, all the lights at their end of the warehouse went dark. Then the spotlights hit the scrim and a lush tropical rain forest appeared as if by magic. A sigh of utter delight escaped from Susie's open mouth.

"It still needs a little work." Renny tried to veil his pride with his modest remark. "I gather you like it," he prodded his silent companion.

"It's gorgeous!" Susie exclaimed. Already she had visions of her elegant giraffe creation emerging from this dense forest. "It's spectacular," she gushed as the tall young woman joined them.

"This is Germaine Concienne," Renny said, introducing his co-worker. "She's a drama student at Tulane and is picking up money for college by working on this stuff. Germaine, this is Susie."

"You do wonderful work together," Susie complimented both of them. Germaine nodded in satisfaction as she surveyed their creation, her thick dark braid swaying.

"I'm a technician, not an artist," she noted. "My part is pretty well finished now. Renny still has to work on all the others. The painting is the time-consuming part," she explained. "I don't have to do a whole lot until we move these things into the ballrooms. Then I get to help set up the lighting systems again." From the look on Renny's face, Susie could tell he was not pleased that Germaine's role was ending, even temporarily.

"Does that mean you don't get paid again until the balls?" Susie inquired.

"That's what it means." Germaine's pretty face puckered into a frown. "If I could paint well, I could stay on and help," she added. "And I sure could use the money. But I'm more adept at the technical stuff—I work better with wires and pliers than with a paintbrush." A slow smile began to spread across Susie's face.

"Would you like a part-time job with pliers and a soldering iron?" Susie realized what an asset a pair of competent hands would be in the headdress workroom. "We're building the frames for all the collars and headpieces, and we're swamped," she professed.

"Sounds like my kind of job," Germaine said, accepting eagerly.

"I could help, too," Renny's hasty offer came out a bit more obvious than he expected. "I mean, I could always use some cash.... If you need the help...." By now Germaine had slipped her arm around Renny's waist in an attempt to ease his embarrassment. The affection in the gesture was unmistakable. Somehow amid the paint and electrical paraphernalia, a romance had blossomed between the co-workers.

"I can use both of you." Susie was more grateful than they realized. With such talented helpers, she might even be able to arrange some free time for herself. "Germaine, do you have transportation?" Susie asked. "The workshop is in Chalmette and that means commuting.'' Now a silly grin formed on Renny's face.

"My friend here has wheels,'' he tilted his head toward Germaine. "Remember the motorcycle?'' He arched his eyebrows. "Well, this is the owner.''

Susie recalled her mother's dismay when Renny had arrived in their front yard on the roaring cycle. Now the thought of the slender, elegant Germaine stepping off that machine seemed even more bewildering. "Wait until my mother sees this.'' Susie laughed.

"The cycle actually belonged to my brother,'' Germaine explained. The massive Harley cycle with its double seat and large side cases seemed more appropriate for a leather-jacketed, tattooed biker, than for the almond-eyed, exotic-looking theater major. "My brother had a little difficulty with the law. I paid his fine for reckless driving and ended up with the cycle. It's a bit flashy for my taste, but it gets me around inexpensively—and it was the only way I could think of to keep my brother off the road. Hopefully, when he earns enough to buy the bike back, he may also have acquired enough sense to operate it safely.''

"In the meantime,'' Renny gloated, "you have two new employees who can get out to Chalmette and assist you whenever you want us. We'll even park that ferocious-looking machine behind your parents' house so they won't be scandalized.''

"If the workmanship on the headpieces is as good as I expect it will be, my parents won't care if you arrive in a tank,'' Susie responded. Before Renny could reply, she warned him playfully. "Now don't go looking for a tank. . . .''

The threesome proceeded from the jungle scrim with

its curving plant forms to the other hanging panels for the two other balls. The backdrop for the Krewe of Sirens was similar to the first, but blues and silvers had replaced the lush greens. This one suited the theme "Mysteries of the Deep," and would provide a splendid setting for the aquatic costumes Susie had designed. One lacy sea fan in the back drop was a deep lavender and would highlight the stand-up collar and train that the Queen of Sirens would wear. "I hope you don't mind...." Renny spoke cautiously as he noticed Susie was inspecting the sea fan. He had lifted the design from her drawings.

"Mind?" Susie shook her head. "I'm delighted. Everything you've done so far, will only make my work look better."

"Wait till you get a look at the ramps and columns that are going to frame these hangings," Germaine commented. "There are seventeen palm trees—each more than twenty feet tall—just for the "Jungle Splendor" ball alone. They're papier-mâché," she added, "but they look absolutely real."

To Susie, not even huge palm trees sounded unusual. The business of staging elaborate balls had become a highly professional and extremely profitable one in New Orleans. Certain studios, like particular costume makers or mask makers, had reputations for excellence and had grown into vast corporate structures. Renny and Germaine were only two of thousands employed in creating and assembling the scenery, props, lighting and doing the carpentry needed to transform a cavernous auditorium into the massive and elaborate settings for the city's fabulous carnival balls. Susie had seen everything from live elephants with bejeweled harnesses to erupting volcanoes and shimmering blizzards. The balls were individual theatrical productions in which thousands of visitors could come and view unlimited splendor—if only for an evening.

"The one I'm having trouble with—" Renny said, staring through the warehouse toward the rear of the building "—is this hard-edge work for the Krewe of Hyacinth." Susie and Germaine hurried along next to him, leaving the vast scrims behind. "I'm not too thrilled using just black and white," Renny muttered as he headed for a worktable where the designs were laid out. "They remind me of Rorschach ink-blot tests."

"We're using a lot of black light on this ball." Germaine seemed more enthused than her co-worker. "The theme is "Stars of the Silver Screen," and all these movable panels have to depict famous actors in a particular role." She picked up several small-scale samples to show Susie. "Everything for this ball is either black or white or a combination. It will be really dramatic," she enthused, "but Renny keeps grumbling instead of working."

"I like color," he protested. "Lots of color."

"If you like green, as in money," Germaine stressed, "then you had better get working on these."

"That's why I recruited Susie." A sly smile brightened Renny's face. "She does pen-and-ink stuff for the newspaper advertisements. Black and white are her biggies."

Already Susie had moved from one familiar face to the next, examining the sketches of the stars and noting what had to be accomplished. This was not one of the balls she was commissioned to do costuming for, but she was intrigued by the stark poster images.

"How many of these have to be drawn?" Susie asked quietly. Each drawing had scale markings indicating the panels would be ten-by-ten squares.

"Forty," Renny answered grimly.

"Forty...!" Susie groaned. Renny had asked her for a few hours' work to repay him for his escort duty. What he needed would require months of effort.

"They don't have to be perfect." Renny hastily gathered the remaining sketches from the table. "They're going to rotate on giant turntables at the sides of the stage." He showed her the overall drawing of the setting for the Hyacinth Ball. "All I need is for you to help me with about half of them. If half of them are really good, then the other half I can get through on my own."

"So now we're talking twenty." Susie still thought that was far more than she could handle. Germaine had discreetly slipped away as the discussion became more tense.

"I'll work on your costumes *free*," Renny promised. "I'm in over my head here, and you're the only one I know who looks like a lifeguard."

"When is the Hyacinth Ball scheduled?" Susie hoped it would not be one of the early round of Mardi Gras festivities.

"February 12," Renny stared down at her with wide, hopeful eyes. "The last weekend before Mardi Gras Day. I'd even give you half of the money," Renny bargained, "only I've already spent most of the advance, and I won't get the rest until the work is completed."

"You spent the money?" Susie moaned.

"I had to pay cash for the canvases and paints I

needed for my real work.'' Renny seemed to droop before her eyes. ''I'm sorry Susie, but I got caught in a bind, and now I don't know what to do.''

''You can pass me the rest of the sketches,'' Susie directed him. ''I'll look them over and see what I can do.''

A light of hope glowed in Renny's eyes as he handed her the stack of drawings. Silently Susie thumbed through them, seeing face after face she would have to draw far larger than life. Marilyn Monroe. Shirley Temple. W.C. Fields. Marlon Brando. Barbra Streisand. All distinct and striking images that must be instantly recognizable.

''If you and Germaine catch on very quickly with the headpieces and can help me out with my costumes,'' Susie said warily, ''and if we don't collapse from exhaustion....''

''Then you'll do it?'' Renny's long arms flopped up and down like the wings of an ostrich as it attempted to lift off.

''I'll *help*,'' Susie agreed with marked reservation. ''I believe in your other art,'' she added. ''If this is the only way to finance it, then I'll try to pitch in and help you get these faces done. It will just take more time than I expected.''

The loud whoop of relief that came from Renny obscured her last words. ''Any time, day or night,'' he pledged enthusiastically. ''If you need me, I'll do anything you say. Just get me out of this mess.''

''I gather you two have reached an agreement,'' Germaine remarked cautiously. Renny wrapped one arm around her and whirled her, then clutched Susie with the other, swinging all three of them in a circle.

"We have a team," Renny asserted.

"And a heck of a lot of work," Susie reminded him. Already she was mentally juggling her commitments. Her final shipments of costumes were for the balls of Triton and Satyr in February, but by then the costuming rush would be over and Renny's work would not be due for another week. If nothing happened to disrupt the plans, it would be possible to get everyone's work completed as agreed. There would be time for all the projects—but little else.

"Just like the Three Musketeers." Renny was still overjoyed.

"More like the Marx Brothers." Germaine giggled at Renny's exuberance.

"Speaking of Marx Brothers—" Susie laughed in spite of her apprehensions "—I think they're in here. Maybe we'd better get started. Come on, Groucho, pass the pencils," she teased her tall, gawky friend. Tapping a pencil like a cigar and with the appropriate posture and a leering smile, Renny stalked around the drawing table in an outrageous imitation of Groucho Marx. Immediately Germaine followed, matching stride for stride in her own rendition of the comedian.

"This is going to be interesting." Susie spread the first sketch before her. The large languid eyes of Marilyn Monroe looked up at her, half-laughing, half-melancholy. In Marilyn's expression was an unmistakable loneliness behind a sultry, magnificent face. "A face with character," Sy Avery would have said.

Susie stared at the illustration that she was to draw large scale. The words connected with Monroe—childlike, clever, comical, sensual, vulnerable. . . all applied in some way to Susie herself. Vulnerable, the last word, perhaps most of all. Sy had seen that in Susie. He had stirred the secret longings and reminded her of feelings that she had held in check. Now his words haunted her as she tried to focus on the portrait in front of her. This fragile creature named Marilyn who had become the epitome of sexuality and desirability had died alone, leaving her accomplishments on film forever.

Susie bit her lower lip pensively, wondering what her own accomplishments would be—pages of mundane advertisements from Blaine's department store? Fanciful costumes discarded or stored away each year after the Mardi Gras balls? Drawings like this of Monroe, which would decorate a ball then be thrown away? All of that seemed so foolish and insignificant. But there were moments, Susie knew, when an idea came to life and was transformed into a costume...when someone wore that costume and filled a room with magic... moments that would exist in people's memories as something rare and wonderful. But the hollow aching inside her seemed to undermine her resolve. This time, those moments were not enough. Someone else's memories could not sustain her as they had before. Something in Sy's eyes said it was time for creating moments of her own, if only there was time enough.

"I think I'd better start with something easier," Susie said, sliding the image of Marilyn Monroe farther down the table. Deliberately she chose the bulbous-nosed, mischievous-faced W.C. Fields. This one didn't look at her with eloquent, silent eyes. This one let her retreat again inside herself and hide her uncertainty behind her competence. Susie would draw and hold it all inside her... until there was time.

On Thanksgiving Day, the Costain workrooms were abandoned except for Susie and her two companions. Germaine and Renny had arrived early and spent hours stretching and gluing shimmering transparent fabric over gigantic pairs of butterfly wings. The theme of the ball for the Krewe of Artemis was "South American Fantasy," and Susie had researched and recreated an exotic assortment of rare butterflies to costume the maids of the court. Each pair of wings, extending four feet above the shoulder of the wearer and tapering off into an elegant train several feet behind, was intricately braced at the waist and shoulder to make the weight almost insignificant.

"You should have studied engineering." Renny marveled at the balance and delicacy that had been achieved with the wings.

"Wait until you see the set for the queen of the ball," Susie cautioned him. "Her wings are twice as large, and they're battery operated. They actually flutter as she moves."

"Are you folks still up there?" Rosie's concerned voice echoed through the room.

"We sure are." Susie held the fragile orange fabric of the monarch-butterfly wing while Germaine tightened metal clamps to press it into the glue.

"You finish what you're doing and come down," Rosie insisted. "Uncle Leo just called and wants us to get over there and enjoy some of his Thanksgiving turkey."

"I'd rather stay here and work," Susie replied. By now her mother had climbed the stairs and stood watching them.

"You may want to starve," Rosie said, giving Renny a knowing look, "but your friends here might prefer some succulent turkey, thick brown gravy, tangy oyster dressing, your Aunt Jo's famous Greek salad, steamed shrimp, roasted potatoes...." Rosie continued with the menu as Renny began to groan aloud.

"Okay, okay," Susie calmed him. "We'll stop for a few hours and eat." They could still be back by mid-afternoon and continue working into the night.

"Then there's coffee, chocolate cake, Key lime pie, croissants, a soufflé or two..." Rosie listed enticingly.

"This may take more than a few hours," Germaine advised. "The man has an enormous capacity for food."

"Just quit for the day and enjoy," Rosie hugged her daughter. "You've worked every evening here and taken up your lunch hours with Renny's scenery. Take some time today to be with your friends and the family. Michelle will be there, lots of cousins and nieces and nephews...friends."

"Just how many people does your Uncle Leo expect?" Germaine asked uneasily. "We don't want to impose."

"Uncle Leo and Aunt Jo stopped counting years ago," Rosie laughed. "Whoever comes is welcome and well fed. In New Orleans, a family get-together includes everyone and goes on indefinitely. You just jump in and fend for yourself," she concluded.

"Just point me to the food!" Renny put away the pots of glue and washed off the work counter.

"No one will have to point." Rosie hurried the three workers along. "All you'll have to do is sniff the air... your nose will lead you there."

"What about the way we're dressed?" Germaine looked down at her loose shirt and blue jeans.

"In New Orleans," Rosie began her usual reassurance, there are times to dress well, and there are times to enjoy. Occasionally they overlap. This day is for enjoying," she declared. "No one cares what you wear, they only care that you come and you share the good food and the friendship."

"And if Uncle Leo dances on the tabletop or offers you some alligator stew or if you are invited into the closet by one of my cousins," Susie teased, "don't be concerned. In New Orleans—" her voice sparkled with laughter "— you can expect... and get... almost anything."

"Susie!" Rosie turned to shush her daughter. Then a ripple of laughter followed. "Uncle Leo did dance on the piano once," she recalled. "Then there was the time Aunt Jeanette came all the way from Baltimore and brought her third husband...."

"Who turned out to have been Cousin Rita's *second* husband...." Susie watched the bewildered expression on Germaine's face. "You're about to find out why I don't attend these functions very often," Susie confided. "But once in a while... they can certainly give one a definite change of pace."

SUSIE HAD NO SOONER PARKED her car among numerous other ones in Uncle Leo's driveway when a small boy darted toward her.

"My dad said you might be here." Tony Avery was

very pleased to see her. "He's out at the back taking some pictures of Michelle and some other ladies," the boy explained. "He left me with all those old people in there, and all of them talk to me like I'm just a kid," he grumbled. "I'm glad you're here so I'll have someone to keep me company."

"I'm glad you're here, too." Susie reached down and hugged the boy. Somehow the sight of his bright face and the thought of Sy Avery being near made the prospect of the midday meal and the socializing afterward seem much more appealing. "My other friends and I were planning to start with the food." She turned to introduce Renny and Germaine to her new companion. However, Renny's instinct for survival had already directed him through the crowd of middle-aged folks standing in the front yard and into the midst of a throng of younger friends and relatives who preferred eating to talking. Just behind Renny, following closely, she could see the smooth-chignon-topped Germaine.

"My friends seem to be quite capable of taking care of themselves," Susie said laughing. "So that leaves you and me."

"I'd be glad to eat with you." Tony took her hand. "Then I'll have to find my dad and let him know I found you."

"He'll run into us sooner or later," Susie remarked as she led the boy through the crowded room. "It will be nice to see him again." She found her own gaze skimming over the familiar faces of the Costain clan hoping to see the bearded countenance of Sy Avery. She began to feel that peculiar sense of apprehension and pleasure that her moments with Sy had brought. It was as if something inside her were opening again in spite of her diligent efforts to keep her feelings locked within.

"So you still manage to find time to eat?" Sy's voice caught her by surprise. While she had been scanning one side of the room, he had appeared behind her. "It's like old times with you and me and good food. How have you been, Susie?" The way his dark eyes locked on to hers made Susie feel as if everyone else had abruptly vanished from the room.

"I've been fine," she managed to reply. "And busy." She felt the words tumble out. "I've been helping Renny with some of his commissions and he's been working on costumes with me." While she spoke, she realized that Sy didn't really seem to listen. He simply stood there, absorbing her with his eyes.

"I brought you a plate." Tony interrupted the meeting by tugging Susie's hand. "Hi, dad," he added brightly. "Do you want to eat with Susie and me?"

"I'll visit with you both for a while," Sy replied without taking his eyes off Susie. "I'm here semiofficially," he explained. "I'm supposed to take a few photographs of Michelle and her court. She suggested I bring Tony along so he could play with the kids while I work. I had a feeling that if you were here, he'd be with you instead."

"Does that mean I qualify as one of the kids?" Susie smiled.

"In some ways you do," Sy agreed. "Then in other ways...."

"How about some turkey?" Tony urged them both to move with the flow of traffic and select their food from the huge buffet. "You two always talk instead of eating," he grumbled.

"We can do both." Sy stepped aside and eased Susie along. "I can't take photographs, and you don't have to be so defensive if we each have a plate of food to balance," he assured her. "No one will suspect there's anything extraordinary going on between us."

Susie turned to give him a curious look.

"You and I know differently." He spoke the words so softly that only she could hear. "All I have to do is look at you...." He didn't have to complete the sentence. Susie knew all too well that in spite of her reservations, there was a compelling attraction between them that didn't take words to communicate.

"I was working on some posters the other day." She moved the conversation on to less threatening territory. "Huge black-and-white faces of movie stars." She described her work with Renny. Tony looked up at her with great interest, then continued heaping food onto his plate. Sy smiled and watched her. He nodded and listened, but for now he had nothing more to say.

Midway through their meal, which Sy, Tony, and Susie were enjoying picnic-style on the sunny back patio of Uncle Leo's home, a slender, reddish-haired young lady interrupted them. "Michelle's father says he'd like to see you." She focused wide, heavily mascaraed eyes on Sy's handsome face. "We're going to change and play some badminton, so he wanted to get a few pictures, Sy...." The way her voice trailed off and her eyelids fluttered made Susie suddenly uncomfortable.

"I'll be right there, Traci." Sy's businesslike manner seemed to indicate that he was unaffected by the flirtatious manner in which the message had been delivered. Tony was less tactful. He looked over at Susie and rolled his eyes dramatically as if both the young woman and the interruption were unwelcome impositions.

"This happens a lot," Tony muttered confidentially to Susie. "They all act so *cute*." Nothing in his tone was complimentary.

"They all also pay the bills," Sy reminded his son. "At least, their fathers and mothers pay the bills," he corrected himself. "And when one is commissioned to do a job, one does it well. And with a pleasant attitude." Sy looked down at the still-displeased expression on Tony's face.

"But they sound so phony," the lad argued.

"If you're eighteen and your parents can afford to pay for Mardi Gras debutante balls and costumes—" Sy tousled the boy's hair affectionately as he spoke "—I suppose it is possible to get a little carried away with all the glamour and even to act a bit phony at times. But it goes away eventually." His dark eyes now looked meaningfully into Susie's. "And when the fantasy is over, what is real and genuine is still there, son." There was no mistaking that much of his comment was intended for her. "Just be patient with the pretending and the silliness. You and I know there is much more to life than that." Without another word, Sy left Susie and Tony alone on the patio.

"He's always working." Tony had waited until Sy was out of earshot before he made his final comment. "Every time the phone rings, it's someone else wanting him to take their picture."

"Your dad had quite a reputation for excellent photography when he worked here before," Susie noted. "I guess people are spreading the word that he's in New

Orleans again. Everyone wants the best, and that means pictures by Simon Avery.''

"My dad said something like that about your costumes.'' Tony speared a fat strawberry with his fork. "He said your company is one of the best.''

"And when did he say that?'' Susie was curious about any discussion Sy had held with his son.

Tony avoided looking at her. "He was trying to explain why we haven't seen you for a couple of weeks,'' Tony confessed. "I don't understand how you two can like each other and then not ever see each other. All we ever see are those girls in their fancy clothes.'' Now he managed to raise his eyes to meet hers. "They remind me a lot of my mother.'' He paused. "All they're interested in is how they look. I'll bet those girls don't really play badminton.'' His tone became an accusation. "Let's go see. I bet they just stand around with their rackets and don't even get sweaty.''

"Let's see if you're right.'' Susie collected the plates that now were empty and deposited them in the kitchen on the way through the house. She was actually more interested in watching the muscular, bearded photographer at his art, but Tony's bet offered an excellent excuse for an investigation.

On Uncle Leo's side yard, surrounded by a hedge of blooming white and scarlet poinsettias, seven of the court including the queen, Michelle, were standing by the badminton net. Sheltered from the crisp November breeze, the young women, all clad in skimpy shorts and designer T-shirts, were radiant as they stood in the sun-drenched portion of the yard. Their full, elegantly coiffed hair glistened in the sunlight. Flashes of light bounced off slender gold chains and bracelets.

"Look at the shoes on that one." Tony nudged Susie. The young woman he'd indicated had three-inch heels on with her shorts. Susie smiled and nodded. There was definitely an incongruous side to this "badminton game," but in the faces of the maids and queen was another, more touching element. There was an eagerness to be beautiful—a joy in having that beauty held forever on a piece of film or in a scrapbook. It was as if all of them knew they were playing another game, and that game would soon be over. So for now, they celebrated their youth, their good fortune and their moment of magic. Even in high heels.

Sy divided the girls into pairs and assigned them to particular sides of the badminton net. He carried his camera as he moved among them, having one girl serve the bird several times until she put it correctly into the opposite court. Then he told them to play. For the first few serves and returns, the girls were more conscious of where Sy stood with his camera than where the bird was. However, a crowd of onlookers began gathering. Aunts, uncles and cousins began cheering on their favorite players, and the game became more earnest.

Now Sy switched to his zoom lens and shifted position, following the players' expressions and movements and catching them in midair: lips half parted, hair blowing, eyes bright with the challenge of competition. Sy held these real moments in the click and whir of his camera. Susie couldn't take her eyes off him as he ducked and swayed.

"I really don't know why Sy insisted we bring everyone out here." Aunt Jo moved beside Susie. "Why did he need spectators? I thought we'd have some pretty shots of Michelle and the others by the flowers." She sounded less than pleased. "Now look at her," she said quietly. "Her hair is all messy... and she's ruining her makeup."

"She looks great," Susie consoled Aunt Jo. "Michelle will have enough of the posed and pretty shots. Just look at the vitality and the excitement in her face in these." Now Susie directed her aunt's attention to the action near the badminton net. The girl in heels had come in to play on one team. Only now she plunged across the court in pursuit of the little plastic bird, and she actually made the shot. She was also barefoot. Sy had slyly manipulated the circumstances so he could get photographs worth cherishing. He had requested an audience, started the momentum of the game and let the enthusiasm of everyone take over. Somewhere in the midst of the action, the pretense had disappeared, and a new radiance had touched the faces of the young women.

"That one with the bare feet is pretty good," Tony acknowledged.

"She's even sweating," Susie noted humorously.

"I didn't think models ever sweated," Tony marveled. "My mother never does. But she doesn't play badminton, either," he added.

Aunt Jo remained on Susie's other side, watching her daughter slam the bird across the net. "Don't overdo it," Aunt Joe called out. "You have a fitting tomorrow." Michelle gave her mother an exasperated look, then passed her racket to another girl. Almost immediately the composed smile returned to Michelle's face. The game for her had ended and another one was beginning. The Queen of the Krewe of Triton had been reminded who she was.

"Your Mr. Avery might enjoy a cool glass of wine." Aunt Jo's voice had a peculiar edge. Before Susie replied, she turned to see that the statement had been directed to Michelle, not to her. "Get a large wine cooler for him and touch up your makeup, sweetie." Aunt Jo hurried Michelle along. "You don't want to let him out of your sight for long." Susie fixed a pleasant expression on her face as she overheard the exchange.

"I do wish she would keep after him," Aunt Jo confided to Susie after Michelle left. "She isn't really interested in college, and she isn't talented like you." The middle-aged woman gave Susie an affectionate hug. "I don't know what will become of her if she doesn't find some nice young man."

"She's only nineteen..." Susie protested.

"I really don't think Simon Avery is too old for her." Aunt Jo missed Susie's point. "He's very good-looking. He's got money. Of course, he is divorced." She obviously disliked that part. "But he has a darling son. Michelle has always wanted to be a mother."

"Don't you think Michelle should have a say in all this?" Susie was only half joking. "Not to mention Sy Avery!"

"Michelle really doesn't have a practical side." Aunt Jo dismissed Susie's comment. "She kept insisting she was in love with a scruffy fellow from school. Paul something-or-other. A geologist." Aunt Jo made it sound like a disease. "This fellow would disappear for weeks on expeditions. Totally unreliable. He missed two dinner parties. Now, Simon Avery is another matter." Aunt Jo turned her soft brown eyes back toward the badminton area where Sy was dismantling his camera.

Tony had joined his father and was swinging an abandoned badminton racket back and forth.

"He certainly is," Susie admitted. Then Michelle appeared with a frosty wine cooler in one hand and her makeup impeccably restored. Every hair was once more in place.

"I really think they make an attractive couple," Aunt Jo remarked. "I've lined up so many functions for them to attend," she confessed. "Of course, he's there to photograph her, but part of the time they do socialize." The smile of satisfaction on her face sent a chill through Susie. "If Michelle is smart, she won't let this one slip away. Someone else will come along and snatch him right out from under her nose. You know how men are." Aunt Jo shook her head. "They won't go looking around if you keep reminding them something pretty good is right on their doorstep."

"So the trick is to stay on that doorstep." Susie felt the tension in her chest. Aunt Jo had set her sights on making Sy her son-in-law, and she would use every trick in the book to get him. So while Michelle would be available for every function—and would always look spectacular—Susie would be up to her neck in sketches and costumes. There would be no time for doorstep-sitting. Aunt Jo's words echoed in her mind: "You know how men are."

WITHIN MINUTES after the picture-taking session, the crowd of relatives and guests at the home of Leo and Jo Costain redivided into separate activities. Most of the men congregated in Leo's family room in front of a wide-screen television set to watch one of the numerous football games that would be telecast throughout Thanksgiving Day. Many of the women moved into the kitchen for a cup of coffee and some gossip as they took turns helping put away the food and wash the dishes. The younger guests lingered in groups or couples on the patio, or mingled in the game room, playing loud music on the stereo and standing transfixed before the video games. Susie found Renny bent over the controls of Mindboggle, a maze game in which the patterns continually fluctuated, forming a kaleiodoscopic effect.

"He keeps losing," Germaine said, laughing, "but he certainly is enjoying the colors." Just as she spoke, a beeping sound indicated that Renny's little man had once again fallen victim to the maze.

"At least I got a few good ideas for some paintings." Renny focused his attention on the two ladies. "These computer graphics really get to me. Hey...it isn't time to leave yet, is it?" His eyes widened in anxiety. "I promised some short people that I'd play a little rag-tag football."

"Next to you, everyone could be considered 'short people,'" Susie said. "And you don't have to worry, we aren't leaving yet."

"Did that Avery fellow leave?" Renny gave her a smug smile. "We saw you eating with him and the kid. Naturally, we didn't want to interrupt."

"I'm not sure where he is," Susie replied noncommittally. She refused to let on that it was Sy, not Germaine and Renny, she'd been hoping to locate on her wanderings.

"Well, he's supposed to play, too," Renny explained. "Let's take a look around and see where this game is going to take place. If we can't round up enough guys for a team, maybe you two can join in."

"Maybe!" Germaine sniffed. "I want you to know that I was the ace quarterback on my brother's back-yard team for years. When you're talking football, you can count me in—enough guys or not." Germaine smiled at Susie and caught her by the arm. "We may even get up a girl's team and take you on," Germaine declared.

The trio rounded the corner of the house in time to see an assortment of individuals collecting on the side yard where the badminton net had once been. These were the people who had grown restless during the tele-vision games or who simply found the prospect of a good old neighborhood football game too much fun to pass up.

"How about you two joining our team?" The lovely maid from Triton's Court who had removed her high heels and played barefoot invited Susie and Germaine to play on her side. Apparently she had the same idea about the females playing against the males.

Sy had changed clothes and now sported a tattered knit shirt with New Orlean's Saints written across it and a pair of cutoff blue jeans. The shirt was definitely one rounded up from Uncle Leo, but the jeans must have belonged to one of the male cousins. Standing with a wide grin Sy waited for Susie's response.

"I'll play," Susie volunteered.

"Me too." Germaine was right beside her. Two other young women who had been standing off to one side looked at each other, then giggled and came along.

"How about you, Michelle?" Susie called to her cousin. Michelle hesitated for a moment as if she wanted to join them, then with a slight frown, she declined.

"I'll just watch." She moved to a lawn chair and sat down, carefully crossing her legs. Susie felt a sudden twinge of jealousy. Michelle could sit there looking cool and elegant while she raced around like a juvenile. Then another emotion supplanted the jealousy. It was a trace of that same melancholy she had felt when she looked at the portrait of Marilyn Monroe. There was a sense of tragedy—of something valuable being wasted. Susie turned away in time to see Sy studying Michelle. Then his dark eyes flashed back to Susie.

"Let's play ball," one of the fellows who was a bit overweight called out. He had offered to act as referee. "No body-tackles. Instead of tackling, just grab the cloth." He was referring to the strips of fabric that were being passed around to be slipped into belts and waistbands. "And watch where you put your hands!" He made the last comment with a leer.

Germaine made it clear instantly that her reputation as star quarterback was well deserved. With relentless accuracy, she managed to throw passes to the barefoot Andrea, the fluttery-eyed redhead Traci and Susie. Holding on to those passes had been another matter. Renny had leaped in front of the pass receivers, waving his long arms and bellowing like an aborigine. Traci had been so startled that she actually handed him the ball. Two other men had charged Andrea and intimidated her so much that she backed up and dropped the ball. Only Susie had held on long enough to gain any yardage.

"We'll have to use you as a decoy," Germaine told Traci, "and we'll let Susie run with the ball. All the rest of us have to get in the way of the guys so Susie can slip on past them.'' The young women all nodded solemnly at the plan.

When the play began, Germaine handed the ball to Susie, then pretended that she still had it and was planning to pass. As all the players shifted to one side, expecting a pass play, Susie slipped around the right side and took off with the ball as fast as she could.

"Look out, Susie," Tony's high squeal pierced the assorted grunts and groans and huffing and puffing. Then a pair of muscular arms closed around her. Susie rolled onto the grass with Sy clinging to her.

"I like this almost as much as dancing," he said, chuckling as the referee blew his whistle.

"You can't body-tackle!" the heavyset fellow reprimanded Sy. "Just grab the belt flag."

"I must have gotten so carried away that it slipped my mind," Sy apologized halfheartedly. "Let me help you up, my dear." He rolled off Susie and tugged her to her feet.

The referee marched off a penalty and gave the ball back to the women's team.

"Maybe we'd better try passing again," Germaine suggested. "Just to keep them off guard." By now, word had spread that the game was on, and several more players had joined the separate teams. "I think we need to work on defense," Germaine coached the women. "Just go for their flags."

The additional players made the game more confusing as fellows delighted in the opportunity to grab both flags and posteriors and the penalties continued to be doled out. The women scored one touchdown, followed rapidly by two touchdown scores by the men. When the referre inadvertently stepped on Andrea's bare foot, the women's team lost one good player and the game fell apart. On every play, there was more laughter than yards made and Sy rolled Susie to the ground whether she had the ball or not.

"This is really becoming a memorable experience," he declared after graciously accepting his fourth penalty for body contact. "There is something absolutely delicious about holding on to you."

"I'm not one for public displays but this does have its appeal," Susie admitted as they walked back to the line of scrimmage. Within the amiable spirit of the game, she had enjoyed the close physical contact with Sy without feeling conspicuous.

"I can arrange something private anytime you're interested." He let his hand rest on her shoulder momentarily. "I have some more subtle techniques that I'd be glad to demonstrate."

"Sy...." Michelle walked out onto the playing area before Susie could reply. "Mother says she has to see you right away," Michelle insisted. "It has something to do with the fittings tomorrow. Sorry to interrupt the game." He nodded, then gave Susie a good-natured smile. "I'll get back to this discussion later," he promised, as he followed Michelle into the house.

Susie glanced briefly at the many windows that overlooked the playing field. Undoubtedly, somewhere inside, Aunt Jo had stood watching, worrying that the "perfect catch" for Michelle was having too much fun playing backyard football against a team of women. Aunt Jo was not about to let this one slip away, so like it or not, Michelle had come to divert him. It was apparent that Germaine was not the only good coach in the area. Aunt Jo was calling some excellent plays from the sideline.

CHAPTER FOUR

THREE DAYS AFTER the Thanksgiving festivities, Michelle arrived for her fitting at the Costains accompanied by Sy, cameras and Tony. "I'm sorry we had to reschedule," she apologized as Rosie brought down the sea-green satin gown she had begun. "I didn't feel very well over the weekend."

"We're used to all kinds of rearranging," Rosie assured her niece. "Just don't you worry. It's not every year we have a queen of our own. A little touch of the flu isn't going to spoil anything."

"Mother insisted that Sy take some pictures of this for the album," Michelle explained the presence of her companions, "to show the progress from the first fitting to the final stage of the costume."

"That makes perfectly good sense to me," Rosie replied. "How about you setting up your equipment in the fitting room down the hall—" she directed Sy to the rear of the house "—and I'll get Michelle into this dress very carefully. It's only basted together now, but if it's going to come apart, I don't want that in the album. Once we have her secure in it, I'll bring her down for pictures."

"Good idea." Sy started along the hall, summoning Tony along with him.

"Is Susie here?" The lad paused to ask Rosie.

"She sure is." Rosie removed the plastic covering from the gown and slid the dress from the hanger. "She's in the workroom out back. Just go out the door and climb that stairway. It may be a lot more interesting to see what she's doing than it will be watching me making chalk lines and sticking pins in this thing. Go on," she urged him with a gentle pat. "Just don't sneak up on her. Call out and let her know you're on the way up."

"Try not to get in the way, son," Sy cautioned.

"Oh, dad," Tony muttered in exasperation as he trudged out the door. "I told Susie that I'm good with glue and staples and stuff. I won't be in the way. I'll help."

Sy turned into the fitting room. Outside, the young boy's voice cut through the silence of the dark night. "Susie," Tony called. "I'm coming up. It's me...Tony."

In the far end of the workroom, Susie was bending over a bizarre, spiny column of metal, carefully curving certain pieces back toward a heavier part of the frame. "I could use an extra hand here," she greeted the boy. "You came just at the right moment. Grab hold of this." She pointed to one metal strand.

Happily, Tony did as she instructed, bracing the piece while Susie went to get the soldering iron. "What is this?" Tony asked. "It sure is weird."

"Let me solder these in place, and then I'll get the rest of the frame. We'll see if you can figure it out for yourself." Susie touched the joints with the solder and the hot iron. One by one, the spiny pieces became graceful curves looping back and connecting with the main frame.

"Are you ready for me?" Bernie came out of the storage area carrying another skeletal structure. "Let's put this together and see if it flies."

"You mean this is supposed to fly?" Tony said dubiously.

"That's my father's way of saying we'll see if the underwiring does what it's supposed to do. It doesn't fly," she assured the bewildered boy. "It only has to hold the shape of a design and not be too heavy for a person to wear comfortably."

"Can I still help?" Tony approached Bernie and cautiously took one side of the framework.

"Hold it right there." Bernie supervised as the three of them moved the structure on top of the piece Susie had completed. "Now we guys will brace this, and Susie can do the honors with the solder." Bernie winked at the boy. "If we train you right, you may come in handy." Tony's face became deliberately serious. As he watched Susie work, he concentrated on looking as efficient as he possibly could.

"So what is it?" Susie finished and put aside the tools. "Step back and take a good look," she suggested. "See if you can figure it out." The frame now curved upward, then hooked over into a shape that was definitely a head.

"It's a snake," Tony guessed. "One with fins on its back."

Bernie placed a large, gentle hand on the boy's shoulder. "You're darn near right. Let me show you where we go from here." Bernie crossed to a worktable and retrieved a brilliantly colored drawing of the final product.

"A sea monster!" Tony breathed with delight. "It's

really neat!'' His wide eyes shifted from the filmy, iridescent details on the drawing to the bare aluminum
wiring that would delineate the structure of the creature.
Now he could see how it would evolve from one stage to
the next.

"It's worn like this." Susie hoisted the frame and
braced it on the tabletop. Then she turned backward
and slid her shoulders under the support braces. Without straining, she could stand and turn with the fantastic creature towering over her, its open-mouthed head
high above her own.

"The King of the Krewe of Triton will wear this
one," Susie explained. "He'll be able to manage."
Susie directed her comment to her father as she moved
from side to side, testing the weight of the piece.

"Right now we have to work on a few other things.
You *are* still planning to help?" Susie teased him.

"I'm ready," Tony replied eagerly. "I like to help
with this stuff." He followed Susie to another section of
the room where other headpieces were lined up in various states of completion.

"You said you were pretty adept at gluing, didn't
you?" Susie passed a pot of creamy white glue and a
slender, stiff paintbrush to him. Tony nodded. "Then
let's do some of these sea fans," Susie suggested. "You
paint the glue all over the frame, and I'll wrap them in
sequins." The massive fans looked like intricate lacework. Covered in glistening sequins, they would be
braced at shoulder and waist and spread for several feet
in a shimmering halo effect, framing perfectly the head
and shoulders of each maid of the court.

"I'll see how Michelle's fitting is coming along." Bernie excused himself. "When we're ready to check her

headpiece, I'll just bring her up here,'' he suggested.
''That way you two won't have to stop working for
long.'' But his words were only received with preoccupied nodding of heads as Susie and Tony created a
silvery masterpiece from glue and glitter. They were lost
in a world of their own.

They were oblivious to the first click and whir of Sy's
camera. Susie and Tony had been working steadily on
the sea fan, talking about the names for the various
Krewes. Almost half the area's krewe names came from
the elaborate mythologies of the Greeks, Romans, and
Egyptians. ''So the krewes chose names like Comus,
Pandora, Venus, Triton—whatever touched the imagination. Often the balls have themes about myths and
legends. Then again, sometimes they choose songs or
movies or exotic places.'' She opened a new roll of silver
sequins and started wrapping another section of the sea
fan. ''This year we've got 'South American Fantasy,'
'Jungle Splendor,' 'Winds of the Orient,' and two
underwater ones—Triton's 'Fantasy Beneath the Seas'
is the one you and I were making the sea monster for.
The other one is called 'Mysteries of the Deep,' and
we're working on it right now.''

Tony listened closely, obviously impressed that he
was actually involved in creating a costume for a real
ball with an actual theme. His hands hesitated a moment, but his eyes never left the strand of aluminum
wire that he was tracing with his glue brush.

''Do you think you could take me to one of the
balls?'' Tony had just asked the question when a second
click and whir interrupted the quiet conversation between him and Susie. ''Could you?'' Tony persisted
more softly as if he hoped for an answer before his

father came close enough to hear what they were discussing.

"We'll see," Susie whispered hastily. Bent nose to nose over the metal lacework, the two of them looked like conspirators hatching a secret plot. Now that image was caught by Sy's camera.

"Will you stop doing that!" Susie finally looked Sy's way. "It really is aggravating to have that darn camera butting in where it's not wanted."

"You should have seen it from where I was standing." Sy refused to excuse his actions this time. "The two of you were so engrossed in this little lighted section of the room. It was really very pretty. Peaceful." He smiled. "So I couldn't pass it up."

"But you're disturbing us," Tony responded impatiently.

"You're going to be even more disturbed," Sy replied. "Michelle felt ill again and decided to go on home. She won't be up for the headpiece fitting after all."

"We can work it in another day." Susie didn't see any reason for concern.

"That does leave us with a conspicuous problem, though," Sy noted. "Tony and I came with Michelle. We now are stranded here unless some generous soul offers us a ride back to our house."

"And I guess I'm that generous soul." Susie got the point. "I suppose my dad already offered my services as chauffeur," she guessed.

"He did. However, if it's too much trouble, or if you can't spare the time...." He was clearly enjoying himself.

"I'd love to drive you two anywhere. But I also would

like to finish this before I call it a night. Can you wait about twenty minutes before we leave?''

"I can wait," Sy replied. "I'm a very patient fellow, as you'll come to understand." There was a softness in his voice that made Susie smile. "You two just go on with what you're doing, and I'll just amuse myself up here. I've never had a look at the inside of this costuming business. I usually only see the finished product. I'm sure I can learn a lot from prowling around your workroom." Camera in hand, he began moving between the tables, pausing to examine a sketch or a partially constructed form.

From time to time, Susie looked up from her sequin-gluing and glanced over at the tall bearded man who surveyed with rapt attention every corner of the room. When the click and whir again began, Susie wrinkled her nose in displeasure. She finally put her work aside and sighed. "I know this may sound a bit picky," she stressed, "but I really don't like you taking pictures of the projects that we're working on for this year. I keep all the original drawings and fabrics up here so no krewe member ever sees what another krewe is wearing. I just don't feel comfortable about any of this being taken out of here—even in your photos."

"I see your point," Sy acknowledged. "I never meant to infringe on your professional secrets. I simply won't print the film," he promised. "In fact, after I develop the shots I took of Michelle, I'll give you the negatives of these. One day you may want them. You and your family do exceptional work. You have a real gift for this type of thing." The admiration in his voice swept over her like a warm breeze. "I've seen what you do at Blaine's," Sy commented, "but *this* is inspired." He turned to regard her with dark, penetrating eyes. "You can trust your secrets with me," he said quietly. "And I will not betray you."

Susie stood motionless, staring at Sy's face. In that one instant she could feel the tension of years of holding things inside her begin to ease. This man seemed to understand so much about her. He seemed willing to wait to learn more. But while he waited, his eyes and voice caressed her and warmed her. Without touching her in any way, Sy was making love to her, confirming with his quiet smile that he saw in her all that she could not express in any way except through her art.

"Finished!" The triumphant voice of Tony shattered the fragile spell that disappeared as magically as it had begun. "Susie," he called, "I've finished all the gluing. Hurry and put on the sequins before it dries."

Susie left Sy standing on the far side of the workroom solemnly contemplating her sketches. She returned to the side of her young co-worker and expertly wound the string of shimmering sequins over the final wires. "Good job," she congratulated Tony. "This is going to look lovely isn't it?" She stepped back to admire the sea fan.

"Just like you drew it." Sy moved closer with the sketch of the silver sea-maid costume in his hand. "This existed in your imagination long before it moved into reality," Sy commented. "You made something exquisite—just with your mind." He emphasized the words. "Now that is lovely."

"Well, I helped," Tony huffed indignantly. "I glued."

"And you glued marvelously." Sy hugged the boy.

"Maybe I'll hire you out to Susie—child labor at a low price," he joked.

"You bring him by anytime," Susie insisted. "I can use his kind of help."

"And Tony could use a good night's sleep." Sy frowned at the glazed expression on the boy's face. Tony had worked diligently, but he had also worn himself out. "School night." He took the boy's hand and started downstairs. "If our chauffeur is ready, son, 'I think we'd better get you home."

Susie put the lids on the glue and glitter containers then hurriedly checked the rear door. Assured that everything was secure, she grabbed her purse and followed the others.

"See you tomorrow, folks," she called as she caught a glimpse of Bernie and Rosie from the hallway. Several other clients had arrived and more fittings for gowns were scheduled until almost midnight, but for Susie, the work schedule was put aside. She had a tired little boy to deliver to his home, and finally, she had a little time to spend with Simon Avery.

On the brief drive from the Costain's house in the suburb of Chalmette back into the center of New Orleans, Tony leaned against his father's chest and quietly drifted off to sleep. In hushed voices, Susie and Sy spoke fleetingly of their various projects, but something about the sleeping child between them made it strangely pleasant to say nothing—to simply share the quiet drive and watch the beautiful city spreading out on all sides in a carpet of lights.

"I could use a few hours of work in my studio," Sy said softly. "If we drop Tony off at home, would you like to have a late dinner in the Quarter? Then I could make sure you get into your place safety, and I can walk to the studio.''

"I'd like that," Susie replied. "I did miss eating tonight. Skipping meals becomes an occupational hazard once I get busy."

Sy's home was a narrow two-story brick house partially obscured in the front by an ivy-covered brick wall and tall trees. The back, however, had an unobstructed view of Audubon Park, named after the famous naturalist and painter John James Audubon. In the center of New Orleans, Tony had a zoo, pony rides, a children's train ride, a swimming pool and an incredible assortment of trees and flowers right at his doorstep.

"You'll have to come over and see it in the daytime," Sy insisted as he lifted the sleeping child onto his lap. "I didn't want Tony to grow up around cement playgrounds and skyscrapers, and the Quarter isn't a good place to raise a child, so I was lucky enough to find this."

"It's just perfect," Susie agreed.

"Open the door and help me out of here, and I'll give you a quick inside tour." Sy obviously needed help to lift Tony out of the small car. "Besides, you can meet my other woman—Francine," he teased.

Francine Sebron was just as Sy had described her— "about fifty, slightly overweight and one heck of a housekeeper." She was also barely five feet tall, had brilliant red orange hair, and a large nose. Susie's first impression was that she looked like a chubby clown temporarily out of costume. But when the clear dark eyes assessed her, Susie felt the immediate chill. Francine was clearly the protectress of both the Averys and their home.

"This is Susie Costain," Sy whispered before carrying Tony upstairs. "Costumes. . . doubloons. . . lunch at the Napoleon House. . . ." He added the few words that would help Francine identify the dark-haired young woman.

"You're Tony's friend." The spark of recognition immediately changed the black eyes from aloof to welcoming. "He likes you a lot." Now a broad smile made that clownish face as endearing as a leprechaun's. She started to add something else, then apparently changed her mind. "Come into the kitchen and I'll get you some hot tea." She bobbed her head eagerly. Susie wasn't sure she had time for a cup of tea, but something about the buoyant Francine made Susie willing to follow her anywhere.

"Now sit by the window and I'll take care of you." Francine directed her to a bench and table set cozily in a lighted bay window. "In the daytime we look out at all the birds and squirrels, and in the nighttime, they look in at us." She talked nonstop as she placed cups and saucers on the table. "I'll bet they'll be relieved to see a new face for a change. Usually all they get is Tony and me."

"Perhaps I should put on a little lipstick and powder my nose," Susie replied with a slight smile. Francine turned and fixed her shiny dark eyes on her guest. Again, the broad grin sparkled.

"You might spoil them," Francine replied, cackling. "Then when they only have me to look at, they might get very disagreeable—throw nuts and make rude noises." Now it was Susie's turn to giggle.

"If she starts calling the teacups by name—" Sy came to join them "—don't be too disturbed. Francine thinks everything has feelings. If we don't use one cup just as often as another one, she actually apologizes to it and gives it extra duty to make up.'' His eyes twinkled as he revealed Francine's idiosyncrasy.

''I used to feel that way about silverware,'' Susie confessed. ''I'd make sure each night when I set the table that the forks and knives and spoons on the bottom of the drawer were used just as often as the ones on top.''

''The world is full of strange ones like us.'' Francine wriggled her penciled-on eyebrows melodramatically. ''Watch your step, Mr. Avery,'' she said with a leer, ''you're surrounded!''

''I'm also hungry, and I've got some developing to do in the studio,'' he responded. ''Apologize to the teacups for us—'' he made a slight bow ''—and tell them we'll join them another time. I'm taking Susie to dinner, and we've got to get going now. If you can get along without me, I'll just spend the night at the studio.''

''Listen to him.'' Francine playfully directed her complaint to the unused teacups. ''If we can get along without him...'' she huffed. ''He's gone so much of the time, most of us don't even remember his name.'' She managed to keep a straight face.

''It's on the mailbox.'' Sy took Susie's arm and led her toward the front door. ''And my phone number is in the book,'' he called back to her.

''She's absolutely wonderful.'' Susie was still smiling when Sy slid into the car next to her. ''Tony must adore her!''

''I adore her, too,'' Sy declared. ''She's extremely efficient as a housekeeper, but it's her bizarre sense of humor that makes her priceless. I couldn't have made the move back to the States if it hadn't been for Francine. There was no way I could spend the time I needed to get my business started again, unless I had someone special to look after my son. As you saw, Francine gives 'special' added meaning.''

By the time Susie drove into the Quarter and found a parking place, Sy had told her a great deal about his attitude to parenthood. ''When I met Felicia, she was just starting out as a model, and I was pretty successful doing photography here in town. She was beautiful. I did a portfolio of pictures for her, and it seemed as if we had a perfect combination. When her career took off, she had a lot of offers in Europe. Magazine editors saw my work and wanted me, too. So the perfect team went to France and Italy and Spain. We had plenty of money and not a responsibility in the world, until Felicia got pregnant with Tony. Then we both grew up and faced reality. We got married, Tony was born, and we tried to act like a perfect married couple—but the freedom was gone,'' he had said with a trace of sadness. ''Now we worked to pay the bills, and there were no more all-night picnics with champagne and caviar on the beach. The romance was gone, but the child was very much there.''

Sy had stayed in Switzerland with Tony while Felicia returned to modeling. Eventually, they divorced and Sy was given custody of Tony. ''Felicia didn't want to be a mother,'' Sy said simply but without bitterness. ''But Tony was three before she actually had to admit that.''

''Does she ever visit him?'' Susie asked as they walked through beveled glass doors into the dimly lighted restaurant on Bourbon Street. The masses of lush trailing plants that hung from the rafters and the deep golds and reds of the antique stained-glass lamps added an increased element of intimacy to their conversation. Seated in a booth sleek with burgundy leather, Susie watched Sy's solemn face.

"Felicia comes and goes," he said without rancor. "When she has a few weeks off, once or twice a year, she may come for a few days. She brings presents, and she really seems to enjoy being around him. Within a couple of days, they both get pretty bored with each other. She goes off to another job. He goes back to his schoolwork and his toys."

"And what about you?" Susie questioned. "How does this affect you?"

"I'm not carrying around any deep psychological scars," he assured her. "I'll never forget some of the good times—" his face was serene "—but I don't feel any resentment. I just try not to categorize people or judge them as readily as I once did. Felicia wasn't a bad wife or a poor mother," he said calmly. "She's just who she is—and she wasn't meant to be a full-time parent. She gives Tony what she has to give—and I try to do the rest. I'm the one who takes him to the dentist and to karate lessons."

"And carries him up to bed," Susie added with a smile.

"That's one of the good parts." Sy returned her smile. "But the rest of it could have been tough if it hadn't been for that red-headed eccentric I have for a housekeeper. She relieved me from having to handle everything myself. She gives Tony affection and good company when I'm not available. I have the peace of mind of knowing he's in good hands. Then I can concentrate on my work. Which is what I'll be doing as soon as we eat." He tapped the menu in front of her to remind her to make a selection. "We didn't come here to discuss me." He grinned. "We're here to eat."

Over creamy, thick-crusted quiche and tangy Greek salads, Sy and Susie talked of other things. Susie found herself telling him about her engagement to Richard Martin and the night he tried to force her to make love with him. She had never said a word about it to anyone, but in the seclusion of their booth, she felt that at last she could let it out without so much anxiety.

"You are a very sexy lady," Sy observed. "I can see how someone would want to touch your body and make love to you. I've wanted to hold you and feel your skin against mine from the first time we spoke in the park." He reached across the table and rested his hand on hers. The gesture was soft as a caress, yet the contact sent an immediate surge of warmth through her. "And I will make love with you one day," he added softly. "We both already know that." There was no reason for Susie to reply. In many ways, she and Sy had already touched each other and loved each other. And they both understood the passion that was drawing them together would eventually be expressed in yet other ways.

"But when we make love," he said, tracing the back of her hand with his fingertips, "it will be completely— with no busy schedules harassing us, no distractions, no doubts. I want all of you lying next to me." His voice mesmerized her. "I want the childish giggles and your marvelous mind, but I also want to feel the intense sensuality you possess. I want you to want me as totally as you are capable of feeling. You have so much you hold back now. When you trust me and when you hunger for me, then we will make love. And it will be worth waiting for," he said huskily. "You touch my heart already."

Sy looked into her eyes. "One day, you'll send your magic through my body, and you'll shake my soul." He lifted her hand and pressed her open palm to his lips. "*That* will be no fantasy," he assured her. "It won't fade away."

Susie stared with half-parted lips at the incredible softness in Sy's expression. His words had touched her more completely than any physical gesture could have. The deep sense of sexual longing and anticipation that Sy had described now stirred within her. Yet in Sy's gaze, she was free to feel her sexuality without having to fear that he would demand too much too soon. He wanted her to savor the desire, to enjoy the wanting, until the time was right for them. "And you'll shake my soul...." His words foretold what she knew to be true. When she could respond to him with her entire being, his soul would not be the only one shaken. It would be a sensation they would share—an unconstrained, uninhibited celebration of each other, and a total acknowledgment of themselves.

"Finish your dinner." Sy released her hand and turned her attention to the unfinished food before them. "I want you to take very good care of yourself," he urged her. "No more skipping meals. Don't underestimate the stress that carrying two jobs puts on you...or is it three?" He narrowed his eyes warily. "Are you still doing work with your friend Renny?"

"It's three," Susie confirmed. "I've got about fifteen more faces to do for him."

"Then start taking vitamins." Sy smiled. "Super ones."

"You sound like my mother." Susie shook her head.

"I am concerned for you," he acknowledged. "But

there is a lot more to it than the desire to play mother hen. I want you healthy and rested for selfish reasons. I want you to feel so good. . . ."

"I know the rest." Susie felt the color rise in her cheeks.

"As long as we understand each other," Sy replied. "Now, eat your dinner and I'll take you home." There was nothing brusque in his tone. It was a gentle request, spoken with affection. Susie understood perfectly.

After dinner and a cup of strong chicory coffee thick with cream and sugar, Susie drove the few blocks to her apartment. "It doesn't look like your bodyguard is home." Sy looked up at the adjoining apartment. "And it is very dark between here and there," Sy added. "I think I'll walk you to the door and wait until you're safely inside."

Side by side they passed through the metal gateway into the walled courtyard. Then they climbed the narrow stairway to the upstairs apartments. Sy hesitated on the balcony while Susie opened the door and flicked on the light.

"Now I'm safe inside," she said, returning to the doorway. "You don't have to worry." The chilly wind from the river swirled along the street below, sending scattered pieces of litter looping and tumbling from one soft circle cast by the streetlights to the next.

"Then I'll get to the studio and see what develops." Sy tugged his overcoat closed and surveyed the scene below. "I wish I had my camera," he murmured, contemplating the desolate effect of the litter on the cobbled street. Susie stepped out beside him.

"It has its own peculiar beauty," she agreed, following his gaze. Then she stepped back inside her apartment. "You can have this." Susie returned with a pen-and-ink sketch she had made of the scene months before, when the breeze had been a summer one and the air scented with jasmine. "I liked it, too." She handed the framed drawing to him.

He held it before him, letting the light from her doorway illuminate it. Then, without a word, he stepped forward and enclosed her in his arms. "Take care of yourself, lady," he whispered. "You're a once-in-a-lifetime phenomenon." Then very gently, Sy kissed her. First on the tip of her nose, then on her eyelids, and finally, when their warm breath made a pale cloud in the chilly air, he lowered his lips to hers.

Susie slid her arms around his neck, letting her fingers brush the rough, trimmed beard then descend to the warm, smooth column of his muscular neck. The contrast in textures of skin and beard both beneath her lips and fingertips sent a sudden shudder of pleasure through her. Without releasing her, Sy pulled open his overcoat and enveloped her in its warm interior. Pressed against him, Susie felt again the power and tension of his taut muscles. Sy held her even closer so she could feel his body responding to the contact with her own.

"Don't worry," he said softly, sending a ripple of heat against her ear. "I'm certainly no exhibitionist. I'm not going to make love to you out here. But I want you to remember this night. I want it to float into your mind as you go to sleep at night, and I want you to wake with it each morning. Then one day. . . ." He eased her away so he could look into her eyes. "One day, you won't have to remember."

"Hey. . . Susie?" Renny's lanky form came loping up the stairs. "Is that guy still hanging around here?"

Renny grinned as Susie and Sy shifted apart. "I really hated to interrupt you guys, but I stood around downstairs until I thought my posterior would drop off. I know an artist can live without a posterior, but when my fingers went numb—" he looked at them apologetically "—I had to quit being tactful and come in out of the cold. Tomorrow is the first of December, you know." He hung his head like a scolded puppy. "Sorry..." he mumbled, ducking past them into his own apartment with a final helpless flap of his arms.

"Before you freeze—" Sy nodded for Susie to go on into her own apartment "—get a good night's sleep." He touched her cheek softly. "And think about me. We may not have an evening together again for a very long time."

Long after Sy left and Susie was snug in her warm bed, she lay awake still smiling with delight. He did not have to ask that she remember. Every detail of their time together was indelibly etched into her consciousness. She could play it again and again in her mind, like a sensuous, undulating melody. "And when you hunger for me," Sy had said, "we will make love." Like so many of her artistic creations, she could create the vision in her mind long before it became a reality.

"Hunger for me...." The words still echoed in her dreams.

CHAPTER FIVE

"READY?" RENNY CASTELOT poked his puff of lavender hair through the transom between his apartment and Susie's. Fortunately he had warned Susie earlier in the afternoon that he had "gone mauve" for the week. The beginning of the festive Christmas season generally brought an influx of visitors to the French Quarter, and Renny was setting up a display there each day in the hope of moving some of his easy pieces—small, brightly colored scenes of New Orleans. Amid all the other artists who lined Jackson Square vying for the attention of passersby, Renny found being a foot taller and a striking shade of light purple from head to foot generally brought him more attention and more sales. Next week he'd try another color.

"Just a couple more minutes." Susie stalled him. She had just heated a cup of soup in her microwave, and while she sipped the steamy broth, she read once more the captions under the numerous photos on the social page. December was the month when the party spirit escalated. The society section ran on for additional pages to accommodate all of the social events and gossipy commentary.

On page two, Michelle Costain and Sy Avery were dancing cheek-to-cheek. The caption below suggested that "much-sought-after bachelor photographer Sy

Avery has found his business is a pleasure." It went on to add that Sy had been commissioned to do photo albums and portraits of the most affluent debutantes and Mardi Gras royalty, but he had been Michelle's escort as well as her photographer on several occasions. Susie took another sip of her warm soup and tried to dismiss the implications of the article. Then she looked again at the photograph of Michelle and Sy. Michelle looked exquisite—young, vibrant, with a cloud of blond hair perfectly framing her face. Only a portion of Sy's face was visible in the picture, but the set of his shoulders and the deep shade of his jacket brought back memories of the time she had danced with him at Michelle's coronation party.

Sy had been Michelle's escort that night, too. Susie shook her head to push aside her misgivings. At the same time, she remembered the look in her Aunt Jo's eyes as she plotted to catch Sy for her daughter and Aunt Jo's words, "you know how men are." If her aunt continually arranged to have Michelle and her unmistakable charms thrust into Sy's arms, would he be able to resist? Would he want to resist? Susie peered more closely at the picture in the paper, wishing she could have seen the expression in Sy's dark eyes. Then she would have known instantly that everything between them was just as he had said. The silly, provocative commentary in the newspaper would not bother her at all. It had only been three days since Sy had held her in his arms and talked of making love with her. Susie angrily pitched aside the paper. That society writer was not going to upset her, she decided. There was a private side to Sy that would never make the social column, and that quiet, intense part of him had made promises that only Susie would share.

"Hurry up, Susie!" This time Renny came through the front door of the apartment. "I've got five panels all set up ready for you. If we get started early enough, we might make it through all of them before midnight."

"Midnight...." Susie finished the last of her soup and put the mug in the sink. "I've got to be back before then," she declared. "I have to be at Blaine's to do some advertising layouts early tomorrow. I'm yours until ten," Susie countered. "Then I'm coming home and going to sleep."

"I'll settle for that." Renny lifted her coat from the chair and held it open for her. "I'd settle for anything if it helps to get these panels completed." Susie thrust her arms into her coat, then diligently locked the door. When she turned toward the stairway, her eyes lingered a moment on the street below. It was early evening and the streetlights were not on yet, and there were people and vehicles moving past. It was not the solitary, poignant scene she had sketched. Right now it was too busy; it was just another street. But in the darkness, Sy had looked upon it with the same sensation as Susie had. He saw its beauty and its pathos all at once. "Kindred spirits...." The phrase suddenly came to mind. It described quite perfectly the sense of immediate comprehension, that wordless understanding that seemed to charge the air when she and Sy looked into each other's eyes.

"Susie...." Renny had already reached the courtyard gate below and now waited impatiently for her to follow. With a slight smile on her lips, Susie hurried past him and unlocked her car doors. Rush hour was over and the traffic would be light. Across the river, in the warehouse, others were waiting for her touch. Katherine Hepburn, Bette Midler, Judy Garland, Bela

Lugosi and Edward G. Robinson would be appearing on ten-foot-square panels as soon as Susie gave them form and line.

It was Judy Garland's hands that brought Susie to a frustrated halt several hours later in the night. She had already drawn four of the five "Stars of the Silver Screen" on their respective panels and Renny was rapidly filling in the appropriate portions with solid black. From time to time he would step back and tilt his head and nod as the large blotchy patches gradually captured the essential features of the stars who would revolve high above the dance floor at the Krewe of Hyacinth Ball.

"You sure are good," Renny would say again and again with obvious relief. "When this thing is over, I'm gonna see if we can get these back and show them somewhere. They're too good to throw out. Man—" he framed one with his hands "—they'd look great in a bar or a restaurant...."

"They'll look even better if they're finished." Now it was Susie's turn to prod him back to work.

She struggled again to get the slightly graceful, slightly grotesque hands in the portrait of Garland to do what they were supposed to do. In films of performances by the singer-actress, Susie had been enraptured by the power of Judy Garland to elicit a tear or a smile from her audience. There was such emotion in the uplifted face of the aging pixie that each performance had the impact of a self-contained melodrama, but it was the erratic, eloquent contortions of Garland's hands that now caused Susie such difficulty.

"I'll have to come back to this one." Susie finally surrendered. "I'll have to think about it for a while, then I'll try the hands again." Renny came and stood behind her, looking over her shoulder at the striking image.

"The face is perfect," he said softly. "We can wait for the rest of it. I sure wouldn't want you to mess it up now. It's too good to take any chances with." Renny concurred with her. Wait until the inspiration is right.

"Nice work..." a distant voice echoed from the dimly lighted far end of the warehouse. When Susie first glimpsed the bearded form emerging from the darkness, she thought it was Sy. But in the brighter glow from the worklights, she saw that the man was younger and more slender. Only the dark, trimmed beard was similar.

"Susie, this is another one of us 'real' artists who work on these projects for the big bucks," Renny said, introducing his friend. "Pascal Danos is a sculptor," Renny noted, "when he isn't working on floats. And Susie, as you see," he added, "is—"

"Very talented. These are really nice," Pascal continued. He looked from one panel to the next. "When you hit them with the black light, they'll be dynamite!"

"Thank you," Susie responded, accepting the compliment readily.

"We just hit a dead end." Renny started washing the brushes and putting the tops back on the paint containers. "How's it going over in the float business?"

"It's just about time to wrap up for the night." Pascal gave Renny a nudge. Renny let out a low moan and rolled his eyes in mock anguish.

"You don't get the joke?" Renny quizzed Susie. "Wrap up," he said the words slowly. "Maybe you have to have seen the inside of the float warehouse to get the point of that rather droll comment," he said with a low chuckle.

"I'd be glad to let you take a look around, if you're interested." Pascal seemed eager to have the opportunity to show off some work of his own. "It won't take long," he offered. "I could also use a hand wrapping up." This time a row of slightly uneven teeth were visible above the dark beard. Susie looked more closely at the ragged edges of the fellow's shirt collar and the ill-fitting sweater he wore over it. Perhaps Pascal was more in need of money than even Renny realized.

"I have fifteen minutes," Susie announced, glancing at her watch. "If that's enough to see the floats, then I'd love to have a tour."

Pascal glanced at Renny for confirmation, then beamed with delight as Renny finished storing the paints and joined them. "Fifteen minutes is a start—" Pascal hedged a bit "—but you'll see enough to get the idea."

Once they had crossed the asphalt parking area to the adjacent warehouse, Susie began to understand why her fifteen minutes would only "be a start." The huge, cavernous warehouse extended far beyond what she had imagined. Inside, the lower floor was lined with rows of flatbed chassis, motorized rolling platforms on which the detailed designs for the floats are set up. Each krewe would have an elaborate, regal float for its king, followed by fifteen to twenty-five other floats depicting the theme for that year. At the end of each parade, only the king's float would be retained for the next year. Each of the other floats would be "struck"—stripped down to the flatbed or the understructure.

"Thse guys have some really effective ways of recycling the floats." Pascal began explaining the procedure. "The company does the floats for nine krewes—nine complete parades on different days or nights." He

directed them between two flatbeds near the center of
the warehouse. "Since the flatbeds are the biggest ex-
pense, they've designed them on a standard series of
patterns." Now Pascal preceded his companions onto a
twelve-foot observation tower that dominated the center
of the huge work area. From that vantage point, Susie
and Renny could look over the sea of partially constructed floats that would ultimately thrill the crowds
who lined the streets of New Orleans during the peak of
carnival season. There were more than fifty flatbeds in
the vast warehouse, but that was not enough to stage
nine separate parades.

"There are the other floats." Pascal directed their attention to the rigid metal platforms suspended high
above their heads. On these platforms, each of which
had motorized pulleys and an identifying number connected to it, were gigantic packages and objects
wrapped in sheets of brown paper. Gradually it was
becoming clearer what Pascal had joked about when he
said he was "wrapping up."

"As we finish the figures for one float, we send them
up there." He pointed skyward. "They're safe and out
of the way until they're needed. The floats are set up so
that after one parade, we can roll them in here, strip off
the outer designs, then lower the new structures and
connect them. The pieces that are supposed to move
have the same internal workings, so we can have the new
character or creature connected in a matter of an hour.
Then we respray the lower base to match the new designs, and an entirely different parade is ready to roll."

"Assembly-line pageantry." Renny wiggled his fingers like a magician performing an act of levitation,
raising one spectacle and lowering another. "But if you

really want to be impressed—'' Renny gestured mysteriously to an enclosed portion of the warehouse ''—let's go into the shop where all these things are born. You do have a few more minutes.'' He winked at Susie.

It was already ten o'clock. Susie wrinkled her nose, knowing that she needed sleep. But the closed workroom enticed her, for she knew that beyond the doors was a side of Mardi Gras that she had never experienced. ''I'll take the time.'' She couldn't conceal her curiosity. Besides, she consoled herself, one artist could always learn something from another.

The fifteen men and women working at lighted work centers along the inner walls of the ''den''—the inner sanctum where the scenery and figures for the floats were constructed—reminded Susie of production lines of her own. Some were involved in the first stages of construction, others were applying the final touches. Several workers looked up suspiciously at the two newcomers, but the presence of the bearded sculptor apparently eased their concern. Pascal would not have brought along someone who could not be trusted.

''Pascal wouldn't tell you this, but he's the genius behind these monstrosities.'' Renny patted a huge papier-mâché head, an exotic male face beneath a twisting turban. ''He sculpts the original form out of clay and supervises the making of a plaster mold from his design. These other workers can press the papier-mâché into the mold and wait till the thing dries. The rest is right in front of you.'' Renny pointed to a couple of young men fitting one new figure onto a wooden armature to support it. The rough edges and seams would be covered. The next set of workers would apply the undercoats of paint according to the initial sketches.

Then somewhere at the end of the assembly line, again under Pascal's expert eye, more skilled painters would complete the detailed artwork. Finally, the head or arm or whatever the completed form might be would be wrapped and given an identifying number, then sent aloft to await the final assembly procedure.

"These are for the Krewe of Comus parade." Pascal now radiated pride. Comus was the oldest of all the Mardi Gras organizations and was the most recent krewe to hire the float-building company for which Pascal worked. The Mystic Krewe of Comus, which took its name from the Greek word for "revelers," was the first to form a carnival society in 1857. Reviving an old celebration, Comus added innovations: theme parades and pageants, culminating in a magnificent ball. To be selected to design the floats for this historic krewe was the supreme compliment to the company and to the artistry of Pascal Danos.

"The theme of the parade this year," Pascal explained, "is simply 'Wishes'...thus we have this genie here, and farther along there are four-leaf clovers and leprechauns, magic lanterns and rainbows...." Pascal began pointing out the drawings along the walls depicting various float designs on the theme. "I think you'll really like something down a little farther." He guided Susie into a second workroom where rows of motionless figures were poised like fairy-tale sentinels until their final coats of paint dried. "You and I have much in common." Pascal tried to keep his lips together as he smiled so his chipped teeth would not show, but the attempt only made his self-consciousness more apparent. "Perhaps my solution could be of some help to you." At the end of the second row, Susie saw the figure that

Pascal had wanted her to examine. It was an eleven-foot-tall model of Judy Garland as Dorothy, the pig-tailed "wishful thinker" from the movie *The Wizard of Oz*. She stood towering above Susie, sparkling ruby shoes and all, with a less-than-perfect face. But the multijointed arms and hands, which would connect to the machinery on the float and would gesture as the parade moved along, were beautifully done.

"You did a better expression up top," Pascal conceded. "The older she got, the more there was to her face. But I got the rest," he said quietly.

The hands of the figure seemed too large to be in proportion with the body, but it was that oversize, awkward design that made them perfect. "They're marvelous." Susie said, acknowledging his expertise.

"You'll never guess what I used as a model." Pascal chuckled. He waited for Susie to insist he tell her. However, Renny had moved beside them and now lifted Pascal's own arm. The bare extended forearm of the slender sculptor, with his slightly protruding joints and long, powerful fingers seemed no more suited to Pascal's slight build than the hands of Judy Garland were suited to her. Yet there was that same eloquence, a graceful quality that could express emotion and tension so skillfully.

"Now I can go to bed and sleep in peace." Susie shook the hand that she would eventually draw. "Thank you, Pascal."

"But I'll lie awake and see the painting that you made. And I'll wish I had seen your version of her face before my work was completed here," Pascal replied.

"That's the nicest compliment of all." Susie was deeply touched by the sincerity of the remark. "I'll re-

member how good you made me feel—when I drag myself into work tomorrow and try to stay awake.''

It was almost midnight when Susie finally collapsed
into her bed. In her dreams huge faces loomed before
her—some were studies in black and white, others were
mammoth figures in bright colors, which waved and
grinned down at invisible crowds. Through it all, there
were arms reaching out and grasping at her, other arms
waving, and yet others trying to embrace her. In this
fluctuating forest of arms, the smiling face of Pascal
kept disappearing as another bearded countenance, with
dark beckoning eyes, tried to come to her. But other
arms entrapped him, and Sy was swept away by a faceless female whose laughter rippled in the night and who
moved in a billow of golden hair.

Susie sat bolt upright in the dark room, clasping the
covers tight around her as the soft laughter persisted.
She stumbled to the window and stared down into the
courtyard. Just beyond the wall, parked next to her car,
Susie saw the hulking Harley-Davidson motorcycle.
Germaine. Susie breathed the name of Renny's friend
with relief. Now the laughter came again and Susie
knew at once its source. On the other side of the
bathroom transom, a sliver of light indicated that Renny was working through the night, probably on one of
his ''real'' pieces for the show he would hold eventually.
Apparently Germaine was over there with him, watching him work, even in the middle of the night.

Susie's smile wavered as the sliver of light abruptly
disappeared and the apartment next door became suddenly quiet. There was a soft muffled sound of voices
then the dull, creaking sound of Renny's bed. Susie
closed her bathroom door silently, hoping to cut off all

sound and to avoid the feeling that she was encroaching on their intimacy. They had all been so busy lately. A few minutes or a few hours together were rare and very special.

Susie tugged her pillow over her head to further block any sounds that might cross the narrow barrier between the apartments, but it was the deep, steady beating of her own heart that filled her senses. Pressing her eyes closed, she tried to bring back Sy's dark, smiling eyes. She longed for the warmth of his gentle hands. She did not want to be a bystander, an eavesdropper or a voyeur. She could feel the desires that Sy wanted her to feel. The aching eagerness made her press her face against the sheets to muffle yet other sounds—the weary, rasping sobs that she could no longer hold inside. Exhausted and alone, her body trembled and her soul whispered to her—enough, enough. At last in new dreams, a hand reached out to caress her. Finally, someone understood.

WHEN THE TELEPHONE RANG in her cubicle in Blaine's advertising department, Susie picked it up, hoping to hear Simon Avery's voice. She had been deluged the entire morning with post-Christmas sales items, but she had tucked Sy's card under her clipboard. She intended to call him as soon as she had a break.

"Susie?" The worried voice belonged to her father. "I hate to bother you at work, but I need to know if you can get out here a bit early today. It looks like someone tampered with the lock in our workroom. I can't tell if anything has been disturbed."

"Someone actually broke in?" Susie was mystified.

Other than the few tools they used, there was little that any thief would be able to turn into quick cash.

"It *looks* like it," Bernie said to qualify his statement. "Before I call in the police, I think you'd better come and take a look for yourself. I have a friend on the police force who will drop by unofficially and go over the place with you. If it looks like we have something to report, he'll take it from there."

Already Susie was wiping off her pens and lining them up. She had completed enough drawings to appease her supervisor, and a break-in at home definitely qualified as an emergency. Susie had to ascertain what an intruder could have wanted in her workroom. "I'll be out in thirty minutes," Susie told her father. She picked up her purse and tucked it under her arm. With a slight frown, she retrieved Sy's business card and once more tucked it into the zippered compartment of her purse. Calling him would have to wait. Right now, she'd have to tell Ella Jenkins she was leaving.

"Don't touch anything," Bill Terrebonne cautioned Susie as he accompanied her up the stairway that led to her workroom. "If anything is missing, we'll call in a lab team and dust for fingerprints." Terrebonne, a short, wiry fellow in his fifties, had been on the police force for years, and now that he had made detective, he wore no uniform and drove an unmarked car. His presence at the Costains would draw no attention from neighbors or from Rosie's seamstresses until it became apparent whether any crime had occurred.

"Whoever worked on this lock was pretty clumsy," Terrebonne said as he pointed to the gouges in the wood surrounding the lock plate. "But if he actually went inside, he sure got neater," the officer noted. He had looked in before Susie had arrived. "Of course, there may have been more than one of them," he added. "But it sure is hard to tell what they were after." He reached in with his handkerchief over his hand and flicked on the lights. "Take a look around, Susie." He let her pass. "Just point out anything that doesn't look like it did when you left it."

A peculiar uncomfortable feeling crept over Susie as she stepped into the room. This had been her sanctuary, her personal studio, where she could dream and create with absolute freedom. Other people—friends, visitors, workers—had come and gone, but this time Susie felt a different presence. Her sanctuary had been violated. Someone unknown and uninvited had trespassed into her domain. Susie walked from table to table, examining the work in progress at each station. She checked the supply shelves where spools of sequins and bolts of fabric were stored. The metal wiring was intact; the soldering equipment was undisturbed. Shaking her head slowly from side to side, she tried to identify what had been tampered with that made her feel so oppressed by this invader.

"It's something to do with the sketches." Susie finally halted by one large display area where rows of tacks held her costume designs on a huge cork bulletin board.

"Some are missing?" Terrebonne came closer to her. Susie stood with her arms crossed over her chest as if she was guarding herself.

"No..." she replied cautiously. "They're here. It's just that something about them is changed." Even with the overlapping and crooked placement of the sketches, Susie had her own sense of order. Now that had been altered although she was not certain what was different.

There were almost two hundred individual designs for this year's costumes, but Susie knew that some hand had rearranged the master designs that she had posted. "I think someone took these down and then put them up again." She hated to sound so foolish, but that was the only disruption she could identify.

Terrebonne stared at the designs thoughtfully. "If someone copied all these, maybe took pictures of them," he wondered aloud, "would they be worth anything?"

Susie considered the possibility carefully. "I guess they could sell the ideas to a krewe that needed costumes." She now recalled the defensive feeling she had that night when Sy was snapping photographs while she and Tony worked on a headpiece. Sy had been merely recording an event. Whoever tampered with Susie's bulletin board may have been stealing her creations. Susie didn't feel defensive now; she was getting angry. "But I'd like to see anyone try to build them," she snapped. "My dad and I are the only ones who could put together these headpieces and collars." She pointed to the fabulous structures that were worn over the gowns—the wings, the creatures, the sea fans—that carried out each theme.

"But the designs *alone*," Terrebonne inquired, "are they worth money?"

"The designs are worth several hundred dollars for each set," Susie responded. "But they would be worthless to a krewe *now*," she explained. "It would be impossible to duplicate the gown and construct the collars and headpieces before the Mardi Gras balls begin. They start in a month," Susie stressed. "No one could order all the fabric and plumes." She dismissed the possibility. "We plan our materials a year in advance." She fluttered her hands to emphasize her lack of concern over such a threat. "What is even more of an obstacle to some copycat costumer is that none of these drawings show the understructures for the costumes. There are no clues about how to motorize the butterfly wings or how to keep the sea monster from collapsing. If others tried to duplicate my designs, they'd end up with something too heavy for a person to support—or something so weak it would droop."

"So the worst that could happen is that someone might try to pick up some cash by selling just the designs," Terrebonne concluded.

"Even if they sold them," Susie remarked, "they would be most likely to sell them to a krewe for next year since they couldn't be completed for this carnival season."

"It will be pretty obvious if they show up." A tight smile brightened the leathery face of the officer. "Clumsy idea—like the clumsy job on the lock," he muttered. "We see all this stuff paraded by on our television sets. How many sea monsters like this one would there be? Just one." He'd answered his own question.

"Unless the designs were sold out of town." Now Bernie crossed the room to join his daughter and his old friend Terrebonne. Bernie had followed them up sometime during the examination of the room and had heard their discussion. "There are a lot of other cities that have Mardi Gras balls," he observed. "Not just in Louisiana. They have 'em in Alabama and in Florida."

"So what do you want to do?" Terrebonne asked Bernie. "Do we call in the lab team and see what we find?"

"No—" Bernie shook his head "—I agree with Susie. Even if they sell the designs, what good are they? No one can build them. So what I intend to do is to change the locks and put in a burglar alarm. I may not have been able to stop these guys, but I'll make sure nothing like this happens again. We're not even sure what did go on up here." Bernie looked once more over the room. "All this design-stealing stuff is just conjecture. Someone may have fiddled with the bulletin board, then just left."

"Whoever broke in here had to have something more in mind than that," Terrebonne said evenly. "You let me know if anything else looks peculiar or if something is missing. And go ahead and change the locks." He voiced his agreement. "They may change their minds and come back."

"How reassuring. . . ." Susie shuddered at the idea of some mysterious intruder returning, particularly since she would be spending more and more time there at night. "I may have to get a watchdog."

"I'll put the birds up here." Bernie brightened at the thought. "Your mother is always complaining about the parrots squawking while we have visitors in the house, especially now that we have clients in for fittings every evening. So at night, I'll put the birds up here. Lord help the fool who tries to break in when Rosalind and Marcel are loose." Bernie laughed aloud at the turmoil that would result. "Those birds would make such a commotion—shrieking and squalling like they do. Poor fella would have a heart attack," he said, chuckling.

"Watchbirds." Terrebonne found the idea amusing. "I'll have to pass this on to the guys downtown."

Long after the two men had left her alone in the

workroom, Susie still wandered from one table to the next wondering if she had missed spotting some detail that would help make some sense out of the break-in. Finally she lifted Sy's card from her purse and strolled over to the telephone.

"Sy...this is Susie." She was relieved that he answered the phone at his studio. From the pleased sound of his response, she could tell he was glad to hear from her.

"This is a major breakthrough," he said with delight. "You actually called me. Now tell me that you have the evening free, and you want to spend it with me."

"I don't have the evening free," Susie replied. "But I wish I did. However, I do have a couple of hours before I'm scheduled to do some fittings for costumes. Do you have the negatives of those shots you took in the workroom?" she asked.

"You still don't trust me...." There was a sudden chill in Sy's voice. "Of course I have them—under lock and key."

"We think there's been a break-in here," Susie hastily explained. "I'm at the shop, not at the department store. I thought that if you printed up the pictures you took, that might help me to determine what has been disturbed up here. It has nothing to do with not trusting you."

"I'm sorry for snapping at you the way I did," Sy apologized. "If you can come down here, I'll have some prints made by the time you arrive. I can't leave the studio now, since Tony is coming here right after school."

"Then I'll get to see both of you," Susie replied. "Maybe we can grab a quick sandwich together."

"Just get here." Sy's low voice warmed her. "Believe me, we'll think of something to do. I just want to see your face again."

"Right," Susie answered. "I'm on my way."

By the time Susie reached the Simon Avery Studios on Royal Street, the French Quarter was slowly emptying of tourists and afternoon strollers. Instead, the deep shadows of the elegant old buildings and passageways were stirring with the local crowd, barmaids and dancers, waitresses and busboys on their way to work. Soon the rush-hour traffic would fill the streets with crowds of early diners on their way home from the near-by shops and offices. Still later into the evening, those who lived outside the Quarter would populate its distinctive byways in search of good food and entertainment. But it was this "in-between" time that Susie liked best, when people smiled as they passed by, and a golden glow still touched the rooftops with a special light.

"Hey, I thought you were going to work for me!" Susie teased the young boy who was diligently slipping glossy photographs into neatly trimmed mats.

"I'm helping my dad." Tony looked up and smiled.

"I've done a turn at helping my dad, too." Susie gave the boy a quick hug. "And look where it got me." She moved next to Tony and easily assisted him, holding open the slits between the mat and the backing while he inserted the photo.

"Nothing like a little teamwork to get the job done faster."

Sy came out from the rear of the store where he'd been working on Susie's pictures. "Nice to see you," he greeted Susie, then planted a surprising kiss on the tip of her nose. He duplicated the gesture on the upturned face of his son.

"Your photographs are ready." Tony tapped the last of his assigned work into a neat stack.

"And so are Susie's," Sy replied. "I'll take these into the back and you two start thinking about somewhere to eat. I'll bring along the glossies that I printed," he called back to them as he disappeared into the rear of the studio. "We can look at them over dinner." He returned with a large envelope and his jacket. "We'll have to make this quick." He hurried them out the door. "I've got a couple of appointments later on."

"Are you sure you want to take the time?" Susie didn't wish to complicate his plans. "I can just take these and go."

"I want to spend some time with you," Sy replied firmly. "I've learned to make the most of any occasion when our paths cross." He wrapped one arm snugly around her shoulders as they walked along the narrow, uneven sidewalk. "Are you hungry?" His innocent question brought a surge of color to Susie's cheeks. "And we're both booked solid for the night." He grimaced as he understood that she had been thinking of a different sort of hunger. "But this is more and more encouraging," he said, pressing her closer to his side. "You're not going to get out of this." He laughed confidently. "You are hooked. We both are." His dark eyes flashed with pleasure.

"Would you two hurry up," Tony urged. "I'm starving, and I want to see the pictures," he added pointedly.

"The kid is a real ham," Sy commented. "He loves to see himself in photos. Wait until you tell him that it's

the room and not his beaming countenance that you're
so anxious to look at.''

"Do you mean that you never mentioned to him that
we had a break-in," Susie asked.

"I think it would be much more exciting for him to
hear the details from you," Sy replied in a matter-of-
fact tone. "And while you talk to him—" he smiled
"—I can enjoy looking at you."

Throughout their dinner, Sy rarely took his eyes off
Susie. While she studied the pictures taken in her workroom, he examined them with her, making comments
and pointing out details. Mostly he watched her with
soft, dusky eyes that seemed to savor every movement
she made. Occasionally Susie's eyes would meet his and
linger there, then she would talk again with Tony or
concentrate on her meal, certain that Sy's luminous eyes
would be watching. The undisguised desire Sy worldess-
ly communicated to her, the frankness with which his
deep-hued eyes roamed the hollows of her throat,
paused to study her lips, then again riveted to her own
gaze sent recurring waves of pleasure softly pulsing
within her.

"I think about you often." Sy's softly spoken comment was one of the few personal things he said during
the entire meal. Susie smiled in reply, wondering if he
had any idea how often and how intimately she had
been thinking about him.

"I'll take these back to the workroom and compare
them to the real thing." Susie patted the series of pictures Sy had blown up for her. "I just can't put my finger on what it is that disturbs me," she sighed. "Maybe
once I see the room and the photos side by side it will
help."

The dinner concluded rapidly, and the threesome hurried off before the evening crowd converged on the Quarter. "Since I don't know when I'll see you again—" Sy caught her by the arm "—you take good care of yourself. Don't take any chances with this funny business at your shop. There could be more to this than just some confused prowler who likes the way you draw."

"My dad has already planned some preventive measures," Susie assured him. "I'll be all right."

"You notice that it's getting harder and harder to say good-night to you." He reached up and brushed his hand against her hair. "And the times in between are getting to seem emptier and emptier." Susie knew too well what Sy meant. In the soft glow of his eyes, she felt her body awakening to an increased awareness of her own passions. Leaving him now loomed ahead as an unavoidable and austere form of exile.

"Can I stay here with you, dad?" Tony's question almost verbalized Susie's own longings.

"I'll keep you here for a while," Sy agreed, "but later I have to drop in at a cocktail party and get some shots. I'll take you home when I go back to change."

"A party...tonight?" Susie sympathized.

"Another debutante affair," Sy explained. "I'm becoming a regular fixture at them. I don't suppose you've noticed that I'm making ripples in the social scene."

"It's more like waves." Susie tried unsuccessfully to keep the sarcastic edge from her voice.

"So you *have* been keeping up with the gossip," he noted. "Believe me, there's likely to be more."

Susie narrowed her eyes as she regarded him closely. "Now just what does that mean?"

"It means that I plan to be very busy and very conspicuous over the next few weeks. Just keep in mind that you're not available—and I have to be visible." Sy stressed. "This is something I simply have to do."

"Business." Susie nodded in understanding. Over the holidays everyone would be feeling festive—and preserving those moments forever would call for a skillful photographer. Sy would conveniently be on hand.

"Something like that." He looked at her solemnly. "Just don't get carried away by the press commentaries," he reminded her. "I'll see you whenever I can."

Susie hurried back to her car, still clutching the photos as Sy's words kept echoing through her mind. They had sounded almost like a warning, as if he knew in advance how sly and insinuating the comments and captions under pictures would be. Susie recalled the impact of the earlier picture of Sy and Michelle and dreaded the effect that other ones would have on her. Yet there were his soft words and the reflection of herself in his smoldering eyes. "I just won't read the paper," she resolved. Almost immediately she discarded that idea. The social articles were about her clients—parties they attended or gave, gowns they wore, krewes to which they belonged. Following the social news was part of her own job. It was something she could not avoid. "Business," she had said to Sy. It made demands on both of them, demands that were becoming increasingly painful.

CHAPTER SIX

BERNIE COSTAIN was crouched by the doorway with screwdriver in hand when Susie returned to the costume workshop. He had already removed the old lock and was absorbed in the intricacies of installing a new, heavier lock with a sliding bolt. Susie left him to his labors while she proceeded into the work area.

While Susie placed the photos Sy had taken on the wall and studied them, Bernie hummed contentedly. Occasionally he would look over at his daughter and smile. "Well...." He finally finished and stood to admire his handiwork. "This should discourage any others." He tugged the door closed and demonstrated the new device.

"I never thought we'd have to worry about anything like this," Susie said, staring at the formidable lock. "It makes me feel uneasy just thinking about it. This has always been mostly fun."

"It still is fun, Souci." Bernie hugged her. "But we've become a pretty sizable business. I guess this is a relatively inexpensive lesson in safeguarding our investments. I was looking around—" Bernie's thick gray eyebrows furrowed into almost a single line across his forehead "—and I was calculating just how much money we've got tied up in fabrics and trims...." He continued talking while Susie followed him. "Then I started looking at the costumes we've pretty well completed." He paused by the adjustable shelves along the side wall. Already several "heads" were lined up with their headpieces placed next to them. Except for the application of majestic plumes, which were now on order, these headpieces were finished. The fragile, flowing plumes would go on at the last minute.

Farther down the wall, the shelves became even more irregular to accommodate sinewy serpent forms and butterfly wings. These collar-and-train adaptations still needed more work before they would be stored in the attic above the workroom.

"We're talking *big* money." Bernie turned to face her. "It sort of crept up on us," he observed. "Each year a few more clients, another set of designs. But we're dealing with a huge inventory now. If someone stole a few of these," he said, pointing to the more elaborate costumes, "they'd be looking at *thousands* of dollars."

Susie didn't need any time to multiply that figure by the number of designs contracted for that year. The little family business had built a reputation for excellence, but it had also become a sizable company with inventory, assets, and employees. They had increased their storage area and their insurance gradually each year, but now, standing beside her father, surrounded by fabrics, designs and fanciful costumes, Susie realized that the very reputation that made them so successful may have also made Costain Costuming Company a target for grand theft.

"Hey, up there," Rosie summoned. "We have fittings in five minutes. Start bringing down the costumes."

"We'll have everything down in a few minutes," Bernie called to his wife. "Do you need anything else?" Often an additional bolt of fabric or the original design was required.

"Sure. Bring one of your books of swatches," Rosie answered. "One for each krewe," she amended. "We have so many scheduled for tonight, we'll eventually need them all."

Susie started around the room locating the thick stacks of fabric swatches—sample cuttings of every piece of material and every trim that would be used in a certain series of costumes. Susie had picked an armful of the swatch booklets, each labeled by krewe and by number, then plopped them onto the worktable by the door. When she started along the next worktable, there were no more swatch booklets. An abrupt, clammy feeling made her draw in a sudden breath.

"What's wrong?" Bernie whipped around to see his daughter's rigid stance. "What is it?" He rapidly rounded the table and hurried toward her.

"That's what's missing," Susie said, examining the pictures Sy had printed. They confirmed her observations. The swatches were clearly shown in the pictures. Now, they were definitely gone. The booklets had been put together for the convenience of the costumers. They had no value other than the easy access they provided to all materials to be worn by a specific krewe.

"Now what would anybody want with fabric swatches?" Bernie sniffed with indignation. "Maybe some kind of nut...." He shook his head. "I'll call Terrebonne in the morning and have him come over for another look. Maybe he'll know what to make of it." It was a little late to investigate the theft officially, but

Detective Terrebonne would be able to offer some unofficial advice. "For now, let's make a list of the sets that are missing and start putting the remaining swatches together. We can make a replacement booklet for each krewe," Bernie grumbled, "but it's just a pain in the neck. I'd rather they walked off with my soldering irons," he professed.

"I'll take the first few headpieces and collars downstairs and see if mom is ready for our part of the fittings," Susie suggested. "Then I'll come back up here and help you with the booklets." At least this way, the flow of customers scheduled for the evening could proceed smoothly, oblivious to the temporary inconvenience that the theft upstairs had caused.

"Maybe I'll get us a guard dog," Bernie was still fuming.

"A guard dog might not be compatible with Rosalind and Marcel." Susie tried to cheer up her father by reminding him of his two outlandish parrots who would be spending the nights protecting the workroom. "Marcel isn't very fond of two-legged creatures let alone four-legged ones," Susie noted. "A dog wouldn't stand a chance."

At last, a reluctant smile crossed Bernie's face. Those two parrots could be vicious as well as loud if someone encroached on their territory. "Watchbirds." Bernie chuckled in spite of himself. "We'll forget the dog."

BY THE END of the week, Susie was beginning to understand Sy's warning to disregard the society pages and the articles discussing "who was with whom." Sy was everywhere. His elegant bearded face and broad shoulders appeared amid clusters of both debutantes and dowagers, but the recurring image was of Sy and his companion, Michelle Costain.

"That friend of yours really gets around," Renny remarked, breaking the silence in the workroom. He and Germaine had been working since morning with three other employees on the new day shift. Since classes for Germaine at the university had let out for the Christmas break, she had taken over as day manager for Susie's business. Renny had come along because it was a dull, drizzly day and there would be no tourists in the Quarter. Besides, he owed Susie hours in exchange for the work she was doing for him, and it gave him time to be with Germaine. But now the day workers had gone home, and only the three friends remained under the low fluorescent lights.

Germaine gave Renny a threatening look when he mentioned Sy's social itinerary. Susie's friend was none of their business.

"It's all right." Susie appreciated Germaine's concern. "Sy has to keep the same hours as his clients," she answered wearily, "just like we've been doing. Only for him, that means going to all the teas and parties."

"He seems to be holding up well under the strain," Renny commented sarcastically. He had seen the pages with Sy's photo. He had also read the sugary prose about Sy and Michelle.

"I guess your schedules are about as busy as ours." Germaine twisted a metal coil into place and soldered it neatly. "Renny and I hadn't seen each other in days until now," she sighed.

"It will only get worse." Susie tried to sound unperturbed, but exhaustion and the tension of the routine were taking their toll. She managed to keep a cheerful exterior, but inside she longed for time to herself. . . and time to see Sy again. She kept recalling the late-night lovemaking that she had inadvertently heard when Germaine had come to spend the night with Renny. Somehow they had managed to form an intimate relationship in the midst of all their conflicting activities. But Susie could hardly bear the solitary nights without Sy as it was. If they did find one night to share, she would have even more to recall, more to yearn for, more tension as she waited until the next time. "When Mardi Gras is over, things will fall into a saner perspective," she consoled them, as much for her own reassurance as for her companions.

"And we'll all be rich and famous." Renny tried to lighten the mood. "I'll have my gallery showing, Germaine will get a scholarship, and Susie will throw caution to the winds and take over the Costain Costuming Company. Then we'll all sit back and sip Sazerac and listen to down-home New Orleans jazz."

"Is that before or after we collapse from insufficient sleep?" Germaine joked. "It's after midnight already, and here we are still plodding along with this conglomeration of metal." She stood to stretch her limbs. The huge swirling nautilus shell was the final structure in the series of sea-creature theme costumes. The spectacular spiral of metal would be encased in shimmering iridescent fabric, then would become the combined headpiece, collar and train of one royal member of a krewe.

"Then let's call it a night," Susie suggested. Rosie had insisted that the three of them stay in the various bedrooms downstairs instead of driving back into the city. "I'll lock up," Susie insisted. "You two go ahead."

"I'll have this finished by tomorrow night," Germaine promised as she gave the shell frame a final adjustment.

"Then we'll move on to the next set," Susie replied. "One by one, we'll get them all finished on time. Good night, you two." She tried to busy herself with the few remaining tools so Germaine and Renny would have a head start. Rosie had put them in separate bedrooms whose walls were lined with more shelves and more costumed heads. However, Susie suspected that only one of those rooms would be needed. There would be time enough for Renny and Germaine to disappear to the privacy of one room if Susie delayed a few minutes. There was so little time for love, Susie noted, and if Renny and Germaine wanted this night, Susie could discreetly arrange to be occupied until the decision was made. What they decided was no one's business.

Wearily Susie turned off all but one of the workroom lights. That one would remain on all night as part of Bernie's security plan. She had to go back to the new power switch and turn on the connection for the burglar-alarm system, which operated on a timer throughout the night. This new piece of equipment had been the suggestion of Detective Terrebonne after Bernie had told him about the missing swatch booklets. Now all the windows as well as the doors were wired in case of a burglary attempt.

"Good night, you folks." Susie directed her farewell to the rows of big-eyed mannequin heads that stared blankly out amid the headpieces and collars. "And good night to you two," she said, lifting the curtain that enclosed the cubicles Bernie had constructed for the parrots. Marcel didn't even pull his head out from under his wing. He took his sleeping seriously. But the pastel gray Rosalind winked her yellow eyes and raised her salmon-hued beak. "Kiss..." Susie agreed and leaned down to touch her lips to the upturned beak. As Susie closed the door for the night, Rosalind scanned the abandoned workroom with cool authority, then she chuckled low in her throat and settled down to sleep in her new quarters.

THE RAIN FROM THE DAY BEFORE had caused the ink to smear and the fold lines to tear, but the note Sy had left on Susie's door still made her smile. All it said was "Any time?" Then below that was "Anytime!" and his initials.

Susie glanced at her watch. She had thirty minutes before Renny would be meeting her for their next round of painting posters of the movie stars. Susie changed out of her office clothes and into her faded jeans and sweat shirt. While she heated a small crabmeat quiche for dinner, she had time to put up her feet and make a phone call.

"Hello...." The low, melodious voice that answered at Simon Avery's residence was no one Susie had expected.

"This is Susie Costain," Susie said politely. If it had been the roly-poly housekeeper Francine Sebron, she would have recognized Susie's name, but the woman on the other end obviously did not.

"Are you that lovely little blonde Simon has been seeing?" The tone of voice was so patronizing that Susie had to think twice before speaking.

"No, I'm a dark-haired cousin of hers," Susie replied sweetly.

"Then you must want Simon on business," she concluded. Susie did not miss the amused lilt in the voice. "He seems to be partial to blondes socially. You may be able to catch him at his studio. He's been very busy."

A number of succinct, uncomplimentary names came to mind as Susie tried to control her anger. "Thank you, I'll try him there," she finally managed, keeping her voice even. "How rude..." she muttered as she kicked the newspaper with her toe.

At Sy's studio, Susie was greeted with a recorded message when the phone stopped ringing. "Just called to say hello." Susie followed the beep with a brief message of her own. "Try me for lunch—evenings are overbooked. This is Susie." She added the last comment self-consciously, wishing it was not necessary. Surely when Sy heard her voice, he would know who was calling. Yet, if Sy was as busy as he seemed, there was no point in taking chances. Even now she could imagine Sy surrounded by predatory women, all of them gorgeous and blond like Michelle, and all of them making themselves very available. Susie watched the digital seconds changing on the microwave clock as her quiche neared completion. Grimly she wondered who was that woman who'd answered Sy's phone and whether she, too, had blond billowing hair.

Over her solitary dinner, both questions were answered. In the Holiday Wear section of the New Orleans *Times Picayune* was the first in a series of articles featuring "former Mardi Gras Queen" Felicia Voison Avery modeling designer gowns. This was no wide-eyed debutante posing and smiling for a family album. Felicia was an exquisite, elegant woman with curving sensuous lips and provocative eyes. And she was definitely blond. Tall, willowy, almost angular in the style of high-fashion models, she was just as Sy had described her—beautiful.

While Susie skimmed the article below, she remembered Sy had said that Felicia visited her son on special occasions, once or twice a year. This was Christmas. It was the peak of the social season. What better time for her to make a spectacular return to her hometown?

Susie stared dismally at the lines of print that stated Felicia would be in New Orleans for a few weeks "visiting relatives." Perhaps that included Sy as well as young Tony. Christmas was a time when deep emotions and old traditions brought an increased emotional response to the surface. Everyone felt more vulnerable as well as more generous. Through all this season, Susie's workload would be greatest. With the New Year, the rapid succession of parades and balls would begin. This Christmas more than any other, Susie felt trapped by the work she also loved.

Now the quiche sat forlornly, abandoned on the tabletop. Susie didn't feel like eating after all. Instead, she popped two multivitamins into her mouth and washed them down with a glass of milk. "Maybe later. . . ." She replaced the lid on the dish and put it back into the refrigerator. Renny's footsteps sent out notice that he had arrived. It was time to paint. Tonight, she would finish Judy Garland. She would get the hands right at last. Then one more task would be completed. One more creation would exist.

FOR THE NEXT WEEK, there was no break in the hectic pace from one day to the next. The aisles of Blaine's department store were packed with Christmas shoppers all determined to find some special gift bearing Blaine's distinctive golden label. Susie's schedule at the costuming company was so demanding that she began taking energy bars and a carton of yogurt for lunch so she could work straight through, putting in her time at the store so she could manage to leave an hour early. She could avoid the congested traffic caused by shoppers and the usual rush-hour commuters and spend some time with the day shift before she and her father took over. The teenage son of one of Rosie's seamstresses had again agreed to work as a part-time custodian. This year, between shifts, Eugene would sweep and take out discarded fabric scraps as usual, but since he was now taller than Susie and considerably more muscular, Eugene had also offered to help build shelves or do any of the heavy lifting and storing labors.

"We absolutely have to increase our storage space." Susie had Eugene following her around as she studied the height of the ceiling in the workroom. "I want you to set up a pulley system so we can put some of these larger costumes on ropes and pull them up there," she said, pointing above them. "They can be easily seen, but they won't be in the way." The plan was an adaptation of the storage system Susie had seen at the vast float-building complex. If it worked as well as Susie expected, it would eliminate the problem of dealing with huge designs such as the trailing sea monster and the majestic butterfly wings, yet they would be accessible when the final fittings were scheduled.

"I can install pulleys," Eugene agreed. "You want me to get hooks or something like a clip to connect the costumes? Or do you want to tie them?"

Susie examined the understructure of several of the

largest costumes. "Get some clips like the ones on a dog leash," she decided. "I can solder loops right onto the frames of the costumes and we can just snap on a line and lift them right out of the way."

"How many of these pulleys do you want set up?" Eugene seemed eager to be doing something that required more than muscle. He looked at Susie with a droopy, shy smile. Susie stood back a pace and tried to appear more businesslike. What she did not need was someone with an adolescent crush following her every move. Eugene may have developed the body of a man, but Susie wasn't flattered by his apparent affection for her.

"Try twenty sets, two each," Susie directed. "I'd say we need twenty feet of rope for each pulley. Make sure it supports about a hundred pounds." With that she returned to the far end of the workroom and left Eugene writing down the list of items.

"I'll be able to move all of those heads and headdresses out of the bedrooms tomorrow," Susie assured her mother between the evening series of fittings.

"Thank goodness," Rosie sighed with relief. The customary Christmas gathering of the Costain clan meant every spare room would be full of relatives over the holidays. Susie's sister Claire and her family would be driving in from Texas, and Rosie did not want her grandson sharing a room with a garish assortment of heads and costumes. With all the changes, Susie's room would be the only one where any costumes would be stored. Since these were all her own creations, she didn't mind the occasional night shared with them.

While several of the repeat customers, members of krewes that had commissioned the Costains many times, came by for Rosie to check the fit of a gown or for Susie and Bernie to help them don their structured costumes, the gossip flowed freely. Susie heard the same stories with slight variations repeated again and again. The talk shifted from parties to newly arrived visitors, from caterers to furriers, but when photographs and portraits were mentioned, Simon Avery's name always came up.

"I saw that his *ex* is in town," usually came next. Then an assortment of rumors would ensue.

"He's been seeing my niece Michelle rather steadily," Rosie would counter. "From what her mother says, it's really quite serious."

Susie continued with the fittings, not entering into the discussion at all. She had been the center of an extremely unpleasant cycle of gossip when she had severed her engagement to Richard Martin, and no one ever knew the true details. There was just talk. With her pliers in one hand to adjust the waist and shoulder braces, and her efficient, businesslike smile fastened securely in place, she proceeded from one client to the next, concentrating on the costume instead of the conversation.

Rosie was the one who loved to talk. She also loved to hear the most minute details of each client's existence. News of a sick puppy could reduce her to tears, but she could recall the name and address of an expert at shoe dying or a dentist who capped teeth for a reasonable price in the same instant that she brushed aside the tears. Her heart was as soft as a marshmallow, but inside her head the wheels were always turning. She knew her business and cared for her customers.

"My daughter Claire is coming this week," she announced with pride to a few old-timers who had accompanied their daughters to the fitting. "She was a ball queen once...."

It was midnight again before Susie collapsed into the bed she had loved when she was just a child. Even surrounded by the glistening creations stored on the high shelves inside her room, Susie knew that this was no longer her home. She had held on to her work as long as she could, and she could always find some refuge in it, but much of her was no longer satisfied with keeping a true commitment at a distance. Like a weary runner, she had tired of the race even though she excelled at her craft. Work had protected her; family had protected her; she had protected herself. Now she longed to smile because she was happy, not simply to camouflage her feelings or to seem polite. To be happy, she needed someone of her own who understood her and allowed her to know herself. Simon Avery had come along as the answer to a question she had never realized she was asking.

"Only talk." Susie chased away the rumors and the gossip that the name Simon Avery generated. She tried to shake the image of the blond-haired beauties who vied for his attention. Susie had not seen Sy for almost a week. "Tomorrow." She vowed to get a call through to him before she slipped away to a dreamworld hung with pulleys, where Judy Garland floated past on gossamer butterfly wings.

WHEN SUSIE ARRIVED at the Costains' the following evening, the six automobiles parked in front heralded the arrival of Claire and her family, home for Christmas. Gaily wrapped packages were still stacked in the rear of the car with the Texas license plates. The other cars were all familiar ones; they belonged to Uncle Leo, Aunt Jo, Michelle and two women who had been school chums of Claire's while she was growing up in New Orleans.

"Wait till you hear the news." Aunt Jo passed Susie in the hallway. Already the aroma of coffee and the sound of laughter and joyful conversation indicated that the gathering had been going on for some time. Before heading into the kitchen where everyone else seemed to be, Susie hurried into her bedroom to freshen up. The strain of keeping up with several jobs and not getting enough sleep had drained the color from her cheeks. Nothing at Blaine's had been on schedule. Her call to Sy once again connected only to his answering machine. All considered, it had been a rotten day. But Claire was home for a visit, and Susie was determined not to diminish the festive spirit.

"Welcome home!" Susie worked her way from Claire to husband, John, to sandy-haired John Jr, hugging each one in turn. "You look wonderful." Susie's comment to her older sister was sincere. Claire had always been beautiful, but with her deep golden brown hair falling in rippling cascades and her aristocratic features softened by either maturity or a few additional pounds, she no longer looked like the beauty queen she had been. She looked soft and lovely and aglow with happiness.

"Motherhood agrees with her." Rosie was beaming at her eldest daughter.

"I couldn't agree more," Susie replied. Then from the assortment of faces, all sporting knowing smiles, she began to comprehend what "the news" was about. Claire was expecting another child.

"Congratulations!" Susie began a new round of hugs and kisses.

"I'm going to be a grandmother again." Rosie pretended to be aghast at the idea that someone who felt so young would be a grandmother—for the second time. Yet the news had brought a radiance to her face. Susie laughed along with the others, but deep inside came that nagging feeling that Claire, "the golden one," had done it again. The model daughter with the perfect family was expanding it right on schedule.

While the conversation revolved once again to talk of old friends and all the marriages and children and changes over the past months, Susie got a cup of coffee and munched on a few brownies left over from the informal gathering. Michelle hovered around Claire, drinking in the advice and recollections of the time Claire had been queen of a Mardi Gras ball. Then when Claire, Rosie, and Claire's two married friends started discussing the intricacies of child care and the antics of their offspring, Susie discreetly eased out of the room. Michelle still sat entranced by her older cousin as if she found the discussion of pregnancies and child-rearing as fascinating as the social news.

For the next few hours, Susie divided her time between headpiece and collar fittings downstairs with Rosie and setting up the pulley system for storing costumes upstairs with Eugene diligently working at her side. Germaine and Renny had worked the day shift again and left before dark, but Bernie and one part-time employee stretched, cut and soldered metal underwiring late into the night.

"I think Michelle has been bitten by the marriage

bug,'' Rosie confided to Susie during a pause between fittings. "It wouldn't surprise me if she and Simon Avery make some sort of announcement over the holidays. You know how Christmas and New Years always seem to bring people together. All those engagement announcements....." Rosie was referring to the pages of pictures of newly engaged couples who had chosen the holiday season to announce their betrothal. "Your Aunt Jo would be so pleased...." Rosie was so preoccupied with pinning the alterations of one gown that she didn't quite complete her thought.

Susie was relieved to finish her part of the fitting and get back to the workroom. Here at least, she felt that she was in control of the situation. Here she didn't have to listen to the speculation about Sy.

"I'll help you lock up.'' The round, hangdog face of Eugene wore a hopeful smile. Bernie and his lone worker had stopped work earlier, and Susie had spent the last hour setting out materials and lists of directions for Germaine and the day crew. Only because Susie was occupied with paperwork had Eugene kept quiet while he swept up and disposed of the trash.

"You can start by checking all the windows,'' Susie indicated, accepting his offer. "Then make sure all the soldering equipment is disconnected and cooled off. I'll take care of the alarm system.'' She finished her pages of notes and went from station to station leaving the directions next to every piece that was under construction. As an extra precaution, Bernie had installed a cabinet with a sturdy lock in which all the most expensive and fragile trimmings were stored. Susie left the key for that under a potted plant at Germaine's worktable.

"Are you stayin' here with your folks tonight?''

Eugene now stood in the center of the large room watching her.

"No." Susie didn't want any more family for the time being. She simply had to get back to her own apartment and her own bed. This was Claire's time to be the center of attention, and Susie needed a little solitude.

"Then I'll hang around and walk you to your car," Eugene insisted. The added security precautions in Rosie's dressmaking studio on the second floor of the house as well as the changes in Susie's workroom had made Eugene increasingly protective. All the workers in both shops had heard that some type of break-in attempt had been made, so Eugene had volunteered as bodyguard as well as general handyman.

"I'd appreciate that." Susie knew Eugene would be hurt if she refused. Carefully she connected the burglar alarm, dimmed the lights and pulled the cover from the compartments of Rosalind and Marcel so they could come and go as they pleased.

"Do you really think those birds would do anything if someone did get in here?" Eugene sounded unconvinced.

"I hope we never have to find out," Susie replied. "I've seen Marcel snap a steak bone with his beak," she noted. "I'd hate to see what he'd do to a finger or to someone's nose. And Rosalind can peel the paneling off a wall with her claws. If she attacked an intruder...."

"But they're just birds." Eugene shook his head dubiously.

"Shhh..." Susie joked. "They think they're people just like the two of us. Good night, Rosalind." She bent over and gave the bird a quick kiss. "You two, Marcel." Susie stroked his head. Marcel was simply not a kisser. One did not put one's face too close to that parrot, unless, of course, one was Bernie. Marcel made exceptions for Susie's father. They were old buddies. They could kiss.

SUSIE ALMOST TRIPPED over the large, prickly obstacle that stood on the narrow balcony by her apartment door. She had been so exhausted on the drive from Chalmette back into the city that she had opened all the windows and let the cool damp air chill her into alertness. Now, shivering from the cold, she found a large, thorny bush hidden in the shadows.

Once she got inside and turned on the lights, she cleared the newspapers and mail from the threshold and pulled the bush to the open doorway where she could see it clearly. The tall, neatly trimmed rosebush had been clipped so that its deep green leaves clustered into a ball shape atop a long straight trunk. Deep currant-colored blossoms, barely open, sent a rich fragrance into the cool night air. Susie quickly pulled the rose tree inside and closed the door. Attached to the large pot that held the plant was a note.

Since you apparently haven't had time to decorate your own tree for Christmas, I thought you might enjoy this. Love to get those recorded messages from you, but they don't make up for the real thing. Eventually....

The message was deliberately unfinished. But all Susie had needed was to see the sprawling "Sy" at the bottom to understand the rest.

SUSIE CALLED SY'S HOME the next morning to thank him for the rose tree. The dusky, languid voice of Felicia Voison Avery answered on the first ring.

"Please...call later, much later," she said sleepily. Then promptly she hung up. Susie stared at the receiver a moment, then slowly placed it back in its cradle.

In the corner of the apartment, the lovely rose tree stood with its crimson buds opened more fully in the morning light. The sweet, penetrating scent hung in the still air like an invisible perfumed cloud. Susie contemplated the exquisite gift while her mind echoed with all the tidbits of gossip and speculation that had been circulating about Sy. Apparently Michelle believed she was the focus of Sy's attention. Then there was the sultry Felicia staying in his home, answering his telephone, disposing of callers in a sleepy, sexy voice. And then there was Susie, alone and bewildered. "What in the world is going on?" Susie voiced the question to no one. If Sy's hours were filled with photography and keeping up with two beautiful blondes, it was no wonder Susie had not seen or spoken to him in more than a week. And if rumors of an engagement to Michelle or a possible reconciliation with Felicia had any truth to them, why on earth did he persist in leading Susie on? The conflicting messages sent angry tears brimming over in Susie's wide brown eyes. "Why me?" she muttered as she poked her arms into the sleeves of her coat and strode out the door.

She already had more on her shoulders than she could handle. The art department at Blaine's was in chaos, since several other illustrators had taken sick days, which suspiciously coincided with holiday festivities.

With Claire's family visiting, there would be additional congestion in the Costains' household, and business there would be delayed. And now this. Susie rapidly walked the few blocks to work to let out some of the tension. If Sy had decided to shift his affections to Michelle, or if his feelings for Felicia had been revived by her presence, the least he could do is to let Susie know. She could stand the truth. She had survived in the real world before Sy had come into her life. She would survive after he left.

What she hated was the uncertainty. He had seemed to be so solid, so straightforward and sure of himself—and of her. She had managed to ignore the publicity and endure the days without seeing him, but only because she had believed what she had seen in his eyes. "You know how men are...." Aunt Jo's casual remark echoed once again inside her head.

"I really hate this." Susie's brisk footsteps emphasized each word. What she hated the most was the thought that she could have been wrong about him. He had touched her mind and her heart and her body—and all of her had responded, gradually accepting, caring and desiring him. She had been wrong about a man once before. Now she could feel the walls of self-protection rebuilding as she steeled herself to disappointment.

Midway through the morning, Ella Jenkins paced next to Susie's drawing table, anxiously awaiting the completion of a final sketch. Susie had been assigned several additional drawings to complete since the workload had been backed up. The post-Christmas sales campaign had to be completed by noon to meet the deadline. Even though the paper would not carry them for several days, the layouts had to be finished and submitted to the printers early. When Susie's telephone rang, Ella Jenkins did not leave.

"How about meeting me for lunch?" Sy's voice brought the motion of Susie's pen to a halt.

"I'm trying to meet a deadline," Susie replied. "I have until noon." She watched the impatient tapping of her supervisor's fingers.

"So I'll meet you at noon," Sy suggested.

"Then I have my own work to get to." Susie tried to keep her end of the conversation as impersonal as possible. Then Ms Jenkins moved on to another cubicle.

"I've got to see you. We have to talk," Sy replied. Susie had the ominous feeling that she didn't want to hear what he had to say.

"I think I understand," she said quietly. "You have enough women in your life." She tried to keep her voice from quavering. "We don't need to go into detail."

There was a long pause on the other end of the line. "You meet me at the front door of Blaine's at two minutes after twelve," he said in a controlled, clipped voice, "or I'll come up after you. I know how you hate scenes, and if you want to avoid a really spectacular one, you'd better be there. We have to talk," he repeated.

"That will be fine." Susie forced a stiff smile and replied politely, since Ella Jenkins had once again come within hearing. Susie hung up the phone and fastidiously cleaned and re-inked her drawing pens. She didn't trust herself to touch pen to paper until the trembling in her limbs subsided. Slowly breathing in and out, she willed the tension in the pit of her stomach to unknot. She would have to face Sy after all and hear his explanation of his entanglements with other women. He was going to put her through this face to face. She had to meet him or he would humiliate her by bringing something very private into her office.

"I think I need to get a glass of water," Susie mumbled, excusing herself for a moment. Ella Jenkins looked as if she were about to issue some type of reprimand, but then reconsidered. Susie was the best artist on the staff. The deadline was an hour and forty minutes away. Now was not the time to pull rank.

Susie stood before the mirror in the employees' bathroom pressing cold towels to her temples and throat. If Sy thought it was more humane or courteous to disillusion her in person, he was sadly mistaken. *I'll get through this,* Susie told herself. She would hear him out and assure him that she appreciated his concern. She would hold it all inside just as she always had. But in public, she would conduct herself with dignity...and silently lament her vulnerability. She would mourn the loss of moments that had slipped away. No one would understand the devastation; no one would know—except Susie.

Sy was standing outside Blaine's at two minutes after twelve when Susie approached.

"You haven't been getting enough rest," Sy announced, looking at her critically. Susie had barely stepped through the heavy glass doors of Blaine's when he'd caught her arm and started propelling her along the sidewalk toward Jackson Square. "You're probably skipping meals, too." He sounded angry. "I should have known you would let all this crap about Michelle and Felicia get to you. Anyone who can create things as lovely as you can simply doesn't have a thick skin.

There are a few times when being sensitive can be a damn nuisance!''

They reached the corner entrance to the old square. Sy led her along the pathway to the low bench where they had first spoken. "Now sit here and tell me just what has made you head for cover." He stared at her with clear, uncompromising eyes.

Susie could hardly speak. Nothing in Sy's manner was either patronizing or apologetic. His anger did not fit into the dismal parting speech that she had imagined. Hesitantly, she started telling him about the numerous comments she had heard about Michelle and him. Sy didn't deny any of them. He shook his head and listened. Then Susie told him of the calls she had made to his home.

"You caught Felicia between job assignments," Sy replied coolly. "She gets a little nervous when she doesn't have any bookings. She dreads everything from getting old to getting up in the morning. So she plays games.''

"Games?" Susie gasped. "You call being bitchy a game?" Sy finally smiled at her blunt language.

"You assume Felicia actually knows what's going on in my life?" Sy asked. "That's one kind of playacting she sometimes uses.''

"She's staying with you, isn't she?" Susie responded. "She certainly knows about you and Michelle.''

"Felicia is staying at my house, all right," Sy conceded. "But I have been staying in the studio. Occasionally I go home to pick up Tony or to change clothes," he informed her, "but Felicia and I rarely cross paths. She is feeling very maternal right now, so

I'm letting her spend as much time with Tony as they both enjoy. When her agent calls with a modeling assignment, she'll be gone again. Frankly,'' he continued, ''she couldn't have come along at a more convenient time. I've had more work than I can keep up with. I've had poor old Francine running her already short legs off doing my errands, and I'd have been feeling guilty if Tony had to spend his time alone.''

Suddenly Susie felt very foolish. ''I just began jumping to conclusions along with everyone else,'' she confessed.

''Sometimes false conclusions come in very handy,'' Sy said perceptively. ''Except in this case, they backfired. There's a lot going on right now that doesn't really involve you,'' he added, ''or it shouldn't involve you. Some of it is leftover details from the divorce.'' He waved one hand brusquely as if he were pushing aside some unnecessary complications. ''Anyway,'' he finished, looking at her now with the familiar softness that seemed to soothe the hurt that had oppressed her, ''I had to see you. I just wish it hadn't been like this.'' He closed his hand over Susie's fingers, warming them with his touch.

''The rose tree is beautiful.'' Susie's chin trembled slightly as she struggled to hold back the tears. She'd promised herself to get through this confrontation with dignity, but now a single errant tear trickled down her cheek.

''I wanted you to have something to remind you that we have a special deal, you and me.'' He cupped her cheek in his hand and wiped away the tear with his thumb. ''Roses in December seemed appropriate. And if we take care of it, it will bloom for years.''

"I didn't need the roses," Susie sniffed and gave him a brave smile. "Everything reminds me of you."

"Including the newspaper and your relatives," Sy said with a wry grin. "I'd rather you have the rose tree. I've got some traveling to do over the next week, and I'll be out of touch for a while." He watched her expression closely as he talked. "So if you get a little shaky, just smell the roses." He stood and tugged her to her feet. Then right in the middle of the walkway, he pulled her close to him. His gentle, persuasive mouth pressed against hers, as the warm, inviting contact sent erotic messages gliding through her limbs.

"You're lucky we're out here where there are witnesses." Sy's ragged breath rippled across her lips, mingling with her own. "If we were alone. . . ." He lowered his mouth to hers, again breathing in her responsive sigh. Susie felt the boundaries between them slip away as she seemed to flow into his body and become a part of him. When the tip of his tongue slid languidly against her lips, Susie savored the soft pressure then received the gentle invasion with a sense of abandon. She could trust this man who held her within his strong arms yet didn't demand to possess her. She could delight in her growing passion without worrying about where it was leading. Right now, in the midst of Jackson Square, with curious pigeons strutting about, it was leading them nowhere. It was a singular act of indulgence that let them enjoy the moment and anticipate the possibilities that awaited them.

"I think we'd better simmer down before we draw a crowd," Sy teased, easing back, "and I'm not talking about pigeons. What I want to do when I feel you smoldering like this is no one's business except ours." His voice was low and husky. "Where is that reasonable and rational female who could put everything on hold until Mardi Gras ended? We're going to have to reexamine our game plan before too long," he declared.

"And where is the good-hearted soul who said he could wait?" Susie smiled. She glanced around self-consciously, aware now that the park benches were filling up with lunch-hour nature-worshippers. She pressed her hands against her flushed cheeks. Several passersby who had been watching now smiled with amusement as the color in her face deepened. "The world seems to fade away when I'm with you."

"Keep that in mind." Sy wrapped one arm around her shoulders and steered her along the path beside the towering statue of General Jackson. "For now, all I can offer you is a quick lunch in the French Market and a rather inadequate wish for a Merry Christmas. The roses will have to hold you until—" his voice dropped to a whisper "—until I can."

CHAPTER SEVEN

"THE FIRST SHIPMENT of plumes has arrived." Susie's father called her at work with the information. Each of the bright-colored delicate feathers would have to be unwrapped and air-blown to restore the downy softness. That meant all other work had to stop for the night while they stood the plumes upright all around the workroom and "fluffed" them.

"I'll be there as soon as I can," Susie promised. "It's schizophrenia time here," she added wryly. "The store is filled with post-Christmas shoppers elbowing their way through the sales counters, and I'm working on the January White Sales." Keeping two weeks ahead of the calendar always made everyone in advertising feel a bit out of synchronization with the real world. "I've even got some Valentine's items to start on."

"By Valentine's Day, this will all be over," Bernie reminded her. "But we have to take this one day at a time, and today we're up to our rafters in feathers."

"See you in a couple of hours," Susie confirmed, adding a few more minute fleur-de-lis on the set of sheets and pillowcases she had drawn. "Keep your wings up," she joked.

In the corner of her cubicle, a slender bud vase held a single currant-red rose, the most recent blossom on the rose tree. Except for one brief phone call, Susie had not heard Sy's voice in days. Between jobs photographing partygoers in New Orleans and several side trips to Baton Rouge and Grand Isle for balls being held there, he had not been able to see her at all. For the upcoming weekend, including New Year's Eve, he would be in Mobile, Alabama, holding photo sessions with several krewes that had agreed to pay all his expenses if he would arrange to photograph the queens and kings and members of their ball courts.

"I'll be back early next week," Sy had told her. "Felicia is flying to New York on a modeling assignment," he added, sounding genuinely relieved, "and I'll be able to settle in at home again. Even if I have to come and help you glue like Tony did...I'm going to see you."

Susie leaned forward and sniffed the sweet fragrance of the rose. One after another, Susie had brought the flowers to the office with her each day, and just as Sy had said, when she felt a bit low, their scent cheered her up. She didn't need a rose to keep Sy on her mind. Day and night his husky voice and his dark eyes drifted through her consciousness. The delicious taste of his lips seemed so vivid that Susie often felt the warm, pulsing ripples of desire gradually sending a secret glow through her. At night, regardless of the hour, she had chosen to drive from her parents' home back into the city so she could delight in the solitude and sleep surrounded by the aroma of roses.

By the time Susie climbed the stairs of the costuming workroom, Bernie had already begun to unpack the elaborate plumage that would provide the final touches to the majority of the headpieces. The delicate, fluttering feathers were an expensive and exotic trim for any costume, but the elegance and graceful movement they added was inestimable.

"Looks like some kind of forest from a fairy tale," Susie commented with a smile, as she walked between the rows of feathers. When she moved through them, the cascading, weblike vanes of the feathers swayed gently like a silent, underwater garden rippling with the movement of the current.

"There are more in the back that need to be un-wrapped," Bernie said, eagerly turning that task over to her. "I'll get started with the dryer. I'm afraid this may take us quite a while." He surveyed the mixture of colors and textures of the plumes already awaiting the fluffing process. Spread out like this, they were an awesome reminder that the business had indeed grown beyond his expectations. And this was only the initial shipment. Bernie clicked on the pistol-shaped dryer and lightly blew warm air over the slightly flattened plumage. "One day at a time." He recalled his motto. This day's work was going to spill over into the wee hours of the next one.

"WHAT DO YOU MEAN Michelle cancelled again?" Susie stormed into the kitchen where her mother was preparing dinner. Five hours sleep the night before had decreased her patience quotient. Susie had left work an hour early to help Bernie and Germaine attach the feathers to the elaborate headdresses of the six costumes that were scheduled for a final fitting that night. Michelle had already missed the collar-and-headpiece fitting set up the night she had become ill. She had tried on her gown so Rosie could make the adjustments to it, but the costume for her presentation as Triton's Queen had to be balanced and adjusted so she could promenade through the ballroom arena without stumbling under the weight.

"I'm sorry." Rosie knew how crucial the fitting was. "She called while you were upstairs and said she couldn't make it tonight."

"When can she make it?" Susie responded testily. "Even if she is family, we can't disrupt all the other clients' schedules just to accommodate her. This is ridiculous!"

"She didn't say. Why don't you call her and see if you can work something out?" Rosie had fittings of her own to see to that night. "She really should be a little more considerate."

Michelle was not at home when Susie called. Aunt Jo suggested calling Traci, the redhead who was a maid for Michelle's court. "They're spending the night with Traci's parents, then they're going to a beach house on the coast for New Year's," Aunt Jo explained. "They're planning to rest up for all the parades and parties that start next week." Susie knew only too well that the beginning of January meant carnival time was under way and the Mardi Gras balls and pageants would begin. All through the month and midway through February, they would continue night after night until the final celebrations on Fat Tuesday, official Mardi Gras day. When the two prestigious krewes, Rex and Comus, toasted each other at midnight, Mardi Gras would end for another year. The roller-coaster effect had taken hold and Susie knew there would be no slowing down until that night.

"Traci...I really need to talk to Michelle." Susie waited for her cousin to come to the phone.

"She isn't here right now," Traci replied. "Can I take a message?"

"We have to schedule a fitting before she leaves for the beach," Susie insisted. "I have everything, including the plumes for her costume, and she simply has to try it on so I can complete it. When do you expect her back?" The impatient edge to Susie's voice made it clear that she wanted action.

"I really shouldn't tell you this," Traci said guiltily, "but I don't want you to get upset. Michelle isn't really spending the weekend with me." Her voice became almost a whisper. Apparently Traci did not want to be overheard on her end of the line.

"Then where is she?" Susie asked.

"Promise you won't tell anyone..." Traci pleaded. "I told her I would cover for her."

"I'm not interested in causing trouble," Susie assured the girl. "I just need Michelle's body for half an hour. Where can I reach her?"

"I don't know," Traci confessed. "She went to Mobile for a few days. She didn't want anyone to know. It was a sudden, last-minute thing, so I let her pretend she would be with us. I'm pretty sure she went with Simon Avery. At least, he came by here and picked her up."

Susie felt as if all her limbs had suddenly gone numb. Apparently Sy had forgotten to mention all that he had planned during his few days in Mobile. Susie did manage to conclude the conversation with Traci and hang up the phone normally, in spite of the stunned state of her mind.

Standing in the hallway, Susie tried to focus on some rational explanation for Michelle's sudden departure. Sy was an intensely passionate man with a powerful body that was both graceful and eloquent. When they had danced or played touch football or walked through the French Quarter, there was an undeniable physical magnetism that Susie had responded to in spite of her caution. Susie was aroused by Sy's sexuality. No doubt other women were drawn to him. Some would not hesitate to make their willingness known. Sy and Michelle had been conveniently accessible to each other for at least two months. Perhaps they had finally found that opportunity had offered an irresistible temptation. Who would ever know of their passionate interlude in Mobile? Who would be harmed by a weekend of intimacy a hundred and twenty miles away?

"I would." Susie answered her own question, even while attempting to excuse their actions. "I would be hurt." If Sy was capable of having a casual affair with someone else while he professed such strong feelings for her, Susie was better off knowing about it now. The intensity of her pain and disappointment already made it difficult for her to even breathe freely. As the color drained from her cheeks, she stood pressing her hands against the tight pressure in her midriff. *What if we had made love already,* she wondered. Would that have prevented Sy from seeking intimacy with someone else? The sinking, cold feeling that threatened to overwhelm her became even more oppressive with her next thought. *What if we had loved each other and he had still taken Michelle away for the weekend?* Then could Susie withstand the betrayal?

The relentless accelerated pounding of her heart was answer enough. Sy was someone special, someone with whom she could share herself and her dreams. A commitment to him would be complete and exclusive. Unless he could make the same commitment to her, unless his body and soul were entwined solely with hers, there was no reason to trust, to love, to hope. Apparently she had expected more of Sy than he was capable of living up to. *Let go* now. Susie willed herself to face reality. Sy was not the man she'd hoped he was. She could not cling to an ideal that simply did not exist.

Wearily Susie started out the back of the house toward the workroom stairway. She remembered how accepting, how generous Sy had seemed in understanding the limitations of his ex-wife, Felicia. When Felicia had wanted to pursue a career rather than try to fit the role of mother, he had let her go without bitterness. When Felicia returned occasionally, even though they were divorced, he had let her live in his house and spend time with their son, again without bitterness. He accepted Felicia for what she was. But they had dissolved the marriage. He didn't try to hold on to something that was an illusion.

I'm not that forgiving. Susie knew that was true. She could be hurt too deeply by infidelity or disillusionment. Unlike Sy, she would be bitter. So she would let go now, before the bitterness could begin.

"Did you get Michelle?" Bernie had lifted down the elegant costume for Triton's Queen. The queen's costume was another spiny sea creature, an elegant version of a sea horse. Susie had softened the design by adding distinctly feminine features to the head—fluttering eyelashes and bejeweled eyes. "I'm afraid we'll have to finish it without her," Susie replied. "Michelle won't be back in town for a few days."

"So what do you suggest?" Bernie was as perturbed by the inconvenience as Susie was.

"Michelle and I are about the same height," she noted. "I'll put on the costume, and you can adjust the shoulder and waist supports on me. When Michelle has to wear it, we'll have to hope that we've guessed right. There won't be much we can alter after the plumes and jewels are in place."

"If we can put up with her irresponsibility, then she can definitely make it through the ball in a less-than-perfect fit," Bernie declared. "Try it on, and we'll give it our best shot."

Susie slipped into the fantasy form and stood in the open area of the workroom. With pliers and padding in hand, Bernie molded the waist cinch and the shoulder supports until the sea horse was so precisely balanced that its weight was negligible. Beneath the jeweled collar and train that Rosie had incorporated into the gown, the supports would disappear, and only the spectacular beauty of the costume would be seen. Susie stood erect, biting her lower lip thoughtfully while her father worked. *There is a certain irony in this,* she thought as she watched her reflection in the wide shop windows. While Michelle was driving to Mobile with Sy, here Susie stood in Michelle's place. Susie was completing her cousin's fantasy, just as surely as Michelle had usurped Susie's dream. Surrounded by a room full of bizarre and wondrous designs, Susie felt strangely unreal herself. She would have several days to regain the objectivity that would enable her to end this entanglement with Sy. Right now, she would have to endure the anguish of being a stand-in while Michelle was so near the man who sent red roses and spoke of ecstasy.

"You can't stay in on New Year's Eve." Renny had caught Susie before she left the apartment the next morning. "A bunch of us are going down to the Quarter tonight to sip a few beers and watch the action. Come on with us and ring in the New Year," Renny insisted.

Susie considered refusing. After lying awake most of the night in her rose-scented room, she knew she would be exhausted at the end of the day. Yet the prospect of working on costumes or spending the evening with her family seemed grim. Somewhere in Mobile tonight, Michelle and Sy would be together, celebrating. Susie didn't want too much time to think about them. "Sure." She had finally agreed to join Renny and his friends.

By ten o'clock, Susie was regretting her decision. Renny had arrived with a group of characters as colorful and exotic as some of Susie's wildest sketches. Wearing anything from a sombrero and hot pants to a leather breastplate and ballet slippers, they assembled in the courtyard below. "You didn't mention that this was a costume party." Susie was only half joking when she looked down from her balcony.

"We don't want to attract too much attention," one of the fellows replied. "Where we're going, this is standard chic."

"Let me take another look in my closet and see what I can come up with," Susie replied. Obviously her sweater and slacks would not blend with the wardrobes of the others. With uncharacteristic bravado, Susie pulled out her high-heeled boots and flame red prairie skirt. She donned a short-waisted Russian-cossack-style jacket, then tucked one of the few remaining roses behind one ear. With her glistening black hair and honey skin, she looked like a Gypsy.

"Now you look like one of us." Germaine applauded the transformation. She had let her own long dark hair loose, spiraling down to her waist. Germaine had also worn her brother's heavy motorcycle jacket, complete with thick linked chains and zippered pockets. The effect was startlingly softened by the pink satin knickers and ruffled peasant blouse worn beneath the jacket. Every outfit was a good-humored attempt to be colorful and outrageous—definitely the spirit for New Year's Eve in the French Quarter. It was a time for letting loose and gearing up for the upcoming carnival season. Then every night the streets would be filled with costumed revelers and impromptu performances.

"I'll be your escort, if you don't mind the difference in our height." Pascal Danos, the bearded sculptor, had taken the night off from float building to join them. In her dark boots, Susie stood at least three inches taller than Pascal.

With all the other incongruities of color and costume, a variation in height would hardly be cause for concern. "I'd be delighted," Susie replied cheerfully. Then Pascal smiled. Instead of the irregular row of chipped teeth, he now boasted a beautiful smile with even, polished white caps.

"I got them for Christmas," he said, flushing slightly when Susie noticed the dental work. "This is their first big night on the town." He chuckled.

"They look great," Susie commended him. "I guess we'll have to take a guided tour of the Quarter and show them the sights," she teased, joining in on his joke.

"Take the teeth to town," Renny said to proclaim the

mission for the evening. "Let's go." He took Germaine's hand and led the procession through the courtyard gate.

Pascal and his teeth thoroughly enjoyed being the center of attention. They were toasted in every bar and even had some tunes dedicated to them by several of the small bands playing in various clubs in the Quarter. As midnight approached and the streets were filled with music and people, the procession increased in number as old friends and new joined Renny in his walking tour. Surrounded by the exuberant crowd, Susie became so embroiled in the laughter and frivolity that she even danced the hora in the midst of Bourbon Street with Pascal and a group of Israeli sailors whose ship had docked in the New Orleans' shipyard. It was a rare, carefree evening filled with friends and familiar places.

Long after midnight, the group had dwindled to four—Renny, Germaine, Susie and Pascal. The teeth had ceased to be a separate entity, and the joke had been forgotten along with Pascal's self-consciousness. Beneath the old streetlights, they strolled along Royal Street in pursuit of a final round of hot coffee and pastries.

Susie had almost passed Simon Avery Studios before she realized where their circuitous route through the Quarter had led them. The framed portraits displayed in the window were barely visible in the dark window, especially since the heavy mesh window guards had been installed. They were another sure sign that Mardi Gras festivities were about to begin. With the influx of tourists and partygoers who mingled with New Orlean's locals in the increasingly congested streets of the Quarter, there also came the vandals and troublemakers who broke windows and damaged buildings under the guise of high spirits. To protect their property, merchants and shop owners temporarily installed metal grids over their windows.

"I guess the party's over," Renny decided, as he strolled along beside Susie. "Your friend there," he said, indicating Sy's studio, "hasn't been around lately. Anything I can do?"

"You did just the right thing tonight," Susie answered. "You brought me out here with some very delightful people. I guess working so much was turning me into a bit of a hermit. The party isn't over," Susie assured her tall, lanky friend. "I think it's just beginning again. I'm not going to let work or Sy Avery or anyone else turn me into a recluse."

"Does that mean you'd like to go to a gallery showing?" Pascal had pretended to be absorbed in the contents of a shop window, but now his wide smile revealed that he'd been listening. "Nothing elaborate," Pascal cautioned her. "I'm not hoping for a passionate entanglement, although I wouldn't turn down an indecent offer." He grinned impishly. "But I sure would feel better showing up with you on my arm. With you and my new teeth, I could face the critics. I'd even dress to look civilized," he promised.

"Do you mean it's a showing of your sculptures?" Susie was impressed.

"In a manner of speaking," Pascal replied modestly. "One of the galleries is opening a Mardi Gras wing. Some of my float pieces will be on exhibit."

"The guy has three pieces purchased for a permanent display." Renny stressed how prestigious the honor actually would be. "He's the only artist with that number of works in the exhibit."

"So would you like to accompany me?" Pascal asked again. Tuesday night. Formal dress."

"I'd be delighted," Susie accepted. By Tuesday, Sy and Michelle would be back from Mobile. Susie knew she would be too preoccupied to concentrate on her costumes, but she would prefer to see the exhibit and avoid being too accessible if Sy tried to contact her. If she wanted to start the New Year right, she would have to involve herself in more than her work, and she would have to find other interests besides Sy Avery.

"BEFORE YOU LEAVE," Bernie said when he met Susie in the hallway the next day as they were passing in opposite directions, "your mother would like to see you in the fitting room. She's having trouble with Michelle's gown. Apparently the queen is here, but the dress doesn't fit right." His gray eyebrows arched in a distressed grimace. It was bad enough that the fittings for the evening had been rescheduled to accommodate Susie's cousin, but now this delay would further inconvenience the clients who would have to wait until the problem with Michelle's gown was solved.

"I'll see what I can do," Susie offered, as she placed over the back of a chair the long beige dress she had selected to wear to Pascal's showing that night. Since Michelle had now returned from Mobile, that meant Sy was also back in the city. Susie wanted to get on her way before he had a chance to call her. Fitting Michelle's dress was one thing, but having to face Sy was another. This was to be a special night for Pascal, and Susie didn't want anything to spoil it for him. He needed someone to show off, someone who would lift his spirits, and if Susie intended to do that, she didn't need any contact with Sy to upset her equilibrium.

"What seems to be the problem?" Susie wore her pleasant-but-efficient smile as she entered Rosie's fitting room. The floor-length mirrors on three sides of the large room enabled them to view the gown from every possible angle. There was no disguising the fact that that gorgeous sea-green satin gown with its sculpted neckline and cascading train was too tight. The seams from bustline to hip pulled at their stitches causing rows of tiny wrinkles across the once-smooth waistline.

"I just don't understand." Rosie shook her head as she paced around Michelle. "When we tried it before the holidays, it was perfect. Have you gained some extra weight with all those Christmas goodies?" She tried to smile, although her worried eyes still remained riveted to the midsection of the gown.

"I haven't weighed myself," Michelle replied in a strained voice. Apparently the reflection of herself in the mirrors had distressed her as well.

"Regardless of what's happened," Susie commented, examining the gown closely, trying to locate a place where some additional room could be made," if mother tries to take out any of these seams now, the lines of the dress will be ruined, not to mention the fact that the stitch marks might show. If you'd come in when we had you scheduled," she continued, intending to sound a bit harsh, "we might have caught this before it reached this point. Now all that can be done is for you to lay off the hors d'oeuvres and cocktails and go on a crash diet. Otherwise, we'll have to risk ruining the gown. There's a lot of money tied up in this already,'' Susie added, as she unzipped the back of the gown to ease the strain on the seams. "I think you can deprive yourself of calories for a week or so in order to spare the dress.''

"I don't think a diet will help." Michelle finally turned to face Susie. "I don't think anything will help.'' Large, bright tears welled up in Michelle's blue eyes. Before they trickled down onto the gown, Rosie hastily passed her a box of Kleenex. While Michelle daubed her eyes and sniffed, Rosie helped her step out of the luxurious garment.

"There are lots of quick ways to lose a few pounds,'' Susie assured her cousin. "I'm not suggesting you starve yourself,'' she consoled the young woman. "But you do have to think of the complications. It's a little late to rework the entire design. A diet and some stretching exercises and you'll look fine." Standing there in only her bra and panties, Michelle finally burst into tears.

"This isn't going to go away,'' she sobbed, resting her hand on her abdomen. There was no doubt that she had indeed added a few pounds to her midriff. "I just didn't think it would show so soon." Instantly the room was ominously silent. Rosie looked at Michelle's slightly rounded midsection. Then, wide-eyed, she met Susie's own alarmed gaze.

"Oh...my goodness..." Rosie breathed at last. "You don't mean you're pregnant?" She rushed forward and wrapped her arms around the weeping Michelle.

Susie stood in stunned silence, unable to move. Her mind raced back to the afternoon gathering when Claire had returned home for Christmas with the news of her pregnancy. Michelle had listened attentively to all the talk about babies and child-rearing. Susie now recalled the look of eagerness on Michelle's face at the time. Aunt Jo had often complained that Michelle didn't take her studies seriously; all she wanted was to be a married lady with babies. The baby part was already happening.

"It's really all right." Michelle finally stopped sobbing against Rosie's shoulder. "It's not the baby that's the problem," she insisted. "It's all this fuss about the ball and the parade and everything. My parents have wanted this for me for years," Michelle lamented, wiping away her tears. "All I've heard about is what an honor it is to be queen of a ball. I didn't want to be queen...." Her voice broke as another series of deep sobs erupted. "*They* wanted me to be queen. I just wanted to get through all this for them, so they would have something to be thrilled about." Michelle shivered as she spoke. "They're going to be so disappointed."

Finally Susie made herself move. Quickly she retrieved a soft velour dressing gown from the corner clothes rack and draped it around Michelle's shoulders. "Come on and sit down," she soothed, helping Rosie guide Michelle through the hallway and into the kitchen. Here they would just be family, no longer surrounded by the uncompromising walls of mirrors. Here Michelle was no longer on display. She was no longer a queen; she was a woman in anguish, sharing her troubles with her cousin and her aunt. For now, business would have to wait.

"My father has spent so much money on this already," Michelle said sincerely. "Please don't tell him or my mom until I've had a chance to sort some things out. I want them to hear about this from me." Again her hand rested gently on her tummy. "If they only understand how happy I am," she said softly, "then it won't seem like such a disaster. I wanted this child," she affirmed. "I just hoped that I could keep it a secret until Mardi Gras was over. I guess I miscalculated." The frown on her face did not make her any less lovely. Now calm and free from the tension of keeping the pregnancy to herself, Michelle seemed more mature and confident.

"What about...the father?" Rosie hesitantly asked. "Is there any problem there?"

"The father will be elated," Michelle replied knowingly. "It's my parents who worry me." Then, as if she were drawing back within herself, Michelle took a deep breath. "I'll need some time." She looked evenly at Susie and Rosie. "Promise you won't worry, and promise you won't tell anyone about this. I'll take care of everything. Really," she stressed. "I can't keep up the pretense. Just give me a few days."

Rosie was the one who promised what she asked. Susie only smiled sympathetically.

"I'm feeling a little queasy again." Michelle stood to leave, then paused, bracing herself on the kitchen counter until the unsettled feeling within her subsided. "I think that once this is all out in the open, I'll be a lot better," she said good-naturedly. "Even the baby is confused. All my morning sickness seems to come in the evening."

"You let us know if there's anything we can do," Rosie said in her most maternal tone.

"I'm the one who has to do something," Michelle replied. "I've done most of it already, I guess." She smiled sheepishly. "Just don't say a word until you hear from me."

"Certainly, dear." Rosie went with Michelle to locate

her clothes while Susie remained in the kitchen, staring glumly at the chair where Michelle had been seated. Outside in the foyer, she could hear Rosie greeting other clients who were waiting for their final gown fittings. Rosie was resuming her scheduled appointments. For Susie, it was time to leave.

"Oh, Sy..." she whispered softly to herself as she drove into New Orleans to keep her date with Pascal. "What have you done?" His past was repeating itself— another beautiful blonde, another love affair and another child. But this time Michelle was the mother-to-be, and she said she had wanted this baby. Then the solemn face of Sy came to torment Susie. She remembered the softness in his eyes and the affection in his voice when he was with his son. Sy loved the boy. He accepted his role as a parent as both pleasure and responsibility. Now there was another child to care for. "How stupid. How careless!" Susie's angry outburst was directed at no one there. It was the frustrated outcry— part anger, part pain—that signaled the loss of hope, the total dissolution of her defences. "You fool!" She meant to condemn the man who had let his passion for another separate him from Susie forever. But the words echoed back with a relentless chill that started slow tears of grief trickling down her cheeks.

She was the one who had held off. She was the one who felt the power of their attraction and still delayed. She had let her old wounds cripple her for so long that she couldn't open her life to a man with eyes of velvet and a soul so like her own.

"You fool...." The words tormented her. She had met a man who could stir her passions with his words. He promised her a tomorrow that would never come.

She had loved him more than she suspected, more than he would ever know. There was not one fool in this tragedy, Susie admitted. There were at least two.

CHAPTER EIGHT

IN HIS TUXEDO and black tie, Pascal Danos looked more cosmopolitan and self-assured than he felt as he waited on the balcony outside Susie's apartment. Finally he emitted a sigh of relief when Susie's sports car pulled into the parking place below. "I came early," he blurted unnecessarily. "I know that we honored guests are allowed to show up fashionably late," he joked nervously, "but there isn't anyone to talk to over at my place, and the walls were beginning to close in on me." He stopped abruptly and stared at Susie's face.

"Did the world end while I was dressing, and I just failed to notice?" he asked with great concern. Susie had been weeping steadily for the last ten minutes of the drive from the Costains' house. Her eyes were puffy and red, and the tip of her nose was deep pink.

"I've had a minor setback." Susie tried to make light of her disarray. "All this can be repaired," she assured the sculptor. "It may take some ingenuity," she admitted, "but I will look presentable."

"Are you sure you feel like going out at all?" Pascal followed her into the apartment. "Don't feel trapped into this."

"Out is precisely where I want to be," Susie declared. "I'm not the one who should be feeling trapped at this point," she added grimly. "And I could use someone to talk with, too.'' She placed the long gown she would wear that evening on a hook by the closet. ''So if you're still willing,'' Susie continued, taking a washcloth and running cool water over it, ''I'll fix my face... while you step next door to visit Renny. As you can see—'' she waved her hand in a sweeping gesture ''—privacy in here is a problem.'' Her apartment was small. Only the bathroom had a door.

''I'll go next door then,'' Pascal agreed promptly. ''Just let me know when you're ready.''

''I'll send a paper airplane through the transom.'' Susie smiled weakly. Already the cool water on her face was soothing away the ravages of the tears.

When Susie appeared at Renny's door, both Pascal and Renny leaped to their feet. In spite of their pleasant expressions and compliments, both men still looked at her with a wariness that made it clear they had been speculating about the cause of her sadness.

''It's that Avery guy again, isn't it?'' Renny literally bristled with anger. His frizzy hair, this week a daffodil yellow, quivered like the tail feathers on a baby duck. ''I should have nudged him off the balcony the first time he showed up looking for you.''

''Please, don't get me started again,'' Susie warned him. ''I have a new face, and I don't want to waste all the effort I put into it.'' She raised her chin and fluttered her eyelashes. ''Simon Avery isn't the bad guy in this story, anyway,'' she insisted. ''There are no bad guys. It's just like one of those Greek tragedies,'' she observed quietly. ''Sometimes we get caught up in things, and before we know it, we can't get loose.''

''Sounds like you're talking about my scenery commissions,'' Renny commented. ''Accepting the money was so easy,'' he chastised himself. ''If I'd only known what I was getting myself into. . . .'' He shook his head thoughtfully. ''Getting us into,'' he amended, including Susie in his scenic-design enterprise.

''Now you're getting me depressed again,'' Susie teased him. They still had not completed all the designs for his ''Stars of the Silver Screen'' ball. The remaining work would have to be squeezed in various evenings whenever the opportunity arose. But not tonight. She had promised herself an evening out. Renny, however, would be working all evening in the warehouse. ''Let's leave before we all become maudlin.'' She beckoned Pascal to accompany her.

''You do make a drab, but otherwise handsome, pair,'' Renny playfully called after them. ''Black and beige. . . really!'' He rolled his eyes in mock disapproval. Susie had deliberately chosen a subdued color for this evening, something that would complement yet not detract from the formal attire Pascal had grudgingly worn. Together, with her dark hair and his sandy-colored beard, they were the image of understated elegance. The only touch of vivid color was the deep crimson of Susie's lipstick and the final rosebud from the rose tree. Susie tucked it into Pascal's lapel and wished him well. This was his evening, but she would stay by his side for moral support. If she concentrated on alleviating his nervousness, she would not have a moment to dwell on troubles of her own.

''I am simply not a public person.'' Pascal didn't need to explain his discomfort to Susie. Throughout the brief ceremony honoring the craftsmen whose work had been selected for the Mardi Gras exhibit, Pascal stood like a convicted man facing a firing squad as each artist was introduced. His expression, which Susie later told him looked like one of his sculpted models, remained rigid and solemn throughout, even though his eyes occasionally shifted from one face to another in near panic.

"I don't like to be stared at, either," Susie consoled Pascal as they drove back to her apartment. "It's one thing to have people admire and critique my costumes," she noted. "But when it's me they're looking at...."

"Exactly." Pascal tugged at his tie and began loosening the collar of his ruffled shirt. "Leave me out of it—that's how I feel."

"Still," Susie reminded him, "the presentation will give you some positive publicity. People who read the articles in the paper will see that you have other works in progress. Maybe a bit of public exposure isn't too great an ordeal to endure—for your art. Besides, we did enjoy the rest of the evening."

"We did, didn't we?" Pascal grinned elfishly. Once the presentation had ended and Pascal and the other honorees were free to circulate among the museum patrons, the evening had taken on a different tone. There had been pale bubbly champagne, hot spicy hors d'oeuvres and a remarkable collection of old photographs and models to view. The earliest carnival parades and costumes were recorded in lithographs from the 1850s and late 1860s when glittering pageants and tableau balls had become a tradition in New Orleans.

Susie and Pascal had moved from one display to the next, carefully reading the detailed history of the Mardi Gras celebration. In one glass-paneled case were elaborate, inventive invitations to balls throughout the years. In the adjacent display cases were rows of parade "throws"—strings of colorful beads, toys and trinkets, painted coconuts, artificial flowers, plastic cups and doubloons—stamped metal coins of every imaginable color.

"I almost forgot," Susie said quietly as Pascal bent down to read the dates on some of the doubloons. "I have a friend who asked me to collect some throws for him." Even though Sy had to be put out of her life, his son still deserved some special thought. She had promised him throws. Susie intended to keep that promise. Then there had been a conversation about going to a ball, Susie recalled. Tony wanted to see some of the costumes when they were paraded about during the presentation of the courts. It would be a marvelous, lavish ceremony that would thrill Tony, just as Susie had been thrilled when she was a child and began viewing the Mardi Gras balls.

"If you're after parade throws," Pascal offered, "I have some connections of my own. I'd be glad to pick up some trinkets from the krewes that I'm working with."

"That would be great," Susie accepted eagerly. "Tony is such a special little kid," she added. "I'd love to see his face if I could hand him a sack full of bizarre and gaudy throws. His eyes have a way of lighting up when he's pleased. . . ." Susie's voice quavered. In addition to everything else, she had been putting aside her feelings for the boy who always broke into a grin the moment he saw her. She had missed him.

"You're aren't going to cry again." Pascal had fumbled nervously for his handkerchief.

"I'm not going to cry," Susie promised. "But I am going to start gathering parade throws. Then I'm going to deliver them personally to Tony."

The remainder of the exhibit had been equally impressive, particularly a few costumes donated by several past ball kings and queens. "From what I've seen of your artwork," Pascal commented, "I can only guess at the quality of your costumes. But if my judgment is correct, maybe the next honoree at one of these functions should be you. Wouldn't you like to see one of your extravaganzas on display here?"

"Not if I had to stand up on a platform like that and have someone go on and on about how wonderful I am." She cringed at the thought.

"We'll see." Pascal glanced once more over the costumed mannequins whose jewels and plumage had lost much of their beauty to the passage of time. "Now that I'm an exhibitor, I could pull a few strings," he teased, arching his brows mischievously.

"Use those strings to get me parade throws." Susie diverted his attention. "And if she isn't spoken for," Susie continued, "I'd like to have that papier-mâché Judy Garland you made for the Comus float. If all they plan to do is dump her in the trash, "I'd like to buy her or have her donated to a cause of my own."

"What on earth would you do with an eleven-foot Judy Garland?" Pascal asked.

"I'd put her in my workroom," Susie responded. "She could stand by the design bench like a guardian angel and inspire me when I work on ideas for costumes. Besides that," Susie joked, "I would be honored to have an original Pascal Danos sculpture for my very own."

"If you get me the black-and-white drawing you did of Garland for Renny's scenery commission," he bargained, "then you can have Judy, the rainbow, and I'll throw in her dog, Toto."

"Let me check with Renny," Susie was as flattered by Pascal's desire for her work as he was with her appreciation of his. "If Renny can get the poster back after the ball, you have yourself a deal." Arm in arm, they had completed their tour of the new museum wing, then they had unobtrusively slipped out the side door and made their way to the parking lot and home.

"Thank you for the evening." Pascal stopped at the bottom of the staircase and made a polite bow. For a moment, he looked at Susie as if he was about to kiss her goodnight. Instead, he took her hand and held it in his. "Whoever this guy is who has caused you so much heartache," Pascal said with difficulty, "he's an idiot not to treasure you. I just want you to know that if you were mine . . . ."

Susie pressed her fingertips to his lips to stop him from continuing. "Please . . . ." She shook her head.

"Beneath this modest exterior," Pascal persisted, "lurks a knight in shining armor." His deep blue eyes sparkled with conviction. "Granted, this knight is an inch shorter than you if we were both in our stocking feet," he conceded, "and I may look more like Dudley Moore than Christopher Reeve, but I have certain qualities that are worthy of your attention."

"I can give you my attention," Susie stated gently, "and I can give you my friendship. What I can't do is will myself to fall in love with you or with anyone else. That's something that simply happens. I didn't choose Simon Avery. I certainly wasn't looking for romance, either. Now that I'm determined to get over him, I may need a little help along the way. But I won't play games with your feelings or anyone else's," she said, taking a stand. "We're all a lot more vulnerable than we care to believe. Right now, I don't need a knight in shining armor. I don't want a romance. I could use a friend.''

"I still say he's an idiot." Pascal shrugged. "But I'm not. If you want a friend, I'll volunteer. And unless you change your mind and notify me *in writing* that you find me irresistible," he informed her with a lopsided smile, "I will not crowd you or make advances or do anything to make you feel uncomfortable. I don't play games, either," he assured her. "But I'll make one heck of a friend."

Susie placed both hands on Pascal's shoulders and leaned forward slightly. With great affection, she kissed the slender fellow squarely on the mouth. It was not a kiss of passion, but one of sincere appreciation. It was a kiss Pascal would not misunderstand—or forget. It was his night, and Susie had made it a memorable one.

"WHO IS IT?" Susie had barely gone inside and undressed before the knock came at the door of her apartment. It was almost three in the morning and Pascal had left several minutes earlier.

"It's Sy Avery," came the low, clipped reply. "You know," he added, "the one your friend called an idiot."

Susie jerked open the door and stared at him. "You heard?" she gasped. "You were listening!"

"I certainly was." Sy stepped past her and stalked into the center of the living room. "You can't imagine what a surreal experience it was watching you and that guy come through the gate and stand there holding hands...and talking about me. I don't even know the guy, and he's calling me an idiot. What the hell has been going on here while I've been in Mobile?" In the darkness of the room, Susie wasn't sure if his voice shook with anger or bewilderment. Quickly she closed the apartment door and crossed the room to switch on a light. In its soft golden glow, she could see Sy clearly. He was angry.

Susie motioned for him to sit down, but he didn't move. He remained in the middle of the room, regarding her with remote, demanding eyes. "Maybe we should discuss what went on in Mobile," Susie countered, settling into her rattan armchair and tucking her bare feet under her. She wore only a soft apricot nightgown that clung to her like a second skin. It was hardly the proper attire for a confrontation, so she tugged an afghan from the sofa and snuggled under it.

"You told your friend down there you didn't play games," Sy shot back at her. "I worked in Mobile. Just what are you after? What kind of game is this?"

"I saw Michelle today." Susie decided to face Sy with the details straight on. "She's pregnant."

"I know." Sy seemed unperturbed by the fact.

"You took her to Mobile with you, didn't you?" Susie felt the muscles in her face stiffen as she forced out the words.

"Sure. She called before I left and wanted to go along," he acknowledged. Then he stopped and gave Susie a solemn look. "I see. . . ." He moved over to the sofa and sank into it with a weary groan. "You think I'm the one who got her pregnant."

"Aren't you?"

"How much do you know about Michelle and what's going on in her life?" Sy had answered her question with one of his own. "Has she ever said anything that suggests she and I have been lovers?"

"She doesn't confide in me," Susie answered. "But I doubt if she would talk about that kind of thing to anyone."

"So you really don't know what's been happening?" Sy's dark eyes were leveled accusingly at her.

"Apparently quite a lot has been happening," Susie replied.

"Michelle and I made an agreement months ago. And not for the reasons you may think." Sy rubbed the back of his neck to relieve the tension. "Actually, it has more to do with Felicia than Michelle. I knew Felicia was facing a slump in her modeling career, and I know how she reacts at those times. She becomes very insecure, and then she becomes highly domesticated. She wants to come home—not just to Tony, but to me." Sy kept massaging his neck, half closing his eyes and rocking his head from side to side. "I've been through it before, and I knew the danger signs. I needed someone to act as a buffer. If you recall," he reminded Susie softly, "you were not available at the time. You were booked up with your work."

As Susie tried to follow the story and Sy explained the dilemma they were in, she watched with fascination the slow, steady movement of Sy's hand against his muscular neck. In spite of her resolve to forget this man, she felt her self-control falter. She longed to sit beside him and let her own hands ease the tautness in his shoulders. Now, when they were separated by so much, she wished they could touch each other and take away the pain that was keeping them apart.

"Michelle needed someone, too," Sy continued. "For reasons of her own, she wanted an acceptable escort, someone conspicuous, to satisfy the demands of a hectic social schedule. So we made a deal. A mutual defense pact of sorts,'' he stressed.

Susie clutched the afghan more closely around her body. Even the softness of its woolly texture could not dispel the sudden chill. The arrangement between Sy and Michelle sounded so cold-blooded and casual. "A deal," he'd called it. That was just what he had called his promise to her. In February, when all this frantic Mardi Gras activity was over, he and Susie had "a deal," too. He said he'd be after her like a moth to a flame. But now the flame had been extinguished. There was nothing left but the ash.

"Contrary to what you may think, I don't take sex lightly," Sy said. "I must admit that I used to," he confessed. "I'd go ahead and enjoy it without hesitating. I loved the pleasure, and I loved the freedom. Then one day, I grew up. What I called freedom was actually irresponsibility. I looked into the face of my son. I took to the role of parent; Felicia felt trapped by it. The story isn't unique," he observed somberly, "only the names of the characters change from city to city, year to year." Now he arched his back and stretched slowly.

"Michelle and I were never sexually intimate." Sy looked into Susie's sad, uncertain eyes. "She would not try to put the responsibility for her child on me. And I will never let myself or any other person go through that trapped feeling that comes when a child is conceived and unwanted. Sex is not like playing Russian roulette. A kid has a right to be conceived on purpose—not by chance. When I make love to you, we'll both know what we're doing. The experience is complicated enough without adding the risk of an unwanted pregnancy. We'll be making love, Susie. We won't be making a mistake.''

Susie's mind was reeling from the sudden shift the conversation had taken. It had begun with her tormented by Sy's sexual exploits with Michelle. Suddenly he was looking at her with a pensive, serious expression and talking of making love with her.

"I agreed to be camouflage for Michelle, and she agreed to do the same for me. It doesn't alter the fact that I want you so profoundly. I want to take the time with you to try again, Susie. I want a life so full of passion that it sizzles." His rugged, bearded face finally softened with a slight smile. "And I want it with someone whose intelligence and sensitivity constantly replenish me. I'm very selfish, Susie. I see all that I want in you. So I'll go slowly to make it right, but it sure isn't easy," he sighed. "I put up with all the gossip so I could buy some time. And you're the one who got hurt." He reached out one hand to her in a silent invitation to sit beside him. Still clutching the afghan to her chest, Susie slid out of the armchair and lowered herself next to Sy. Protectively, he drew her within the circle of his arm, holding her against him.

Susie closed her eyes and breathed in the familiar scent of his body. She felt his warmth gradually engulfing her. "I didn't think we would ever be this close again." She had barely whispered the words before Sy grasped her with his other arm, pulling her forward tenderly until he cradled her across his lap. Very gently, he tugged the afghan from around her and draped it so they were both under it.

"I wake up at the most ridiculous hours—thinking of you, wanting to hold you." Sy's voice was low and husky. "I can close my eyes and feel the pressure of your lips on mine. Making love to you will be the easiest thing I'll ever do," he added hoarsely. "It's the not making love that tests my strength." He stroked her shoulder through the thickness of the afghan as if he didn't trust himself to let his hand brush against her bare skin.

"I tried to call you tonight, but there was no answer here," he reported. "I called your folks' house. Your dad said you were out and you wouldn't be back there tonight. I went to the studio and worked for a while. I even sprawled out on the bed in the back and tried to sleep." The slow, steady pressure of his hand against her back sent waves of pleasure coursing through Susie's half-reclining body. "So I came here and leaned against the courtyard wall, waiting for you to come back. You stay in my mind every minute of every day." He pressed his face into the silky softness of her hair. "I had to hold you again."

Susie slid her arms out from under the woolly covering, reaching upward, opening them to bring Sy closer to her. "Then hold me now," she breathed against his cheek. The tension in his muscular shoulders returned as he studied the weariness in her face and tried to resist, but the gentle pressure of her hands against his body melted any resolve he may have had. Sy exhaled a long breath, then wound his arms around her, shifting his weight and pulling her beneath him full length onto the sofa. When it became apparent that the inadequate space between the arms of the sofa could not accommodate them, Sy simply held her more tightly, sliding both of them, still in each other's arms, onto the soft carpet.

Through the filmy fabric of her gown, Susie could feel every texture acutely. Sy's coarse sweater and the rough-woven fabric of his slacks rasped against her sensitive skin. Brushing against her throat and neck, Sy's beard seemed natural and silken by comparison, exciting her with its surprising softness. The heavy garments now became insufferable artificial barriers separating them as their bodies pressed closer.

"Let me touch your skin." Susie reached beneath Sy's sweater, dismayed to find her progress blocked by another fabric, a smooth knit shirt, beneath it. Gliding her hands over the tight muscles in his back, Susie shook her head in frustration. "Please let me feel your skin against mine," she insisted, seeking reassurance through her sensitive touch.

Sy moved away from her only long enough to pull off the heavy sweater and the shirt beneath. Both fell into a discarded heap as Sy pressed his bare torso against the insubstantial fabric covering her waiting body.

"I love to feel your hands on my body." He moaned with pleasure. "I love it that touching me gives you pleasure, too." Susie pressed her open palm into the hollows of his back, absorbing the feel of him through every pore.

Almost breathless from the delicious joy their bodies aroused in each other, Susie thought a gasp of delight was about to escape from her lips, but the sound was more one of relief than excitement. It was like a sob of surrender. Emotionally and physically, Susie was overwhelmed. She felt as though a flood was overflowing the riverbanks, as the strain of maintaining control and putting on a calm front was finally over.

All the urgency left Sy's touch as his hands roamed her body with great gentleness, caressing, comforting her. Susie clung to him, sobbing uncontrollably while Sy stroked her, whispering her name again and again.

"Oh, Susie." He leaned her back and regarded her closely. "You have so much passion in you, but you hide it. Yet you care so deeply and you hurt so desperately. You don't want to trouble anyone." His smile acknowledged so much about her. "You ask only to touch again, to be held." His voice cracked with emotion. "Then you catch fire simply from touching my skin. I want to bask in the glow you radiate." He lowered his mouth to hers in a languid, lingering kiss that offered not an invitation, but a promise.

"I will love you so totally." He let his hands glide over her body, not demanding but discovering a response. "I will explore your body and share its secrets. I'll teach you to trust me so completely and to be so sure. When you want to make love to me, you won't need to whisper my name or brush me with your fingertips. You'll just look at me, and I'll know."

"Make love to me now, Sy. . . ." Susie had subdued her weeping and felt closer to this man than she had to anyone before. "I want to be a part of you." Her words rippled against his lips. "I want you to surround me." But the tremble in her arms gave her away, hinting at a weariness of body and of heart.

"Now I really am going to sound like that idiot your friend called me." Sy backed off and pulled himself into a sitting position. The tremor in his voice had revealed his conflicting passions. Now his majestic eyes appraised her. Suddenly, he grabbed the afghan and wrapped it securely around her. "You're a bit too irresistible for your own good," he declared. "But I will not make love to you tonight. God knows, I want to," he admitted. "But I don't want you coming apart totally. You've been through too much, and you're simply beat." He eased her up and cuddled her against him. "I'll hold you, and I'll stay with you tonight. I'll help chase away the shadows, but I'll wait until you've had a chance to think this through before I make love to you. I want our first time together to be so awesome that turning to each other will become instinctive." He pulled the afghan up to her chin, tracing her jawline with a gentle stroke. "Without being too clinical," he added with a trace of discomfort in his tone, "I doubt if you have equipped yourself with any precautions, and I sure haven't. That brings us right back to the old Russian roulette syndrome. I want you to wake up the next morning feeling good and feeling free, not worried or trapped. I care too much about us to take chances with your body or your mind."

"I understand." Susie glanced up at him, studying his profile. "I don't feel rejected." A flicker of a smile crossed her lips.

"You and I will do a lot of loving just for ourselves," Sy promised, taking her hand. "We'll take our time to find out just what direction our life together will take. I see the magic in your eyes when you want me, but I've also seen the same magic in your eyes when you talk about your work. It's the inspiration and discovery that's part of your artistry. It's a life-force of an intensity few ever know. I saw a hint of it years ago in Felicia's eyes when she was modeling. She could be amazing at times." He spoke of Felicia's work with a sense of awe. "Then there was Tony and diapers and duties. And choices she never had to consider before. Being a mother was an accident. It extinguished that special light in her eyes and left a cold gleam in its place. That isn't going to happen to you," he insisted. "Felicia had the courage to get out of a situation that could have destroyed her and damaged all of us. But she's lost that creative edge, that instinct that sets her apart. She has her bouts with insecurity and guilt, and she'll probably spend the rest of her life second-guessing herself, but she did make that choice. Life is tough on anyone with a slightly unconventional calling.''

Susie slipped her hand free and reached up to rub the back of Sy's neck. Just as she suspected, the tension had mounted, making the column of taut muscle rigid. With strong, sure fingers, Susie began massaging the ropelike cords, working out the knots with her touch.

"I don't want you second-guessing yourself," Sy said evenly. "And I don't want you regretting anything we do with each other. You're such a complicated creature." He smiled as he closed his eyes and sighed at the movement of her hands on his neck. "You come at things from so many angles. Tonight you thought you wanted to make love," he said softly. "Tomorrow, you would be seeing this from a totally different perspective, especially if there is a chance that one act of love could begin a new life. Maybe one day we will want to have a child together. I think it might be a really nice idea," he acknowledged as he brushed aside a wisp of hair that fell across Susie's cheek. "But that choice is one to be made at some point in the future—after we've had time to ourselves. I couldn't bear to see the light go out in your eyes, Susie. So no Russian roulette," he concluded. "And that's the most difficult speech I've ever had to make. But while we're being so calm and rational, I sure as hell prefer that you don't go around kissing any guy with a beard besides me. Being called an idiot is one thing, but when you kissed that guy. . . ."

"And I'm the one who thought you indulged in casual sex." Susie joked. "Here you turn down the only offer I've ever made."

"Nothing with you is casual." Sy laughed. "Nor is anything predictable or convenient. We don't even get to see each other enough. This is one heck of a way to conduct a romance."

"Is that what you call this?" Susie teased.

"I don't call this anything." Sy became serious. "No labels. I just want it to keep going. It's something special, and I never thought anything like it would come my way again. Proceed with caution, lady." He kissed her lightly on the lips. "This one is ours and we have to take special care."

The sun was coming up when Sy descended the stairs to the courtyard. Bleary-eyed, he paused to contemplate the empty street where the solitary streetlight stood. In the morning mist, the scene acquired a new beauty, a fragile quality sparkling with dew and the promise of a new day. Characteristically, he framed the shot he visualized between his upturned fingers then muttered once again, "I wish I'd brought my camera."

CHAPTER NINE

BY THE END of the week, the final shipment of plumes arrived, ordered from a South American firm that specialized in exotic feathers. For Susie it meant that the entire weekend would be spent fluffing and sorting the exquisite plumage and completing the costumes for the first of the krewe balls.

With the onset of the balls, Sy had been forced to turn his schedule upside down. During the daytime, he would sleep, then from midafternoon to dawn he was on the run from one final costume sitting to another, from one ball to the next. When Susie left work at Blaine's, Sy would be packing his photo gear for the evening. While she labored on costumes, he dressed in formal attire and attended the balls, unobtrusively taking photographs of the courts and the partygoers for krewe yearbooks and for personal albums. With at least two balls scheduled each evening, Sy would work until dawn. As he collapsed into bed, Susie would be rising for a day of fittings and working on costumes or a workday in her cubicle at Blaine's.

"This is awful," Sy had said groggily as he called her at Blaine's the afternoon the plume shipment arrived. "Tony is going to forget what I look like," he complained, "and I only get to hear your voice on the telephone. How about playing hooky from work next week and spending the day with me?"

"If we were really daring," Susie offered conspiratorially, "we could keep Tony out of school that day. All of us could play hooky and go on a picnic."

"We could ride the riverboat." Sy obviously liked the idea. "Tony hasn't had a chance to hear the calliope while cruising along the old Mississippi," he added. "Great idea. Pick a day."

"Wednesday," Susie suggested after a quick look at her calendar. "I'll become dreadfully ill," she promised, already rehearsing her excuse in her mind.

Wednesday seemed like a distant oasis as Susie spent all Friday night unpacking and storing the feather shipment. Saturday morning, she awoke with her arms already aching. Throughout the day, she and her father carried one elaborate costume after another down the stairway to Rosie's fitting room. There the clients tried on the entire outfits—gown, headpiece, collar or backpiece and train. In addition to the elaborate headgear for the spectacular presentation, Susie had made a smaller tiara for each lady in the court. If everything fitted at this sitting, the client would take home the gown and all the coordinated costume pieces. "We could sure use the space." Susie had surveyed the already completed pieces. "Let's hope we measured everything accurately."

"Let's hope we hear something from Michelle," Susie's mother had whispered to her. Just as she had promised, Rosie had kept the secret of Michelle's pregnancy. In the four days that had passed, the opulent Triton's Queen gown had been hanging, still unfinished, in Rosie's workroom. That krewe ball was still a month away, February 5, but if Michelle would not be able to serve as queen, Rosie would have to start again with someone new. That meant new fabric and more fittings. Time was simply running out.

Saturday night, Susie wearily conceded that she was too exhausted to drive back to her own apartment. The trip would be pointless, since all the next day Germaine and the day crew were coming in with Bernie and his two trainees. Sunday would be a hectic workday with Susie supervising and assisting the application of hundreds of feathers. But by nightfall, the entire series of costumes for two krewes, Sirens and Artemis, would be ready. Susie sat quietly while Bernie rubbed a soothing muscle liniment on her shoulders and arms to relieve the soreness.

"We're going to have to come up with another system for getting these costumes up and down the stairway," Bernie stated. "When we started with these big pieces," he noted, "we also created a problem with weight and bulk. Trying to carry the pieces down a flight of stairs just isn't feasible, and I don't want to sacrifice any of our storage or work space in order to get a fitting room upstairs."

"I've already asked Eugene to come in tomorrow with some extra ropes and pulleys." Susie had been mulling over the problem herself. "If we take out a couple of windows and replace them with a single hinged large one—" she drew an imaginary sketch with her finger in the air "—then we can swing the big items out the window and lower them to ground level."

"If we really want to get serious," Bernie suggested, "you can take over the business full-time. We could convert the lower floor of the garage to fitting and storage, install an elevator setup of some sort, and you could take as many commissions as you like. Of course, you'd have to quit your job at Blaine's," he said, carefully watching his daughter's face for reaction. Susie listened calmly but made no immediate reply.

"Souci," he said quietly as he put the cap back on the strong-smelling liniment, "you're already doing this work full-time, and you and I both know it. We've been partners in every way except on paper," he said reasonably. "But you've poured your talents into this enterprise so much over the past couple of years, and you've designed such marvels that you could leave Blaine's tomorrow and double your income. We've had to turn down krewes who asked for your expertise. And this year—" Bernie rested his hand on his daughter's shoulder "—when the newspapers and television show the balls you designed the costumes for. . . we'll be deluged with more requests. The question is, my talented coworker, do we go for it, or do we muddle through another year, exhausting you with two jobs?"

Susie deliberated on what her father had said. The opportunity was there, to be sure. If she concentrated just on the costuming firm and made it a year-round business, she could indeed be secure financially. Redoing the first floor of the garage-workshop to accommodate fulltime employees and all the innovative pulley and storage ideas would allow for a less hectic production period. And fitting rooms in the new addition where Rosie could adjust the gowns while Bernie and Susie fitted the costumes would free more space inside the house for Rosie to work. "We could double the business," Susie acknowledged.

"We could," Bernie said hopefully. He had seen this coming for a long time. He had watched his daughter grow from a talented teenager to a clever, artistic designer. Her keen imagination and acute eye for structure and mechanics had surpassed any expectations he might have had. Bernie had also seen the other side of his daughter, the intense, thoughtful woman who kept so much of herself private. He had not intruded into her personal affairs; he had just loved her and accepted her and now looked with respect at the woman she had become.

"Let me think about it," Susie finally responded. "We'll have to survive this year before we plan the next one." She arched her back and groaned at the dull ache between her shoulders.

"If you had just this one business," Bernie persisted, trying to add some incentive to the plan, "in the off-season, you could actually go on a vacation, spend time at the beach, take a trip. When you're the one in charge," he emphasized, "you have no set hours, no regular routine. When you work till two in the morning," he said, glancing at his watch, "you can sleep in the next day."

"Does that mean I can sleep in tomorrow?" Susie teased.

"We're talking about the off-season," Bernie replied. "Now—we have to keep going, sleep or no sleep." A glint of mischief came into his eyes. "Unless, of course, we were a big operation. Then you'd have a trained staff to take over occasionally—"

Susie cut him off with a sigh of exasperation. "I think I'd better get to bed. Since you and I and Germaine are the only trained staff in charge tomorrow, you had better get some rest, too. This 'big operation' talk will have to wait until I can actually sit down and think straight."

"That should be sometime late next month," Bernie

concluded with a sly smile. "It sure is tough with two jobs," he repeated, getting in his final comment before closing the bedroom door.

BY SUNDAY NIGHT, the new pulley system was installed and operating flawlessly. Susie had to rewire a section of the burglar-alarm system, diverting it around the plywood panel that was temporarily replacing the two windows Eugene had removed. The two parrots, Rosalind and Marcel, had to be returned to their old roosts in the kitchen while the work on the windows had been done, to prevent either one of the adventurous creatures from flying out the opening. But once the wood panel had been fitted, the two birds were reinstated as sentries.

"I think all these feathers make them a little nervous." Bernie had tried to calm Marcel. The large green creature paced back and forth along its perch, muttering indistinct messages to the plumage still standing in holders and cascading from ceiling hooks.

"Maybe he knows them." Germaine walked past with an armful of tiaras and poked fun at the disgruntled parrot. "One of your cousins?" she asked him.

Bernie had laughed and pulled the curtain over the front of the compartment. If the feathers or the shift in housing had upset the birds, there was always one solution. Cover them up and they would take a nap. "I'll wake you two up when we close shop," Bernie promised. At least Rosalind and Marcel would face the night duty well rested.

Long after the workroom had been locked up for the night and the impressive assemblage of costumes for Artemis and Sirens had been completed and stationed along one wall, Susie retired downstairs and soaked in a tub of hot soapy water. Rosie had persuaded her to spend the night at the Costain home, and there was no reason to resist. Susie was exhausted. There was nothing back at her apartment except two goldfish, which Renny would gladly feed, and a rosebush that no longer had any blooms. Sy would be working through the night, either taking photos or developing them. Tonight, Susie would stay in her old room and sleep. Tomorrow it was business as usual back at Blaine's.

When Susie rolled over for the third time, it became apparent that, tired or not, she couldn't sleep. In the quiet darkness of the Costain house, she walked barefoot from room to room, pausing to contemplate the sea-green gown that Michelle could no longer wear. Michelle had seemed so confident that she could work out the situation once she'd broken the news of the pregnancy to her parents, but still there had been no word from anyone to indicate that Uncle Leo and Aunt Jo had been informed.

"So what will happen to you?" Susie spoke softly to the satin dress as she spread out the graceful skirt and let it flutter back into place. Year after year, gowns just like this had been worn in the balls and then again in the parades that would follow during the two weeks leading to Mardi Gras Day. Susie knew that after carnival these dresses would hang in closets, then eventually be sold, given away or discarded. But at least they had their moments of magic. Susie viewed the gown sympathetically. At least the other dresses had been worn and photographed and would be admired and remembered for years to come. Not this one, Susie thought with regret. This one missed out on all the excitement.

Somehow the tragedy of the gown sent Susie's

thoughts spiraling in all directions as thoughts of other incomplete dreams haunted her. Felicia Voison Avery still pursued a modeling career that had almost been curtailed by a pregnancy. Leo Costain and Aunt Jo had wanted their daughter to go to college and to be a Mardi Gras queen, and now all that would be lost to another dream—Michelle's longing to have a baby. Susie shook her head, thinking of the women who knew so well what they wanted to do with their lives. *And what about me,* Susie wondered. The advertising work she did at Blaine's paid adequately and provided a routine she had needed, a secure position with a promising future. But it had no magic.

Susie walked into the kitchen and peered into the refrigerator. Then she heated a glass of milk, hoping that it would relax her and help her to sleep. Leaning by the back door of the house, Susie sipped the milk, glancing out into the moonless night at the huge two-story building that could be expanded to accommodate a more efficient costuming business. If platforms were built into the floor, ones that could be raised or lowered.... Susie was considering modifications that could indeed make that building functional.

Upstairs, a gleam of light flashed across the workroom ceiling, then was gone. Susie stared intently at the upper-story workroom. As tired as she felt, she knew she could have imagined the gleam of light. It could have been the reflection of car headlights or a streetlight.

"I forgot to let the birds out." Susie suddenly remembered that the closing procedure had been repeatedly interrupted by last-minute details. No one had uncovered Rosalind and Marcel.

She finished the last of her warm milk and placed the glass in the kitchen sink. If she didn't go upstairs and remove the cover from the bird roost, she knew that she would lie awake worrying all night. Susie paused a moment by the doorway to study the workroom windows. Nothing stirred. She started for the stairway to wake up the watchbirds.

Susie had unlocked the door, clicked on the far light and walked the full length of the workroom before the uneasy feeling drew her to a halt. Something in the dimly lighted room wasn't right. Susie stood in the center of the lighted area scrutinizing the shadowy outer edges of the room. Like a squadron of airborne specters, the costumes suspended on pulleys hovered above her, while row upon row of butterflies and sea creatures awaited the krewes of Artemis and Sirens. Occasionally the motion of air currents in the room would enliven the eerie scene as plumes trembled and sequins caught the light.

"Is anybody here?" Susie strained to detect some other presence. The only response was the reproachful grumbling of Marcel, still confined beneath the striped cover.

"If there's anyone here—" Susie talked to the birds to soothe their anxiety and her own "—you have my permission to rearrange their faces." Rosalind raised her beak for a kiss while Marcel stretched his wings and gave Susie an indignant look. Then the feathers flew.

With an ear-piercing shriek, Marcel went straight up. Rosalind caught Susie squarely across the eyes with her outspread wings. When Susie whirled around to see what had startled the creatures, the huge figure plummeting toward her threw up an arm that caught her chin and slammed her into the bird roost. Susie dropped slowly to the floor as the pale circles of light above her shimmered then faded into black.

BERNIE AND ROSIE took turns pacing to the doorway and back while the dark-haired man stood below, waiting anxiously by his car, its hazard lights blinking a grim yellow signal in the night. Sy's dark eyes shifted from the roadway to the upstairs workroom where he wanted to be.

"Don't move her," Bernie barked. Somewhere in the black cocoon that engulfed her, Susie heard her father's voice.

"But she looks all crooked." Rosie leaned down and gently pressed her hand against Susie's cheek. "Let me just straighten out her legs a bit."

"No." Bernie fought to conceal the tremor in his voice. "When the paramedics get here, they can decide how badly she's hurt and they can move her. She hit her head and back. We don't want to twist anything and make it worse than it already looks."

Susie tried to focus her eyes on the figures crouched over her, but again the images blurred and became dark. The next voice she heard belonged to Simon Avery.

"Just lie still, Susie. The paramedics are here. You're on a stretcher ready to take a quick trip to the hospital. You hit your head." She could now feel the warmth of Sy's hand clasping hers. "They'll take you in for some X rays," he informed her in a calm, even voice. "You'll be fine, but they're going to make sure."

"Souci...." Bernie moved back into view with the same peculiar luminescent aura surrounding him. "You were knocked out," he whispered. "Bruises and a cut on your head. A goose egg on the back of your head where you hit the bird stand—but nothing dangerous. You'll be all right.''

Susie blinked slowly, trying to make the images before her come clearer. But the faces all seemed to recede into featureless golden orbs that moved and shimmered and occasionally spoke. Then she felt herself being lifted and carried from the room. Other indistinct faces with unfamiliar voices stopped to glance at her. The last thing Susie heard before they bore her out into the night was Rosie's hushed voice. ''I want to ride with her in the ambulance.''

''Sorry, ma'am,'' one of the white-clad paramedics responded. ''Just me and the victim are allowed back there. State law, I'm afraid. You'll have to follow in your car.''

Sy watched the paramedics slide the stretcher with Susie carefully secured to it into the emergency vehicle. Rosie stiffened noticably when he walked over to her. ''Mrs. Costain, I'll be glad to drive you to the hospital,'' he offered.

She shook her head slowly and walked back into the house.

After the ambulance pulled away, Sy rejoined the uniformed officers who stood conferring with Detective Terrebonne, Bernie's short, graying friend.

''Inside job,'' Terrebonne muttered. They all nodded in agreement. The alarm had not sounded. The window board had been tampered with, and it was apparent that the finished costumes had been moved toward the new pulley device that could lower them to ground level unseen by anyone in the Costain household. ''Someone had to know every detail of your schedule to pull this off,'' Terrebonne went on in his low, rich Southern drawl. "The only flaw in the plan was Susie returning to free the birds."

"When we went through this before with the break-in," Terrebone said to Susie's father, "you said that some fabric swatches were stolen. What's the connection between this stuff—" he pointed to the headpieces and trains that were completed "—and those swatches? Do they go together?"

Bernie looked over the collection of costumes for Artemis and Sirens. He remembered only too well having to reassemble the swatch booklets for each of those krewes. "They're the same ones, all right." Bernie realized that this scheme had been laid well in advance. "They're also two of our earliest shipments," he added. "They had to be ready first. If someone planned to sell them this year," he noted, "they have four weeks of balls still ahead."

"It would be stupid to try anything like that locally," Sy interjected. "They'd be too easy to spot."

"And how do you figure in this?" Terrebonne turned a suspicious eye on the tall bearded man who still wore a tuxedo from the evening's festivities. Sy had been there when Terrebonne arrived, but they had not met until now.

"I'm Sy Avery. I'm a photographer," he introduced himself. "I'd finished doing a ball and came out here hoping to locate Susie. I pulled into the street just as a big rental truck came barreling out of the side alleyway. When I got here," he said, pointing to the gouges in the grass next to the workroom, "I could see where the truck had been. All the lights were on, and Bernie was upstairs on the phone calling the rescue squad. Susie was out cold."

"You go visiting at two o'clock in the morning?" Terrebonne questioned Sy further.

"Only during the carnival season," Sy replied. Terrebonne simply nodded. A peculiar lighthearted madness took over New Orleans during carnival season. Nothing surprised the experienced officer anymore.

"Tell me about the truck." Terrebonne methodically began jotting down details. Sy described the size, gave the rental company name and two details that would distinguish that truck from any other—it had a broken left-rear taillight, and there was a deep indentation in the driver's door.

"We'll get with the rental agencies." Terrebonne was obviously pleased. "We'll start in New Orleans and work out from here. If someone has that truck rented, then there has to be paperwork on it. In the meantime—" Terrebonne turned to Bernie "—I'll need the name and address of anyone who has access to the workroom, everyone who works with you and anyone who would know your production schedule. If they were planning on stealing the costumes for an entire ball, or two balls, you're talking grand theft—not to mention the assault charge for attacking Susie."

"Has anything else been disturbed?" a second officer, this one in uniform, asked.

"How about the dresses that go with the headpieces?" Sy asked. "Wouldn't they go after them, too?"

"I doubt that." Terrebonne sent an officer with Rosie to check her work area just in case. "Dresses have to fit too well. The rest of this stuff is what's worth all the money, and it can be put on by anyone of any shape."

Bernie thought his friend Terrebonne had over-simplified the situation, but he did see the officer's point. Under Susie's elaborate costumes, the original gown wasn't absolutely necessary. As long as the colors were close enough and the fabric compatible. "So they took the swatches—they could match the dresses later." Bernie breathed between his teeth. It was a risky, one-shot deal, but if the thieves had pulled it off, they would have driven away with thousands of dollars worth of headpieces and accessories. The sick feeling in his stomach was not simply caused by his concern for his daughter or for their designs. It was something cold and full of horror. Someone had set them up for this. Someone betrayed them, and that someone had been a person they trusted.

"Renny Castelot lives in the apartment next to Susie. Germaine Concienne, student at Tulane. Eugene Tanner lives in Kenner." Bernie began listing all the workers who were most involved in the costuming. Each time Terrebonne wrote down a name, Bernie's throat became tighter. These were Susie's friends, his friends, people he had worked and laughed with. Now Bernie felt like the traitor, exposing his helpers to the scrutiny of the police. "Avery here, of course." Bernie felt his face redden with discomfort. But Sy had been in the workroom. He had taken photos that had helped determine what had been taken in the first break-in. Now his name was added to the others in the interest of being thorough. "I really don't like this." Bernie apologized to the bearded man who stood by his side.

"I don't like what someone did to Susie," Sy said pointedly. "And I don't mind anything it takes to get the bastard."

Minutes later, Sy walked through the upper story with Bernie and two policemen, carefully rechecking every section to make sure it was again secure. "You two settle down and take it easy," Bernie said, pausing to stroke the two parrots. It had been their loud, maniacal screeching and their hysterical flapping that had brought Bernie and Rosie racing upstairs. Neither of Susie's parents had seen her assailant or the truck careering into the night, but the police lab specialist had removed several human hairs and a tiny piece of skin tissue from Rosalind's claws.

Still ruffled and wild-eyed, Marcel whistled and chortled incoherently, pacing back and forth on his perch. Rosalind sat very still, her pale gray wings pressed against her sides. Only when Bernie picked her up and tucked her under his robe to warm and comfort her could the rapid staccato of her heartbeat be felt. "Easy, baby." Bernie stroked the creature. "You did all you could." He stood holding the parrot until she no longer trembled beneath his touch. Then he put her back in her cubicle above Marcel's perch. Bernie had consoled the birds enough. Now he had to drive Rosie to Chalmette Hospital to sit by Susie's side until she could speak to them and tell them she was all right.

CHAPTER TEN

"WHAT ARE YOU DOING out of bed?" Rosie rushed to grasp Susie's arm. "The doctor said you may have woozy spells, and you shouldn't wander around like this. You could fall and hit your head again." She led Susie into the kitchen and sat her in a chair. "A concussion isn't anything to fool around with." Her earnest look made Susie smile.

"Mother, really..." Susie protested. "I'm not fooling around. I'm hungry. I thought I'd get myself something to eat." Susie had spent the two days since the attack recuperating under the care of her parents, but this morning she had decided that being a patient was a role she no longer wanted. "I'm going to get dressed and look around in the workroom to see if there's anything I can do," she stated.

"I think you should take it easy," Rosie cautioned her. "I'll whip you up an omelette and you can see how you feel after that."

"I'll feel like getting back to work." Susie remained undaunted. "How's dad doing without me?" Bernie had been in and out of Susie's room over the past two days, bringing her soft drinks and filling her in on the details of the break-in. The police had been following through on every clue they had, but still neither the truck nor her assailant had been located.

"Your father is doing fine," Rosie answered a bit too quickly. "It's you I'm worried about." Other than the bruises on Susie's back and occasional moments of dizziness, the effects of the attack were still unclear. Susie had been pushed against the parrot enclosure with such force that she had received a concussion. The doctor had recommended Susie avoid exerting herself unnecessarily, even though he was convinced the concussion was a mild one.

"Has Renny come in today?" Susie asked. Rosie cracked an egg and nodded. "How about Germaine?" Susie inquired. Again Rosie nodded. What Susie really wanted to know was if Sy had called or dropped in, but every time she had mentioned his name, Rosie had avoided looking her in the eye and had reported no sign of him.

"Today is Wednesday. . . ." Susie didn't really need confirmation. This was "hooky" day when she and Tony and Sy were supposed to have skipped work to take a ride on the riverboat together.

"Wednesday." Rosie nodded, occupying herself with the omelette.

"Any word from Ms Jenkins at Blaine's?" Susie inhaled the chopped scallions and cayenne pepper sautéing in the pan. Even Rosie's omelettes had a spicy touch of Creole cuisine.

"Nothing other than that they all wish you a speedy recovery," Rosie reported. "And come back to work when you feel up to it."

"Any other calls?" Susie felt as if she was having to drag each bit of information from her mother.

"None, except for family." Rosie wouldn't even look up on that one. Susie decided it was useless to continue to dig for any word of Sy. She would try another approach.

"Have you heard from Michelle?" Susie lowered her voice just as Rosie did whenever Michelle's condition was discussed.

"Not a word." Rosie folded over the steaming omelette and slid it onto a plate. "It's just two weeks until Ernest Dufrene is giving the King's Champagne Party. Something has to be decided by then." The king's party was a traditional gathering limited to the king and queen and the members of the court. Generally the king and queen presented court members with lovely gifts as mementos of their reign. Uncle Leo had already made the purchases that Michelle was to give out. "I wish I could say something to Leo," Rosie was extremely worried.

"Maybe Michelle has already told him," Susie said hopefully. "They may already be trying to find a replacement for her."

"I think she may be having trouble with the father." The way Rosie said "the father" made Susie look up at her. "If he was supposed to be as delighted as she had hoped," Rosie reasoned, "he wouldn't be stalling like this. There would be some kind of announcement." Now all the pieces were beginning to fit together. Rosie had assumed Sy Avery was responsible. His public appearances with Michelle made him the logical partner. Until Rosie knew otherwise, no philandering womanizer was going to get near her Susie. One distraught Costain female was more than Rosie could bear.

"I know there has been a lot of talk lately, but it was just that—talk. Simon Avery is not the father of Michelle's baby," Susie said bluntly. "And he isn't the one who's stalling. Now—'' she enunciated each word precisely "—has Sy Avery tried to call me?''

Rosie looked at the uncompromising expression on her daughter's face. "You're sure?''

Susie nodded.

Then Rosie frowned and walked out of the room. When she returned, she was carrying a florist's box containing a dozen red tulips. They hadn't even been fully unwrapped.

"He sent these." Rosie passed them to her. "And he did call—a few times, but I asked him to stop," she confessed. "He hasn't called today.''

"Well, if he should call," Susie replied with a firm tone, "I'll be in the workroom. I'd like to talk to him.''

"I'll get a vase." Rosie busied herself with the flowers in an attempt to ease the tension between them. "Just how did you and Sy Avery become so chummy?" she finally had to ask. "Or is it too nosy of me?''

Susie could tell her mother's feelings were hurt. Rosie had only been protecting her.

Susie paused between bites of the delicious omelette and gave her mother a forgiving smile. "It's not too nosy," she conceded. "I've seen him every once in a while in the Quarter." Susie was remembering the afternoons in Jackson Square.

"The Quarter," Rosie muttered. "I should have known.'' But the image conjured up in Rosie's mind was not the sunlit square or the lovely shops on narrow streets overhung with iron-lace balconies. She had stayed away too long from the quaint old section of riverside New Orleans. To her, the Quarter had become something different—an address given in crime reports in the news. The raucous nightclubs of Bourbon Street and the haunts of derelicts and drunks had convinced her that Susie should not live in that questionable section of town. But Susie had moved there anyway, and she claimed to love it. Now Susie had met a man there, a dark-eyed, sophisticated divorcé whose name had been mentioned again and again in the holiday gossip columns. The weary sigh that Rosie finally expelled was one of submission. Susie was in charge of her own life now. Rosie couldn't protect her from her own mistakes. "You just be careful." She couldn't hold back a final caution.

"I'll be careful." Susie slipped her used plate in the sink and scooped up the vase of tulips. "And I'll be upstairs working." She kissed her mother's cheek. "Just in case anyone comes looking for me...or happens to call."

The man who came looking for Susie was Detective Terrebonne. "If you two can spare about an hour—" he could hardly stand still as he spoke "—I have something you might like to see." Bernie and Susie stopped work and looked up at the man. "We traced the truck," Terrebonne announced with a tight grin. "And we found out what they were up to. You gotta see this...." He urged them to join him.

"What about me?" Renny poked his head up from behind a massive horned headpiece for the krewe of Minos ball. Renny looked like a creature himself with his bush of kinky hair sticking out like an electrified halo. The wiry little detective looked at the tall artist whose yellow hairdo and lean form gave him an inhuman appearance.

"We're goin' down to a part of town where flakes like you might get us in real trouble." Terrebonne chuckled at the spectacle Renny would be in the section of run-down apartment buildings. Having the police descend on the area was something the residents were accustomed to, but a six-foot-four, daffodil-crested scarecrow of a fellow would bring them all out in the streets to gawk. There were people involved who wouldn't appreciate the attention. "Nothing personal," the officer insisted, "but we're going to do this as discreetly as we can."

"I'll wear a hat." Renny produced a knit stocking cap from his coat pocket. With one energetic tug, he yanked it over the bright yellow cloud of hair, squeezing it close to his head.

"Now you can come along," Terrebonne agreed. "This is really something out of Charles Dickens." Renny was impressed that the detective had even heard of Charles Dickens, but he had learned to expect almost anything from the little man. In checking over the list of employees that Bernie had supplied, Terrebonne had not only spoken with Renny's co-workers at the scenery warehouse, but he'd even called Renny's art instructor at a junior college he'd attended back in Alabama. Renny had been cleared as a possible suspect, but the thoroughness Terrebonne demonstrated inspired an unqualified respect for the unpretentious detective. He knew his stuff. He had also tracked down the real thieves.

Terrebonne parked his unmarked police car in the street beside an abandoned grocery store with boarded-up windows and an array of candy wrappers and empty beer cans littering the doorway. "We go in the back way." He led Susie, Renny and Bernie through a narrow walkway between that building and the next, carefully stepping over more trash and old blankets, which some homeless soul had transformed into a sleeping pallet.

"You sure we're not walking into something dangerous?" Bernie saw nothing to indicate that other police officers, or any kind of security, would protect them if trouble broke out.

"I have some uniformed men inside." Terrebonne directed the trio hurriedly through the unlocked door at the rear of the old building. "We just want it to look like business is going on as usual," he explained. "These folks have been coming in all morning." Now he stepped past one uniformed officer who had been standing unobtrusively by the back door and led the group past a wooden partition into a large open room.

"My designs!" Susie stared at the rows of glossy photographs tacked along one wall. Obviously someone had photographed them during the first break-in. Several racks of completed dresses hung in one corner of the room while five sullen-faced black women sat stonily on a bench beside them. In the center of the room several grocery counters had been converted to cutting tables and now stood strewn with fabric remnants and paper patterns. The stolen fabric-swatch booklets sat in tagged plastic bags. Crammed along the remaining wall were eight vintage sewing machines where the gowns had been sewn together.

"I assume these folks aren't making the minimum wage." Renny eyed the silent women who apparently had been the seamstresses. Now he knew what Terrebonne had meant about Charles Dickens. This sweatshop for putting together the stolen designs was as dismal as the workhouses Dickens had written about in his novels. The putrid smell of decaying garbage permeated the building. The lights by which these women worked were bare bulbs suspended over the tables and sewing machines. The floor in the building was cold and damp; no heating system alleviated the chill in the room.

"These women were simply trying to eke out a living doing piecework for the shop manager. They aren't in any real trouble," Terrebonne insisted. "From what we can tell, they had no idea they were working on stolen designs."

"Then if they aren't in trouble—" Susie glanced over at the five women "—what are they doing here?" She had assumed they were under arrest for being involved in the theft.

"They don't want to leave yet," Terrebonne replied. "They say there are four other women who will be bringing in work they finished at home. These women don't want the others to walk in here and get frightened. They asked if they could wait."

"What about the guy you mentioned, the one who runs this place. Where's he? For that matter—" Bernie bristled at the prospect of facing the man who'd injured Susie "—who is he?"

"His name is Ralph Tanner," Terrebonne disclosed. He watched with bright, curious eyes to see if either of the Costains made a connection. When they didn't recognize the name, Terrebonne continued. "Your handyman Eugene has an older brother—Ralph. He also has a sister-in-law who occasionally worked for your wife," he told Bernie. "Between the two of them, they came up with this scheme. They copied the designs for about twenty costumes, duplicated the patterns for the gowns from the ones Rosie had, then sold the whole set to a krewe from Houma," Terrebonne said, naming a city sixty miles from New Orleans where lavish Mardi Gras celebrations were extremely popular. "I wouldn't be surprised if the sewing machines and all the material turn out to be stolen, too. We're checking on it."

"Then they waited for a chance to steal the head-pieces and all the fancy stuff." Renny nodded thoughtfully. "Pretty slick."

"If they had taken the costumes Susie made all the way to Houma," Bernie noted, "there wasn't much of a chance that we'd see them in the news and recognize them."

"If you ever did," Terrebonne added, "the Tanners would be long gone with a heck of a lot of money. Backtracking from the Houma krewes would have been tough. If it hadn't been for Susie here—" Terrebonne patted her shoulder "—walking into that workroom before they took the costumes, the scheme might just have worked. Ralph Tanner may be a coolheaded thief, but having to deal with an assault charge scared him off real quick."

"What about Eugene?" Susie wondered what role her affectionate helper had in the plot. The big fellow with his droopy smile and hangdog expression had not seemed like the type to get involved in anything illegal, but Susie wasn't sure. All she had seen of her assailant was that he was big.

"Eugene is being held as an accomplice of sorts," Terrebonne reported. "He wasn't actually there during the crime. He had inadvertently bragged about the security and pulley system to the point that Ralph knew the setup inside and out. Ralph's wife knew the production schedule from looking at Rosie's records. When your dad and Eugene put in the big window pulley, Ralph put the pressure on Eugene to disconnect the alarm system for the night. Eugene insisted he didn't know what Ralph was up to, and he sure didn't think you were in any danger. He really isn't very bright," Terrebonne added with a frown. "Unfortunately stupid and innocent aren't the same."

Two more women carrying papers bags full of completed sewing stepped in through the rear door, then froze in their tracks when the uniformed police officer stepped out of the shadows and directed them into the lighted workroom. Wearily they looked from the officer to the five other seamstresses, then to Susie and her companions. "Relax, ladies." Terrebonne proceeded to explain the situation to them.

They listened to him, wide-eyed, then one of the women stared forlornly at her bag and burst into tears. "You mean we ain't goin' to get paid for all this?" she whimpered. "I've got young'uns to feed. I do such lovely work." In her grief, she fumbled in the bag and withdrew a gown. The beadwork on the bodice had been done with a cheap grade of sequins and glass beads, Susie noted, but the needlework was exceptionally well done. Susie moved close to the woman and nodded appreciatively.

"You did excellent work." She felt her own eyes fill with sympathetic tears. The woman had to have spent hours laboring on the garment, and now she would receive nothing.

Before Terrebonne finally took the Costains and Renny back to the costuming company, a reporter from the *Times* arrived with a photographer at his side. Word of the arrest of Ralph Tanner and his wife had been passed on to them from the crime bureau. With Mardi Gras balls already under way, the story of the costume theft would make an intriguing news feature.

Terrebonne managed to block any photographs of the women who had worked on the garments, insisting that they had suffered enough. They didn't need their misfortune made public. However, the shop itself was photographed. They even got a shot of Susie examining the completed gowns.

"How about them, miss?" the reporter pressed her. "How does the copy compare to the original?" In spite of the inferior materials and the cost-cutting omissions in interfacings and linings, the gowns were passable. Beneath the lavish headpieces and collars that Susie had made, the gowns probably would have worked.

"I'd like my mother to see these," Susie replied honestly. "She would be impressed by the skill and the effort these ladies put into their work." Susie took a moment to point out differences in the details between these gowns and the original designs, so both the reporter and the photographer could get the information. Later, while they interviewed her father, Susie knelt by the row of dejected seamstresses, carefully taking down their names and addresses.

"If my mother could possibly use you," she promised the women, "I'll have her get in touch with you. All of you should be making decent money when you do such careful sewing." Even with her encouraging words, the women's expressions were somber.

When the story appeared in the newspaper that evening, Susie became acutely aware of other victims in the scheme—the krewe members from Houma who had already made an initial payment on the gowns and costumes. They had unwittingly been taken in by Ralph Tanner and his wife. With three weeks remaining until their scheduled balls, there would be no way to begin again.

"Could you do anything to help us?" Three Houma krewe members and their wives arrived at the Costains' the next day. "We've been working all year with car washes and dinners to raise extra money for this year's ball. The families of all the court members have put so much money and effort into this already...." Each of her visitors dreaded facing the families if they returned to Houma without some hope.

When Susie called Detective Terrebonne, he said that the dresses were needed for evidence, but since the krewe had paid for them, it was reasonable to have the costumes to wear for the balls. He also agreed to turn over to Susie all the fabric that had remained in the sweatshop. "I guess this means those Houma folks got to you," he teased Susie. "They called me, begging me to do something," he told her. "Since they were your designs, it's up to you what happens to them. Are you going to try to finish the costumes?" He already knew the answer.

"I can't do the same designs as I did for the krewes that ordered the costumes originally. They ordered something unique." Susie cautioned the Houma krewe members who had sat anxiously while she made the phone call to the detective. "And I'll have to check with my dad to see if he can work on some underwiring. The designs will have to be simple...." Susie didn't need to go on. Already two of the wives were daubing tears of relief from their eyes.

"We'll take anything you do," they agreed.

"And next year, we'll come to you early and have you do the whole thing for us. We were so impressed with those designs...." The wistful look on the woman's face was praise enough.

"YOU HAVE TO BE CRAZY." Sy Avery's indignant response wasn't quite what Susie had expected. He had finally managed to arrange a break in his schedule that coincided with hers. "You're going back to work tomorrow, *and* you've taken on twenty more costumes?" His deep brown eyes examined her expression closely. "Your doctor suggested you take it easy." He shook his head in bewilderment. "What you're doing is suicidal. You'll exhaust yourself."

"You should have seen those people, Sy." Susie stood in the kitchen of her apartment, scooping ground coffee into the paper filter. While the aroma of brewing coffee began to fill the air, Susie tried to explain why she could not refuse to help the Houma krewe members. "They've been planning this all year," she stressed. "Some of them have daughters or granddaughters in the courts. For them it's a once-in-a-lifetime thing. They're not after costumes that are stupendous—just costumes. A lovely, fancy headpiece—anything to make the evening memorable."

Sy's jaw muscles flexed as he listened to her. The uncompromising look in his eyes eased momentarily. "I admire your motives," he said quietly. "I also question anything that puts an added strain on you. I even hesitated to come over tonight because I didn't want to tire you by keeping you up late. You're supposed to get a lot of rest."

"I'm glad you came." Susie hoped her gentle response would erase some of the concern in Sy's expression.

"I missed you." He came toward her and took her in his arms. "The last time I saw you was when those guys were carrying you out for X rays. That was really grim." He held her close and stroked her smooth dark hair. "Of course, I did see the photos of you in the paper in that feature on the robbery. However," he said in a low voice, "it is less than adequate to hug a newspaper."

"I missed you, too." Susie could hear the deep steady rhythm of his heartbeat. "I guess you noticed that my mother was not too pleased when you called to ask about me."

"That's putting it mildly."

"She thinks you're the father of Michelle's baby—at least she thought so until I cleared that up. She was afraid for me." Susie looked up at him. "She wanted to protect me from you."

"I'm trying to protect you from you." Sy looked at her solemnly. "You've got dark circles under your beautiful eyes, my lady." He kissed her lightly. "You look like you've lost more weight. You're recovering from a concussion—and you decide to go back to Blaine's and add twenty costumes to your already ruthless schedule. Why is it that you can't say no to anybody else but me?" He smiled at last.

"If I recall, I was saying yes in our last close encounter," Susie corrected him. "And you were saying no. Have I wasted away so much that you've lost interest?" She slid one hand seductively up his chest and slipped a fingertip through the closure at his throat so she could feel the softness of his skin. Instantly the pulsing beat beneath her touch seemed to accelerate.

"Don't play games." Sy caught her wrist firmly. "All it takes is the sound of your voice or that soft glow in your eyes to make me want to lose myself in you. I've made it pretty clear how I feel about making love with you. Touching you, loving you," he said in a voice far softer than the grip he had on her wrist, "is something I take very seriously."

"I'm sorry," Susie realized that she had chosen the wrong time to be playful. Sy was genuinely worried about her health. He was not about to start something that it would not be wise to finish.

"Besides," he continued, loosening his grip and slipping his hand gently over her arm. "I don't intend to be loving you one moment, then leaving you the next. When I finally hold you, I'll hold you the entire night. When I wake up, you'll be there beside me, sweet and warm and beautiful. And before the sun rises, if you look at me like you are right now, I'll love you all over again." Susie stood spellbound listening to him.

Sy indicated the kitchen. "Remember the coffee?" he asked her. "One cup and I'll be on my way, and you can get some sleep." Almost as if she were awakening from a trance, Susie forced her eyes from Sy's handsome face. There would be a time when it would be the last thing she saw at night and the first thing she would wake to see in the morning light. But right now—the coffee.

CHAPTER ELEVEN

THE NEXT WEEK the roller-coaster pace accelerated as costumes for two more balls were completed and picked up, and the additional twenty for the Houma krewes began to take shape. Susie had telephoned New York asking one distributor after another for any available imported plumage. She had finally located one importer who was able to ship her a freight-damaged assortment from which she had salvaged enough usable feathers to add some elegant touches to the new pieces. Sympathetic local suppliers had searched their supply shelves for sequins and beading to add to her stock.

"Next year..." Susie had promised each of the cooperative suppliers, "I'll remember how you helped me, and I'll give you some big orders." Even with the additional materials, there was no way Susie could match the excellence of the costumes she had designed and worked on throughout the year, but they would do. Like the dresses beneath them, they would be passable. If the lighting was carefully placed and no one inspected the work closely, the costumes still would make a fantasy come true for the courts and families of the Houmas krewes. "Next year...." Susie repeated what had become a litany. "Next year...we'll do it right."

"We've been asked to attend the King's Champagne Party." Rosie was white-faced when she reached the workroom where Susie and Bernie were using the hot-glue machine to apply trimmings to the new costumes. It wasn't the technique they preferred, but it did save time.

"Why should we be there?" Susie asked without looking up. "That's a closed party—just the court."

"Maybe Uncle Leo and Aunt Jo want some family there," Rosie said pointedly. "They may have something to say." Susie now glanced over to see the anxious look on Rosie's face. It would be difficult enough for Uncle Leo to make public Michelle's pregnancy. In all the years that Leo and Bernie Costain had been involved with krewes and parades and balls, the rest of the family had always participated in the activities and the work. Having to be the one to disrupt a tradition would be an ordeal Leo and his family shouldn't have to face alone.

"We'll go," Bernie said calmly. "Whatever they've worked out, we'll be there to stick by them. I just hope Michelle is going to get through this all right." Bernie said it so softly that Susie almost missed his statement. Her mind had been racing ahead, trying to estimate how much time the party would take and how her costume production would be affected by an evening taken up elsewhere.

One look at Rosie's face made it apparent that Rosie had told one person Michelle's secret. Susie reached out and squeezed her mother's hand with affection, relieved that Rosie had not kept the worrying to herself. Telling Bernie, sharing with him, was not a betrayal of Michelle. It was an intrinsic part of their marriage—a combining of their strengths to face the world. "Someone who understands...." Susie's thoughts turned to Sy. "Someone who is always on my side...." She recalled how he'd cautioned her against too strenuous a work load, how he responded to her touch but would not let his desires threaten her health—or her future. Sy was a remarkable man, and he had seen in Susie something remarkable, too.

"I'll call Leo back and tell him we'll be there." Rosie pressed a gentle kiss on the top of Bernie's head. "I guess that means another round of adjusting the fitting schedules," she added. "There's always something..." she murmured to herself as she walked through the workroom, heading back to the headless, legless dress forms that had stood in for so many human shapes over the years.

"Have you thought any more about giving up your job at Blaine's?" Bernie had broached the subject again. "These Houma krewes will be back next year," he noted. "That newspaper piece on the sweatshop has made a lot of people anxious to see our work and find out why it was good enough to try to steal. We could be in for a big year."

Susie had been going nonstop since she had resumed work in the advertising department. "Right now, my stool at the store is the only quiet place I have to sit down all day." Susie avoided a direct answer. "There I can sit and draw without having to concentrate so much. My cubicle is my retreat from the rest of the world." The words were intended half jokingly, but Susie realized that Blaines's was precisely that—a place where she could spend an entire day absorbed in detailed drawing—without being required to exert either her talents or her emotions. It was not the "career" she pretended it was; it was actually just a job that let her put so much of herself on hold. It gave her a sense of external order to her life that contrasted drastically with the hectic, erratic pace of the costuming business. It demanded very little, except for her time. Now there wasn't time enough.

"Just keep your options open." Bernie backed off the subject. "That concussion business may have been a blessing in disguise," he observed. "Now if you find that you want to quit at Blaine's, you have a good excuse. No one would fault you for taking care of your health."

"I'm really not too concerned what anyone thinks," Susie answered, without any element of defiance. "If I decide to leave Blaine's," she asserted, "I won't need an excuse. I'll make a choice and stick to it. Grown-ups don't need excuses," Susie chuckled. "Or a note from their parents."

Bernie looked at her thoughtfully, then turned his attention back to the project they were gluing. He could tell that in his daughter's mind the wheels were turning. Expanding the business to a full-time occupation meant that Susie would assume final responsibility for everything, from designs and stock orders to dealing with clients and keeping accounts. There would be a staff of employees to recruit and train, and increased storage and equipment to oversee. It was a formidable prospect. But the wheels were turning, Bernie noted with a slight smile.

ON FRIDAY NIGHT, Susie stood before the mirror, puckering her lips and making a disapproving scowl. The dinner dress she had planned to wear to the King's Champagne Party hung loosely on her body. She had been losing weight again. There had been too many skipped meals and late hours, and her slim body was showing the consequences. Skillful makeup and a lot of cheek blush had been able to conceal the weariness in her face, but the few missing pounds couldn't be camouflaged. Hastily she slipped out of the dress and returned it to the closet. There were other dresses in smaller sizes to choose from. Deliberately Susie picked out one with inset lace at the waist and puffed sleeves. It was a bit fussy for her taste, but the style would alter her proportions and make her appear less slim.

When the Costains entered the dining room at the Country Club reserved for the champagne party, the atmosphere was not the somber one they had expected. In addition to the king, white-haired Ernest Dufrene, and the court members, there were a number of other invited guests mingling with the Triton krewe honorees. A string quartet played lilting music, and the table was lavishly bedecked with cascades of flowers and with candelabra. This was not going to be the traditional court gathering, nor was it going to be a solemn occasion. The beaming faces of Uncle Leo and Aunt Jo were not forced. This was a celebration.

"The reason we've made some changes in the customary party," Uncle Leo announced, as the krewe captain, to the gathering, "is because this is not what one might call the normal run of events. For years, I've looked forward to the day that my daughter would be honored on the court of a krewe such as Triton. Having her become its queen was an even greater honor." He looked over the assembled guests as he spoke.

Susie glanced around the room looking for Michelle, but she was not present. From Leo's cheerful countenance, Susie had to conclude there was nothing negative about Michelle's absence, but it seemed very peculiar to be going on without the queen.

"Well," Leo continued, "Michelle went along with the dreams her mother and I had woven for her. From time to time she talked about dreams of her own, but I guess we were just too caught up to listen." His smile became more pensive. "We were busying planning a life *for* her, not *with* her." His eyes now seemed to light on the face of every young woman in the audience. "Fathers are like that." He said good-naturedly. "We want to make dreams come true for our children."

Susie didn't have to turn her head to know that her own father would be standing next to her, nodding in agreement. Rosie would be holding his arm, gently squeezing it, acknowledging that mothers are like that, too.

"I guess time sneaked up on us, and the dreams Michelle's mother and I had must be put aside. Michelle has been living her own life in the real world," Uncle Leo said. "She found a man she loves, went off to Mobile and married this fellow, and now she's expecting a baby. She's also resigning as Triton's Queen."

Nothing in Leo's statement was unexpected, except for the mention of Mobile. Susie knew that Sy had taken Michelle along on his trip to that city, but he had never discussed what Michelle had done there. Sy had said he'd worked, taking photos for certain krewes that had commissioned him. In the past month, he had gone back again to show the proofs and to meet with those krewes for final orders. He had not mentioned anything about Michelle on the second trip. *This has* nothing to do with Sy, Susie said to herself. All she had to do was to recall his warm embrace and the pulsing of his heart, and her own pulse settled down to its normal rate. What she hated most was that she felt the familiar suspicion building again, and that somewhere deep inside she feared he would let her down. *Just like Richard did....* She regretted the presence of the old memories. She wished she could control them and keep them from plaguing her, but they still had a hold on her. She could relive in vivid detail the harrowing night when Richard had tried to force her into lovemaking, knowing she was passionate and trusting—and not ready. *Old scars....* Susie pressed her hands over her chest to subdue a new barrage of anxiety as the face of Richard Martin loomed in her mind.

"My new son-in-law is a bit difficult to keep track of sometimes," Leo Costain continued, looking expectantly at the rear door of the banquet room. "They were supposed to be here." As Leo spoke, the door opened and Sy stepped in.

"I'm not late, am I?" He strode up one side of the room and joined Leo on the raised platform. Susie stood frozen in horror as the two men greeted each other.

"Oh, no," Rosie breathed as she reached over and grasped Susie's arm.

Sy turned and scanned the faces of the guests. He stopped when he located Susie. In an instant his smile vanished, then he leaped forward. "Are you all right?" He grasped her by her shoulders. "You're as white as a sheet." He held her right arm while her mother steadied Susie from the other side, and they led her over to a

chair and made her sit down. Leo came right after them
with a glass of water.

"It's that concussion. I know it is." Bernie's
alarmed voice came from behind Sy. The chilly glare in
Rosie's eyes indicated it was something else completely.

Susie felt the entire room receding, just as it had the
night of the attack. She couldn't take her eyes from
Sy's face. She couldn't even draw a breath. Confront-
ed with something too painful to absorb, her mind had
rebelled, cushioning her with a wall of dull sensations.
Everything moved in slow motion. Sounds were
muffled and a feeling of numbness gripped her whole
body.

"Get me a paper bag," Sy called without releasing
her. "Quickly!" He watched her breathing again and
again, but not seeming to catch enough air to fill her
lungs. "She's hyperventilating," he added, as he
grasped her hand, feeling its icy coolness.

Susie heard a high-pitched sound, like the wail of a
distant siren. The next object in her line of vision was a
large brown bag being thrust over her nose and mouth.
"Breathe into this." Sy calmly talked to her while the
bag rose and fell with each gasp. "Steady now. Try in-
haling through your nose and exhaling through your
mouth." The bag expanded and contracted as Susie followed his directions. Finally the feeling of panic eased,
and her breathing slowed to a steady, even pace. The
ringing sound faded away, and the peculiar bright haze
that had surrounded everything disappeared. Defined
forms took the place of the shimmering patterns of
color.

"Now will you believe me when I say you've been pushing yourself too hard," Bernie said as he knelt at Susie's side, while she leaned against Sy's arm. Rosie still hadn't spoken a word, nor had she relinquished her protective hold of Susie's hand.

"Just what I've been telling you," Sy concurred. "So soon after your injury—Susie, something has to give."

From behind Sy, Leo peered over at Susie's face. The color was returning, so he gave her a relieved smile. "If you don't mind getting back to business, they're here," he said as he tapped Sy on the shoulder.

"Can you manage?" Sy directed his comment to Bernie. "I've got to shoot some pictures."

"We've managed for years," Rosie said under her breath. Bernie ignored her comment and nodded and smiled, feeling the crisis was over. "Go on. Go ahead," he said, waving Sy off reassuringly. "We'll stay right here with her."

Once again, the party atmosphere resumed as Leo signaled for the string quartet to play. Their rendition of "The Wedding March" brought everyone to silent attention. This time, the banquet-room doors opened to admit Michelle, who walked in on the arm of a slightly balding young man whose smile was as wide as her own.

"My son-in-law, Paul Asprodites. He's a geologist working with off-shore oil rigs in the gulf," Leo said to introduce the young man.

Susie stared at the fellow, while the impact of Leo's statement slowly sank in. Amid the wave of applause and joyful wishes, Rosie's and Susie's eyes met for a single solemn instant. Susie looked over at Sy, who had been snapping pictures of the happy couple. In the moment his gaze met hers, his expression shifted from one of affection and concern to a remote mask of controlled politeness. He had seen the transformation when the alarm and distrust in her eyes had changed to relief— then to guilt. Susie had doubted him again—and he knew it.

Sy continued with professional diligence, taking pictures of Michelle and Paul. Leo talked with Bernie, reminding him that daughters sometimes pick the unlikeliest candidates for husbands. "When Michelle and this guy were dating at Tulane, her mother and I thought he was a real oddball. He'd go off on expeditions searching for oil or looking at rocks. He missed Michelle's birthday party and showed up late for everything. Then he dropped out of sight for a few months. We thought we were rid of him. But he was just working on some off-shore rigs. Michelle was so set on him, she went on and married him before he left. We were talking when we should have been listening again," Leo confessed. "Turns out he's a hotshot consultant. He makes more money than I do." Leo was obviously reconciled to the fact that his son-in-law, the oddball, was going to take good care of his daughter. Nothing else mattered.

Susie stayed close to her mother throughout most of the photo session. When the next speaker stood, the Krewe of Triton was no longer Uncle Leo's concern. Ernest Dufrene, Triton's King, had an announcement of his own.

"Since Michelle can no longer be Triton's Queen," the elderly gentleman said with a sparkle in his eyes, "we and the krewe council met and discussed our difficulty. The ball is three weeks from tonight, and the parade will follow the next Wednesday. There are costumes to think of and rehearsals for the ball...and always—'' the wrinkles around his eyes deepened as he smiled ''—there is the problem of money. However, we did come up with an excellent solution.'' Now the pale blue eyes of the distinguished man sought and found Susie.

''There is one among us who embodies the spirit of Mardi Gras.'' Ernest looked squarely at her as he continued. ''She has helped create more wonders than I can estimate. Her costume designs are so fine that as you all know they were almost stolen recently. I understand that Susie is very busy, but for someone who is so familiar with Mardi Gras, it would take very little to step into the role.'' He paused a moment then added. ''Of course, it does help that Susie wears the same size gown as Michelle—and the title would stay in the family, so to speak.'' By now every face in the room was turned toward Susie. She could not see Sy's expression. His face covered by the camera that clicked and whirred and was aimed directly at her.

''Would you honor us, Susie Costain, by serving this year as Triton's Queen?'' Ernest accompanied the offer with a grand sweeping gesture of his hand. It was extended to Susie.

There was a moment of silence as everyone awaited her reply. Susie couldn't move. All she wanted was the eyes to look elsewhere—anywhere but at her. Then the applause began as cheers of approval and encouragement filled the room. Several people rushed forward to congratulate her, as the tension in the room dissolved into renewed gaiety. Susie glanced over the shoulder of one well-wisher at the grinning face of her father. "Why fight it?" he mouthed the words with a good-natured shrug.

There never was an opportunity for Susie to regain control of the situation. The assumption was made; she was the perfect one to rule as Triton's Queen. Even if she was given another chance to respond, she knew she could not refuse. Everything would work out so smoothly, from the costuming to the family pictures. A tragedy would be avoided, and a tradition would be upheld. A Costain would save the day. Susie shook her head slowly as she remembered Sy's declaration—that she couldn't say no to anyone, except to him.

"I'd like to talk with you," Sy whispered, after he had completed several pictures of the new queen and her court. They were informal shots of Susie and the others, but even so, Sy had worked with patience, tilting a chin or altering the lighting in order to get the effect he wanted. Now his official duties were over, he wanted to see Susie alone.

"You did it again, didn't you?" He looked at her steadily. "You started putting suppositions together, and you created a monster. For an instant that monster was me." Sy had guessed the cause of her hyperventilation spell. It was no leftover reaction from the concussion; it was another kind of trauma.

"I'm so sorry." Susie could hardly speak. The pain and anger in Sy's eyes made her ache all over. "I don't know why I felt that way. It simply happened. I couldn't stop it."

"It tears me apart to see you like that." Sy's voice

quavered slightly as he spoke. "I get so angry at that Richard creep for betraying you...for shaking your confidence and starting all this mess. If he walked up here, I could do something about it. I could punch him out and feel like we've evened the score." Sy's dark eyes seemed to burn with hostility. "But the Richard I'd meet now isn't the one in your head. He's still frozen back there in time, still hurting you and still making you frightened. Here I am, loving you so much and watching you suffer. You have to let go of him, Susie." Sy was almost pleading. "You have to put *his* face on the monsters you imagine—then you have to drive them out. You're punishing me and yourself for something that happened years ago. It has to end."

"I know it does." The anguish in her voice echoed his own.

"I used to think he'd just made you cautious about sex." Sy spoke more steadily than before. "But he was much more thorough than that. He's made you so aware of your special vulnerability that you don't trust your own instincts. Your instincts are right—but because you were wrong before, you're afraid to believe in your own judgment." After a brief pause, he went on. "You don't want to end up like Felicia—second-guessing every move you make, or every move I make. You're so damaged by what he did, you bury yourself in work or with things that don't require a real choice. You live by default, Susie. *You* are the last priority on your list."

Susie brushed away a quivering tear that had formed along her lower eyelid. Her lips were drawn in a tight line in an attempt to steady herself.

"Making an intimate commitment is not what scares

you, my love." He took her hand and pressed it to his chest. "In spite of that creep, you have already made a commitment to me. It's trying to make it survive in the real world that's the scary part," he noted. "That's the part I hate him for. He makes you recoil every time you feel threatened. Its not enough that his ghost makes you miserable, but he's got you dragging in *my* ghosts as well—Felicia, Michelle—and he's turned them into monsters as stupid and manipulative as he was. And it's all in your head. I can't meet him in there and drive him out. You have to do that, Susie," Sy stressed. "You have to take some time to think, to put your priorities in order. Then become a fighter. Go after what you want. I can't run interference for you. I've been holding off and trying to wait this out," he admitted. "I didn't want you to make any mistakes or take any risks," he added softly. "But now," he said evenly, "I'm going to do what you do—bury myself in my work for a few weeks. You take charge. Drive out the monsters once and for all. Decide what you want. Take responsibility for your own well-being. Then come after me."

Susie studied Sy's solemn, uncompromising face. The melancholy expression in his eyes was like the one she had seen there months before, when she had told him she was too tied up with work to have a serious relationship with anyone. Sy had then made his deal with Michelle to become public companions so she could keep her marriage a secret and still fulfill her obligations as Triton's Queen. Now as Susie saw the resigned sag in his broad shoulders, she regretted all that he had gone through in order to let her come to love him at her own pace. She had moved too slowly, and with every step she took, the specter of Richard Martin had taken one, too.

"Look how thin you are—" Sy trailed his hand up her arm "—and how tired you are." He slid his arm around her and held her against his chest for a moment. He pressed his cheek against her smooth dark hair, then released her. "It's your move, Susie Costain." He spoke with a distinct hoarseness. "You and I don't belong at the bottom of your list, not separately or together. Don't come looking for me until you've put us at the top. I'll even take second ranking to you." He managed to smile. "But I want to know that you've sorted out the rest of your concerns, too. I'm on your side," he emphasized. "But it's your turn to run the show." He didn't touch her again. He stood and looked at her closely, as if he wanted to imprint her image on his mind. Then quietly Sy left her alone.

Back in the banquet room, the court members and guests made their farewells. Bernie was holding Susie's coat and looking around the room for her when she returned. "You look tired, Souci." He draped the coat around her shoulders. "I think you'd better check in with the doctor tomorrow and let him have another look at that concussion. That bout of hyperventilating really scared me." He waved across the room for Rosie to hurry along.

"I wasn't too thrilled about it, either," Susie answered. "And I'm not thrilled about being Triton's Queen," she added. "I feel like I was railroaded into it, with everyone waiting and staring at me."

"You'll survive it all, Souci," he insisted. "Sometimes being in the spotlight has its advantages." Bernie escorted her to the exit. "It makes us find out just what we are capable of doing. Having an audience may have pressured you into a position of honor that you've ducked successfully for years." Bernie hugged her as they walked. "But they couldn't have picked a better queen, and we both know it. Your whole life revolves around the Mardi Gras. This isn't going to change you. It's just going to be another moment in a very special life."

When her father put it that way, Susie could feel the tension ebb. If she were just a young debutante, being Triton's Queen would have seemed like the high point of her life. After that, all other social events would seem anticlimactic. But Susie was a grown woman with talents spilling out into two careers. She'd been on the other side of the spotlight for years. She could appreciate the pageantry without being overwhelmed by it. She had other concerns far more significant—ones that extended far beyond a social season. Now she could accept the position for what it was—a temporary honor, a moment of magic—then she would proceed with her life.

"We'll have to start feeding you or the gown won't fit." Rosie was already making plans as she joined Susie and Bernie at the door. "Now what has to be done with the backpiece?" She recalled the arching sea-horse structure that surmounted the head and shoulders of the wearer with imposing elegance.

"It already fits," Bernie said with a wry smile. Susie had stood in for Michelle when they adjusted it. "See how easy this is going to be." He paraded his ladies to the car.

BILL TERREBONNE picked Susie up in front of Blaine's the next day in his unmarked police car. Susie was scheduled to testify at the Grand Jury hearing against the Tanner brothers and their accomplice, Ralph Tanner's wife, Elizabeth. The jury would decide whether there was sufficient evidence for the burglary and assault charges to be brought to court. If so, the jury would make an indictment, and the trial would be scheduled. Then Susie would have to testify again.

"The attorney who's representing these three is hoping to have the assault charge dropped." Terrebonne told her what to expect. "He'll try to get you to say that you may have slipped or fallen back into the bird roost when you tried to back away from Ralph Tanner."

"I didn't have a chance to back away," Susie replied. "I didn't even see him coming until he slammed into me."

"That's just what you have to tell the jury," Terrebonne recommended.

"But I also didn't see the face of the man who hit me." Susie was worried. She remembered seeing the shape of a man's body. "I can't identify Ralph Tanner as the one who did it." She didn't want to be a poor witness, but she couldn't accuse a man whose face she'd never seen.

"We have other proof that it was him," Terrebonne assured her. "Your parrots had hair and skin from the guy. There are fingerprints. All you have to do is tell the jury exactly what happened, just like you did when we took your deposition. Don't worry about helping the system work," he comforted her. "We've done all the groundwork. The law may work a bit slow at times, but it does work. There will be hearings and more hearings, then a trial, then appeals, and these folks may be walking around out on bond for months.'' He parked the car and turned off the ignition. ''But they are the ones who did this. We have the proof. Sooner or later, they'll serve their time.''

Susie had not seen her former helper Eugene Tanner since the night before the assault. Like his brother and his brother's wife, Eugene had been charged with his part in the crimes, but none of them spent any time in jail. Just as Terrebonne had said, they were out on bond. The only restriction was that they were not to contact Susie or the Costains in any way, and they were not to go into the vicinity of the costuming company. Now Susie walked into the hallway next to the room where the Grand Jury was convening, and four somber faces turned toward her. One was the attorney that Terrebonne had mentioned, the others were the Tanner brothers and Elizabeth.

''Don't let them rattle you.'' Terrebonne turned into an antechamber where Susie would wait. ''They aren't even supposed to be here, much less have any access to you. Let me see what the heck is going on.'' He left her while he went out into the hallway again. Susie could hear the indistinct exchange of comments as Terrebonne challenged the attorney for having his clients standing there. Then the conversation became more subdued, and Susie couldn't hear whatever they were saying. When Terrebonne finally returned, she was pacing back and forth, trying to suppress the urge to peek into the hall.

''Supposedly they have a timing conflict,'' Terrebonne said, sounding unconvinced. ''I'd hoped to get you in and out of here without any confrontation,'' he apologized. "Don't worry. They won't be bothering you."

Susie saw the Tanner brothers once more before she left the building. She had done what Terrebonne had said; she went in and told the Grand Jury what she could remember of the assault. She identified items from her studio and from the sweatshop that Elizabeth and Ralph Tanner had operated. Then she was excused. As she stopped at the water fountain to sip some cool water and relieve the dryness in her mouth, the Tanner brothers came into the hallway from another room.

Eugene only looked at Susie apologetically and hung his head. Other than casting a fleeting glance, he could not let his eyes meet hers. He had liked her; once they had been friends. Ralph Tanner was another matter. Tall and broad like his younger brother, Ralph looked at her with cold angry eyes, as if he were the injured party and she the villain. He shifted his eyes from side to side, scanning the halls for any other occupant. For a moment Susie thought he was going to charge at her again.

"I'm right here." The wiry Terrebonne strutted up and stood by Susie's side, but his gaze was riveted on the face of Ralph Tanner. "Something you wanted to say, fella?" He looked steadily at the far larger man. "Just breathe at her and I'll have your tail in a cell," Terrebonne snapped.

Eugene took his brother's arm and tugged at it. Without changing his hostile expression, Ralph Tanner turned and stepped back into the side room.

"He wouldn't try anything," Terrebonne assured Susie. "He's just a chicken thief. A sneaky dude who got in over his head. We think his wife may have been the brains behind the whole operation. He's trying to blame someone besides himself so he picked *you*. He's probably facing a prison term and is just plain scared.''

''*He's* scared,'' Susie finally gasped. ''I was pretty scared myself,'' she admitted. ''Did you see how he glared at me?''

''All bluff.'' Terrebonne led her out to his car again. ''He's too much of a coward to make a move. He's a thief. He's beaten a couple of shoplifting raps, and he was thrown out of the army for stealing. Thieves are sneaky, but they aren't dangerous.''

''But he did hurt me before.'' Susie couldn't shake the feeling that her encounter with Ralph Tanner had brought.

''That was a fluke,'' Terrebonne assured her. ''He got caught in a room with you and he panicked. Guys like Tanner don't have the guts to come face to face with anyone. But if you ever see him hanging around,'' Terrebonne advised emphatically, ''you call me or call any cop. That will be the last time. He'll be in jail for harassment.''

''Just how long do you think this whole process will take?'' Susie was still uneasy knowing that Tanner would be strolling around New Orleans until he was convicted and sentenced.

''The way that the courts are booked up, it may take months.'' Terrebonne wouldn't pretend otherwise. ''But you have to do what the rest of us do,'' he stressed. ''Show up for the dates when you're called in to testify, and between times, forget it. Forget him. He's made this mess, and it will all work out. You go on with your life, and don't give him a minute's thought. What happens to him is *his* problem." Terrebonne spoke with authority.

"I've just never been looked at like that." Susie glanced back once more at the courthouse.

"The world is full of crazies," Terrebonne remarked. "But we can't let them scare us off the streets. The good guys have to tough it out and even stick out our chins once in a while." His wise, somber eyes reflected years of experience. "You may find it a bit scary to do your part in getting guys like Tanner off the street, but think how much more scary it would be if he went free because you *wouldn't* testify. He'd be out there with all the other creeps that people were too frightened to face in court. If you do your bit, another citizen will do his. That's how we keep the odds in our favor."

"I wasn't thinking of backing out," Susie assured him.

"Then don't let Tanner spook you." The detective opened the car door and let Susie slide into the passenger seat. "He just isn't worth it."

When Terrebonne pulled up in front of Blaine's again, Susie felt as if she had returned to civilization. Surrounded by the elegant merchandise and well-dressed shoppers, she made her way back to the elevator, pushing the courtroom and the Tanners out of her mind. There were people and projects that did deserve her attention, and Susie would follow Terrebonne's advice. Between court dates, she would try to forget. Sooner or later, the legal process would take care of the Tanners. It was their problem now, not hers.

CHAPTER TWELVE

"I'VE GOT SOMETHING you're going to like." Pascal leaped out of Renny's apartment when he saw Susie coming up the stairs.

"I hope it's edible." Susie smiled at the dapper sculptor. Instead of his sloppy workclothes, he wore slacks and a shirt and tie. "I'm starving. I know," she teased, "you brought dinner, and that's why you're dressed so nicely." Pascal stopped in his tracks and glanced down at his outfit.

"This is my successful-ish sculptor costume," he grinned. "I entered several designs to a big computer company that's bought up a block of prime downtown condemned property. They're going to rip everything down and build a spectacular new building on the site. Of course," he added casually, "they're including open gardens in tiers, and they were after pieces of sculpture to enhance the environment, so...."

"So they commissioned you to do them," Susie said excitedly. "Congratulations. You brought the designs to show me," she guessed.

"Actually I brought you a sack of parade throws." Pascal presented her with a neatly tied package made from a paper bag. "Renny and I are going down to the French Market to sit in the sunshine and get some sand-wiches. Care to join us?" Susie glanced at her watch.

She had left Blaine's a few minutes early. She had planned only to change clothes and drive straight out to the costuming company.

"When is the last time you saw sunshine like this?" Renny came out onto the balcony to join them. "Or should I say when did you stop long enough to enjoy the sunshine?" January had been filled with an unfortunate series of cold, rainy days punctuated only occasionally by sunshine. Most of those were missed while Susie sat in her cubicle at Blaine's.

"Put yourself on the top of the list." Susie imagined Sy's quiet voice whispering the words. She'd been considering his admonition to get her priorities in order and to take better care of her health.

"I think I will join you," Susie told her two friends. "And thank you for the parade throws." Susie took the package inside her apartment. She had collected a few herself from various clients. With the assortment Pascal had gathered, she would have an impressive delivery to make to Tony. For now, she had herself to think about, and watching the sun sink over the Mississippi from an outdoor café in the French Market was a special New Orleans treat that she would give to herself.

When the threesome strolled along the colonnade walkway of the French market, pausing to watch the women in one candy store pour out a batch of nutty syrup that hardened into the famed New Orleans' praline, Susie caught a glimpse of their reflection in the windows. With tall, frizzy-haired Renny on one side, dapper Pascal with his trimmed beard and slight build on the other and Susie in jeans and a loose-knit pullover, they looked like a very mismatched group. "Look at us...." Susie nudged her friends. "We look like we're going to a come-as-you-are party."

"The bizarre, the beautiful and the bourgeois." Renny pointed from one reflected image to another. "You've gone conservative on us." He explained his choice of bourgeois for Pascal. "In that bland outfit, who will ever know you're an oddball artist?" he teased. "With incipient fame?"

"My creditors," Pascal responded. "They'll notice when I start paying off all my bills."

"Come on, you two." Susie laughed as she moved farther along toward the outdoor café. The round metal tables with blue and red umbrellas fluttering in the breeze were already filled with groups of people as mismatched as Susie and her friends. Early evening in the Quarter brought all types together to watch the sun set and to enjoy the good food. Businessmen and shop owners sat elbow to elbow with artists and antique dealers. Accents and languages were as varied as the clothing. Tourists were the only ones who would stare when young men in pastel jeans and makeup strolled by, seeking one another's company. But the people who frequented the Quarter had a live-and-let-live attitude that neither judged nor ignored the passersby. It was a feeling of reserved respect for the differences that exist among people in a world that often demands conformity.

Over cold beer and hot gyro sandwiches oozing olives and cheese, Pascal sketched on paper napkins the designs for the sculptures he would do. "They wanted something particularly suited to New Orleans," he explained. "So I simply gave them some of the things I've used on the floats." There were giant elfin heads, beasts of varying degrees of ferocity and characters from myths and storybooks. They were done with the same exaggerated detail and altered proportions that Pascal had used so effectively on the floats. "For the folks who miss the Mardi Gras parades," Pascal noted, "there'll be some sense of it all year round. And these will be in bronze, not papier-mâché," he added. "We won't have to worry about being rained out."

"I think they're marvelous." Susie slid each sketch closer, then lined them up neatly. "Congratulations again." She leaned over and kissed Pascal on the cheek.

"Some guy is heading this way..." Renny muttered as he glanced over Susie's shoulder. "Looks like one of those creditors you were talking about," he teased Pascal. "Maybe he heard you had money and wants to get in line early to collect."

Susie tried to turn inconspicuously to get a look at the so-called "creditor." Instantly she realized that the man in the three-piece suit was not seeking Pascal, he was coming to see her.

"Susie," the slightly balding fellow said, smiling down at her, "I read about the theft in the newspaper. The Grand Jury indicted the guy for burglary and assault. It said you'd been knocked out. How are you?" Susie held her sandwich in midair. Very carefully she lowered it to her plate.

"I'm fine, Richard, just fine," Susie replied calmly. She was learning to take indictments and depositions in stride. Just as Detective Terrebonne had said, there would be lot of loose ends to take care of. The man who stared down at Susie was another loose end that she had never quite managed to file away and forget.

"These are my friends, Pascal Danos and Renny Castelot.'' Susie made the introductions smoothly. ''This is Richard Martin.'' As Pascal and Renny each rose slightly from their chairs and shook Richard's hand, Susie noted with relief that she felt only a peculiar detachment when she looked up at the man who had once been her fiancé. ''If you can find an empty chair, you're welcome to join us,'' Susie offered.

''Who is this guy?'' Renny whispered while Richard moved amid the outdoor tables trying to find an available chair.

''We used to date,'' Susie explained rapidly. ''He's an accountant.''

''Told you he looked like a creditor,'' Renny cackled.

''I guess your little business is going quite well,'' Richard commented, after returning with a chair. ''If your designs are good enough to steal, they must really be something.''

''The company is growing,'' Susie acknowledged, ''and the designs are good.'' She wasn't about to underrate herself. Richard simply smiled politely. Obviously he had nothing more to say about her work. Now that he was seated and had a closer look at Renny and Pascal, he didn't appear quite as confident as he had when he'd approached.

''Do you both work down here in the Quarter?'' Richard tried to get a conversation going. Pascal and Renny had each just bitten into their sandwiches and looked helplessly at one another while they chewed.

''They're both artists,'' Susie answered for them. ''Renny paints and Pascal sculpts.''

''Oh,'' Richard smiled and nodded again. He had nothing more to add.

"So how have you been?" Susie filled the awkward silence.

"Fine, just fine," Richard replied, obviously relieved to have a topic he could talk about. "The company is doing great. We've moved into new offices. Bigger and better," he boasted. Susie closely regarded the man who had once betrayed her trust. He was not aging well. Even in the few years since she'd last seen him, he had become heavier and lost enough hair to transform him from the handsome fellow she had loved into a sedate, rather innocuous-looking individual.

"I heard you'd married and have children." Susie gave him another opening.

"Boy and a girl." Richard nodded. "Fine kids. My wife really has her hands full," he finished, grinning contentedly.

By now, Susie had wearied of playing moderator. She really wasn't interested in what else Richard might have to say. She was hungry. While Richard sat with his all-purpose smile, she joined Renny and Pascal eating the delicious gyros.

"I want to leave you my business card." Richard reached into his jacket pocket and lifted out a printed card. "If your company is growing as well as you say it is—" he put the card on the table in front of her "—you'll be needing a good accounting firm to handle your books. Keep me in mind." He tapped the card with his forefinger. "Nice seeing you again," he concluded as he stood. "Pleasure to meet you gentlemen." He offered a hand to Renny, then to Pascal. Hurriedly they wiped the cheese from their hands and shook his in farewell. "See you again." He made the parting comment to Susie. "Don't forget the card."

"He's a real smooth operator," Renny sniffed in disgust when Richard had left the café. "How are you, Susie, and how about doing business with my company?" Renny mimicked Richard's businessman smile. "What a jerk."

"You used to actually date that guy?" Pascal rolled his eyes. "Perhaps he's had a lobotomy since then. Surely he would have bored you to death. Imagine, referring to 'your little business' like it's some kind of amusing hobby. He's obviously not a patron of the arts, and he can't have seen your work."

Susie finished her sandwich and poked at the business card with her greasy fingertip. Then she picked it up and methodically ripped it in half. "So much for old flames," she said jokingly as she deposited the pieces on the stack of crumpled napkins that would be discarded. Susie looked over the heads of the others seated in the café at the disappearing form of Richard Martin. He had said to keep him in mind. She had kept him in mind, far longer and with more devastating effects than he would ever realize. He still had no concept of what was important to her. "What a jerk," she finally said, echoing Renny's comment.

"Now how about some ice cream—my treat," Pascal offered.

"Too bad you didn't mention to that Richard guy that you were such a plutocrat," Renny teased. "He might have given you one of his cards, too."

"Then we'd just have two more pieces of garbage." Pascal pointed to the destroyed card. "Although I think I would have torn mine horizontally, just to add a little pizzazz." He winked. "You know how we artists are...."

Susie didn't wait to see the sunset. She sat on the levee looking down on the Mississippi and eating an ice-cream cone while the river sparkled with gold. Nice as the scene was, she decided she had indulged herself enough for one day. "I'm working on a couple of really tricky headpieces," she told her friends. "I'm anxious to see how they turn out. Then I've got to try on a gown and see if it fits yet. I think the gyro sandwich may have improved the chances of that." Rosie would be glad to know that Susie had picked up a little weight. She had not wanted to alter the sea-green queen's gown until the very last moment, and she had given Susie orders to eat, and eat well.

"You are going to get us tickets to this ball of yours?" Pascal reminded her. "I mean, it's doubly important, since not only are they your costumes but now you're the queen. We do take an interest in each other's work."

"You'll get tickets," Susie assured them. "And I'll even make you dance with me."

"An honor and a privilege," Pascal called after her. "Just remember to take off your shoes. I refuse to be dwarfed by a sea horse."

Susie found her long strides turning to leaps as she hurried back to her parked car. "Talk about being a jerk." She chastised herself for all the years she had let Richard Martin's betrayal make her retreat into herself. Now he was out hustling new business in the guise of friendly conversation. She couldn't believe she had let someone like him undermine her self-esteem. He was a manipulator. He was no monster. As Renny had said, he was a smooth operator—and a jerk.

Susie breathed in the river air and strode along the

street, feeling better with every step. She had met the ghosts and vanquished them. Now it was time to get on with the rest of her life. "Look out, Simon Avery," she said aloud, laughing. "I'm coming after you...like a moth to the flame," she repeated Sy's words. "And goodbye Blaine's," she whooped. "This lady is making some changes!"

"LOOKS GOOD TO ME, young woman," the doctor said, switching off the lighted panel after checking the latest X ray. Susie had asked the nurse to schedule a few additional minutes for the weekly checkups she had been undergoing since the assault. "Now what else did you want to talk about." He sat down at the desk and jotted a note to her medical records.

"I need some vitamin pills," Susie began. "I've been on the go a lot lately and I don't want to wear myself down."

Dr. Bennett nodded. "I'll give you the name of an excellent vitamin-mineral supplement that I use." He wrote down the information. "And I'd like a prescription for birth-control pills," she added, hoping her voice remained steady. Without looking up, Dr. Bennett pulled another piece of paper from the notepad and wrote the prescription. "We'll try these for now," he said, sliding the two notes to her. "If they don't cause any side effects, you can stick with them. Maybe later we'll try something else if they don't seem to suit you. As long as you're coming in for checkups, you should do quite well."

Susie stepped outside the office and let out a sigh. For Dr. Bennett, her request was simple enough, but for Susie, it marked the end of a long period of doubt. *No*

Russian roulette. She agreed with Sy that a child had a right to be wanted. Having sex was one matter; having babies was a totally different commitment. She was ready to take responsibility for the first choice. The second decision would have to be carefully weighed when the time came. This was Susie's time. It was her choice now to avoid leaving a child up to chance.

In the back seat of her car, Susie had stowed the package of parade throws that Pascal had acquired. Now she had added to those numerous other beads, doubloons and plastic souvenirs from the krewe members whose costumes she had made. Her customers had been generous, and the items they had supplied filled a large plastic bucket that had once been used for a shipment of spools of threaded sequins. Susie smiled as she drove into downtown New Orleans. She would go out to the lovely brick house on Audubon Park and light up the eyes of a young boy. Perhaps she would have a moment to speak with his father.

"Is Tony home?" Susie tried not to look surprised when Felicia Voison Avery opened the door instead of Sy's housekeeper, Francine.

"Surely you aren't one of the neighborhood children looking for a playmate?" Felicia's sultry face was less attractive when she smiled. There was a coldness in her eyes that made her smile into a chilling contradiction.

"I'm a friend of his." Susie refused to be intimidated. "I brought something that I had promised to give him."

Felicia's long lashes fluttered as her gaze settled on the paper package and the plastic bucket. "So I see." She made no move to invite Susie inside. "I'll make sure he gets them." Felicia's long nails gleamed a deep garnet color as she reached for the items.

Without thinking, Susie pulled the packages of parade throws closer. "I'd rather give them to him myself," she replied with the most polite tone she could sustain.

"Tony is ill with the chicken pox," Felicia explained with an impatient sigh. "He can't have visitors, but I'll be sure he gets the things you brought. Who should I say came by?" She held her arms out again to take the containers. This time Susie reluctantly surrendered them.

"Susie Costain. Tell him I'll call him tomorrow and that I hope he gets well soon."

"Costain...." Felicia pursed her lips thoughtfully as she placed the package and the bucket inside the doorway. "Didn't you call once before? Only you were after Simon...." A sly smile accompanied the comment. "Are you sure it isn't Simon you'd like to see now?"

"Is Sy here?" Susie brightened. He was precisely the person she'd like to see now.

"He's sleeping." Felicia seemed to enjoy delivering the news. "His schedule has been very strenuous lately, and he has to sleep in the afternoons since there are all the parades and balls going on. I really don't think he should be disturbed. This isn't urgent, is it?" She obviously knew it was not.

"No." Susie maintained her dignity. She knew Felicia was toying with her, but she was not about to lose her temper. "I'm sure I'll cross paths with him eventually." She stepped away from the door.

"I'm sure you'll make a point to." There was a sharp edge to Felicia's parting statement. "I do wish you wouldn't use my son as a means to get to his father. It's

a tactic that Simon would resent just as much as I do.''
Susie had turned to leave but that remark brought her
swirling around to face Felicia again.

"I don't use anybody." Susie bridled at the accusation. "In the first place, I came to deliver these to Tony
because I'm very fond of him. He will really enjoy them
now if he's confined to bed. I would have liked to have
seen his face when he opened the parcels. But since I
must miss out on that, I would have liked to have Sy
share that moment with him.'' Susie's increasing fury
did not cause her to raise her voice. Instead, she spoke
more softly to retain her self-control. "In the second
place," she continued, "I don't need to use any tricks to
get to see Sy. Adults don't manipulate each other. If
he's sleeping, fine. I couldn't agree more that he has a
hectic schedule. But if you'll be kind enough to tell him
I was here, I'm sure he will not resent anything about
that. And when I do see him,'' she finished, with an
iciness that matched the frost in Felicia's eyes, "I will
tell him how graciously I was received at his home.''

Felicia's smile never wavered. She simply turned away
and closed the French doors without another glance
through the beveled glass.

"Aaargh," Susie growled as she stormed over to her
car. "That woman...." She slammed the door behind
her. Then recalling there was a sick child and a sleeping
man inside, she controlled the urge to squeal the tires
and race the engine. As quickly as possible, she drove
out to the street and turned toward the river.

GERMAINE CONCIENNE SKILLFULLY uncorked the bottle
of chilled champagne and filled the three plastic cups.
Then Renny, Susie and Germaine raised the glasses to

the two huge panels that had been the last ones needed for Renny's movie-star series. "Congratulations," Germaine exclaimed, toasting the artists. The panels with Humphrey Bogart and Katherine Hepburn in their *African Queen* costumes glistened with the still-wet paint. "You did a marvelous job." Germaine praised the workmanship.

"Thank goodness we're through." Susie sipped the cool champagne and surveyed the portraits with satisfaction. "Remember, when the ball is over," she said, turning to Renny, "I'd like these two myself. Please don't let them get thrown out."

"What on earth will you do with ten-foot panels?" Germaine wondered. "Two of them!"

"Later in the spring, when we remodel the garage, I'll put them on the wall of my new office," Susie proposed. She had given Blaine's her two-week notice that she would be quitting her job right after Mardi Gras. She had decided to follow through with her father's suggestions and utilize both floors of the huge garage for the costuming business. If she were jumping into a full-time career as a costumer, she would like to have Humphrey and Katherine along for moral support.

"And what about that papier-mâché figure Pascal is supposed to save for you?" Renny recalled that Pascal had agreed to give Susie his huge float decoration of Judy Garland as Dorothy in *The Wizard of Oz*.

"She'll fit in nicely," Susie asserted. "I want the place to capture some of the spirit of Mardi Gras—the ball and parades, and not just the costumes. If we're going to be working on ideas all year round, then we'll need lots of inspiration. I'll start a museum of my own eventually."

"Is that what Pascal gave you all those parade throws for?" Renny asked. "Are they going into your museum?" He was sorry the minute he'd said it. Susie's smile quickly disappeared.

"I took those and some others to Tony, Sy Avery's son," Susie explained. "He's got the chicken pox, and he'll miss most of the fun. No parades, no balls. Just spots."

"I bet he loved the trinkets you gave him." Germaine tried to cheer her up. "He's probably got them all over his bed."

"I hope so." Susie smiled fondly at the thought of Tony with his body all polka-dotted with chicken pox running his hands through clusters of brilliantly colored glass beads and stacks of stamped doubloons. In the three days since Susie left the throws with Felicia, she had not heard any response. Her only call to Sy's son had been intercepted by Felicia who'd asked Susie not to call again. The ringing phone disturbed Tony's rest. Susie's calls to Sy's studio only reached his recording machine. All she received in return was a brief note on her apartment door saying that Sy had stopped by, but she'd been out.

"When Tony gets better, we'll get together and rummage through them," Susie added, wanting to erase the worried look from Renny's face. "For the next ten days, I won't have much time to play, anyway." The Mardi Gras parades had already started and would proceed day and night until the Tuesday before Lent. There would be a steady succession of final fittings, last-minute alterations and costume pickups. At the same time were the rehearsals for Susie's own presentation, the Triton Ball, then a week later, the Triton parade and the postparade party. All this had to be accomplished in the hours Susie was not working at Blaine's.

"I've still got some work to complete on those back-drops." Renny looked forlornly at the huge canvas hangings that would be needed for two others balls for which he had been designing scenery. "I guess I got kinda hooked on these black-and-white panels after all, and I'm really behind on the others."

"Considering that one set is due this weekend, and you have two more after that—" Germaine promptly recorked the champagne bottle "—I think Susie and I had better leave you here sober so you can get in a few hours more of uninterrupted work."

"You're leaving me!" Renny wailed in protest.

"I've got to work tomorrow," Susie reminded him. "You can sleep all day."

"I've got classes," Germaine chimed in. "Cheer up, though." She stood on tiptoes to hug his neck. "To-morrow afternoon I'm free." The look that passed between her two friends made Susie glance away. With their irregular work schedules, Renny and Germaine had to take whatever time they could to be together. From the glow in Renny's expression, an afternoon with Germaine would be as romantic as a night beneath the stars. Even now, the quick hug and kiss they shared made Susie long to see Sy. She had taken charge of her life, but sharing that life with someone special made each moment more magical.

"See you two later." Susie left Renny and Germaine behind as she strode out of the scenery warehouse into the cold, clear night. She had finished the work she had promised to do for Renny, and now all that was left was to complete her own. Within the next ten days.

Across the parking lot, the doors of the float warehouse were opened wide to let in the fresh breeze as workers scrambled like industrious ants over the huge floats that had returned from a parade earlier in the evening. The laborers were busy dismantling one set of float upperstructures and lowering the new pieces that would transform the same chassis into an entirely different theme.

Susie stood watching the skillful maneuvering of pieces and studied the platform and pulleys that she had modified for her own use. "In the new workroom..." Susie mused as she thought of other ways to make her operation more efficient. Bernie had grinned the night Susie told him that she had decided to make costuming her career full-time. Then he had called his lawyer to draw up the official partnership. "I'll give you fifty-two percent," Bernie had decided. "That means if we have a difference of opinion, Souci—" his eyes had glowed with respect "—you make the final decision. And while you're at it, plan a little vacation time for all of us."

"Vacation time." Susie glanced back once more at the float warehouse as she pulled away. Eventually there would be vacation time, but what she wished for now was a few minutes with a dark-eyed man who had waited for her to grow up.

CHAPTER THIRTEEN

ROSIE COSTAIN'S FACE was streaked with tears when Susie arrived at the houe the next afternoon. "I've got to go to Houston. Claire's baby. . . ." Rosie tried unsuccessfully to complete her sentence. "There's some trouble. She may be losing the baby. . . ." Then she pressed her hands over her face and sobbed. "I want to be there with John, Jr. I want to be with Claire. But there are so many gowns."

Susie hugged her mother and comforted the distressed woman, assuring her repeatedly that everything would be taken care of when Rosie was gone. "Just fill me in on the status of every gown to date." Susie started making notes for herself. "I'll call the airport and get you reservations, and we can talk while you pack. Claire needs you more than those gowns do. So calm down and let's get organized."

By the time Bernie arrived, Rosie's bags were packed and in the car, Susie had all the notes she needed, and had even called ahead to Claire's husband to arrange for Rosie to be met at the Houston airport. "Dad can drive you." Susie kissed her mother's cheek and let Bernie take over. "I've got to make a few calls and recruit some help." Bernie's look of concern for his wife was enough to let Susie know that the two of them needed time alone before Rosie departed. The drive to the airport would enable them to console each other and share their concern for their child and the baby she hoped to bring into the world. Susie had done all she could to ease Rosie's doubts about leaving the unfinished gowns. Now it was up to Bernie to see her safely off.

"Is this Rosa Powell?" Susie said into the phone. "This is Susie Costain. Yes, the lady who designed the costumes." Susie had tracked down her list of seamstresses who had worked in the sweatshop duplicating her costume designs. "I admired your work then," she reminded the woman, "and I certainly could use your skillful hands now." Susie recruited one woman after the other to augment Rosie's staff. With so much beading to do and so many silk flowers to construct, Susie would be unable to concentrate on her own work if she didn't bring in additional help. With the large staff, Susie could divide them between the headdress department above the garage and the dress shop in the house. There would be a lot of going back and forth for Susie, but she could concentrate on supervising the work, not doing it all herself.

"I'll see what I can do about arranging transportation," she promised another one of the women who had agreed to work. "This may turn out to be a year-round job," she assured the lady, "so we may as well set up a car pool so you can get here regularly. I'll get back to you with the details," she told the hopeful woman.

Susie was still on the phone at ten that night, but by then she had lined up a used van that would seat eight, a retired bus driver who would enjoy making the rounds for a little extra money, and she had drawn out a map and a time schedule for her new employees' pickup and return. Germaine had agreed to come in every day after classes and several nights to work on headpieces and collars, acting as Susie's fill-in when Susie was needed elsewhere.

"Ella, this is Susie Costain." She had put off this call to her supervisor at Blaine's until last. "I can't continue coming in to work. I know I was supposed to give you a full two weeks." Susie didn't back down. "I could call it my vacation time and draw pay for it," she reminded the woman. "However, I don't intend to. My sister in Houston is ill, and I'm taking over for my mother while she's gone. I simply cannot be in two places at once." Ms Jenkins uttered an official-sounding reprimand in spite of the circumstances.

"If you feel you must make a note of that in my personnel folder, you go right ahead and do it," Susie replied. "Since I'll be running my own company, I doubt if I'll need to consult your records to determine whether I am a responsible employee. I'm sure you'll find a replacement who will do an excellent job." Susie tried to conclude as rapidly and cordially as she could. When she finally placed the receiver back in the cradle, she expelled a long-controlled sigh.

"Nice job." The voice that came from behind her in the kitchen was Sy's.

"I'm so glad to see you." Susie almost leaped into his arms.

"I've been calling here off and on for hours." Sy hugged her. "When I drove by, I found your dad working upstairs on some costumes. He said I'd find you here." Bernie had returned from taking Rosie to the airport hours earlier and had found solace for his own anxiety in the work he loved. But true to his word, he was letting Susie make the operation run more efficiently, so while she made phone calls, he soldered and glued.

"My sister is having trouble. . . ." Susie didn't have to finish. Bernie had already explained what had caused the current havoc in the Costain household. Then she looked more closely at Sy's face. The strain and weariness in his countenance could not be concealed by the handsome gladiator beard. In spite of his pleasure at seeing her, Sy's shoulders sagged. The man was exhausted.

"One of us has things under control," he remarked, trying to joke, "and it's not me." There was a touching vulnerability in his attempted smile. Susie placed her palms on either side of his face and gently pressed a kiss on each eyelid as if to kiss away the fatigue she saw there.

"How about some coffee or something to eat?" Susie urged him to sit down and relax in the cosy kitchen. "I didn't really skip dinner, I'm just having it later than most folks." She glanced at her watch. It was ten-thirty. She hadn't eaten since noon.

"I am hungry," Sy acknowledged. "I went to two parades tonight in two different parts of town, and I haven't stopped to eat."

"Good." Susie started rummaging through the refrigerator, pulling out Polish sausages and crusty buns. "How about onions and green peppers?" She intended to sauté them New Orleans' style and pile the vegetables on top of the sausages.

"Sounds great," Sy agreed. "If we both eat it, we won't offend each other."

"Speaking of being offended. . . ." Susie vividly recalled her encounter with Felicia. "I haven't heard whether Tony got the parade throws I delivered. How's he doing with the chicken pox?''

Sy didn't answer immediately. Susie turned to find him staring at her incredulously. ''Tony had chicken pox when he was two,'' Sy informed her. ''So he's doing just fine.'' Then his eyes took on a new light as the muscles in his jaw tightened. ''And about the parade throws,'' he said in a tight voice, ''it seems as if some of us were misinformed. Tony thinks Felicia solicited them from all her old chums who happen to be in Mardi Gras krewes. He's been playing with them constantly, but he's also been thanking the wrong person.''

''Oh, my. . . .'' Susie realized now how devious Felicia had been. ''I guess that means you weren't really home resting the day I brought the parade throws by,'' she guessed.

''Felicia had another round of maternal devotion just about the time one of her modeling assignments fell through. She came back, I had a busy schedule, so I let her stay with Tony and I moved into the studio again. Francine ran shuttle service with meals and messages from one place to the other. No, I didn't sleep in the house with Felicia,'' Sy said coolly. ''Did you assume that I had?'' He wanted to know if she had doubted him again.

''I didn't worry about where you slept,'' Susie said truthfully. ''I wasn't even concerned over Felicia's attitude. All I know is that I was relieved you were resting. I didn't jump to any conclusions.'' Susie now realized she had not mistrusted Sy in spite of conditions that could have caused her anguish only weeks ago. ''I figured you would need your rest when you finally heard what I had to say.'' She swirled the chopped onions and peppers around in the cayenne and garlic-flavored butter, then scooped them out onto the sausages.

"What were you finally going to say?" Sy looked up at her. Silhouetted in the golden glow of the kitchen light, Susie stood in an oversize apron holding two plates, each stacked with steaming food.

"I'm coming after you," Susie said the words softly. "I'm taking control of my life, my priorities are lining up nicely, and you're on my list." She slid the plate in front of him and put her own at the next place. Then she went to the cupboard and returned with a wine bottle and two glasses.

"Just how high up on your list am I?" Sy suppressed the smile that was forming.

"You were right at the top." Susie looked at the deep eyes that had become the center of her universe. "And I'll put you up there again," she insisted. "Right after you're fed and rested and. . . ."

"Don't make conditions, Susie." Sy placed his hand over hers. "I'll know and you'll know when that time is. It just isn't here, and it isn't tonight." There was nothing critical in his tone. They had already talked so much about the "right time." Now they were both sure that it would happen, there was no need to discuss it further. Even with the concern, the precautions and the responsibilities, Sy wanted to let the magic take over when that moment arrived.

"I realize that this may sound as if I've totally lost my mind—" Sy leaned back in his chair after they'd eaten and studied her face "—but I've never taken a formal portrait of you in all your queenly finery." He was referring to the traditional full-length photograph that was taken of every Mardi Gras ball queen. It was a solitary, regal pose made before the elaborate gowns and costume showed any signs of wear. Generally they were taken in the Costains' fitting room or in the photographers studio immediately after the costume was completed. "How about doing it now?" Sy suggested seriously.

"It's late." Susie looked at the kitchen clock. "Eleven-fifteen."

"So?" Sy no longer looked quite as weary as he had before. "You look lovely," he insisted. "And I feel steady enough to do a decent job. All my equipment is in the car. How about it?" he urged her. "Let's make it official. Put on your costume, and we'll make you timeless."

Susie wrinkled her nose as she considered his offer. Granted the queen's photo was something that Rosie and Bernie would want to have. They could hang it next to the one made when Claire was queen of a ball. Still, Susie would have to pose for it. She would have to stand in full regalia while Sy adjusted lights and position and peered into the camera. When she had longed to see him again, it was not supposed to be under these conditions.

"I'll make it bearable." Sy guessed some of the reasons for her discomfort. "With just you and me there, we can get everything right and over with quickly. All the photos at the ball will be done in front of an audience. This one will give you a chance to practice in private. How about it, Susie?"

Bernie cleared his throat as he approached the entrance to the kitchen. When Susie looked up at him, she wasn't quite sure what he might have overheard or what he might have imagined they were talking about.

"Sy suggested getting out the Triton's Queen costume and doing the formal picture tonight," she hastily explained. "What do you think, dad?" Bernie thought for a minute as his gaze shifted from their faces to the clock.

"I was thinking about going to bed," he joked. "But I was also worrying about Claire and your mother, so I doubt if I'd do much sleeping. So," he continued making the connection, "if I bring down that sea-horse costume and help you get into it, I just might wear myself out. Then I would be able to get some rest. Besides that—" the anxious look in his eyes softened "—your mother would love to have that portrait. With the schedule we've got, we might as well take advantage of having Sy here and willing. To heck with the time. Let's get started."

Each of them went off in a different direction. Sy went to the car to bring in lights and his tripod. Bernie headed back up to the workroom to lower the magnificent sea-horse backpiece down to ground level, and Susie brought her gown from the storage room into the fitting area and began dressing, carefully applying makeup and brushing her hair into a smooth, silky sheen. By the time Bernie brought in the seahorse costume, Susie and Sy were already set up in front of the long drape that had served as a backdrop for so many official photographs over the years.

"We'll do one in the full costume and one with just the gown, train and tiara." Sy prepared her for the procedure. At the ball itself, Susie would be presented first in full costume, but once the tableau part was completed, she would put aside the huge backpiece, which would be saved until the Triton parade. Then in gown and train, Susie would be able to move freely and enjoy the dance.

"This is really beautiful." Sy held one side of the sea horse while Bernie held the other. Deftly, Susie slipped the shoulder and hip supports under the panels of her gown. Then miraculously the creature that seemed so formidable became a part of her, perfectly balanced as it flared out behind her shoulders and arched above her head. The green iridescent fabric shimmered in the light. The subtle trailing plumage swayed, giving the eerie appearance that the fantastic sea-horse and the queen it sheltered were drifting in a mythical world beneath the waves.

"Spectacular...." Sy stepped back, marveling at the spellbinding finery.

"The costume and the costumer." Bernie offered an appreciative nod to echo Sy's praise. "Both are spectacular."

"Will you two stop staring at me." Susie broke the silent pause of contemplation that both men had fallen into. With bemused smiles, Sy and her father glanced at each other, then shrugged apologetically for gaping at her. Sy stepped over to his camera, adjusting the tripod height, occasionally peering through the lens, lining up the range. Once the portrait camera was set up, Sy picked up the smaller, hand-held one, then slid the strap around his neck so his hands would be free to direct.

"Now let's try revolving you full circle." His hands made graceful arcs in the air as if he were rotating a crystal ball, but Susie knew that within the imaginary sphere, Sy held her suspended in a vision of his own. Slowly she began to pirouette before him so the angles, curves and textures of the exotic sea horse caught the light and shadow in a dramatic display of motion and form. An atmosphere of intense concentration prevailed as one artist offered to another what they both possessed: an intangible but unmistakable gift for seeing a reality that they alone could bring to life.

"I guess you two can manage without me." Bernie shifted his eyes from the photographer to the resplendent queen, but neither responded. Sy swayed and studied the creature before him, snapping momentary glimpses with the click and whir of his camera. Susie's dark gaze was locked on to the mesmerizing movements Sy made with his hands, which silently beckoned for a tilt of the head, a sway of plumage or a slight pause before continuing the full circle of her turn.

"I'll be in my room if you need me," Bernie offered, waving good-night. Discreetly he eased out of the door, leaving the two artists facing each other in hypnotic preoccupation, their images dancing to an unheard melody across the mirrored walls.

"Around again." Sy waved his hand in a sinewy spiral that Susie instinctively duplicated with an arching of her back and a slight tilt of her shoulder. Sy's dark eyes narrowed in concentration, gleaming brilliantly as he waited for the instant when the motion and illusion combined to form the precise fairy-tale quality that he was determined to capture. "Dance for me, marvelous sea horse," Sy whispered to the exquisite creation Susie had crafted.

The luminous beast obeyed, parading with an arrogance and grandeur of its own. Susie felt as if she were a being apart from this costumed queen and the magnificent sea-horse guise. The lights and the fantastic costume allowed her to move into another realm, that of

artist and creator, while the creation itself swayed
before the gleaming mirrors. Sy's own creative intensity
forced her to act out the vision of the sea creature as she
had imagined it, infusing it with an elegance that it had
possessed in her mind. The creature and the queen were
roles that she could assume for a period of time, smiling, posing, pirouetting for Sy, while the real Susie, for
whom such spectacle would be difficult, remained happily and snugly inside herself.

"Dance again, gentle creature," Sy murmured. This
time he moved behind the portrait camera as the vision
he awaited came closer to the movements Susie made.
"Glide...glide...." His low voice guided and controlled her. Like a being adrift, she repeated the subtle
motion as Sy urged her, barely moving to one side with
slow, easy steps. Susie knew precisely when the image in
Sy's imagination coincided perfectly with the position
she assumed. Everything suddenly felt enchanted. The
sorcerer had swirled the ingredients together and
conjured up a charmed fragment of time. Within a
breathless few seconds, Sy signaled that he had it.
"Spectacular...." He blew out a puff of air, chasing
away the tension that had held them both enthralled.

"I feel as if I've been rudely shaken awake in the
midst of a pleasant dream," Susie sighed. "I can imagine how an actress must feel, trying to unwind after a
performance. This is very hard work," she acknowledged.

"Only if you want it to be good." Sy emitted a low,
amused laugh. "Surely you didn't think I'd just settle
for mediocre. Not with you. Certainly not with what
you designed." He shook his head and laughed again as
he moved behind her to help her remove the massive

creation that had once again become a framework of sequins and feathers and metal. "Lady, you have such a unique talent. I had to match it with my best effort."

"Thank you, sir." Susie bowed slightly, realizing how accurately Sy's perception of her work reflected her own sense of herself. He understood the complexities of any creative act, and he knew the unspoken pride and awe an artist feels for his work. He had drawn it out of Susie with his gentle words, and he had made it immortal with his camera.

"I wish Tony could see you in this." Sy moved the sea-horse backpiece to the rear of the room while Susie slid two hooked rods through the support rings and suspended it from the ceiling brace. It could dangle there throughout the night without any danger of being crushed or wrinkled.

"I really wish that you'd bring Tony to the ball," Susie replied. "He could see me along with everyone else, and we'd have a marvelous time. After all his help gluing on sequins, he deserves to see how it all turns out. I'll even arrange for him to sit at our ringside table on the ballroom floor." She had hoped to take Tony to one of the other balls just to sit and admire the costumes, but the fictional chicken pox had deterred her. Now the only ball Susie had time to attend would be her own. Tony would love it.

"If you can arrange two ringside seats, it would help." Sy obviously wanted his son to see the spectacular show. "I may have to send him with Francine. I'll be photographing two balls that night, so I won't be able to chauffeur him. Francine would resign as housekeeper if I passed up an opportunity to get her into one of these affairs, especially yours." His glance lingered on the suspended sea-horse costume. "I'd like them both to see this side of you. It's something they should experience."

"I can arrange two seats," Susie assured him. "Francine's cheery face will be a welcome sight that night. She and I can get together and talk to the table settings." Susie giggled.

"I'm not sure if a queen should display her idiosyncrasies in public," Sy teased. "Certainly not wearing anything as conspicuous as your sea horse there. You and my housekeeper can have your offbeat conversations after Mardi Gras is over. For the time being, we'd better keep your regal aura intact." He tilted his head back toward the camera and lights. "We have more pictures to shoot," he reminded her.

"I'll need a little help with the train." Susie slipped the plastic covering from the floor-length train, which would take the place of the backpiece after her presentation. Sy held it extended while Susie connected it at the shoulders, letting it trail behind, resplendent with wavelike patterns of glistening sequins in deepening shades of green. Then Susie placed the matching tiara on her head, lifting and spreading strands of her dark hair so it covered the combs holding the tiara in place. Sy held her hand, leading her onto the photo platform beneath the lights. This time she was alone in the light, with no sea horse to divert the attention or conceal her self-consciousness.

"I can almost feel you tensing up," Sy said, adjusting the train so it swirled slightly to the side, displaying the elegant design more effectively. "This may seem like a different setup," he said easily, "but it will work just like before. We worked together then; we'll do it now.

Only this time, you're the queen, not the sea creature. We're after a totally different persona," he noted. "But she does exist in your head somewhere. We just have to invite her out to join us for a brief instant."

Sy adjusted the white-screened overhead lights, then stood back to examine the effect. "Turn this way a bit," he indicated. Susie obliged. Sy smiled, but his eyes were detached and analytical. The artist was not satisfied with what he saw. The queen he visualized had not yet emerged.

"I feel so artificial. . . ." Susie tried to put into words the uneasiness she was feeling. "Like a mannequin."

"Maybe I'm going at it the wrong way," Sy apologized. "I don't want this looking all stiff and phony," he insisted. "Give me a minute to line this up again and think it through." He shifted the tripod and readjusted the lights while Susie stood motionless, watching him.

"Getting back to the subject of Francine and Tony—" he talked casually while he changed lenses in his hand-held camera "—I assume that I should tell her to come in formal dress. I don't suppose you have anything hanging around here that would happen to fit her." Susie smiled at the thought of the short, very plump Francine with her flaming red hair. Delightful as she was, there would certainly not be any garment in Rosie's collection of gowns that would fit her unique shape.

"If you can't come up with a gown for her, how about lining up a date for her with one of your buddies?" Sy peered through the viewfinder of his camera, then moved the overhead light again. "How about Renny? I can see the two of them on the dance floor."

Now Susie broke into a wide grin. The idea of tall, lanky Renny dancing with Francine with her chubby, leprechaun body brought an effect that Sy was after. He fired off two shots of that view of Triton's Queen.

"You tricked me," Susie protested.

"These are just warm-up shots." Sy chuckled. "I just liked what I saw. Shall I tell Francine that she has a date?" he persisted.

"Not with Renny," Susie responded. "He's already overwhelmed. He's actually going with Germaine, but he's going to escort me back to the throne after the presentation. I knew you would be taking pictures of the event, so it would have been a bit tricky to have asked you," she noted. "But between his official duties assisting me and his social ones with Germaine, I'm afraid Renny is taken. However, Pascal will be there, too," Susie brightened. "Height-wise, he and Francine are in the same league."

"No one is in the same league with Francine," Sy insisted. "But don't worry about Francine. If she gets in the door, she'll have a wonderful time. Once the dancing starts, no man in the place will be safe. She'll wear them all out before the evening is over. But while we're on the subject of dancing—" his voice softened as he raised his camera again "—it seemed to work for us before—" the warmth in his eyes reassured her before the camera totally obscured them "—so dance with me again, Susie. Let me see the queen." He moved in an arc before her, camera focused on her shimmering form, like a partner in the grand waltz, coming forward to bow and rise again. "Dance with me, Queen of Triton," Sy urged. "Step into this world and fill it with enchantment. Come dance with me."

Just as the dark lens of the camera concealed the face she knew so well, the facade of Triton's Queen was one that Susie could put on for a moment. To the camera-masked courtier who invited her to dance, Susie could play the elegant queen, extending her hand and flashing her dark eyes with delight. With each graceful turn of her shoulder or provocative tilt of her chin, Susie heard the whisperings of the camera shifting on to another frame.

"Lovely, lovely, my lady...." Sy's words supplanted the sound of the camera as his body followed the movements of hers in eloquent harmony.

Susie slowly turned around, just as she had when she'd worn the sea horse, but this time she felt another transformation as one part of her assumed an attitude of sophistication and elegance that every fairy-tale queen possessed. The regal bearing of countless goddesses and nymphs immortalized in legends and art and even in the pageants Susie had designed now became a part of her. All she had tried to articulate in her creations became a part of her own regal stance.

"Queen of Triton." Sy was invoking her presence, calling her to become that entity. "Come to me," he breathed. Triton's Queen turned toward him, half smiling as she did. Sy's camera whispered a greeting, welcoming her into its world. One. Two. Three shots in succession. Then the eyes that came from behind the camera-mask issued a message of their own. The camera had wanted the queen. The eyes burned for Susie.

"Dance with me." Sy clicked off the large reflector lights and came toward her. Only one fluorescent light at the far end of the room remained on, giving the impression that Sy was stepping from the bright space filled with cameras and equipment into a dark mystical world where Susie waited. With the same distinctive bow of a courtier, he dipped, then rose again to take her hand and draw her near.

"I will always dance with you." Susie cupped her hand around the base of his neck and pressed her temple against the soft mat of his trimmed beard. The goddess and the gladiator. Locked in each other's embrace they swayed and turned in the silent, mirrored fitting room. Like the changing patterns in a kaleidoscope, the image of the tall, bearded man in loose-collared shirt and slacks and the satin-gowned lady in his arms reflected in one mirror after another.

"Are you still up...?" Bernie's weary voice came rumbling down the hall ahead of him. He stopped at the doorway of the fitting room and stared in at the two dancers, still turning to an unheard melody. "You're both crazy." Bernie stood in his pajamas and robe gawking at them. "I'm going to bed...again," he muttered good-naturedly as he wandered off. "Good night."

"I guess we'd better say good-night, too," Sy said, without loosening his hold on Susie. "You feel so warm and soft." The pleasure in his voice elicited a deep surge of desire that made Susie hold him even closer. Silently, they danced on and on.

Sy's breath fanned her cheek, inviting her to turn toward its origin. With almost dreamlike motion, Susie sought his lips with her own. The tender, languid pressure of their kiss held them suspended in a world of their own as each one wordlessly responded to the increasing intensity of the sensations they shared. With almost imperceptible movements, Sy traced the softness of her lips with the tip of his tongue, not demanding but delighting in the texture and tension of the contact.

"Love me, Sy...." Susie breathed the words so softly they were almost inaudible, but the heat that flooded her being and the pliant invitation in her kiss were unmistakable. He responded with a low groan as his tongue hungrily entered more deeply, with a passion that echoed Susie's own.

The ardent merging of their lips, the slow soft circling of warm mouths and rippling breaths became a dance of gentler rhythm as each caressed and savored the softness he or she had sought. Kisses lingered on half smiles, then inched upward, feathering over eyelids, tasting and teasing in a blend of feeling and discovery. Then the lips would meet again to sample the delicious flavor and tantalizing texture.

Susie rolled her head to one side, her dark hair trailing against her bare shoulders, as the slow, sensuous descent of Sy's kisses followed the curves and contours of her throat. With one hand Susie held Sy to her, prolonging the exquisite pressure of his mouth upon her. Her other hand disconnected the fasteners of the elaborate train, letting it glide to the floor in a confusion of sparkle and iridescent color. Now her bared shoulders invited the searching tracings of lips and tongue, and Sy willingly ventured over the pale, delicate skin.

With a shudder of restrained impatience, he reached behind her, clasping the zipper of her gown, then pulling it easily downward so the sea-green satin loosened and fell away slightly from her breasts. From the folds of luxurious fabric drifting lower, Susie's breasts and slender torso emerged as if she were an alabaster image of a goddess ascending above the ocean foam.

"Susie, you are so lovely...." Sy breathed a ragged sigh as he bowed before her reverentially, embracing each bare breast in his cupped hands, then lowering his lips to explore their exquisite velvety surface.

Susie closed her eyes, clasping Sy's thick dark hair, holding onto the dense mane while the motion of his mouth and the luxurious progress of his lips filled her with a heat that made her gasp for air. His strong hands stroked her naked torso with rhythmic, erotic motion while Susie clung to him, straining to have every inch of her body encompassed by the compelling fire of his touch.

Sy guided the elaborate gown down over her hips and let it fall to her feet. He knelt before her now, burying his face in the intoxicating warmth of her breasts, the dark bristle of his beard, rough and provocative against her skin. Susie could feel the rock-hard muscles of his shoulders tremble as his hands slid lower and caught the silken panties. Susie placed her own hands over his, insistently and longingly urging him to go on. She wanted nothing to separate them. Every part of her being desired to be engulfed in the passion of Simon Avery.

"Hey, you two. . . ." The call came from the hallway. Immediately the images in the mirrors froze.

"I can't sleep," came Bernie's voice from the far end of the hallway. "I'm going to make some hot chocolate. Want some?" Obviously he was unable to subdue his anxiety about his family. From the faraway sound of his voice, Susie thought he had no intention of immediately coming down the hall to the fitting room.

Sy thrust his head back with a series of deep, rasping breaths. He had been totally lost in the ecstasy of the encounter. Susie struggled to form words. The dryness in her mouth made it difficult to speak. For an instant, they had blended into an entity—touching, holding, exploring, savoring the passion they shared. Now they were separate again.

"None for me," Susie managed to call out. "I don't think either of us wants anything. Thanks anyway, dad." Susie steadied herself on Sy's shoulder as she stepped out of the collapsed gown. Then Sy stood and located the discarded train.

"I should have known better," he began apologizing. "I shouldn't have touched you unless we were really alone. This could have been quite a disaster, and that isn't the way it should be for us." He started shaking the wrinkles out of the garments while Susie hastily put on the blouse and slacks she had originally worn into the fitting room.

"I'm the one who should have known better," Susie knew the color in her cheeks now was from embarrassment, not from passion. "I feel like a woman, and I was acting like a teenager—fooling around in one room while my father is in another part of the house."

"We weren't fooling around." Sy looked at her with dark eyes still glowing with desire. "We were making love."

"I know we were." Susie touched his cheek lightly with her fingertips then trailed them downward through the rough texture of his beard. Even this gentle contact sent a tremor of excitement through her. "This may have been the wrong time and wrong place," Susie said quietly, "but I am sure. I know that I want to make love to you. No games, no chances. No Russian roulette," she added pointedly. "No one else should be involved."

"We were lucky that no one else was." Sy took her hand and pressed a kiss into her palm. "I'd have hated to see your father's reaction. Here we were with cameras, mirrors and lights. Not your customary intimate environment." He paused to stroke her cheek lightly. "Touching you lifts me right out of this world," he said softly. "There is a magic between us that makes everything else disappear."

"Almost everything," Susie corrected him. She could hear the distant flip-flop of her father's slippers as he came up the hallway. "Are you sure you don't want some hot chocolate, Souci?" He smiled sheepishly from the doorway, but his attempt at light-heartedness couldn't conceal the anxiety he felt. Bernie looked like a forlorn puppy, aimlessly searching for something he missed. He was worried and lonely; Rosie was away, Claire was still in "guarded" condition. He needed someone familiar to be with; someone who could ease his distress by being there. Susie had turned to him a hundred times. Now he was turning to her.

"Go ahead and fix some for me," Susie said, relenting. "I'll help Sy get his equipment into his car, then I'll be right in to join you, dad." The relieved half smile on Bernie's face indicated that he felt better already.

"I'll tell Tony and Francine to get out their fancy clothes," Sy said as he and Susie carried the lights and camera along the hall. "And I'll straighten Tony out about who actually brought him all those parade throws. His mother always likes to be the one who shows up bearing gifts," Sy said wearily. "Usually they're expensive ones. I guess she couldn't stand to be upstaged by those trinkets, so she claimed they were from her. It was a rotten thing to do."

"Is Felicia still here in town?" Susie hoped that Sy and Tony and their efficient housekeeper had the house to themselves. "I'd like to call Tony and invite him to the ball myself. I just don't want to get Felicia instead."

"She's leaving Saturday." Sy placed the equipment in the trunk and slammed it shut. "Then when I get back, I'll get to relax under my own roof. I'm getting a lot of work done at the studio this way, but I miss being around Tony."

"You're going somewhere, too?" Susie said uneasily.

"I'll be at the ball," he assured her. "But right after that, I have to fly out for a few days."

"But I thought that once the ball was over..." Susie protested. After the Triton Ball, her routine would change drastically. She would have almost a week to relax and unwind, since only one shipment of costumes remained. All that was left of her "official" responsibilities was the big parade and the informal party that followed. She would finally have some time for herself and for Sy.

"I'm coming back," he assured her. "I'll be there for your parade, for sure. This is a photo deal I promised to complete." Something in his voice made Susie apprehensive.

"Does it have something to do with Felicia?" She wished she didn't have to ask.

"It's a deal her agent cooked up," Sy acknowledged. "It's a fashion layout for a big magazine spread. We used to do them in Europe. It will take a few days in New York."

"Couldn't someone else do it for her?" Susie's face had turned into a tense mask. She was relieved that Sy could not see her clearly in the darkness. He would not have liked what he saw.

"The deal is for the two of us," he explained. "I really wasn't interested, but when Felicia came back here to work out the details, it was clear that they were after my work as well as her body. The editors said both of us or no deal.''

"Just like in the old days." Susie did not try to disguise her bitterness.

"It means an entire new start for Felicia in American fashion magazines. It gives me some excellent commercial exposure." Sy outlined the benefits. "It won't take long," he promised.

"It's just that she keeps coming back, in and out of your life. Felicia is never really going to let you go, Sy. One way or another, she's going to keep hanging on." Susie recalled only too well how possessive Felicia had been toward both Tony and Sy. She had not even allowed Susie inside the Avery home. Now, in spite of her lies and trickery, Sy was going off with her alone for days to help rebuild her faltering career. Susie was caught between Sy's past and his future, and Felicia Voison Avery was determined to block the way.

"She can't hold onto something that doesn't exist." Sy turned Susie to face him, grasping her shoulders firmly so she couldn't turn away. "But she always will have access to Tony. That's something you'll have to learn to accept. As far as I'm concerned, this is good business. . . for both Felicia and for myself. This spread will give her back her confidence and it should improve her finances immensely—mine, too. I'm that good at what I do," he said evenly. "My pictures will make the difference. She needs my talent—not me."

"And what do you need, Sy?" Susie challenged him.

"I need some photo credits in American magazines, which I'll get," he replied with increasing impatience, "and I need to get back here to you."

"In that order?" Susie responded crossly.

"Not necessarily," he said, chuckling. "That's just the way it is."

"I don't trust her." Susie felt like a child pouting over being slighted in a game. Only in this game, the stakes were people's lives—Sy's, Tony's, Susie's and Felicia's.

"That makes two of us," Sy agreed. "But that doesn't change anything. I'll go to New York, do my work, then I'll come home."

"Until Felicia needs you again?" Susie wondered if the pattern would ever change.

"I'm exhausted. I'm going to my solitary bed in my studio and sleep by myself." Sy talked to her now as if she were a slow learner. "Good night, my love." He kissed her lightly on the cheek. "See you at the ball, Cinderella."

Susie started back into the house, turning out the hall light as she locked the door behind her. Inside, her father waited, anxious and restless until he could learn more about his daughter and his child, and lonely for the familiar presence of his wife. Sy once had a family with a wife and child he loved, and even after the divorce, that threesome had a unique and undeniable claim on each other. Time and again, Sy had allowed Felicia to return. *It would be so easy....* Susie knew how powerful old emotions could be. Under the right circumstances, with Felicia as cunning as she was, Sy could become the victim of his own sense of honor.

He had said "She can't hold on to something that doesn't exist." All that Susie could do now was to wait and see if Sy was right.

CHAPTER FOURTEEN

"WHY DOES RENNY look so worried?" Susie asked Germaine as they stood backstage at the Municipal Auditorium Basin Street Hall. The reserved tables and chairs around the perimeter for the dance floor were sparsely populated, but the upper tiers for observers, those who would watch but not participate in the elaborate ball, rapidly filled with people.

"He has to leave early tonight and go straight over to the scenery warehouse. He still has a lot of work to do on the backdrops. I even volunteered to help after we finish here," Germaine explained. "You know how desperate he must be if he's putting a paintbrush in my hand," she joked.

"He should have told me." Susie peered at Renny waving wildly into the darkness. When Pascal appeared, she knew who Renny had been signaling. "I could have asked someone else."

"Renny wouldn't miss this for the world," Germaine assured her friend. "He has this peculiar sense of theater. It delights him to be in the center of the show. Besides, he dearly loves you. He wouldn't want you out there with just anyone."

"But having to go to work after the ball. . ." Susie lamented.

"I hate to sound unsympathetic, but it's his own

fault.'' Germaine frowned. "He took a few afternoons off just to spend with me when he knew he was behind schedule. Then he and Pascal started their 'watch the sunset' routine down by the levee. He didn't plan well, and he got caught short.'' The almond-eyed young woman shook her head. "I'll help him, of course,'' she said, softening her voice, "but I'll make sure he doesn't let this happen again. He took eighteen of his paintings in to be framed for the gallery showing. They're finished, but he can't pick them up until he has cash in hand. It's a tough way to learn to be responsible.''

"Susie!'' Rosie rushed up beside the two women.

"You made it.'' Susie hugged her mother with delight. Late the night before, Rosie had called with the news that Claire had been allowed to go home from the hospital. Her condition had stabilized and the baby was apparently developing normally. The threat of miscarriage was over.

"I had a terrible time at the airport.'' Rosie was obviously flustered. "I had to have a porter track down my luggage.''

"But you made it,'' Susie repeated. "And you look elegant.'' Rosie had dressed rapidly, but the results were no indication of the haste. She had swirled her gray-streaked hair into a style that made her look carefree and chic, and the silvery gray dress revealed that the few pounds she had worried away had given her a more youthful figure. But it was the relief of knowing that one daughter was safely home and the other had the preparations for the ceremony under control that gave Rosie the glow that made her beautiful. Tonight, she could relax. Tonight, her youngest child became a queen.

By the time the lights dimmed to signal the beginning of the tableau, Susie was beginning to feel anxious. Sy was not there yet. There was also no sign of young Tony or Francine.

Out amid the tables, Uncle Leo was gingerly moving around with his videotape camera propped under one arm. He had intended to film Michelle's presentation, but when Susie took her place, Uncle Leo insisted on filming her ceremony instead. The ball was a family event, he had stated, and a long-overdue tribute to Susie's contribution to Mardi Gras balls over the years. Uncle Leo's video camera would capture the motion that Sy had so admired in Susie's creations. However, Sy was the official photographer who had been commissioned to preserve the high points of the evening in a traditional Queen's Album. But it wasn't the pictures that worried Susie. This would be her last opportunity to be with Sy before he left on the New York trip with Felicia. Susie had so much she wanted to say to him before he went away.

When the music swelled and the voice of the captain of the Krewe of Triton began the program, Susie ceased to worry about Sy or anything else. She became that "other Susie," the one who could smile and look so serene and survive the attention. She climbed the tall stairway on the stage and took her place on a throne amid the eight beautifully costumed maids. Her king, Ernest Dufrene, was seated across from her on a second throne, with the eight dukes lined up below him. Then the curtains parted so the audience could see the tableau.

This part of the presentation seemed to take forever as the spotlights highlighted certain portions of the huge underwater setting that had been created. Stairs from floor level led upward in two directions toward thrones seemingly sculpted from white coral. Softly blown by overhead fans, glistening draperies in varying sea shades from aquamarine to deepest blue cascaded across the upper portion of the stage, giving the effect that the entire court poised motionless in a marvelous underwater paradise.

One after another, the members of the court were introduced to the audience. That maid or duke would then descend to the floor of the ballroom and promenade the full course around the dance floor. Spotlighted from above, these figures clad in Susie's amazing creations brought forth sighs and applause from an audience delighted by the fantasy.

Then it was Susie's turn. A page in deep green satin had escorted the beaming Ernest Dufrene to the base of Susie's stairway, then climbed up to assist her in making the descent. She'd had one rehearsal in costume that afternoon to prepare her for the evening performance, but coming down the stairway had been much easier than climbing up again, when the weight of the costume impeded her.

With her hand resting on Ernest's, Triton's Queen circled twice around the ballroom floor, greeting her subjects and acknowledging their accolades. Midway through the second promenade, Susie heard the click and whir she had once dreaded. In the darkened area beyond her circle of light, Susie could distinguish Sy's tuxedo-clad form maneuvering between the tables as he focused his camera on her. Instantly, her smile became more radiant and her step more regal, not for the benefit of the camera, but in response to the broad grin of the photographer.

Before the dancing could begin, the members of the court had to remove the spectacular outer costumes that would inhibit their movement. As their circuit of the ballroom ended, Susie and Ernest stepped behind the curtains where the sea costumes were lifted from their backs. Now each of them wore the less cumbersome additions—a mask and crown for Ernest and a tiara and train for Susie. This time, when the king and queen emerged, they would dance together, leading the grand march that would bring the entire costumed krewe onto the ballroom floor.

After that, the costumed krewe members would invite ladies from the audience to join the dancing in a "calling-out" procedure, in which each lady would be summoned by having her name announced. Susie would dance with her father, then with several distinguished members of the krewe and finally with Renny, whose sole official duty was to then escort her back to her throne for a final bow. Then the floor was open for all the guests, costumed or not, and the festivities would continue into the night on a far less formal level. Susie could join her family at their table and relax among her friends. Triton's Queen would simply be one more dancer on the floor, or one more diner enjoying the cocktails and delicacies served on silver trays by white-jacketed waiters.

When the time came for Renny to dance with Susie and then escort her back to the throne, Sy stepped from the sidelines, without his camera. "Could this dance be ours?" he asked. "My flight is booked earlier than I expected. I won't be able to stay much longer, but I do want to dance with you before I leave."

"Fine with me." Renny was pleased to have another chance to dance with Germaine. "Just tap me on the shoulder when it's time for me to do my thing," he suggested.

Susie tried to hide her disappointment with a polite smile. She had hoped that when the formal part of the evening concluded she and Sy would have hours to dance together.

"You're doing magnificently." Sy took her into his arms and beamed at her. "Your hands are as cold as ice, but I won't tell a soul. On the outside you look totally unruffled. For a moment back there, I thought you were even enjoying it."

"I was enjoying it until you said you had to leave," Susie answered honestly. "Oh, Sy. I hoped we could talk."

"You talk." He held her close against his chest. "I'm happy just feeling you near me again. I remember that dress...." The pressure of Sy's hand sent a familiar warmth through her. "You look beautiful in it." He tilted his head back and looked at her with a glint of mischief in his eyes. "But out of it..." he murmured, "you're breathtaking." Susie felt the fiery pleasure that his presence elicited. The vivid memory of their lovemaking in the fitting room had obsessed her for days. All she had yearned for was one more time, one more touch. Now that she was in Sy's arms again, she really did not want to talk. She wanted to make love with him. Instead, they danced.

"Susie, it's time for you to take your throne." Bernie was obviously enjoying the evening. "If you'll take your place up there, we can get on with the rest of this party." He looked at Susie's face and then at Sy's and shrugged apologetically. "You know how these things are," he commented. "No food until the queen is seated. You don't want all your subjects to go hungry."

"I guess this is it." Sy let her go reluctantly. "I'll be around for a few more photographs, then I've got to leave. I'll see you as soon as I get back." He held onto her hand and led her over to Renny.

Susie couldn't say goodbye to him. She couldn't even look at him without fearing she would burst into tears. Queens aren't supposed to cry, certainly not in public, so she tried to steel herself for the moment Sy disappeared.

"Tony and Francine are here," Sy told her. "The presentation had started when they arrived, so they had to wait to be seated, but they are here. I'm not leaving you without representation from the Avery household." He tried to cheer her up by pointing out the twosome that had joined Pascal and Germaine at the reserved table.

"Let's get this over with." Renny stood nervously shifting from side to side and staring at the narrow elaborate stairway he had to ascend. Susie had already told him about holding her train and walking slowly, but they had not actually made the climb together. "Now run through it one more time," Renny said as he took her arm and started toward the center platform. "I just take you up. . . ." Sy stood watching as Susie assumed a regal pose and walked away. Then hastily he retrieved his camera and prepared to take the final shots of the ceremony.

Susie couldn't distinguish faces as she moved through

the royal court, which now stood in line at the base of the stairway. In spite of her efforts to control her sadness, large tears welled up in her eyes and threatened to spoil the show. Renny lifted the back of her train precisely as she had told him and began climbing in step with her up toward the coral throne. When they reached the top, he draped the train to one side while Susie sat down, spreading out the skirt of her gown. He was supposed to take her hand, bow, then leave, but Susie hesitated, pulling back her hand to brush away a tear that could no longer be controlled.

Renny glanced around nervously, trying to look nonchalant about the small delay. "They probably think you're all choked up with happiness," he said as he stepped back and straightened his tuxedo jacket and searched for a tissue to offer her. When he turned slightly to plunge his hand into his pocket, he stepped too far. With only the slightest yelp of alarm, Renny dropped out of sight. The thud that followed brought the entire presentation to an abrupt halt.

"Renny!" Susie peered down the dark chasm beside the royal stairway. The drop to the next platform was about ten feet. Something black and white was moving down there.

From the darkness came a few muttered epithets as Renny struggled to his feet. "How the hell do I get out of here?" he called up to Susie.

"Just duck under the end panel," she told him, pointing to the silvery curtains that had transformed the platforms into the shimmering bottom of a fantasy sea. "You'll come out beside the stairway." She was relieved to see that he had survived the fall unharmed.

By now several krewe officials had raced to his aid

while everyone else stood in near silence waiting to learn what had occurred. Then Renny stepped out and gave a self-conscious bow to assure everyone that he was quite all right. Red-faced and rumpled, he was horrified that he had caused such a scene.

"Everything is fine." The captain of the krewe reinstated order at once. The band began its musical salute to Susie, and the enthusiastic families and friends applauded the entire Triton court. From her throne, high above the heads of the audience, Susie watched Renny weave through the crowd to the table where Germaine waited anxiously. His fall had frightened everyone, but he walked along without so much as a limp.

Sy was no longer there. Susie scanned the crowd and located Tony and red-haired Francine joining the others who had clustered around Renny as he sat by Germaine, apparently recounting the details of his sudden disappearance. Susie waited for the curtain to close so her official duties for the evening would be over, and she could rush down to join her guests.

At last the lights on stage dimmed and the curtains were drawn. The queen and her court were free to join the festivities and visit with their friends. The elaborate costumes would be taken home and stored until the Triton parade, more than a week away. After the parade, at the informal party, finery would be abandoned for more casual clothes, and all that would remain would be the memories.

When Susie finally reached the table where Pascal and Tony stood to greet her, she could tell by the look on their faces that something was very wrong. "I think we have a problem." Pascal took her arm and led her aside. Susie glanced over at Renny who had now changed from his embarrassed reddish coloring to a dismal shade of gray. This time the color change was nothing he could control. The poor fellow was in pain. "It looks as if Renny may have broken his wrists." Pascal spoke in a low voice.

"Oh, no..." Susie moaned. Then the full impact of Pascal's words hit her. "You mean both wrists?" She turned to stare at Renny.

"He wouldn't get up and go to the hospital until the ceremony was over." Pascal said, to explain why Renny had refused to move. "Now we're not sure we can get him out of here without causing more damage to his wrists. If he faints on us...." Pascal shook his head. As tall and long-limbed as Renny was, carrying him out of the place would be a problem.

"I'm on very close terms with the local paramedics." Susie recalled the efficient team that had treated her after the break-in. "The first thing they say is not to move anyone unless you know what you're doing. Since we don't know what we're doing, I'll call them. Renny's wrists are too important to take any chances with. Just keep everyone calm, and I'll be right back."

"Can I go with you?" Tony was enthralled with all the action. If Susie was bringing in the rescue squad with the paramedics, the boy wanted to be in on the excitement.

"Pretend we're taking a casual stroll over to the rest rooms," Susie directed him. "There's a phone over there. We may be able to take care of this without causing too much of a disturbance."

By the time the paramedics arrived, Susie had located two satin robes discarded by krewe members who had chosen to shed their masks and costumes. Clad in these, the paramedics crossed to Renny's table without attracting any notice. By the time they had determined that both wrists did seem broken and slipped support braces under each wrist, the band was pausing for an intermission and the waiters came in to refurbish the food supply. "We're taking you in for X rays," one of the two muscular men bracing Renny on either side said. Arm in arm, they crossed to the foyer and out into the waiting rescue vehicle.

"I'd better follow them to the hospital," Germaine insisted. "If you think he looks sick now," she added, "wait till he realizes that he won't be able to finish the scenery he's doing. *That* will be sick."

"Tell him I'll help," Susie promised. "Just tell him to take it really easy and do whatever the doctors say, and I'll be his hands for a while." She stood looking out into the night as the orange-and-white emergency vehicle took her friend off.

"I can paint even better than I can glue." Tony stood beside her looking up hopefully. "My dad and I painted my room all by ourselves. I can help."

"It means working at night," Susie warned him. "You have school, don't forget."

"What if I do my homework and take a nap?" he bargained. Susie had told him about the scenery warehouse, and he was eager to get a glimpse of it himself.

"Let me check with Renny when he gets home. If he says you can help, then we'll have a deal."

"You can count me in, too," Francine insisted once Susie and Tony had rejoined the others back at the table. She would see to it that Tony got the nap he promised to take.

"Me too." Pascal offered his considerable talents.

"I'm almost finished with the floats. All I do is see that they are assembled correctly. As long as I'm out there, I can hit a few licks on Renny's backdrops."

"Just as we all thought things were calming down..." Susie sighed. "Here we go again like a bunch of monkeys on the loose."

"Keeping busy is the way to stay young." Francine tossed her bush of bright red hair. "That and a hairdresser who knows how to keep her mouth shut." She cackled at her own joke. "And as long as I'm here and ready to boogie," she announced, looking around the room for a likely partner, "I'm going to enjoy this evening immensely." She zeroed in on the gentle Ernest Dufrene, still in his Triton's King regalia. "Introduce me to that one, Susie," she whispered, winking conspiratorially. "I might as well start at the top."

IT WAS ALMOST two in the morning when Susie finally parked beside her apartment in the Quarter. In Renny's living room, a light was on, so Susie tiptoed along the balcony and peeked inside. Spread out on the sofa bed, Renny lay asleep with both wrists in white casts. Next to him, curled up in a chair, Germaine, who had been watching over him, was fast asleep, too. "Just what we needed," Susie muttered to herself as she turned back to her own apartment. "Another disaster."

The package taped to her door didn't surprise her at all. The large brown envelope had Sy's studio address on it. Susie knew at once they were the portraits of her or, more precisely, those of her as Triton's Queen. In the aftermath of Renny's accident, and with Sy on his way to New York, any reminder of the costumes or the man who photographed her in them simply added to her depression. Susie undressed and began brushing her teeth before her curiosity began to take over. She eyed the package that lay unopened on the table, cautioning herself not to look inside. She'd always been less than pleased with any photograph of herself. She wasn't sure that being photographed by Sy would make her feel differently.

Still. . . she argued inwardly as she stood, toothbrush in hand, frowning into the mirror, . . . *they are a part of him.* They were evidence of his talent and perhaps something more.

Susie managed to slide into bed, fluff the pillow and pull the covers up over her before she finally surrendered to her innate inquisitiveness. She sat cross-legged on the carpet, spreading before her the photographs Sy had taken. The large full-color portraits looked up at her like countless reflections in a mirror, with sequins and satin ablaze and her dark eyes luminous.

Susie stared at one photograph then the next, stunned by the skillful job Sy had done. He had captured another Susie, regal and elegant, sophisticated and striking—everything a Mardi Gras queen should be. He had summoned the fantasy queen, lovely and exotic, without exposing too much of the person inside that sultry exterior.

He had also made her incredibly beautiful. The interplay of light and shadow on her features accentuated the bone structure and made her deep brown eyes seem mysterious and compelling. Susie contemplated the photos thoughtfully, trying to decipher her own mixed feelings, part pleasure, part dismay. The queen she saw was lovely, but the image in the portraits was not really her. This was not the way she wished to be seen by Sy. The immobile faces in his photographs were a skillfully wrought product—something apart from her that Sy's expertise and Susie's designs had brought into existence. But Susie didn't want to see herself as a product. Her bond with Sy was far too intimate and intense. There was too much that each photo *didn't* show.

Carefully Susie slid the photographs into a stack and started to place them back in the large envelope. She wanted to see herself in Sy's eyes, not in his portraits. The note that fell out of the open envelope had a brief message on it. "We work together well. You're exceptional, and I told you I'm that good at what I do. Sy."

Susie reread the note. She could see why he was so sought after by other Mardi Gras queens. She could also comprehend that Sy's note expressed the same reasoning that Felicia had used in getting him to do her photo layouts. If Sy could transform an amateur model like Susie into a serene and majestic queen, he could certainly make some impressive shots of a professional like the golden-haired Felicia. Having access to a photographer as excellent as Sy would enhance Felicia's chances of re-establishing a career. One could become very possessive of this kind of artistry. Susie's mind raced back over Felicia's deceptions. Everything from the tale about Tony's chicken pox to the lie about who brought the parade throws could be seen in a different light. They may not have been the conniving of a woman trying to reclaim an ex-husband; they could be the fabrications of a woman who simply wants to hold on to an artist she needs, a friend she respects and a son she loves in her own way.

Susie pressed her hands to her temples, trying to ease the tension and erase the doubts. She tried to focus on the things Sy had said. He had told her that she would have to get used to Felicia's unlimited access to Tony, but implicit in that was a continuous connection to Sy as well. There would always be a complex tie, personal and professional, between Sy and Felicia. Any relationship between Sy and Susie would naturally include Tony, but it would also extend to Felicia, who would resent any erosion of her position. *I'll always have to share him....* Susie couldn't ignore the reality of other claims on Sy's attention, his talents and even his affection.

Sy had said that Felicia "can't hold onto something that doesn't exist." His words took on a new significance as Susie brooded over the complications that their relationship would have. Felicia's hold on Sy might no longer be a romantic one, but it was valid, nevertheless. Susie couldn't hold on to something that doesn't exist, either. She could only trust in what she felt to be true: that the bond she and Sy shared would grow stronger, strong enough to hold them together regardless of the strains of other commitments. She would have to learn to let him go where his unique sense of honor led him, without feeling the uncertainties that plagued her now. Whatever Sy saw and valued in her was enough to make him promise to come back to her. *And I'll be here—* Susie stuffed the photographs and the note into the envelope and placed it on the table once again *—doing the best job of being me that I can.*

IN THE MORNING, the minute Susie stepped outside onto the balcony, she could see that something was wrong. In the parking lot below, her little compact car was attracting an audience.

"Someone sure did a job on her." One tall fellow shook his head when Susie came down to see what was going on.

"Musta done it in the night." A second young man bent down and brushed his thumb over the smear of white paint that wriggled like a caterpillar down the side of her car. "Paint's dry all right," he muttered. Whoever had sprayed the ugly stripe on her silver gray vehicle had done it hours before. The mark wouldn't budge.

"Sure is a shame," the first fellow said sympathetically.

Susie stared at the streak and shook her head dejectedly. "I guess I'd better call the police." She turned and walked away before she said aloud what she was thinking.

"Some wise-ass kids out looking for trouble." The patrolman who'd come to investigate the vandalism wrote out the details of the damage. "There's a lot of transients coming our way for Mardi Gras," he noted. "Some of them don't have anywhere to sleep, so they roam the streets at night. Your car just happened to be in the wrong place at the wrong time." He accepted this as part of the price residents of New Orleans had to pay each year.

Susie tried to place the blame on some faceless wanderer who picked her car at random, but as she watched the officer fill out the complaint, she was haunted by a pair of angry eyes and, for a minute, that faceless vagrant in her mind looked remarkably like Ralph Tanner when he'd stared at her in the court hallway. "Then you aren't going to investigate it," Susie asked quietly.

"Oh, I'll write it up and file it," the patrolman replied. "But unless there is a witness or you have reason to suspect a particular person, we have nothing to make a case. I doubt the guy even touched the car." He looked at the way the paint had been applied. "All he had to do was to hold the can down low and just walk right past it while he sprayed. Without the can with fingerprints and without a suspect, you may as well figure this one's a lost cause," he explained honestly. "If it happens again in the area, we may pick up on a pattern. But, like I said, unless someone can give us a face or a name, you may as well forget it. Just call your car-insurance agent and go on from there."

"Then I guess I'll go to work. But it just doesn't seem fair...." She didn't like the idea that the person who did this to her car would go unpunished.

"It sure isn't fair," the patrolman agreed. "There's a lot of crimes we can't solve." He sounded more philosophical than apologetic. "That's part of the system."

"I understand," Susie acknowledged. "I just don't have to like it."

"It's pretty frustrating," the patrolman replied. "No one likes to feel they're defenseless against stuff like this. Unfortunately, there isn't much we can do."

"I can do something." Susie checked the time on her watch. "I can get to work and take out my frustrations on the drawing board. Only I plan to be a whole lot neater than this guy."

The officer obviously had no idea what she meant, but he nodded politely and watched her walk away. "Sure is a mess," he muttered to himself as he flipped closed his notebook and inspected the car once more. "Crazy time." He walked off to his patrol car with a resolute air. There was another side to Mardi Gras that the street cop knew too well. And it was just beginning.

CHAPTER FIFTEEN

"NOW DON'T YOU WORRY, I'll rinse you out and have you looking lovely as soon as I finish this little orange starfish over here." Francine was talking to the paint-brush she had placed on the tray. Renny sat on the high stool with both wrists lying helplessly on his knees. The one-sided conversation between the short, red-haired woman and the paint-soaked brush brought a smile to his otherwise somber face. His assortment of volunteers had been eager to help complete the scenery, but progress was still very slow. Renny had to translate all the images he had held in his head into words and directions that these helpers could understand.

"I've brought something that might expedite matters." Pascal pulled a dolly loaded with equipment from the float-manufacturing warehouse. "If we spray the entire surface in whatever basic color areas you need, then some of us can work on details while the majority of the space dries. If we don't finish it exactly as you planned, there will still be color everywhere." He lifted out the huge electric paint sprayer that they used to hastily change colors on the floats.

Renny winced at the idea that his designs could be sprayed on electrically. Using machinery for his art appalled him.

"At least this way we'd have a chance of getting these

two backdrops out on time." Susie came around from the far end of one panel where she'd been working. "It may offend your artistic sensibilities, but it sure would ease our tension."

"Not to mention our arm muscles." Germaine poked her head around the other side. She'd been standing on a step stool applying long blue green stripes to a jungle scene.

"The time has come to compromise." Pascal looked up at the huge blank areas still remaining on the two backdrops. They had labored steadily for two nights, and still the panels were not even half completed. "These things have to dry before we try to deliver them. That means, settle for what is possible—not for what you wished could be done."

Renny stared dismally at the unfinished scenes. Then he looked at the crew who had struggled to paint what he wanted where he wanted it. Even with her good-spirited chatter, Francine couldn't cover up her apprehension that the task was hopeless. Tony had given up hours ago, quietly unrolling the sleeping bag that Francine had brought. He was snuggled under a work-table, where he had drifted off to sleep watching the bigger folks work.

"Let's try it your way," Renny finally agreed. Germaine and Susie let out sighs of relief. Tonight they might actually get to bed without aching all over.

"Get a couple of ladders and a board to use as a plat-form between them," Pascal directed the women. "Give Renny that flashlight. You shine it where you want me to paint, and I'll do the honors." Within minutes, the slender sculptor stood on the crossbeam with the paint sprayer in hand. He'd covered his hair and lower face with a gauze mask, making sure that his nose and his short beard were well protected, then he'd pulled on clear goggles to keep the paint out of his eyes.

"You look like something from outer space," Susie teased him as he walked across the board with the sprayer cord trailing behind him.

"If you don't want to turn jungle green, you'd better show a little more respect." He pointed the sprayer menacingly in her direction. "Now, shine that light." He signaled Renny that he was ready to paint.

Germaine taped the flashlight onto Renny's right wrist cast and switched on the beam. All he had to do was aim the light. Pascal skillfully blocked in the area with the color Renny specified. Susie worked behind the panel, mixing new paint and switching one shade for another as Pascal or Renny indicated. Francine settled down beside Tony, propping her short legs up on a paint can while she rested and watched the backdrops take shape. "We should have thought of this to begin with." She watched with delight as the blank spaces became filled with brilliant color. "We have a couple of rooms at the house that could use sprucing up," she joked. "How about tomorrow afternoon?"

By eleven o'clock, the two backdrops were totally colored in. The first panel was already dry enough that Susie and Germaine could brush in exotic flowers and sinuous vines. Francine had fallen asleep next to Tony, and Pascal was Technicolor all over. Every shade that he'd applied to the two backdrops had coated him from head to toe.

"Don't touch me, I may be contagious," he joked as he looked down at himself. Then he removed the paint-speckled goggles. The only part that still looked human was the unblemished area around his eyes.

Then Susie heard the click and whir.

"Your mother told me I'd probably find you here." Sy stepped forward. "I see your helpers from the Avery household have pooped out on you." He shook his head at the sight of Tony and Francine both sound asleep.

"You're back early." Susie started toward him. Then she stopped, recalling her own paint-splotched condition. In all the mixing and changing of colors, she had picked up a variety of drips and streaks herself.

"We ran into a few problems in New York, so I finished what I could and flew back." Sy lifted his camera and clicked a shot of Susie with her paintbrush still in her hand. "I thought perhaps I could take you out for coffee or something...." He looked at her closely. "I'm just not sure where we could go." He grinned at her. "You are a bit messy, my dear."

"I'm also washable," Susie replied. "Come home with me." She moved close enough so only he could hear her words. "I will scrub away all this paint, and you can make the coffee." The soft glow in Sy's eyes intensified as he studied the upturned face before him. The invitation Susie made had a meaning that was unmistakable. "Come home with me." She barely breathed the words. "Now that I'm the boss, I can give myself the morning off," she added with a slight smile. "That means I can sleep late."

"How soon can we get out of here?" Sy's low response resonated with an eagerness that sent a tremor of pleasure through her. The look in his eyes smoldered with a glow of undisguised desire.

"I'll finish up here quickly." Susie's throat was suddenly dry. Then her attention shifted to the boy still asleep beneath the worktable. "What about Tony...?" she said, looking up anxiously.

"I'll take care of Tony," Sy assured her. "You just pack up, lady. I'm going home with you."

Sy gently awakened Francine, who rubbed her eyes and fluffed her cloud of red hair. "I must have drifted off for a moment," she mumbled, restoring herself to order. "I was simply resting my eyes for a minute," she insisted. With her customary efficiency, she helped Sy load Tony, his sleeping bag, assorted thermos containers and a few boxes of snacks into Francine's car.

"I'll put us both to bed." She assured Sy she could handle everything at home. Then she poured a final cup of coffee to sip as she made the brief drive back across the river. "I'm as fresh as a daisy," she declared emphatically. "We'll be fine. However," she added with a sly smile, "I do think your son may be due for another spell of hookyitis. If he sleeps late tomorrow, and you have the afternoon free—" her green eyes sparkled "—perhaps the two of you could spend the afternoon at the zoo?" Tony was long due an outing with his dad.

"Hookyitis...." Sy grinned at her. "I think I feel a case of that coming on myself. You've got yourself a deal."

"We'll be rising rather late tomorrow," Francine added with a wink. "You might want to do the same. We'll not plan anything until midday." Sy looked at her closely, wondering just how much of his conversation with Susie Francine may have overheard. The approving smile on her face indicated she needed no words to understand that two people needed to be together. All she had to do was to watch their faces whenever their eyes met.

"Don't even mention it." Susie halted Sy before he could say anything about the grotesque paint streak on the side of her car. He had followed her back to the Quarter in his vehicle and parked next to her on the far side of the stone wall surrounding her courtyard. Only when he stepped out did he see the damage.

"I've already reported it to the police." She sighed as he bent down to look closer. "They said there's been a lot of vandalism lately, with all the drifters coming in for Mardi Gras. My insurance man has filed a claim. I'll get it sanded off and repainted after the carnival," she stated matter-of-factly.

"You don't think there's anything more to it than that?" Sy asked cautiously. After learning of Ralph Tanner's hostile attitude toward Susie, Sy felt uneasy knowing that the man was out on bail.

"If you're referring to that Tanner fellow," Susie said, addressing Sy's concern, "I called Bill Terrebonne, and he said he'd do some discreet checking. He didn't come up with anything to link Tanner with this mess." She looked glumly at the side of her car. "His attitude is that I should chalk it up to vandals and forget it. Tanner is in such hot water now, that painting a car is small potatoes. They've found the fabric store he stole the satins from," she noted. "He'll face charges on that, too."

"It still is a sneaky, cowardly thing to do," Sy muttered as he stood beside her.

"It can be repaired." Susie refused to dwell on it. "I'm just not in a big hurry to get it done."

"I'm not in a big hurry either." Sy's low voice spread

a cloud of warmth against her ear. "But I think it would be wise to get me inside your place before I embarrass both of us." The bright moon framed everything in silver as they stood there looking into each other's eyes. As they climbed the stairway, they paused simultaneously to glance out over the silent street below. Pale layers of mist hovered above the rooftops, as the distant sound of a bleating signal from a riverboat drifted in on the night breeze.

"The sounds of *home*." Sy smiled at the familiar haunting river noise. Hand in hand, he and Susie reached the balcony where she stopped to unlock the door. Only when they were inside and Susie hurried over to the long mirror on her bathroom door did she realize how understated Sy's comment about her being "a bit messy" really was.

Unlike Pascal, Susie had not worn any gauze covering on her hair or her face during the painting session. She had been caught in the clouds of residue during the spraying. Her hair had acquired a bluish sheen from the tiny particles that had settled over her, and even her eyelashes had collected an aquamarine coating that made them seem darker and longer than before. The overall effect was at once startling and exotic. With the unnatural coloring, Susie looked like some exquisite demigoddess from an alien world.

"This may take a little longer than I expected." Susie knew that removing the paint would be a difficult chore. Sy moved behind her, sliding his arms around her so he could reach the buttons down the front of her faded workshirt. "I'd be delighted to offer my assistance." His easy smile matched the seductive gleam in his eyes. Watching their combined reflection in the mirror, he pressed her back against him, unbuttoning the buttons one by one. "I seem to remember a moment somewhat like this once before," he murmured. "You and I and mirrors all around." He slid apart the front of her garment, gliding his hands over the nearly transparent fabric of her coffee-colored brassiere.

"I remember how you felt then." His hands moved down over the bare expanse of her narrowing torso, where the tips of his fingers dipped beneath the waistband of her jeans. Sy pulled the roundness of her derriere back against his thighs, stroking the flatness of her belly and brushing with his fingertips the dark furred swell below. Susie watched his motions in the mirror, as her own gleaming eyes echoed the passionate yearning apparent in his. "I want to touch you all over." Sy slid one hand, then the other, out from the confining jeans. "But first, I'm going to help you wash away that colorful exterior. I want you au naturel. How big is your bathtub," he asked quietly. "Large enough for two?"

"I certainly hope so," Susie replied breathlessly, already missing the feel of his hands against her skin.

"Then you start the water running, and I'll be right there." He looked at her with unhurried desire as he systematically began discarding his clothes. Susie kicked off her shoes, then padded over to the bathtub. From the outside, she closed the shower curtain that hung on an L-shaped metal rod enclosing the tub, and she reached in and turned on the shower, filling the enclosure rapidly with warm steam. Well aware that Sy was watching her from the doorway, she undressed hastily, reaching into the shower to adjust the temperature.

"Where's the shampoo?" Sy stood beside her, totally

naked, as naturally as if he belonged there already. Susie gazed with fascination at the haze of dusky hair across Sy's chest then followed its narrowing descent below his lean waist. Sy had caressed her naked body before and told her she was breathtaking. With all his manly form visible before her, Susie found her own breath halt, bewitched by his virile beauty.

"Shampoo, Susie. . . ." Sy stressed each word. "We have to get that blue stuff out of your hair and away from your eyes." Susie went to the cabinet and returned with the bottle he'd requested. Sy took it, checked the temperature of the water coursing from the shower, then took her hand, inviting her to join him within the cloud of mist.

"We have all night, my love." His obsidian eyes admired her unclad form. "We will know every inch of each other before dawn." Like a woodland nymph joining her lover beneath a silvery waterfall, Susie stepped into the steady downpour.

Standing under the steaming water, Susie closed her eyes, letting the water beat against her face. Behind her, Sy stood silently massaging the thick foamy shampoo through her hair as streams of blue-tinged water made graceful spirals at their feet, then swirled down the drain. The only contact between them was the strong rhythmic motion of Sy's hands moving over her hair, trailing it through his fingers, then sweeping the sudsy mass upward and beginning again. Occasionally Sy would slide his palms down over her bare shoulders, using the slippery foam to ease the tension as he kneaded the muscles in her back and neck. His hands touched Susie with a possessiveness and sensuous enjoyment that soothed and pleased her. They had loved each other in so many ways that this shampooing ritual became part of a natural progression from one plateau of intimacy to another. For the two of them, time had ceased to be an adversary. Tonight there was nothing but each other.

When the clear warm water washed the suds from Susie's hair, she turned to face Sy. With the steady stream of water beating down on her back, she watched as Sy lathered his chest with her scented soap. The combination of her perfumed lather and the movement of his eloquent hands against his own flesh sent a shiver of erotic possessiveness through her. Willingly Susie's hands joined his, sliding and circling in leisurely spirals over the spray-moistened furred chest hair that spread over his torso. Hypnotically drawn by the enticing textures and contours of his body, Susie caressed the hollow of his throat with her fingertips then glided both hands outward, embracing the muscular column of his neck.

"I love having you touch me." Sy's half-whispered comment rumbled with pleasure. "I love the wonder and the delight that comes into your eyes when you let your senses explore and discover." His finely wrought hands now repeated the motion of Susie's, stroking her wet, glistening body like a sculptor tracing the details of his creation, adding a distinctively human pressure to the steady downpour of the water on her back.

With their eyes absorbing every nuance of expression, each artist wantonly ventured with gentle strokes over sinuous lines and velvet crevices, in a timeless adventure of perception.

"Your hands give me such messages." Sy smiled down at Susie. "I want you to feel my body speaking out to you, telling you of pleasures that you have hidden away too long." Molding breast upon breast, sliding thigh against thigh, they stood locked in each other's embrace while the water streamed down upon them. The gentle kisses evolved into more intense and probing contact as they drank in the taste and warmth each offered with soft parted lips and penetrating tongue. Like sea sprites caught up in a whirlpool they were immersed in a pulsing torrent of sensuality.

Sy's hands moved sinuously over Susie's back, pressing the curves of her spine, then sliding lower over the firm, flaring lines of her derriere. Then he cupped his hands beneath their taut contours, drawing her against his potent form. "We fit together so perfectly," he murmured. Susie tightened her arms around his neck to prolong and intensify the proximity. "Like pieces of the same puzzle." Sy's voice mingled with the steamy rush of the water.

"Oh, Sy. . . ." Susie held more tightly as the quivering eagerness deep within her body responded to the arousal that the skin-on-skin meeting generated. "I want to feel you inside me." The words rushed out in a breathless request. But joining together wasn't all Sy wanted her to experience. He had told her that they would know every inch of each other before dawn, and he intended to take infinite care to summon Susie's passion to a fever heat so she could comprehend her own powers to receive and to bring pleasure.

"I think we'd better get out." His voice came in rasping uneven breaths as if he'd struggled to reach the surface before they were both overwhelmed by the current. They had become so entwined in each other's limbs, slick and scented, gliding against one another, that they balanced precariously in the confines of the antique tub.

The desire to be still closer could not be fulfilled within the limitations of the tub. Sy turned off the streaming water and stepped out, holding open the shower curtain for Susie to join him.

"The towels are right here." Susie reached for a large fluffy pink towel, wrapping it turban-style around her damp hair. Before she could reach for one to dry her body, Sy stopped her.

"You won't need a towel." He carefully unwrapped the turban and dropped the pink towel on to the floor. "I'll dry you." He took her hand and led her toward the bed. Before lowering themselves onto the flat surface, Sy bent over her, his rough beard brushing against her moist skin as he began to kiss away the droplets of water. The steady downward progression of provocative languid kisses and the gentle licking of his warm tongue aroused a new trembling deep within Susie's body. Gently he eased her onto the cool unruffled sheets, still caressing, savoring and probing the musky depth of her body where a new dampness supplanted the scented residue from their shower. Sy trailed his warm fingertips over her skin, touching and tenderly invading her womanly recesses, relishing the feel and taste as she arched her body to welcome his admission and his kiss.

"Sy. . . ." Susie invited and delighted in all the sensations that he generated in her. His whisperings, the fiery ripples of his breath, and the pervasive heat of his touch beckoned something enchanted and powerful in her. All her senses focused on the strain to meet him, to deliver to him the wondrous magic that existed within the complexity of her miraculous body. Barriers disappeared, and she reached beyond any restraint. "Love me now,

Sy. . . ." Susie wanted him to share the tide of ecstasy that was building.

Then Sy rolled onto his back, pulling Susie above him so her open thighs were poised over his own. "You come to me, Susie," he urged her quietly. "It's your body, Susie. You're in control of it. Take me with you." He clasped her hips as Susie gazed down at him with a gleam of triumph in her eyes.

Sy issued a purring sound as Susie lowered herself, claiming the right to her own passions—inflaming his with the tension in her slim body. His hands held her motionless for a moment as the overwhelming sensation of confirmation sent tremors of joy radiating through their merging bodies.

Feeling the fullness within her, Susie gasped in tiny breaths, closing her eyes so the feelings could engulf her. Pressing her fingertips against the dark silken triangle where their bodies united, Susie rocked gently from side to side, feeling the hunger Sy had wanted her to know, but also comprehending the power of her own body to enfold, to excite and to elicit a surge of desire. Sy's body moved in conscious opposition to hers, withdrawing then returning harmoniously, his midnight eyes riveted on the face that hovered above him, enraptured. His hands glided up her body, brushing over the delicate tips of her breasts, then lingering beneath them in the shadowy crescents, holding the soft orbs while her heartbeat pulsed into his palms.

Their bodies moved instinctively, increasing the steady rhythm in an exquisite blending of motion more primal than any ritual dance. Each clasped the other, seeking and giving a satisfaction that only the incandescence in their eyes expressed. Then Susie's dark eyes widened as the smoldering heat within burst into a radiant beacon drawing every part of her toward a fiery release. "Like a moth to a flame." Sy's image suddenly flashed through her mind. She would come to him, inflame him, just as he would come to her and fill her with his fire.

Sy brought her down against him, rolling above her as the wonder and abandon flared in her eyes and reverberated in the short husky breaths that escaped from her lips. He rose above her, whispering as the deep rocking rhythm brought them into closer and closer contact. "Love me, Susie...."

Susie grasped his muscular back, moist from perspiration, as she matched her rhythm with his. They clung together, striving toward an intangible realm of ecstasy accelerating gradually as the irreversible floodtide began its timeless course, sweeping them along in a rush of liberation.

Susie's breathless "Yes..." invited a more insistent, more powerful response in Sy, that brought both to the brink of a primordial realm where sensation answered sensation, and waves of passion held them suspended. There was no outside world. The only reality was the explosive absolution, the giving and the receiving, all-consuming and all-magical. Holding on to each other, gasping while the shuddering torrent erupted with volcanic force, then subsided so slowly into gentle ripples, each listened to the messages that body conveyed to body, soul offered to soul. At last, in a world of shared serenity, Susie and Sy celebrated the joyous creation of a moment that was theirs alone, one that had existed inside each of them—as a hopeful possibility—until this moment gave it life.

WHEN THE MORNING SUN again brought the relentless time of the world back into their lives, Susie's day began more suddenly than she wished. The harsh, persistent rapping on the wooden door insinuated itself into the still soft cocoon of tenderness that had filled their night. Within each other's arms there had been no clock nor schedule, only shared kisses and hushed sighs. The repeated tapping from the adjacent apartment signaled that another day had begun.

"Hey, Susie. . . ." Renny called from the opposite side of the sealed bathroom door just as he had many times during the months before. "Can I have a cup of coffee?" The aroma of the freshly brewing coffee filtered through into his apartment and had been too enticing to ignore. Minutes earlier, Susie had slipped out of bed while Sy still slept. She'd filled the coffeemaker and switched it on, then had barely returned to bed, still drowsy and content, when Renny's plaintive voice called out.

"Just a minute, Renny." Susie tried to answer without awakening Sy. His tousled dark hair and dense beard against the pale floral pattern on her pillowcase made an image Susie did not want to disturb.

"Go ahead, I'll wait right here." Sy cracked open one eye, then spoke as if he had known what Susie had been thinking.

Susie pulled her robe around her and hastily poured a large mug of steaming coffee for her neighbor. She took it into the bathroom to pass it through the only access there was. "Here you are," she called through the transom between the apartments. Standing on the commode, she waited while Renny opened the frosted-glass divider and stuck his hand, still supported by a slightly fraying cast toward the mug. Susie held it steady until Renny got a good grip on the mug, then coffee, hand and cast disappeared.

"Thanks," Renny called out.

"You're welcome." Susie climbed down and closed the bathroom door to seal off that room. If Renny decided he needed a refill, she did not want him peeking through the transom and seeing Sy with her in the room beyond.

"How about a cup for me?" Sy had propped himself up on one arm and lay in her bed, watching her.

Susie poured a cup for each of them then padded barefoot back across the room. Sy held the cups while she paused by the bedside.

"It's warm in here. You won't need the robe." Again, he anticipated her thoughts. With a quick shrug, Susie untied the sash and slipped her arms from the sleeves, laying the robe across the foot of the bed before easing between the sheets next to Sy. "Good morning to you." He presented her with the coffee mug then eased forward to place a gentle kiss on her lips. Then he shifted his position so Susie could lean against the curve of his shoulder, with Sy's arm supporting her back and his hand resting on the rise of her hip. Nestled together, they breathed in the cozy aroma of the coffee and smiled.

"Before we get too accustomed to this," Sy cautioned her, "I'd better tell you that I'll be going out of town again soon."

"Oh, no. . . ." Susie groaned.

"It's not as bad as it sounds." Sy elaborated. "The people from the magazine decided to expand the section Felicia is doing the modeling for. They're planning on making it into a series that they can spread over several issues, which means more pictures and more clothes." He wanted her to understand the reason for a return trip to New York. "Unfortunately, some of the designers couldn't finish the additional garments in time for this photo session."

"So how does that affect your job there?" Susie didn't grasp the implications. She thought that an extended assignment would have made his stay in New York longer, not shorter.

"I shot what they had ready and printed some proofs. Then I told them I had work to do back here. I didn't plan to hang around until they were ready to shoot again, and I knew darn well that the work I'd turned in was excellent." A sly smile crossed his face. "Rather than risk losing me altogether, they offered to fly me back here for a couple of days. I'll go back and finish the job when they have everything lined up."

"You're only here for two days," Susie protested. She had hoped that the time for them had finally arrived and this tranquil morning together was a new beginning. She assumed that he was home to stay, and his business with Felicia was over.

"I may be going back tomorrow," Sy replied. "When they need me, I'll go back, do what I have to do, then that's it." He didn't seem to mind the additional time or travel. "It's their money, and they do pay well," he stressed.

"If this thing with Felicia is to be a series, as you say—" Susie considered the possibilities that would be involved in an extended assignment "—will this trip be the only one left to do, or will there be more?"

"Hopefully more," Sy answered. "It could mean taking a week up in New York every few months," he explained. "Felicia is not the only model involved." He sensed Susie's distress. "She's just the lead-in model. After this, if the series is effective and the magazine continues it, I'll have my name right there on the photo credits under whichever face they hire. If they're pleased with what I do, I'll keep doing it. I told you, I'm that good with a camera," he reminded her.

"You don't have to convince me." Susie realized she sounded a bit petulant. "The pictures you took of me in the sea-horse costume and the ones in the train and tiara were excellent." Her assessment sounded almost clinical.

"I'm glad you think so." Sy was watching her profile curiously. "I notice you didn't say that you like them, though. Just that they are 'excellent.' Is that one artist appraising the efforts of another?" he teased.

"I'm a little uncomfortable with the content," Susie admitted. "The pictures were very effective, very well done. They just didn't seem like me."

"That's because they weren't." Sy laughed. "Those were Triton's Queen, who just happens to be Susie Costain this year." He took another long sip of the coffee. Then his voice became low and no longer teasing. "The real Susie Costain is sitting here next to me, stark naked, in bed. I hardly think you'd want color shots of this on your parents' walls."

"No, thank you." Susie felt her color deepen at the idea of a portrait of her, her body still glowing from lovemaking, next to the formal picture of sister Claire in her queen's gown.

"Your Triton's Queen portraits did what they were supposed to do," Sy observed. "They show you as you were then—at that time, in that role. My job was to preserve that moment. Now if you want me to do the same with this one," he said, passing her his half-empty cup and sliding out of bed. He walked, naked, across the room to get his camera bag.

"Don't you dare!" Susie shrieked. The two coffee cups afforded little for her to hide behind. "Don't you dare..." she warned him as she swung her legs around and looked for somewhere to land the two cups. "Don't!" she insisted more loudly than she'd intended.

"What's going on in there?" Renny's voice came from the next apartment. "Susie, are you okay?" He had apparently heard her protests and was ready to come to her rescue. Since the vandalism of her car, Renny had been keeping a closer eye than usual on both his neighbor and her belongings.

"I'm fine," Susie called out, putting aside the cups and grabbing her robe off the bed. Hastily she slipped it on in case Renny should decide that a face-to-face visit was necessary. Sy stood in the middle of the room grinning at her, completely naked, with his camera still in his hand.

"You still sound upset." Renny wasn't satisfied. "If someone is giving you trouble—" he dropped his voice so he sounded more ferocious "—I'm coming over and help straighten this out."

"No, don't come over," Susie squealed. "I'm not in that kind of trouble. I'm just having a disagreement with Sy.'' She tried to appease her would-be protector. ''We're arguing about photography.'' She realized how feeble that explanation sounded, even though it was the truth. ''I appreciate your concern, Renny, but I'm perfectly safe. We'll just have to keep the noise down in here.''

''Noooo problem. No problem at all.'' From the sound of Renny's drawn-out response, Susie knew that he must have been smiling. Her cheeks slowly began turning deeper shades of pink.

''I really wouldn't do anything to embarrass you.'' Sy lowered his voice so Renny couldn't hear. ''But you seemed so concerned that I'd missed capturing the real you.''

''The real me is not to be put on display for anyone,'' Susie replied angrily. ''I told you before that I don't like having my picture taken.''

Sy nodded. ''No one wants the world to see what they're really like. We're all too vulnerable to show so much of ourselves. So we settle for tiny glimpses of part of what we are or what we pretend to be. It's even better if those glimpses are prettier or more sophisticated or more elegant than how we see ourselves,'' he stressed, ''because then we feel as if we know a secret. The secret is that the wonderful person in the picture is not really us. The secret is that no one can hurt the real you if they are kept at a safe distance by the image on the outside or the person in the picture. That's why I'm so good at my job.'' Sy put the camera aside and walked over to her. ''I take pictures that have just a touch of the truth, but I add that magical distance that lets the subject act out that moment, without feeling exposed or vulnerable. It's a game, and I play it well.''

"You make it sound rather clinical." Susie let him put his arms around her, but she still remained rigid. "It sounds like. . . ." She groped for the right words.

"Like a business," Sy supplied. "That *is* my business," he affirmed. "I step in somewhere between what a customer wants to see and what the subject actually is. I create an illusion that pleases. That's what you do, Susie. You do that when you design costumes. You give them an illusion. It may be exquisite, but it's a *product*. It's your business. You do it well."

"But I feel so much more than that," Susie responded.

"So do I, sometimes." Sy smoothed her hair and tilted her chin so she had to look up at him. "That's what gives my photos or your costumes that element of excellence. The care we take in creating them shows. That excellence is the criterion we set for ourselves. It has little to do with who commissions us or what the subject is. It's a peculiar integrity of our own. My portraits aren't personal, they're professional. That's why Felicia requests me. Don't confuse how I feel about my work with how I feel about Felicia." He led straight to the source of Susie's doubts. "Business is business."

Now Susie leaned against him and wrapped her arms around him. "I'll try to remember that," she promised. "It's just that I love you. I want everything between you and me to be very personal. I don't want to be in your photos. I want to be in your life. I don't need a photograph to make last night last forever."

"Photos may last forever." Sy kissed her temple. "You can put them on a wall or in an album, but you can't hold on to feelings. They change, and when they do change you have to let them go. But you discover new feelings. Loving someone is a risky experience. You put everything on the line every minute just to have that rare magical moment when everything is so perfect that you're afraid to breathe in case you disturb it.'' He was unknowingly describing exactly what Susie had felt when she awoke that morning and watched him lying asleep next to her in her bed with the musky scent of their lovemaking lingering in the still air. She had felt it when they had made love in the darkness and trembled with the awesome power of their passion as their bodies communicated wordlessly in the night.

"I can't promise that we'll always feel this way about each other,'' Sy said with a touch of melancholy in his voice. He had seen love die before, just as he had seen great beauty change and fade. "But I will always be honest with you. I will tell you if the feeling ever ceases to exist. I won't let all the good we are to each other become tinged with disappointment and bitterness.'' He locked his eyes onto hers in somber contemplation. "I won't betray you. You have put your love and trust in me. It's up to me to deserve you. If I can't live up to that, I'll stop right then. I never would have let you love me, I wouldn't have let you commit so much of yourself to me if I weren't convinced that I do deserve you.'' He lowered his lips and brushed them lightly over hers. Then he paused as the solemn look in his eyes dissipated, and a familiar sparkle returned. "I think I deserve you *now*.'' His serious tone shifted as a mischievous chuckle rumbled from his throat.

Catching the sash of her robe, he untied it and the front fell open, so the length of her body was displayed beneath his appreciative gaze. This time when his mouth descended to her throat, Susie began to feel that a dormant part of her was being animated by Sy's touch, as if something that had been only imaginary was now becoming vibrant reality. The appetite he excited in her permeated all her body; every part of her longed to be rediscovered and released. The awakening sensations now emerging were unique and distinctive, full of possibilities that had not existed a fragment of time before.

With each quiver of delight, what seemed familiar blossomed into a new sense of wonder, a new hunger—not to repeat the past, but to strike an image in the present unlike any other. Sy's warm breath fanned the deep rose tips of her breasts, then his lips enveloped one. Susie reveled in the joys her body offered. Threading her fingers through the tousled dark hair that brushed against her flesh, she arched her back, withdrawing one responsive breast to offer and demand pleasure with the other. A new moment flamed incandescently as their acts of love held time suspended once more.

CHAPTER SIXTEEN

WHEN SUSIE WALKED through the vast scenery warehouse the next evening, far ahead she saw the motionless scarecrow form of Renny Castelot waiting alone.

"Where's Sy?" Renny seemed surprised and disappointed that Sy had not come along to help Susie work on the backdrops.

"He's taking Tony to a parade tonight. He wanted to get some pictures of the night parades." Susie unpacked the paintbrushes as she spoke. After they'd parted at midday, Susie had gone to the costume workroom to oversee the finishing touches on the last set of costumes. The staff she had trained, particularly three of the women who had been working in the sweatshop, now followed her directions perfectly. There was no need to check and redo their work. Susie could concentrate on the design end of the business, not the handwork. She had even spent part of the afternoon working on her files for the next year. Sy had gone his own way, intent on spending the afternoon and most of the evening with his son, letting Tony enjoy having his father completely to himself.

"You think Sy may be dropping in here later?" Renny seemed unusually curious. Susie turned to look at her friend.

"Just what is it you want with Sy?" she asked him.

"Oh, I don't know..." Renny hedged. "He's taken a lot of pictures of the bunch of us at different times. I was just curious about some of them." He avoided looking at her. Instead he began mixing some paint and attempting to appear preoccupied.

"Where's Germaine?" Susie suddenly sensed that she had pinpointed the cause of Renny's peculiar behavior. "Isn't she supposed to come tonight and help us finish up?"

"She isn't coming," Renny grudgingly admitted.

"Why not?"

"She said she had to study." Renny poked at the counterclockwise spiral of paint in the container he was stirring. "I tried to call her at the university to see if she might drop by later, but she wasn't there," he confessed. "One of the girls said she'd left with some guy." His dejected look was even more pathetic when he propped one broken wrist under his chin and stared into the paint can.

"Then what does all that have to do with Sy and his pictures?" Susie asked.

"I just wanted to know if Sy has a picture in all his stuff...a picture of Germaine," Renny replied. "I just wanted to have something. I don't even have one picture of her." He sounded bewildered that he could have overlooked such a thing.

"Going out one night with one other guy doesn't mean that she's gone forever," Susie chastised him. "Maybe she's studying with another classmate, and it happens to be a male."

"She wouldn't come over last night," Renny added forlornly. "I wanted to, you know..." he stalled. "Anyway, she told me that I needed to get some sleep, and so did she, so she wouldn't come over. I couldn't sleep,'' he lamented. "I kept missing her. I don't like waking up in the night and not having her near.'' He crouched over the paints with his knees poking out, like a grasshopper getting ready to spring. "I'd like to have a picture of her,'' he concluded mournfully.

"I'll ask Sy to see if he has one.'' Susie patted her friend on the shoulder. "I just think you're giving up on this a little early. You need to talk to Germaine and listen to what may be a perfectly reasonable explanation for everything.''

"Sure,'' Renny muttered without conviction. He was willing to accept the grim reality that Germaine might have found someone else. He just wanted something tangible.

"What happened to all the other helpers?'' Pascal came strutting into the lighted area where Susie and Renny were working. From the look Susie gave him, he knew at once that he'd asked the wrong question tonight.

"The Averys are at a parade,'' Susie explained. "Germaine is studying.'' She stuck with what she had been told. "And Francine was exhausted.'' Susie had skimmed over the details about Germaine rapidly, hoping to discourage Pascal from asking Renny for more information.

"So that leaves just you, me, and the guy with cement bracelets.'' Pascal tilted his head toward the silent painter with the broken wrists.

"I think it's you and me...period...'' Susie corrected him.

"Well, then, let's get on with it.'' Pascal grabbed a paintbrush. "Tell me what you want, and I'll slap it on there," he prodded Renny. "It's now or never, chum. This is the last night."

"The last night...." Renny saw another meaning in the words. "I wish...." He started to say something then simply took a deep breath. "Let's get this finished," he agreed. Stony-faced and emotionless, he described what was left to be painted on the hanging scenes. Then Susie and Pascal climbed on the two scaffolds to complete the upper portion while Renny watched from below. Tomorrow the hangings would be inspected by someone from the scenic studio that had commissioned Renny to do the job. Once they were approved, they would be left for another day to dry. Soon after delivery Renny would get the final installment of his wages and pay off the craftsman who was framing his paintings. As far as he was concerned, Mardi Gras would be over, and he could get back to his "real" art. But without Germaine, it just wouldn't be the same.

Shortly after one in the morning, they put the final touches on the second panel. "Let's all go out and get a drink," Pascal suggested. "Celebrate the end of this ordeal."

"I could use a drink." Renny packed away the paints and dumped the brushes in cans to soak themselves clean.

"I have the day off tomorrow." Susie joined her friends as they started for the door. "I actually have time to sit down with you guys and talk like civilized folk." She was beginning to enjoy her flexible hours. After the months when every minute was committed to one job or the other, Susie realized how deeply she had let herself be buried by her work. But it had protected her until Sy brought her out into the light and made her take charge of her life.

The French Quarter was still alive with post-parade celebrants who were unwilling to suspend their festivities until the next day when other parades would fill the air with doubloons and streamers. Tonight the lanterns all along the streets became the gathering places for costumed mimes or street musicians who joked and played and passed the hat as the passersby thronged the streets. From bars and restaurants one door after another opened, spilling the sound of Dixieland jazz or the heavier bump-and-grind music of strip joints into the streets. It was the peculiar mixture or merriment and madness that made New Orleans an around-the-clock carnival throughout the weeks leading to Mardi Gras Day, "the greatest free show on earth."

"He *looks* the way I *feel*." Renny pointed to one bedraggled fellow in a college sweat shirt, propped in the doorway of a shop. The unshaven young man still clutched an open can of beer in his hand, but it was the numerous ones he had consumed before it that left him immobile, staring dully off into space. "Give me booze," Renny moaned melodramatically. "I want to drown my sorrows in oblivion."

"If oblivion means that Susie and I are expected to haul you back to your place," Pascal said, staring up at his tall, gawky companion, "then the offer is canceled. I'll take you to a real hole in the wall for some gumbo instead. It's spicy enough to get you home under your own steam, not mine."

"I'm not hungry." Renny had spoken the words Susie thought she'd never hear from his lips. "I'm depressed, and I want to be numb."

"I'll buy you a beer with the gumbo," Pascal bargained. "One beer."

Renny gave a thoughtful glance at the inebriated lad still standing in the doorway, then shrugged. "If I'm going to suffer," he lamented, "I might as well do it on a full stomach." Walking in single file, picking their way through the street crowd and the heaps of litter left behind, the trio turned along Bourbon Street in search of native food.

The restaurant that Pascal led them to was a narrow corridor-shaped room with a bar along its length and rows of stools almost blocking the eating area. Even at two in the morning, it was packed with devoted followers who crowded in elbow to elbow while a lone waitress ferried bowl after bowl of rice and gumbo from the small kitchen at the rear of the room. The woman behind the kitchen partition moved her wide lips in song as she stirred a heavy black iron pot in which her seafood gumbo bubbled. She watched as customers came and went, some smiling at her or yelling out "Night, Bekkah." Here the gumbo was the finest—clear caramel-colored roux thick with shrimp, oysters and boiled crabs. Ladled generously by Bekkah over mounds of pure white rice, it was eaten in near silence by the true devotees of New Orleans' fare.

The beer that came in heavy frosted mugs was as cool and bland as the gumbo was hot and spicy. No bill was presented when the food or drink were served. Pascal placed a ten-dollar bill on the counter. To talk when such food was available seemed almost irreverent. When it came time for them to leave, the bill was gone and the change lay in its place. Pascal raised one hand in silent salute to Bekkah. The slight nod of her head signaled farewell in return.

"It's hard as hell to be depressed in a place where no one even talks," Renny muttered as they came out onto the street. "The food was good, though." He realized how foolish he sounded.

"When Bekkah cooks," Pascal cautioned him, "one is supposed to enjoy and contemplate—not sulk. And the food was not merely good, it was great."

"How did you find this place?" Susie interrupted their exchange deliberately. "I must have passed by here a hundred times and never even noticed it."

"Someone has to bring you here." Pascal wriggled his thin eyebrows and made weird gestures in the air as if he were performing some mysterious rite. "That and the fact that the place hasn't been here long. She moved here about a month ago from a seafood market on the other side of the river. Some of the guys in the float warehouse took me to her old restaurant. When she moved into this place, we all followed. This used to be one of those air-brush shops where some guy sat spray painting T-shirts."

"That makes me feel better," Susie conceded. "I hoped I was too observant to miss a place like this."

"Talk about missing something." Renny resumed his earlier mournful tone. "I sure would like to know where Germaine is right now."

"Maybe I could spring for another beer or two," Pascal surrendered. "How about it, Susie? Should we let this poor fellow dull his senses?"

"You two go on without me." Susie didn't want to suffer through Renny's imaginary sorrows. "I'll be on hand with coffee in the morning. You take this shift." She kissed Pascal lightly on the cheek.

"You're not going to walk home alone?" Renny seemed vaguely content now that he had a drinking buddy and a shoulder to cry on. "There's all kinds of bats coming out of the attic this week."

"Walk me over to Royal and I'll catch a bus," Susie suggested. "One runs right near our place."

"We'll walk you home," Pascal insisted. "The jerk who sprayed your car may be lurking around." Even though they had no proof that Ralph Tanner had anything to do with the vandalism, they all still intended to be cautious. "You never know what you'll run into between here and there," Pascal added.

"I hope we run into Germaine." Renny made both of his friends roll their eyes and grimace. For Pascal, it was beginning to look as if three beers wouldn't be enough.

"Hey...." Renny spotted the light in Sy's studio as the three of them passed by the building. "Looks like your friend is in there working." The shadowy shape that moved around in the rear of the store crossed the inner doorway. "It's him all right." Renny sounded hopeful. "I wonder if he's got a picture of Germaine in there." Renny tapped loudly on the locked door.

"It's late." Pascal tried to silence him.

"As long as he's up working—" Renny tapped again "—he might be able to put his hands on one just like that." Renny snapped his fingers. "If I had just one picture...."

"Fancy meeting you three here," Sy said, pulling open the door.

"We're sorry about this." Susie was the first to apologize. "Renny is feeling a little low and we'd started out to cheer him up, but he wants to drown his sorrows in beer, and I decided to go home." Her rapid-fire explanation brought a smile to Sy's tired countenance. "He was wondering earlier if you happened to have a picture of Germaine anywhere in your shots, and when he saw you working inside...."

"Hold it," Sy reached out and rested his hand on her shoulder.

"We shouldn't have interrupted you," Pascal apologized. "We'll take Susie home as we'd planned, and then I'll take Renny out for some remedial booze. The picture of Germaine can wait."

"I just happen to have a picture of Germaine," Sy said very patiently. "And I will be delighted to see that Susie is safely accompanied, so you can save yourselves a long walk. Just step in," he said, leading them into the dim interior of his shop.

While Renny shifted his feet nervously, and Pascal tried not to appear too embarrassed, Sy walked into the rear of the studio and emerged with a glossy black-and-white photo of Renny and Germaine arm in arm, looking up at the huge hanging scenery panel. "I didn't use to like black-and-white." Renny stared down at the picture. "But this is great." His voice quavered slightly as he shook Sy's hand.

"I can blow it up or crop some off or make you extra copies," Sy offered. "And I'm sure I have others. But not tonight," he added pointedly.

"I guess we can be on our way now." Pascal picked up the cue. "Thanks for being so decent at such an indecent hour." He grabbed Renny's arm and escorted him out of the shop. "See you later, Susie," he said over his shoulder.

"Are you sure you don't mind stopping work to take me home?" Now it was Susie who felt as if she was imposing. Sy often processed pictures during the night when it was quiet and dark. It was that reverse schedule that had made it impossible for them to see each other, but during Mardi Gras season, when so much developing and printing had to be done, the reversal worked.

"I didn't say I would take you home." He locked the door behind her. This time he pulled down the heavy shade so no light from inside was visible from the street. "I said that I would accompany you. And I certainly will." He caught her across the shoulders with one arm and walked her into the back room of the studio. "This is where I've been spending most of my nights lately." He pointed to a large loft bed built along one wall. "We have several options," he said as they walked. "You could go back to your place alone. I could close up shop and take you back to your place, which, of course, would take a while. Or we could stay here and pretend that I'm Superman and you're Lois Lane and the loft is our Temple of Solitude at the top of the world."

"I think I'd like to stay here," Susie replied with a smile.

"You can climb a ladder, can't you?" He led her to the wide rungs rising to the loft.

"I can climb a ladder," she replied. "But I was hoping you'd fly me up there."

"That could be a little risky," he said, laughing. "We'll have to climb." Sy walked over to the counter where he had pictures and negatives spread out. He slid a few items into manila envelopes and set them aside. With a press of a button, he switched off all the lights in the room except for a dim lamp up in the loft. From out of the near darkness, Susie heard him say softly, "I should point out that here we have no neighbors, no windows, no interruptions.'' He emerged from the shadows and stood close to her.

"And no bathtub," Susie teased.

"Just a commode and a shower. But next time—" his hands stroked her shoulders then trailed down her arms "—if you give me a little warning, I'll have a plumber put in the biggest tub I can find."

"I think we can rough it tonight." Susie slid her arms around his neck. "I can give up the tub for the chance to spend a night at the top of the world. Besides, we don't want to do the same things again and again."

"It's never the same, Susie." Sy bent to kiss her softly on the lips. "That's part of the magic. Every time is the first time, and when you're away, all I want is for the next time to come. I was thinking of you when you and your motley bodyguards showed up at my door. I didn't want to crawl into that bed alone again tonight. Wait till you see what's up there." He waved his hand for her to climb up into the loft.

"A cape and a pair of pajamas with a big *S* on the chest," Susie guessed.

"Climb, Lois," Sy slapped her fanny playfully. "Superman doesn't need pajamas tonight."

In the loft Susie expected to see some of the favorite photographs Sy had made. Instead there was only one picture on the wall beside his bed—the black-and-white drawing she had made of their favorite streetlight, which they had contemplated from her balcony.

"I've been sleeping with that part of you near me for a long time," Sy said as he settled down beside Susie and began peeling off his shirt. "But after being with all of you—" he unzipped his pants and slid them down "—I hate the thought of being up here alone."

"I guess I wasn't really looking forward to going back to my place by myself," Susie admitted as she unbuttoned her blouse. "Funny how empty a place can become." She looked into Sy's eyes and knew he understood.

"Let me hold you." Sy reached out and pulled her close to him as he eased back onto the pillows. "I want to feel you next to me all night long. I want the scent of you to fill this space with an unmistakable perfume, so I can breathe you in any time. It will never be the same again. It will be filled with you."

For a few moments, they only held each other, while their physical closeness gradually drew them into their world of secluded wonder, apart from the world beyond this quiet room. Susie lay beside Sy, listening to the steady pulsing of his heart as he cradled her in his arms. A peculiar inexplicable sadness settled over her as she realized that every place she shared with Sy, everything they saw or felt or did, would be colored by his presence from this moment on. She had opened up her soul to him, shared her life and her talents and herself. Now that she knew how wonderful everything was when he was close to her, loving her, smiling at her or simply talking with her, the prospect of being somewhere—anywhere—without him was bleaker than she had suspected. Lovers fill their lives with each other and those lives are far emptier when the lovers are apart. Renny's loneliness would be her own if Sy disappeared from her life.

But he is here, Susie thought. She could feel his warmth and inhale his scent. Her hand touched his bare chest just as his arm tightened around her. Then they looked into each other's eyes and found the new beginning, the "once more" that set their hearts pounding in unison. All touch and taste and texture, they lost themselves in each other and in the loving, they were renewed.

WITH THE DAWN, their make-believe world had to give way to the real one where other commitments took precedence.

"It's back to Clark Kent time." Sy chuckled softly as he awakened Susie with a kiss. "I have to fly off to Metropolis in a few hours. On a plane," he added before she could comment. He was trying to keep his tone light, even though both dreaded this parting. "I don't know if I'll make it back from New York in time to see your parade," he went on as he lay beside her, listening to the growing sounds of the traffic outside. The night parade of the Krewe of Triton was three days away. Sy was booked on a midmorning flight to complete the photo assignment. "I've lined up a friend of mine—another photographer—to take some shots in case I don't make it."

"Can Tony ride with me in the parade even if you aren't back?" Susie asked. She hoped the boy could enjoy the excitement while he was safely seated next to her, dressed as the Queen's page. He would not have to struggle with the pushing and crowding of the throngs that lined the roadways screaming, "Throw me something" as they reached up for trinkets and doubloons.

"You can have Francine, too, if you want," Sy said, laughing. "She's so short she won't go near a parade for fear of being elbowed into unconsciousness."

"Then I'll use my influence to get her on the float, too." Susie snuggled close to Sy, resting her hand on his chest. "Afterward, we can go to the party and celebrate the end of a very hectic season."

"And the beginning of a new one," Sy noted. "The cycle picks up again right after the streets are swept clean."

"Only next year will be different," Susie observed. "I have some excellent employees, and the new workrooms will be remodeled."

"And there will be even more clients calling to ask you to do the designs and costumes for their krewes." He fell silent for a moment. In the studio below, the soft persistent ringing of the telephone summoned him. "Now who the heck would have the phone number for the Temple of Solitude," he tried to joke. He swung his legs over the side of the loft and leaped to the floor.

"Hello?" He stood there naked, speaking to the caller. "Yes, she's here," he reassured someone. "She's perfectly safe. I'll be sure to tell her." When he hung up the phone, he looked up at Susie and shook his head. "Apparently he went looking for coffee and found out you didn't make it home last night," he told her, laughing. "Your friend Renny," Sy explained. "He wanted to know if you were all right, and he wants to talk to you as soon as it's convenient."

"I guess that means I'd better get dressed. Civilization calls." Susie sat up and began collecting her clothes. "Did he sound upset?" she asked as she pulled on her blouse.

"He sounded about the same as he did last night." Sy started a pot of coffee. "Depressed...bewildered. Something like that."

Susie finished dressing while Sy showered in the small studio bathroom. Then they shared a quick cup of coffee. Sy dressed in a deep brown European-cut suit, then lined up the suitcase and camera gear he was taking back to New York with him. Susie called Renny.

"I got a note from Germaine." He certainly did sound bewildered. "It says that I have to be at the university tonight at eight. I'm supposed to wear a suit."

"Is that all the note says?" Susie asked.

"It has the name of the building printed on it," Renny replied. "I tried to call her to ask her what's going on, but she isn't in her room. No one knows where she is."

"I think I'll come over there and pick you up," Susie suggested. "We'll take a little ride up to Tulane and see if we can find her. You might try to pull yourself together so you'll look respectable when we get there."

"Okay," he answered. "Do you think this means she still might like me?" The hopeful sound in his voice made Susie smile.

"You'll have to ask Germaine about that," Susie said sympathetically. "I'll be there in a few minutes. See you then."

"Don't you have work to do today?" Sy hugged her. "Here you are driving Renny around, staying out late carousing with the guys, spending the night with me, sleeping in late...."

"I have one krewe picking up costumes this week, then I have to be in the parade. Detective Terrebonne said he needs me one afternoon to give some depositions for a federal hearing. Apparently the Tanners are going to be prosecuted for labor-law violations in addition to the criminal charges."

"Them again." Sy frowned at the mention of the man who had given Susie the concussion. The trial date for that charge had not even been set.

"It doesn't take much of my time," Susie informed him. "As a matter of fact, I'm going to have a lot of uncommitted hours in my days and nights. You picked a lousy time to leave town," she teased him.

"I didn't exactly pick it," Sy replied. "It picked me. It was easier leaving you when I knew you were too busy to draw a breath. Knowing that you have time we could be sharing...."

"Will make you anxious to get back?" Susie guessed.

"It makes me wish you could come with me." He looked into her eyes. "There's nothing worse than sitting in a restaurant or spending the night in a hotel alone when there's someone you'd really like to be with. You can bet I'll be anxious to get back here."

"Call me as soon as you know when you're coming. I'll even meet you at the airport," Susie promised.

"The places we meet." Sy chuckled. "All my ideas about romance, and we end up in your little bathtub or in my cluttered studio. And now it's an airport." His face grew solemn. "You should have flowers and music...."

"I don't need anything but you." Susie silenced him with a gentle kiss. She glanced out and saw the airport limousine pull up in front of the studio. "And you need to get going." She hurried him along. "Give me the studio keys, and I'll lock up for you." She carried one bag to the waiting vehicle while Sy followed with the large suitcase.

After the limousine pulled away, Susie took a final look inside the studio, clicking off the lights and unplugging the coffee pot. She paused and looked at some of the pictures spread out on his counter—countless faces of lovely young women and elegantly clad krewe members from balls that Sy had photographed. There were other envelopes, large manilla ones with handwritten labels naming a particular krewe or a queen of a court member. Sy would compile these later into large, elegant albums that would document a special part of Mardi Gras for each client. There was one folder simply labeled, Susie, set off to the side, but Susie only touched it with her fingertips, then turned away. She didn't need a picture to tell her how she felt or to remember what she and Sy shared. She wanted to see herself in his eyes—not in his photographs.

This time, when the telephone rang, Susie tried to sound official. "Simon Avery Studios. May I help you?"

"Is Simon there?" Felicia Avery's honey-sweet voice cooed into the phone. The hollow sound on the line indicated this was a long-distance call.

"I'm sorry, but he's just left for the airport," Susie replied.

"Oh, dear. I was afraid I'd miss him." Felicia sighed. "Do you happen to know if he packed his tuxedo? Some old friends of ours are having a get-together tonight, and it's formal."

"I'm not sure what Mr. Avery packed," Susie answered.

"I'll just rent one in his size," Felicia decided. "He asked me to meet him at the airport. Do you happen to know the number of his flight?"

"I'm sorry, but I don't know that, either." Susie felt the tension building.

"I'm sure I have it somewhere." There was no final comment, only the dull click when Felicia hung up the phone.

Standing in Sy's studio, Susie fought the urge to slam the receiver back into its cradle. In the very room where she and Sy had loved each other, suddenly an old presence made itself known. Felicia had "dropped in" again as she had before. In the brief time of the phone call, she had made it clear that the ties between them still existed. She was to meet him at the airport. They were to attend a formal party with old friends. She would rent a tuxedo in his size. They were the comments of someone who still held a claim and did not intend to relinquish it.

"Don't let her get to you this time." Susie tried not to give in to the frustration she felt. Just as everything was beginning to feel so right at last, Felicia reappeared. Susie turned and stared at the loft where she and Sy had held each other through the night. Then she slowly scanned the entire room. It was nothing more than a cluttered back room in the daylight. In the night it had seemed like a paradise. "The places we meet...." Susie remembered Sy's words. They had sat in Jackson Square together, and they'd played rag-tag football at Uncle Leo's. She tried to remember all the times they had shared. Most of them weren't very glamorous. Even the Triton Ball was simply something they knew was make-believe. But in the world of Felicia Avery, glamour was a way of life, and it was a life that Felicia and Sy were caught up in again.

But this is his home now, Susie thought. *And I'm here for all his tomorrows.* She would feel their commitment grow stronger with every "once more."

Susie understood that she could not let the past torment her. She had chosen to live her life fully and to love a man who came to her with a history of his own.

All she could do was hope for another time, another moment with him when the magic would be reborn. If Felicia shared the same hope, if she too wished for that "once more," it would still be Sy who made that choice. Susie had already made hers, and she had no regrets.

"THAT'S THE ADDRESS of the Fine Arts Center." Susie read the brief note Germaine had pinned to Renny's door. "They have a huge art show at the university every year during Mardi Gras so the alumni who return or parents who come to visit get to see new works. Maybe Germaine wants you to take a look at some of the displays," Susie suggested.

"She did say that she had to do some special lighting for a show," Renny recalled. "I thought she was talking about a *show*, you know, in the drama department where people move around."

"We can go to the university now and take a look," Susie offered. "Or I can go out to the costume work-room for the rest of the day and then come back here tonight. If you aren't too thrilled about going by your-self at eight, I'll take you."

"I'd rather go now." Renny kept staring at the note.

"Let me call and see if it's open." Susie didn't want to make the trip to the campus and find out that the building was closed. Renny was dejected enough as it was. Another disappointment would be difficult for him to bear.

"That settles that," she told him after she'd made the call. "There *is* a reception starting tonight at eight. Un-til then, no one is admitted. I guess that means we go tonight."

"I don't think I can get into my suit with these casts

on my wrists." Renny rotated them back and forth. "Let's forget it." The mention of a reception was enough to scare him off.

"I'll take your jacket to work and have one of the seamstresses open the sleeves a bit." Susie wasn't going to let him avoid the event. "Whatever Germaine wants you there for must be important. So we're going."

"If it's so important, why is she avoiding me? She could at least tell me what it is. I just want to see her."

"We'll see her tonight at eight," Susie assured him. "I'll be back here in time to help you get dressed. Now get me your suit coat and let me see what can be done about the sleeves."

By seven forty-five that evening, Renny was in near panic. "I called her room all day." He shifted from one foot to the next as Susie knotted his tie. "She didn't even call back."

"I don't usually recommend this, but let's stop and get you a stiff drink on the way there. Maybe it will calm you down a bit." Susie watched him pacing back and forth.

"Where were you last night when I needed you?" Renny threw his hands in the air. "Pascal bought me beer, and all it did was make me need to go to the bathroom. All night long, I was up and down, running back and forth to the john."

"I'm glad I missed it." Susie laughed. There was no way she could have slept through that commotion. "Come on, Renny," she summoned him. "I'll buy you a Scotch on the rocks."

"Wait till I get paid," he muttered as he followed her along. "I'll buy my own drinks."

"Right after you pay for all the framing and pay off

any other creditors," Susie chided him. "Your art comes first," she stressed. "And so do your bills."

The university's massive Fine Arts Center building was surrounded by a vast, tree-lined parking area to accommodate the audience for all types of performances. Theater, music and art displays could be held simultaneously in the various performing centers. Tonight, however, the entire building was devoted to displaying new art from across the United States. As guests and alumni joined local art patrons in roaming from one hallway to another, small groups of musicians played on raised platforms, and refreshments were served in abundance at bars and buffets along the way. It was an evening to meet old friends, appreciate new artists, enjoy the food and drink and buy. All the paintings on display were cataloged and priced with the hope of advancing the artist's career and providing the wealthy guests with a possible tax advantage. Any art purchase donated to the university was deductible.

"I bet Germaine did the lighting." Susie paused to admire a group of performers sitting motionless beneath the dramatic lights. When the musical group on the next platform played, these dancers would suddenly come to life, performing a brief ballet, until the music ceased again. Then farther down the corridor, on another set of raised and lighted platforms, a new group would perform.

"Actually, I did a lot more than the lighting," Germaine said, walking up beside them. "I know this may get me into big trouble," she admitted, "but Renny is such a lousy money manager, I just had to do something."

"What exactly did you do?" Renny had talked Susie

into buying him two drinks. On an empty stomach, they had not only calmed him, they had nearly anesthetized him. He could hardly focus his eyes. As he spoke to Germaine, he swayed forward.

"I knew you wouldn't have any money for this, and you're too hardheaded to take a loan if I offered it, so I put the Harley cycle up for collateral and bailed out all your framed pictures." Germaine backed up a step when she caught a whiff of his pungent breath. "I put prices on them and placed them in the show here."

Renny teetered back, then forward again. "What I want to know," he insisted, moving his mouth as if forming the words required considerable concentration, "is do you still love me?"

"Did you hear what I said about your paintings?" Germaine narrowed her eyes and looked at him closely. "I put them in the exhibit. They're for sale. Maybe you should look at the prices and see if they look fair."

"The damn paintings aren't going anywhere." Renny raised his voice impatiently. "What I want to know is do you still love me." He was oblivious to the crowd gradually collecting around them. Susie looked at Germaine and shrugged.

"Do you think I would risk making you angry and putting my motorcycle on the line so I could get your paintings here if I didn't love you?" Germaine tried to silence him.

"Now let me get this straight, you do love me. You don't love anyone else, but you do love me." Renny bobbed his head up and down as he stressed each thought.

"That's right. But I also think you're a hopeless mess with money, and if we're going to have any kind of life together," she informed him, "you have to stop spending money you haven't earned yet."

"You mean if I had money, you'd never leave me again?" Renny persisted.

"It would help if we could afford things like food, rent and tuition. I've been paying most of my own all along, but I don't think I can afford to support you, too," she explained. "When an opportunity like this comes along, I'd rather not have to barter with a Harley-Davidson to get your work out of a frame shop."

Gradually an idiotic smile spread across Renny's face. "You really love me," he said happily. "She really loves me." He turned to tell the appreciative audience. "All you have to do is buy a painting, and she'll never leave me again." By now the amused bystanders with their cocktails and hors d'oeuvres were caught up in the romance.

"Let's take a look at one of your paintings." A white-haired gentleman with a Phi Beta Kappa key dangling from his watch chain, stepped forward and took Renny's arm. "In the old days, I used to ride a Harley." The elegant fellow hardly looked the type. "If the little lady thinks your work is worth her Harley, it had better be good." Germaine took Renny's other arm and guided him through the corridor to the room where his works were arranged.

Most of the remaining bystanders followed, with Susie mingling unobtrusively among them. Then the next musical group, who had listened intently while Renny and Germaine conducted their conference, began to play. The ballet dancers leaped into motion, but this time they could not conceal their smiles. The tall scarecrow of a fellow with a cast on either wrist and the slim, oval-eyed drama student who walked with the grace of a gazelle had brought something unexpected to those who watched. They had opened their hearts and shown a glimpse of their love in a world that hides feelings so well.

For the rest of the evening, Renny kept Germaine by his side while his newly acquired white-haired patron strolled through the halls bringing his friends and associates in to see works signed by Renny Castelot.

"If you buy one, she'll never leave me again," Renny told each patron who stood to admire the vivid colors and abstract patterns he had painted. It was the excellence of the paintings themselves that made the sales, but the sight of the two lovers and the laughter that accompanied Renny's antics were the touch of romance that made the viewer linger. Once they had taken the additional time to admire the works of art, many of them got out their checkbooks.

"I really thought I overdid the price on some of these," Germaine confessed as the last patrons left the Fine Arts Center. "Then I looked at what the other artists were asking for their works, and I really got confused. That's why I had one of the professors from Tulane come over here with me last night and really look at Renny's paintings. "I told you I was studying," she acknowledged. "That was partly true. I was studying the prices."

"So the guy you went out with wasn't a date?" Renny had sobered up on hors d'oeuvres and orange juice. The large sum that his burgundy-and-lavender abstract brought had also improved his perspective. "I thought what we had was over."

"I don't have time for dates," Germaine laughed, "I hardly had time for you. And what we have needs improving financially and otherwise. I'm not satisfied with a few hours now and then together—and I'm not going to spend my life sleeping in an apartment filled with paint and brushes constantly wondering if we can pay for your materials. If we're going to plan some kind of future, we have to start now—beginning with a studio for you."

"What about your motorcycle?" Renny asked. That had been Germaine's sole form of transportation—and often his as well.

"When you get the money for the scenery, you can pay the man who did the framing, and he'll give the cycle back to me," she explained with a broad smile. "If your apartment can be made to look like a place where people live and we can find you a decent place to work, I'll give up my room on campus. But I will need the cycle to get back and forth to classes."

"If either one of you wants a ride tonight," Susie interrupted them, "my shuttle service leaves immediately. I've got some remodeling of my own to look into."

"If I promise to start looking for a place to put all my paints and canvases tomorrow," Renny said, clasping Germaine's hand, "do you think you could pretend it's all gone and come home with me tonight?" He looked at her beseechingly. "I hate it when you aren't there."

"You've kinda grown on me, too." Germaine smiled at her tall admirer. "I think we can overlook the aesthetics of the place once more." She draped one graceful arm through his. "Let's go home."

Susie knew she couldn't stay in her apartment before she even pulled into the parking place by the courtyard.

"I think I'll go out to my folks house tonight," she said as her two friends stepped out of her car. "I'll be working there all day tomorrow, so I might as well get an early start." The walls between the two apartments were far too thin for Susie to feel comfortable tonight, and the thought of lying in her bed alone, trying not to listen, made her heart ache. But when Susie backed out onto the street, she didn't turn toward the suburb where her parents lived. Instead, she drove deeper into the Quarter and parked in a place marked S. Avery. To her, this studio had become the haven she needed. She still had the keys after locking up for Sy, so she let herself into his shop.

In the dim light of the loft lamp, she undressed alone and slipped under the coverings of the bed still unmade from their night together there. Sy had said that they had made that place theirs, and tonight that was all she had to comfort her. He was somewhere in New York, dressed in a tuxedo, surrounded by his beautiful ex-wife, Felicia, and some of their old friends. That world had a hold on him just as his world with Susie had. But only one of them could feel like home. He could not go back and forth forever. Susie and Sy needed a more stable environment than their fantasy bower. She felt too much as Germaine had. Susie knew that if she and Sy were going to plan some kind of a future, they'd have to sort all this out. But the future wasn't what concerned Susie as she lay staring at her sketch of the streetlight. All she wanted was to get him back from this trip, to have that "once more" feeling, to build a time in the present that could protect Sy from the temptations of his past and open possibilities for their future together.

In the old days in New Orleans, would-be lovers

sought dark-eyed native women like the enigmatic Bek-kah, who brewed gumbo in Pascal's late-night haunt. But then the native women would make another kind of magic, weaving bits of hair and cloth and feathers into voodoo gris-gris charms. Then the lovers placed the charms under the pillow of the one they longed for in the hope that through their dreams, their true love would be known and they would live together happily ever after.

Susie did not believe in voodoo, but her own sense of ritual had brought her back this night to sleep in the bed she and Sy had shared. She had no spells or charms to offer. All she could do was press her cheek upon the pillow and whisper, "Please come back to me." This was the only magic she knew.

Tony Avery was already at the assembly point the next evening when Susie arrived before the Triton parade was to begin. His companion, Francine, was peering under one flatbed, examining its construction while a jeans-clad fellow assured her that it would support her weight.

"Any word from Sy?" Susie asked the two of them as they looked up to greet her. The only message from New York the day before was that he would call them when he'd finished there.

"No word." Francine frowned. "I guess that means there was more to do than he expected. He'll be back as soon as he can." She tried to sound unperturbed. But like Tony and Susie, Francine had hoped that for the big parade and the party afterward all of them would be together.

"What do you think of the floats?" Susie watched

Tony mount the king's throne and pretend that he belonged up there.

"I like them from this side," the boy said, smiling. When he had attended one night parade with his father, he had found the pushing crowds and the towering floats frightening. "Here I can see everything and not get squeezed."

"I have your costumes in the car." Susie summoned him down from his post. "Then I'll show you where you'll ride and help you get wired in."

"Wired in. . . ." Francine arched her red eyebrows. "You mean I have to be tied down on that thing?"

"Tied on, not down." Susie laughed. "Actually they're more like brackets that support the riders so they don't topple over when the float changes speed or direction. There are upright poles to hold on to, but if you're waving or throwing beads, the braces give you a little more stability."

"I plan to *sit* through this." Francine bobbed along after Susie and Tony. "Find me a flat place, and I'll plant myself there. I want to watch the crowd and enjoy the ride."

Very rapidly the number of costumed and masked riders multiplied as krewe members and the court were positioned on the fifteen floats that would form the procession. Several marching bands would parade amid the floats, so the music would provide a festive sound to accompany the fantastic structures. The night parades in New Orleans had an excitement and rhythm distinctly their own. It came from the shuffle and prance of the flambeaux carriers. Black men clad in white robes dance down the street, "second-lining," an original New Orleans style of strutting. While they dance, they twirl and wave brilliant kerosene-fueled torches, the flambeaux, that illuminate the way. The appreciative crowd traditionally throws coins to these magnificent dancers, and punctuates their steps with loud, rhythmical hand-clapping that erupts into applause as the fellows move farther on.

"The flambeaux...." Tony leaped to his feet when the first of them began to form up. It was still not quite dark and the torches were unlighted, but their presence meant the party mood would escalate well before the first motor began and the procession started to move. Tony raced over to watch them as they carefully fueled their kerosene torches and checked them all to be sure they functioned correctly. With each row of dancers, there was one man who was older, and whose expert eye pinpointed any leaks or possible danger to the carrier or to the crowds. These men carried heavy fabric pieces dangling from a waistband like a wide cape. If a flambeau should inadvertently begin to flame abnormally or if a bystander should pitch some paper into the flame, the larger team leaders would put out the fire with one swoop of the treated fabric cover.

"What's that for?" Tony squatted amid the flambeau carriers, watching every move they made with wide, fascinated eyes.

"Fire extinguisher." One young man whose gold tooth gleamed in the torchlight seemed embarrassed to answer. "New precaution." The bright red cannister with the funnel-shaped spout looked out of place with the stark black and white of the dancers.

"We've got 'em on the floats, too." Tony tried to sound as if he were an old hand at float riding. "Just in case." He nodded wisely.

"Time to load up." The voice summoned all the riders to their posts.

The huge theme float moved out onto the street first, followed by the float for Triton's King. Then came the other floats bearing members of the court and all the masked and costumed krewe members, with Susie's float next to the last. The procession would move along Napoleon Avenue then up tree-lined St. Charles, heading toward the Quarter. Within sight of Blaine's department store, it would turn along the divided Canal Street and disband at the new Riverview Hotel. While the floats were taken away to the warehouses to be torn apart and reconstructed for another parade, all the Krewe of Triton and honored guests would move inside the hotel's ballroom and discard their own elaborate costumes for informal wear. They would party till dawn or until their stamina gave out, and it would be time to leave the fantasy behind.

The first few floats had barely moved one city block before the procession stopped. Tony stood on tiptoe, peering ahead, trying to determine what had blocked the progress of the parade. "It's a cop car," he called up to Susie. "Maybe they're the escort," he guessed.

From her throne, Susie could tell that the car was pulled sideways in the road. It was deliberately blocking off the parade route. The krewe members from the first floats had leaped from their stands and converged on the police car. All the parade permits were in order, the police had been alerted, the parade routes had been approved and published well in advance. There was no reason to stop the parade now.

Then Susie saw a second and a third car pull into view. The officer who stepped out and approached the krewe leaders was her father's friend Detective Terrebonne. Susie watched in silence as Terrebonne and a trail of others wound their way toward her float. Susie experienced a sinking feeling. Terrebonne's expression meant there was trouble.

"We got a tip." Terrebonne said, climbing onto her float. "From Eugene Tanner," he continued, moving closer to her. "It looks like his brother Ralph has decided to stop you from testifying at the federal hearing this week. Eugene says Ralph has been drinking pretty steadily over the past few days and has turned mean as sin. He plans to do something to you. Eugene says Ralph is going to get you while you're in the parade."

"What good would it do to hurt me?" Susie had already given depositions recounting everything she knew about the robbery and the sweatshop. All the evidence was filed and tagged and totally out of her hands. Her personal testimony would just reinforce those facts.

"The booze and the pressure must have gotten to him. The guys is nuts," Terrebonne concluded. "He sees it all closing in on him, and he's gone a little crazy. Regardless of what he's doing, we can't take any risks with you or with the crowds lining the streets. We're calling off the parade."

"You can't do that!" Tony's wail of protest was barely out before Susie said the same thing.

"We can't call off the whole parade just because that guy might be planning something," Susie argued. "I remember what you said before about crazies," she challenged Terrebonne. "You said we can't let them scare us. We can't let them take over the streets."

The wiry detective nodded grimly. He had said that to her when Ralph Tanner's angry look was enough to upset her. Now Tanner was up to something more dangerous, and Susie was not giving in to him.

"*I* can drop out of the parade," Susie said evenly. "If he's after me, then he'll be out of luck. But there are so many others waiting on the street and riding floats. If we can be frightened out of one parade, what other crazy will come along next year or the next?" There had been previous incidents when a bystander had thrown a brick and smashed the lip of a famous trumpeter riding on a float. There had been times when a child had been crushed beneath the wheels of a float when the crowd pushed too close. There had even been a shooting when a marching band could not push its way through the unruly crowd of onlookers. In the scuffle that followed, someone pulled a gun. The violent undercurrent was always there, and increased as the jobless and the transient criminal element thronged into the city, making "the greatest free show" into something to be dreaded.

New Orleans had been fighting back, with guidelines for parade behavior, increased police assistance and citizen committees urging cooperation and common sense. If one crazy could ruin one parade, Susie knew that it was a victory she could not tolerate. She didn't want her city to surrender its right to celebrate in its own streets.

"Just what did Eugene say Ralph was going to do to me?" Susie demanded. She was thankful that the young man who had once been her helper had decided to come to her defense and report the threat.

"He made a Molotov cocktail." Terrebonne's steely gray eyes were leveled at her. In the midst of a street crowded with parade floats and observers, an exploding bottle of gasoline would be disastrous.

"A fire bomb...." Tony stepped over to Susie and grasped her hand. The young boy had been fascinated by the fires on the flambeaux, but this time his eyes showed only terror. "Susie...." He was stunned that anyone would try to hurt her.

"If he's walking around with a bottle full of gasoline and he's as worked up as Eugene thinks," Susie said, considering the possibilities carefully, "isn't he likely to use the bomb on something else, if he doesn't have me for a target?" With or without Susie to aim at, Tanner was dangerous.

"I've thought of that myself," Terrebonne admitted. "We have his picture out to every cop in town. He's an accident looking for a place to happen, and we have to get him before he does something fatal. He's got the whole city wide open."

"That doesn't leave us much of a choice. I think we should give him a target," Susie said evenly. "At least then we'll all know where he's aiming."

"I don't like that idea a bit." Terrebonne flatly refused. "You'd be a sitting duck up there."

"It's easier to protect one sitting duck than an entire city full of people and parades," Susie replied with obvious logic.

"You could be hurt." Terrebonne shook his head.

"He might hurt someone else just as badly, only then he would get away. I can see the crowd pretty well from up here," Susie noted. "With a few of your men riding with me and some others riding the nearby floats, we would stand a pretty good chance of spotting someone with a flaming bottle in his hand. You did say that we good guys sometimes have to tough it out," she reminded him.

"They'll have my badge and put me under the jail if this one backfires." Terrebonne's gray eyes were already gleaming with the thought of grabbing Ralph Tanner before anyone was hurt. "Let me make a few calls and talk to my men." The detective climbed down from the queen's float. "And get all the civilians off your float." He looked deliberately at Tony. "Let him ride with someone else."

As Terrebonne stalked off toward his waiting car to phone into his headquarters, his comments left little doubt about what he intended to do. "You guys pull in some extra fire extinguishers. Get the fire chief. I want a crack shot riding up there with her." His directions came one after the other with staccato beats. "I'd better call the mayor."

The Triton Parade pulled out in full array twenty minutes later than it was scheduled. The group of krewe members who had yielded their costumes to the uniformed officers watched with somber faces as the procession moved on without them. Like the others who had been briefed on the possible danger that lay in wait for them, these men refused to be intimidated by one of the "crazies" that Terrebonne described. They would have to miss the excitement themselves so that the police could ride unnoticed on the floats that guarded their queen, but the parade would go on as scheduled. One man would not shake an entire tradition.

"This stuff sprays real fast and foamy." The officer beside Susie handed her a container to hide beneath her skirt. "And the sheet will keep the heat out if he does manage to start a fire." He pointed to the shiny silver fabric draped over the back of her throne. The fire-protective covering would be lifted over her and her sea-horse backpiece if Ralph Tanner was spotted anywhere near the float.

The officers located lower down on the queen's float had similar silver blankets with them to cover any fire or to drop over Tanner if he held on to the blazing container. The costumed policemen on the float ahead of her and the one behind included several from a terrorist team, two of whom were armed with rifles.

Susie spread her skirt out smoothly then bent down to push aside the brace that would have helped to keep her upright if she had intended to stand. But Terrebonne had braced the backpiece, not the queen, to the throne, and he'd insisted on her sitting throughout the procession to reduce the size of Tanner's target area. Then he had made sure that if trouble broke out, nothing would slow her movement if Susie had to leap off the float.

"This isn't quite the way I thought it would be." Susie tried to joke as the band several units ahead began to play. Then the flambeaux bearers lighted their torches and began strutting to the tune. Somewhere ahead, along the parade route, there was one viewer who would not raise his hands with the traditional "Throw me something, mister," on his lips. This man had a parade throw of another sort.

"It's always a little scary out there, ma'am," the young officer at her left replied as his eyes steadily scanned the faces lining the street. "Put someone in a crowd where they think no one knows what they're doing, and you've got trouble. Only this time we're not dealing with pickpockets and camera thiefs," he commented. "We've got a *torch* on the loose."

"A torch. . . ." Susie repeated the police name for a fire bomber. Far ahead in the growing darkness, a flambeau swirled into the air and looped over, then was caught again by expert hands.

"He'll probably wait until the crowd is really thick," Terrebonne had cautioned all the units in the parade. "So we'll spread you out just a little farther than usual to stop him from having two floats in range at the same time. The longer he has to get ready, the more likely someone will spot him."

As the procession moved toward the Quarter, the streets stretched ahead like dark corridors with rows of waving people forming human walls on either side. Some stood on stools and benches to get a better vantage, while small children crouched along the curbs, darting forward with outstretched hands to grab the beads or doubloons that were tossed into the air. Balconies were overflowing with eager viewers who often raised their glasses to salute the Triton krewe. Spotlights mounted on the corners of each float shone upward, enclosing the ornate structure and its riders in a cocoon of light.

"Like a sitting duck...." Susie forced a smile as she realized how very exposed she was. The eyes of the men riding with her constantly searched the crowd while their hands pitched trinkets with the abandon of the traditional float riders. Every time a flashbulb shot its brilliant light into the night or someone lighted a cigarette or tossed a glowing butt into the street, Susie felt her breath catch as her muscles tensed for action, but the sea of people only cheered and watched her float pass by.

When they turned onto Canal Street, the mass of human forms collected there made the color fade from her cheeks. From light posts and traffic signs, from upper floor windows and balconies, people waved and yelled and tossed confetti and tickertape, yelling for the krewe members to return the gesture with doubloons and throws. The lead flambeau dancers stopped to prance and strut as the crowd broke into a loud low roar that sent an inexplicable chill through Susie's limbs. The enormity of the crowd and the encompassing sound they made immobilized her with a fear she could not shake. "He's out there...." Her mind raced. She had refused to be intimidated by a coward who hid in crowds, but now her fingers clutched the armrests of her throne as she tried not to panic and bolt for somewhere to hide.

It was the movement of the gold-toothed flambeau carrier that made her suspect something was wrong. He had cut away from the others, signaling several of them to follow as he backtracked, weaving between the floats and the band units as he came closer to Susie's float. When he passed by the float preceding hers, he pirouetted and twirled his flambeau in an elaborate solitary routine while the progress of the parade halted. Then he strutted near the base of the float where Detective Terrebonne was stationed. When the dancer moved away, Terrebonne turned toward the queen's float and bowed. That was the signal they had set. Tanner had been spotted somewhere in the crowd ahead.

Susie clasped the can of fire supressant with one hand while she waved with the other, but her eyes never left the gold-toothed flambeau dancer who now moved forward along the parade route. He stopped and swayed from side to side, waving his torch and laughing with the onlookers who flipped coins onto the street. Then everything seemed to shift to accelerated motion as the silver sheet unfolded and caught the light. Costumed figures leaped from the float before her, surging toward the crowd.

For an instant, the bystanders cheered and reached up as if they were expecting to be showered with an additional barrage of parade throws. Then the officers, clad in satin costumes and sequined masks, formed a wedge that deftly parted the closely pressed crowd, seizing one crumpled form with fast, pincherlike movement. As they yanked the suspect to his feet, Susie saw a gleam of flame in their midst.

Without a second's hesitation, the gold-toothed dancer stretched his dark, muscular arm into the center of the melee, yanking away an object that he thrust into his heavy black side-drape. In his bare hand, he held the remnant of a charred, twisted piece of cloth. When the officers braced their captive on either side, forcing him against the base of the float, Susie looked down for a mere flash of time into his dull, unfocused eyes. Ralph Tanner lolled his head from side to side, too drunk to steady himself. He seemed to glare right through her, as if she had ceased to be a person but was simply a blur of sea-green color in the midst of so many others. With chilling clarity, Susie knew she had only been a target—an impersonal object—for the irrational anger of a man trapped by his own guilt. If she hadn't been there, she was certain Tanner would have vented his rage on someone—anyone—without the least concern. She had stood her ground, somewhat tremulously, but she had seen too clearly what Terrebonne called a "crazy." The look in Tanner's eyes was something she would not forget.

"No more trouble now." The flambeau carrier smiled up at her. Wrapped in his black cape was the missile Tanner had intended to roll beneath the wheels of Susie's float.

"You're the one who spotted him." Susie reached down to shake the man's hand. "I'm really thankful you handled it so well."

"He was sittin' with the kids, but he didn't have any throws," he explained. "An' he wasn't drinkin' from the bottle he had in his hand." The black man had danced and strutted in parades since he was a youngster. He knew New Orleans' crowds, and he'd spotted Tanner right away. "If you ain't drinkin' and you ain't catchin' throws, then you be up front lookin' to do wrong."

Terrebonne and his men had Tanner shifted to a police unit and hauled off before most of the bystanders were aware that the parade had halted again. To those who stood near the spot where the dancer had smothered the flaming wick, it only seemed as if another drunken vagrant had been taken downtown to sober up. They would eventually learn in news reports that they had witnessed something far more sinister.

High above it all, Susie felt the sickening clammy sensation. Tanner had been no more than twenty feet ahead of her, waiting to explode his gasoline bomb regardless of the victims it might have claimed.

Terrebonne had said Tanner was a sneaky man, a coward who wanted to blame someone else for the trouble he was in. He turned out to be far more deadly than that. As Susie watched the crowd, again caught up in the excitement of the parade, all she wanted was to climb down from her throne and become anonymous again. The limelight she had successfully avoided for so long had nearly turned into a brighter glare, a conflagration that could have claimed her life. The other side of Mardi Gras—the business of creating some of the magic in costumes, not in the pageantry, was where she belonged.

When the parade was over, Tony went into his emphatic recounting of the threat to Susie's life and the capture of the "weirdo" who had tried to firebomb the float. He had spent most of the post-parade party informing anyone who hadn't yet heard about the near-disaster on Canal Street, which he had witnessed from his prime vantage point two floats ahead of hers.

Bernie and Rosie had been white-faced when they met their daughter at the door. They had skipped the entire parade and had instead gone straight to the Riverview party room. The details of the incident had come to them in bits and pieces as the parade riders arrived. By the time the queen's float reached the disbanding point and Susie stepped into the party hall, she was welcomed with applause into the arms of the relieved Costains.

"What a way to end your reign." Bernie shook his head. "And we thought this would be such an easy thing—you stepping into the role of Triton's Queen."

"It's over and done with now." Susie felt as if a massive burden had been lifted from her shoulders. Like the huge shimmering sea-horse structure that would now be stored away, so many things from the past could be discarded. Her life was waiting ahead of her; she would carry the memories, but she would not let them dominate her again.

"Dad!" Tony's high-pitched squeal pierced the air. Susie swirled around to see Sy charging toward her. The anxiety in his expression indicated that word of the excitement on Canal Street had reached his ears.

"On the way in from the airport—" Sy broke off when Susie threw her arms about his neck. He wrapped her close against him, holding her tightly as if to assure himself that she was really safe. When he finally released her and looked down into her eyes, his own glistened brightly with a poignant relief. "If something had happened to you...." His voice was hoarse with emotion. "I had so much I needed to say...." His warm kisses touched her eyelids, nose and finally her half-parted lips. There they lingered, in spite of the attention this reunion had generated in the roomful of paraders and their friends.

"I'd even ordered a new bathtub." Sy now could smile again. "In New York, I spent the evening talking plumbing with a friend of mine who'd just installed a huge pink sunken tub. Everyone else stood around eating canapes and drinking champagne." His words tumbled out in a burst of unrestrained joy at seeing her. "All I could think of was how I could convert the bathroom in the house so you and I—" he lowered his voice abruptly "—so you and I could...."

"I know the rest." Susie silenced him with a kiss.

"I can do without this New York stuff," he said emphatically. "And if Felicia wants a photographer, I'll recommend someone else. I don't want to waste a minute of our lives," he insisted. "When I'm away, I'm miserable. I still do damn good work—" he grinned "—but I *am* miserable. Tonight the taxi driver said he'd heard that someone tried to blow up a float. Then he said which float, and I made him drive like the wind to get me here. You don't know how good it is to see your marvelous face." He kissed her again. "The rest of you feels pretty good, too," he murmured against her earlobe.

Much later in the evening, after Sy had listened with rapt attention to his son's account of the parade events, Susie sat nearby sifting through the large manilla folders that Sy had had Francine retrieve by taxi from his studio. "I was going to put these all in an album—two albums, actually," he informed her as he guided her to a quiet table and insisted she look at what he had produced. "After you look them over, we'll talk." He left her with the folders and went off to join his housekeeper and his son.

The first folder contained the photos of Susie Costain, Triton's Queen. Looking regal and serene, Susie appeared in all the traditional poses, from the formal queen's portrait to the solitary dance at the Triton Ball. Sy had been very skillful and extremely thorough. It was the second folder that made her pensive.

This folder was overflowing with the other Susie— with powdered sugar on her nose; leaves in her hair from the rag-tag football game; a quiet, lovely shot of her and Tony bent in concentration over the costume they were gluing together. There were several of her the night she was covered in paint from working on the scenery with Renny. But the picture that took her breath away was one she had not known existed. It showed her tousle-haired and sound asleep in Sy's loft bed where they had made love. The magic she had hoped would bring him home to her was not in the sensuality of the scene. It was the vulnerability he had caught in her sleeping face. That picture showed Susie as only he could see her—trusting him completely with her dreams, her ambitions, her body and her soul. Implicit in the picture was a promise that Susie could believe in.

"Marry me, Susie Costain." Sy's warm voice drew her eyes to his own. "I don't ever want to face a day without you." There was no one near to take a picture. This one moment would not be held motionless in any album. Susie slipped into Sy's arms. That "once more" feeling began again, as it would throughout a lifetime that offered beauty and joy and moments of magic.

**March's other absorbing
HARLEQUIN *SuperRomance* novel**

TASTE OF A DREAM by Casey Douglas

As rioting beset the Malaysian capital, two strangers sheltered in a basement—and fell in love. The madness of the world was purged with the night. With the dawn they were separated . . . .

Until four years later in Washington, when cultural adviser Danielle Davis and logger Ryan Kilpatrick locked horns at an embassy party. The minute their eyes met, they became the intimate strangers of long ago.

Mutual need made them forget that high-handed diplomats and headstrong loners don't mix. For they wouldn't be content with just a taste of life . . . .

A contemporary love story for the woman of today

These two absorbing titles
will be published in April
by

HARLEQUIN
SuperRomance

A LASTING GIFT by Lynn Turner

Jennifer had been happy, married to Michael Page.
He died after a tragic illness, and now all she
wanted was to be left alone.

Then Nathan Page, Michael's younger brother,
arrived, determined to take care of her. Tempers
flared, but temper turned to tenderness when they
admitted their mutual loss. Something special had
begun. . . .

Nathan was first to realize he was in love—with his
brother's widow. He knew he should leave. But
Jennifer had already lost one love, and she could
not let him go. . . .

RETURN OF THE DRIFTER by Melodie Adams

When Kathryn was seventeen, the fiery excitement
of Judson Taylor's touch had seared itself into her
imagination and flesh forever.

Seven years after she'd been devastated by his
abandonment, she had risen from the ashes of her
painful past. Kathryn finally had it all: her own
boutique, an independent life-style and the love of a
man touted to be Kansas's next governor.

And now Judd had returned, no longer the shiftless
drifter she'd known, but the head of Monument
Oil—a powerful man determined to set the record
straight, no matter what it cost him . . . or her.